Eve's Sins

- Book 3 in the Abomination Series -

By Felicity Thorne

Content Warning: Explicit sexual content. Only intended for mature readers.

Enjoy!

The Abomination Series:
Eve's Monsters
Eve's Curse
Eve's Sins
Eve's Revelations

Check out the accompanying Spotify playlist:

The Abomination Series by Felicity Thorne
https://open.spotify.com/playlist/6rVzdKXwm0lk5Bsz1G3SqZ?si=HgeRqP-KSnyqk7RcltflDg&pi=9X79qnTQQeS8F

"Love is the most twisted curse of them all."

- Satoru Gojo
(Gege Akutami, *Jujutsu Kaisen 0*)

1
Old Habits Die Hard

At the morning meeting after the paper mill incident, there was a lot more chatter than usual. Rumors had already started flying about what went down the night before, and everyone was up in arms about being left out of the loop.

Except for Levi and Kai, of course. They were just exhausted. Kai had his chair tipped back on two legs, his head lolled back with his long, black hair draped like a curtain behind him. He had his eyes closed and his bare foot on the edge of the conference table. Levi had his chin in his hand, his eyes bloodshot and droopy. They'd had a long night.

Eve felt the same. Luc had kept her up well into the early hours of the morning because he was all jazzed up from the fight. Everyone else was exhausted from it, but it had invigorated him. He slept an hour or two, and then he was up again, banging around in the kitchen.

Eve felt like she hadn't had a full-night's sleep in forever. How long had it been? It was catching up with her. She needed a break.

"You look tired," Eoduun said, looking over at her from his seat next to her. He beat Zeke to the only open chair next to her, so Zeke was on his other side. Bo was back at his apartment, watching over Ruth.

"Hm, that's sweet," Eve replied sarcastically. She leaned over to look at Zeke. "You promise you aren't mad about us not telling you about last night?" They'd filled him in at Eve's apartment that morning before the meeting.

"Of course not," he replied good-naturedly. "I mean, obviously I wish I could've helped out, but I understand why you had to leave me out."

Luc walked into the room, and, even behind his sunglasses, Eve saw his gaze gravitate straight to her. He smiled.

"So, is this going to be a regular thing now?" Mendal asked when Luc walked past him. "Are we all about morning meetings and riding the pine exclusively?"

Luc pulled on Kai's reclined chair as he walked past him, and Kai jumped, thinking he was falling over. Luc pushed his chair back down and continued to the head of the table, next to Eve. "I made a strategic choice using the information available to me. And this will be our last meeting for a while, I hope. I'm just as tired of seeing all of your faces as you are of seeing mine."

Everyone was briefed on the events concerning the secret plan and Dizzy's betrayal. Luc told them about Apep's appearance, and, finally, about what happened with Ruth.

"She's *here*?" Celeste choked. "Dude, I don't care if she's been erased. That bitch is fucking certifiable. She shouldn't be here."

"Bo's keeping her under surveillance, so don't panic," Luc said dismissively. "And, like I said, she doesn't even know who the fuck she is. She's not hatching any master plans while she can't remember how to work a spell. She doesn't even remember why she hated us in the first place."

"Hold on, let's back up a minute," Mira said. "Eve brought Ruth *back to life*? As in, Ruth was, for certain, *dead*, and Eve revived her? How the hell is that even possible?"

"Because she's awesome," Luc replied simply, like it was obvious. "And I'm sure she'll continue to push the boundaries of what we thought was possible."

"Is that necessarily a good thing? Isn't that why she requires a Vatican watchdog?" Mira muttered.

"Aw, are you jealous because you've never been powerful enough to earn the attention of the Vatican?" Eve asked sardonically.

"I'd never want *that* kind of attention from them," she snipped, shooting a disdainful look at the wall behind Eve where Isaac was leaning with his arms crossed.

"Leave him out of this," Eve scowled.

Mira leaned in, arching a beautifully sculpted dark brow. "Oh? So, what, has the watchdog become your new pet now that your silver wolf has his beloved sister to take care of? You just aren't happy if you don't have your own little doting shadow, are you?"

Eve scoffed and looked back at Isaac. He returned her gaze with that usual bored, impassive expression on his face. Eve turned back to Mira. "Does he look *doting* to you?"

"Don't worry," Mira replied, leaning back in her seat. "I'm sure you'll have him doing tricks in no time, just like the others. It seems to be the one thing you're good at."

Luc's hands slammed down hard on the conference table, startling everyone. "Mira," he said, his tone deceptively calm, "I'm trying to run a meeting. Do I need to send you out to the hall so you can sit and reflect on your behavior?"

Eve's eyes roved Luc's splayed hands and cabled forearms under his rolled-up sleeves, and she suddenly wanted to be on the receiving end of his wrath. *Punish me, sir. I was misbehaving, too.* She squirmed in her chair.

"No, sir. My apologies," Mira said quietly.

"Good," Luc said, suddenly cheerful. He stood up straight and fixed his sleeve cuff, and the room seemed to brighten. "Now, Roy's still looking into how to kill Apep, and I'm sure he'd appreciate any help he can get with that. Dizzy's in the wind, possibly with Apep, and Lilith's grimoire has slipped through our fingers. But, hey, we still got a big, fat W on Ruth. I'll fucking take it."

Zephlyn spoke up. "If I had only realized that the 'Dagon' in the vision was just Dizzy shifted into Dagon, that could've changed the game. I should've seen it. Sensed it. I don't know how I could've missed his deception right under my nose. But…I never would've suspected Dizzy."

"Don't blame yourself, bro," Mendal said. "I didn't see it either. And I'm fucking pissed. If I ever get my hands on that bastard, I'll tear him limb from fucking limb before I chop his ugly gourd off his shoulders."

"Dizzy will be dealt with when we find him," Luc assured them. "And we *will* find him." Luc opened a folder on the table in front of him and consulted the papers inside of it. "In the meantime, Celeste, I'm going to need to move you to Team Delta, and you three will be headed to Montana. There's a case up there, but I also want you to make a detour to check out a property there that Ruth may have been using as some kind of monster army base. Dizzy might be there. But do not engage. Apep might also be there. Recon only." He passed down a packet of papers for the team to peruse. "Team Gamma, you'll be headed to Florida. Something's lurking in the swamps of Polk County." He handed Roy a packet. "And Team Beta, you're off to Washington state. Go kill some sparklers." He slid a packet to Mira.

"Sparklers?" Eve asked.

"*Twilight*. Vampires," Eoduun clarified.

"Pacific Northwest vampires," Zeke elaborated.

"That's all. Dismissed," Luc said.

"Nothing for Flannel?" Ruger asked, disappointed, as everyone else stood up and started filing out the door.

"Not this time."

Cassie leaned over the table toward Eve. "Girl, we're getting together tonight. I'm taking you shopping for an outfit, and then we're going dancing. You've earned a night out."

Eve's immediate response was to look up at Luc to read his face before answering, but Cassie slapped the table. "Hey, don't look at him. Look at me. You don't need his permission," she said sternly.

Old habits die hard.

"I would love to, but I'm exhausted, Cassie," Eve confessed as she pushed up from her seat. "I'm running on fumes. Maybe we could just hang out at the apartment tonight?"

"Sure, of course. But no boys allowed! I need some girl time. And maybe we can hang out with Ruth, too," Cassie suggested as she and her team also rose from the table.

"Eve, I need to talk to you for a moment," Luc said as she started to walk toward the door. She didn't like his tone. He had bad news.

"I'll bring some takeout later today," Cassie said as she left with Remi and Ruger. "I'll text you."

"We'll wait for you in the hall," Zeke said to Eve. He and Eoduun walked toward the door. Isaac surveyed the situation, then decided to follow Zeke and Eoduun to the hall.

"You're leaving," Eve guessed once she and Luc were alone.

"Sorry, love. Duty calls." He folded his arms loosely around her and pulled her to him.

"When?"

Luc looked at the expensive watch on his wrist. "Soon. An hour or two."

"Where are you off to this time?" she asked with a mildly annoyed sigh.

"My father needs me in Paris."

"Ew, Paris. How unfortunate for you," Eve deadpanned.

"I know. Disgusting. Such an ugly city," Luc replied in kind. "But thankfully I only have to be there for two days."

"And then you can come home?"

Luc hesitated. "For a day. And then I'm off to Michigan for a couple of days."

Eve groaned.

"I know, love. I'm sorry." He smiled sadly at her, then pressed a light kiss to her lips. "Keep the guys in line for me, will you? I've asked Bo to be around as much as he can so you don't have to be alone with Isaac for too long. I've also reactivated the dreamcatcher spell under your bed to keep Dagon out of your head at night. Can you *please* remember to replenish the water in it this time?" he implored.

"I may need to be reminded," Eve admitted. "But I'll try."

"I'm not going to tell you to be good, but I would ask that you don't kill anyone when Isaac is looking. Agreeable?"

"Agreeable."

"Have fun tonight with Cass and Ruth." Luc kissed Eve's forehead, then slapped her ass. "I'll catch up with you before I go."

Eve started toward the door, then paused. "Luc?"

"Hm?"

"Why weren't you at Ruth's graduation?"

Luc's face went blank. "Huh? Wasn't I? Uh...hm." He scratched the back of his head. "God, that was so long ago. I honestly can't remember. Why do you ask?"

"Because she remembered your empty seat."

"Oh. Well, I'm sure I must've had something going on that day. I wouldn't have just skipped it," Luc reasoned.

"Your parents weren't there either. Bo was the only one there when she walked across that stage."

"Yeah, he was usually around. He didn't have a whole lot going on."

He was missing the whole point, Eve realized. "Were they at your graduation?" Eve asked.

"I'm not sure. I don't really remember."

"You don't remember your graduation?"

Luc shook his head. "Not really. Like I said, I had a lot going on, and it was a long time ago. Things kind of blur together." He stuck his hands in his pockets. "What's with the sudden interest in graduation?"

"Nothing. I was just curious. I've been trying to stay out of Ruth's memories, but that one keeps popping up on me randomly. Bo, and three empty chairs. She was heartbroken, you know."

Luc looked genuinely shocked. "Why? It was just graduation. It wasn't like she was getting married or anything."

Clueless. "Never mind. I just thought you should know."

Luc stood there, perplexed, as Eve left to join the boys in the hallway. She hoped he would take some time to reflect, but with everything he had going on, she wondered if he would even have time, or if he would forget about it as soon as he left the war room.

She tried to ignore the creeping fear that she was going to end up like Ruth – vying for his love and attention when he had already moved his focus on to other things.

Old habits die hard.

2
You're Not Bo

Zeke and Eoduun walked on either side of Eve as they walked across the grounds from the bunker to the apartment complex, and Isaac hung a little behind, smoking a cigarette.

Eve turned and addressed Isaac, walking backwards as she pointed at him. She held both index fingers together, then drifted one further from the other. She touched her head and drew it away in a Y. *Why are you so far away?*

He held up his cigarette, then swirled one hand around the smoke rising from the end of it.

Eve signed, *You know smoking will kill you.*

He waved his hand dismissively at her, then took another drag.

"I can't stand the smell of cigarettes," Eoduun complained. "Tell him to walk further away," he told Eve.

She turned back around, walking normally again. "It doesn't bother me. You can walk further ahead if it's bothering you that much."

Eoduun slipped his hand into Eve's. "No."

Zeke saw the display, and took hold of Eve's other hand. "So, we get a rest day today. What should we do with it?" he asked suggestively.

"Rest," Eve replied. "I'm a walking zombie right now."

"Cuddle on the couch and watch a chick flick?" Zeke proposed, swinging Eve's hand playfully.

"You don't want to watch *Hellraiser*?" she teased.

"You wouldn't put me through that." Then concern filled his handsome, innocent face. "...Right?"

She laughed and leaned her head on his massive shoulder. "Aw, of course not, my poor, sweet baby."

"You got the baby part right," Eoduun teased.

Back at the apartment, Eve got into comfortable clothes, losing the bra and donning a pair of sweatpants and a crop top. She came out of her room just as Bo and Ruth were walking through her door.

"What's up, Daddy?" Eve asked as she went to the kitchen to make popcorn.

"How'd the meeting go?" he asked, joining her in the kitchen. Ruth followed along behind him, her long blond hair pulled back in an uncharacteristically boring ponytail, her ears, fingers, and wrists naked of jewelry. She was wearing one of Bo's t-shirts and the same jeans she'd been wearing yesterday. Bo must have washed them for her, because they were no longer filthy with mud.

As Ruth passed through the living room, she looked back at Zeke on the couch and Eoduun sitting on the floor in front of him. Isaac was reading a dog-eared book in the chair. Eoduun had control of the remote, scrolling through the romantic comedies on Netflix.

"The other hunters are pissed about being lied to, and they have concerns about bringing in guests," Eve said as she gave a quick, unintentional glance to Ruth. "But Luc sent everybody off on a case.

Well, everyone except Team Flannel. Cassie's coming over later." She pointed at Ruth. "You should hang out with us, too. Maybe we'll have a slumber party and break into Luc's liquor cabinet. We'll tell secrets and prank call boys." She waggled her eyebrows.

She was going to win Ruth over. Ruth had done some horrible things, but Bo still loved his little sister, and Eve would do just about anything for Bo. Eve had Ruth's memories in her head, and from the ones she'd already accessed, she knew Ruth was a victim of emotional traumas, not entirely unlike Eve's own. Being made to believe you are worthless and unloved does something to a person that isn't easy to repair. Eve knew all about that. She wanted Ruth to know what it was like to have family. To have support.

She needed to give Ruth her memories back, somehow, someday, but she needed to work on building her up first. She wanted her to be emotionally fortified against the traumas she would have to relive all over again when those memories were returned to her.

Eve had caused enough problems. It was time for her to try to fix something for once. For Ruth. For Bo. For Knighco. If Ruth joined them, she would bolster their firepower beyond measure. They didn't have a witch on the roster, and having a witch as powerful as Ruth? Forget about it. Done deal.

Ruth considered Eve's invitation, then she looked to Bo.

Bo nodded at her. "You should," he encouraged. "Eve and Cass are a guaranteed good time."

Eve winked at Bo. "*You* know *I* am, anyway," she teased as she pulled the popcorn from the microwave, then laughed at Bo's annoyed expression.

"Not what I meant. Don't be a bad influence," Bo chastised.

Eve dumped the popcorn into a bowl, then stepped in front of Bo, purposely too close. "Bo?"

He gazed down at her. "Yes?" he replied, his voice low.

"I'm going to be the absolute worst influence on your little sister, and there ain't shit you can do about it," she whispered conspiratorially. "We're going to drink alcohol and talk about sex with boys and practice kissing pillows. Shit, we might even steal a cigarette from Isaac's jacket and smoke it in the bathroom with the exhaust fan on."

The corners of Bo's eyes crinkled. "Wow, you *were* a bad influence, weren't you?"

"Were? Bitch, I still am," Eve laughed.

Bo took a handful of popcorn from her bowl and lowered his mask. Eve took the opportunity to drink in his handsome face in broad daylight. "I know," he smirked, showing one beautiful, sharp canine before shoving the popcorn into his mouth.

Ruth saw the way they looked at each other and said, "Ok, wait. So, you two are together? Because I thought Eve was with Luc yesterday. I'm so confused."

Bo quickly lifted his mask and took a step back from Eve. "What? No," he said with a derisive laugh. "Evie *is* with Luc. Well," he looked at Eve with uncertainty, "sort of, I mean. It's…" He turned back to Ruth. "It's a little complicated."

"It's a team effort," Zeke called from the living room. "Nothing complicated about it."

"Except when it is," Bo mumbled.

Ruth's pretty face scrunched in further confusion.

"We'll talk about it later," Eve told Ruth. "Trust me, my love life is one of Cassie's favorite topics. But be warned: you'll never be able to look your brothers in the eye again."

"Hey, brothers *plural*? What do I have to do with it?" Bo protested.

Eve shrugged innocently, then took the bowl of popcorn out to the living room, holding eye contact with Bo as she walked past him.

She sat next to Zeke, and Eoduun immediately wrapped his arm around the leg she draped down next to his shoulder. Bo sat next to Eve, and Ruth sat in the other empty chair adjacent to the couch. Eve saw her looking across at Isaac in the opposite chair, but Isaac was staring at his book.

"So, he's deaf?" Ruth whispered when she was sure Isaac wasn't looking.

"Yes, but he can read lips. And he's doing it right now, aren't you Isaac?" Eve said.

Isaac glanced up from his book at her, but didn't respond. Then he returned his attention to the book. Eve noticed he was reading *Wuthering Heights*.

"And he can talk, but apparently only to Evie," Bo said spitefully.

"He's selective," Eve explained nonchalantly.

"And he selected you. And I don't fucking like it," Bo grumbled. "I'll be relieved when the Vatican sends him elsewhere."

"He's not a team member?" Ruth asked.

"No, he's a Vatican assassin," Bo said. "They point him at someone and say 'kill.' And they pointed him at Evie."

Ruth's emerald eyes widened, and she looked warily at Isaac again. Isaac looked up at her, then over at Eve. He held his palm up. *What?*

Eve touched her fingers to her thumb on each hand, making a loose O, then waved them toward and away from each other, side to side, shaking her head. *Not important, never mind.*

"That's so annoying," Eoduun said, looking up at Eve from the floor. "I hate your secret little language."

Eve erupted in laughter. "It's not secret. And don't worry, we're not talking about you."

Isaac looked at Eoduun, then Eve. He made a face and touched two hooked fingers to each side of his face and drew them away. *Jerk.*

"Now he's talking about me." Eoduun glowered.

"How about we don't piss off the assassin?" Ruth suggested.

"Ah, he's fine," Eve said with a wave of her hand. "So, what are we watching?"

By the time Jenna Rink started chanting, "Thirty, flirty, and thriving," in *13 Going on 30*, Eve was already falling asleep.

Eve dreamed that she was in Bo's apartment, and the "Bo" she was with wasn't actually Bo. Someone was pretending to be Bo. She didn't know *how* she knew this, but she did. She was certain of it. Was it a spell? A shapeshifter? Mind tricks?

She waited until imposter Bo was in the shower, vulnerable, and she snatched two knives from his kitchen and stalked to the bathroom. She could hear the water running and Bo humming a tune to himself. She quietly opened the door, but he heard her. The humming stopped.

"Evie?"

"Get out of the shower. Slowly. I don't know who you are, but you aren't Bo."

The tap closed, and the towel over the curtain rod slipped down out of view. She took a fighting stance and held the knives at the ready. The shower curtain opened, and there stood a damp-haired, annoyed-looking Bo with a white towel wrapped around his waist. Even if this was an impostor, she couldn't stop her roving eye.

"What's the meaning of this, Evie?"

"Get out of the shower," she ordered.

He sighed heavily and stepped out. "Can I at least get dressed?"

"No. Go to the bedroom."

"That's where my clothes are. Are you sure I can't get dressed?"

"Why? Are you afraid I might notice something off about your fake body that would give you away? A scar in the wrong place, maybe?"

As Bo walked past her and she followed him into the bedroom, he said, "You can look me over if you want, but I'm pretty sure you'd be mortified about it afterward when you realize it's just me."

"Get on the bed. Lay down and raise your hands to the headboard."

He stopped and turned to look at her. "Are you going to tie me to the bed?!"

"Damn right I am. Get over there."

"I'm not sure if Luc is going to laugh or stab me when he hears about this," Bo said as he reluctantly followed her orders. Eve grabbed white cloth athletic binding from the shelf in his room and tied his wrists together around a bar on the headboard. Then she did the same with his feet to the footboard.

She climbed on top of him and straddled his torso, looking down at his bare face. She ran her finger over the scar on his eye, then down the side of his face.

Bo fell silent, and he averted his gaze. If she wasn't mistaken, that was embarrassment on his face. A thrill of panic rattled her brain. What if this really was Bo?

No. It just couldn't be! She poked the knife into his pectoral, just enough to draw a droplet of blood, then started to slowly drag the blade over his skin. Bo inhaled sharply through his teeth.

"No, please don't do that. Stop!"

She leaned forward, getting closer to his face, looking for any kind of change or break in the illusion. "Why, because it's making it hard to concentrate on your transformation?" She taunted. Eve took the knife in her other hand and repeated the cut on the other pectoral.

Bo made a deep groan that thrummed through her core like a plucked cello string.

"No…because I like it," he admitted thickly.

Eve didn't have to look to know that he'd hardened. She felt it against her ass as she sat straddled on his stomach.

Her conviction wavered. Her legs began to tremble, and she knew he could feel it. He clenched his eyes closed, and his breath caught in his throat. "Evie, you have to stop. Now. I'm not the gentleman you believe me to be."

"You're not Bo."

"Yes, I am." His body flexed and strained beneath her, his hips pushing forward. "But I only have so much restraint, and we're just about beyond that point. You need to get out of this room and let me cool down."

She narrowed her eyes at him. "That's exactly what I would expect an impostor who's losing his concentration to say."

20

Bo threw his head back against the pillow and growled in exasperation. "Please," he pleaded.

She scooted back slightly, his erection sliding up her back, and she dragged both knives across the top of his abdominals and ribcage.

His hips jerked forward again, and he moaned deep in his throat – a moan that turned into a humorless chuckle. "God, just stab me before I make us regret this," he begged.

"Who the fuck are you?!" Eve demanded, raising the knife to his throat.

"It's me, goddamn it!"

She was growing desperate. She feared she was wrong now, but after all of this, she *needed* to be right. If she had done all of this to Bo, she would never be able to look him in the face again. If she was wrong...

She'd already gone too far. There was no turning back.

She reached behind him and grabbed his erection. It had escaped the towel, so it was hot, bare skin-on-skin touch. If this didn't reveal the impostor, she was in big trouble.

Bo inhaled and gritted his teeth. "I warned you..." A sudden chittering flash of light leapt from his hands and ripped through the headboard and his bindings. His hands were now free, and he grabbed Eve's wrists and yanked her forward, causing her to drop both knives. She fell forward, her face close to his, and he released one of her wrists so he could grab her jaw with his rough hand. He pulled her into a kiss that ruined her for anyone else's lips.

She had made a deeply, *deeply* egregious error.

3
Why Don't You Two Just Fuck Already?

His hands moved to her bare thighs and slid all the way up to the hem of her shorts while he kissed her. He gripped her thighs tightly, and he flexed and rolled his body beneath her, trying to work himself into a more satisfying position while his ankles were still bound.

Eve pulled away from his mouth and looked down into his eyes, and when she saw that yellow wolf eye gazing back up at her, she knew. "You really are Bo, aren't you…"

"In the flesh," he simmered. He released her thighs and reached up with both hands to forcibly grab the sides of her face and pull her back down to him. His mouth met hers in another incinerating kiss. He brought his lips close to her ear and whispered, "Now untie me."

"No." There was no way she was freeing him, not in this state. At least she hadn't given him any blood, so she still had a shred of control. She could still stop this, even if every fiber of her being was urging her to just ride the fucking lightning.

He twisted the fingers of both hands into her hair and brushed his lips over the ridge of her ear, whispering, "If you don't want this, then you'd better run, little rabbit. Because I'm going to devour you."

Oh, god, but she *did want it*. She wanted it *so* badly. She'd always wanted it.

Eve hesitated, frozen with indecision. Her needs, her wants, her loyalties, her honor, her desires, her heart…she was being completely torn asunder. This wasn't allowed, but it had been a long time coming. Maybe it had been an inevitability that she had chosen not to acknowledge. They'd been building up to this all along, hadn't they? Hello, consequences.

"It's wrong, Bo," Eve said tremulously.

"It doesn't feel like you want to say no." Bo's hands now moved down to her ass, and he lifted her enough to maneuver her atop his hard cock. It felt like a hot iron rod pressed between her legs. He then gripped Eve's hips and held her against him as he rolled his hips into her. "Give up Zeke and Eoduun and take me, instead."

Eve sat up again and looked him in the eye. "What would Luc say?!"

Bo sat up, bringing himself closer to her. His eyes lingered along her lips, and he kissed her hungrily again. "Nothing. He already consented to this."

Shocked, she pulled away from Bo. "What the fuck are you talking about?"

He looked at her, mismatched eyes both blazing with desire. "I'm the backup plan, remember? If you can't trust yourself not to kill Zeke and Eoduun, you're supposed to come to me. And you almost killed them."

She suspected Luc didn't see it going down like this when he agreed to it, though. This was more than just training. More than just casual sex to satisfy the beast inside her. But Bo was right. She didn't want to say no. She didn't know if she could even utter those words right now if she tried to. But…

"There's no going back if we do this," she protested uneasily.

"There's no going back now anyway," he countered. Using the power of his eyes, his ankles suddenly passed through their restraints, freeing him completely. He flipped her onto her back beneath him. The towel he had on had long since worked free of his waist. "I told you, if you didn't want this, you shouldn't have pushed me."

She never had control over this situation. He'd been humoring her.

"You're bleeding," Eve pointed out. "Let me heal you."

He slammed her wrists down onto the bed. "Don't you dare." He thrust his hips against her, then took one of her hands and placed it on his chest wound, using his hand to guide hers through the blood. He then drew her hand down his belly, smearing it through the blood there, too. But he didn't stop. He brought her hand down to his cock and urged her to stroke him, using the slick blood on her hand as lubricant.

But it was getting on her clothes. She released her grip on him and used the opportunity to pull her shirt off. When he saw Eve undressing, Bo wasted no time in assisting her out of the rest of her clothes.

They no longer had any barriers between them. Just skin against skin. He reached down between her legs, his fingers sliding inside of her. Eve rocked her hips slowly, pressing herself against his warm, rough hand. A small groan rumbled in his throat as he kissed down her belly, then her inner thighs, and then…she arched her back when his warm mouth reached her apex, his soft tongue wiggling against and exploring just the right places. That cello string he plucked earlier was now being worked into a vigorous presto, faster and faster, intensity increasing into a steadily building, powerful crescendo, until all the strings were suddenly struck with a thunderous forte chord. Her body convulsed, her core spasming against his tongue, and her unbridled cries of pleasure were released out into the open for everyone to hear.

He didn't wait for the orgasm to finish before he mounted her and sank his cock into her pulsing heat. He slowly thrust a little further inside with every shudder and spasm of her aftershocks, reveling in the way she tightened and squeezed around him as she bucked beneath him. He buried himself deep inside of her and took her mouth roughly with his, the sweetness of her release still lingering on his tongue.

"Tell me you're mine," he demanded in a low, husky voice.

Eve looked up into his eyes. "Bo…" she whispered.

That single syllable, uttered so desperately from her sleeping lips, is what woke Eve. She blinked sleepily, and saw Jennifer Garner dancing to *Thriller* on the television. She shifted slightly, and felt the dampness in her underwear from her wet dream about Bo.

God, what a dream.

She looked up at Zeke's sleeping face, his cheek smushed against the palm of his hand, and she smiled. He was so fucking adorable. She glanced down, and saw that Eoduun was no longer on the floor. He must've gone back to his apartment. Ruth was asleep in her chair, exhausted from yesterday. Isaac was still reading his book.

She raised her head from Zeke's lap and looked over. She had one leg curled and tucked under her, but her other leg was stretched out across another lap. Bo's lap.

He was staring ahead at the television, focused entirely too hard on the screen. He had one hand resting on Eve's calf, and she could feel his fingers gripping into her flesh.

"I dreamt that out loud, didn't I?" she whispered sheepishly.

"We don't have to talk about it," Bo replied, still looking at the TV.

"I thought you were a shapeshifter. I tied you up and tried to torture the truth out of you. You liked it," she said, a sly smile curling her lips.

"I said we don't have to talk about it."

"And then you got free. And then *I* liked it."

"Evie…" he warned.

Eve tried to slide her leg over his crotch, but he kept a firm hold on it, not allowing her to budge. "What did I say in my sleep?" she asked curiously, still grinning at him. "Did I call you Daddy?"

"Drop it, Evie."

"Did I moan?"

Bo didn't reply.

She rolled onto her back, resting the back of her head in Zeke's lap, and tauntingly touched her free foot to Bo's chest. He snatched it up and pressed it down with her other leg. He cast her a stern look.

"Someone needs to put you in your place, little girl," he said in a low tone.

A shiver of desire ran through Eve's entire body. "And you definitely did that in my dream."

"Why don't you two just fuck already?" Isaac grumbled from his chair, still looking down at his book.

Bo shot him a surprised, scandalized look.

"Excuse me?" Luc said from the doorway, walking into the apartment. "The Angel of Death speaks, and *that's* what he says?" He walked up behind the couch and looked down at Eve, spread out over Zeke and Bo.

Zeke roused from his slumber and groaned, tipping his head back to look up at Luc. "I thought you were leaving," he said, blinking against the light.

"I'm not gone yet," he said, looking at Bo instead of Zeke. Then he looked over at Isaac. "What the fuck, padre?"

Isaac just shrugged without looking up.

Luc looked down at Eve from behind his round sunglasses. "Are you causing trouble?" he asked scoldingly.

"Always. It's why you like me."

Luc smirked at her. "Well...you're not wrong. Now, come give me some love. I need to head out soon," he demanded, holding his arms out wide.

She clambered over Zeke and Bo and climbed over the back of the couch, throwing her arms around Luc's neck, clinging to him like his pet monkey.

Perhaps that's all she really was to him.

Stop that.

She was having a harder time controlling these intrusive thoughts now that she had Ruth's memories pushing into her feelings for Luc. But she'd been in Luc's head. She'd *felt* the extent of his obsession with her. It was all-consuming, and a little terrifying. She wasn't just a mere passing fancy to him...at least, not yet.

But feelings can change, especially for someone as capricious and easily distracted as Luc. As long as he still felt like he was chasing her, she would hold his attention. As long as he had competition, he would try to win her, because that's who he was. He had to be the best. Number one. In everything. And he would struggle and fight to achieve it.

Once he won, though? She didn't know.

That's why she couldn't let him win. He knew she loved him. He knew she loved him most, even. But he didn't have her entirely all to himself. And he never would, because she was terrified that his achievement of that challenge would spell the end of his obsession with her.

Even she could taste the toxicity in that philosophy. She sucked. She knew that. Absolute hot garbage that walks, talks, and fucks. Her desperation for love and validation was fucking pathetic.

God, she hated herself.

But, god, she loved Luc. She would do whatever she had to to keep him.

Luc fisted his hand in her long locks and kissed her deeply, making an obvious show of it in front of everyone, and her self-loathing was temporarily pushed from her thoughts. It felt so goddamn good to be loved by Luc. Claimed. Wanted.

She never wanted to lose this.

And yet, the dream about Bo still lingered in the back of her mind.

Greedy bitch.

Luc lowered her to her feet, but she clung to his neck so he couldn't stand back up again. She kissed him again, and he smiled against her lips. "You're making it really fucking hard for me to find the resolve to leave," he said.

"Good," she whispered.

He gave a low chuckle, then untangled himself from her arms. He stood up and looked down at her. "I love you, Eve. I'll call you later. Have fun with the girls tonight." He leaned down with his mouth close to her ear. "And don't forget to feed the monster while I'm away. We can't have you going feral in front of Isaac, now can we?"

Or on *Isaac.* "I'm sure it won't be a problem," she replied, her gaze sliding to Zeke's handsome profile. Then her focus shifted to Isaac, and she saw him watching her.

Always watching her, even when he wasn't looking at her, waiting for her to go full darkside.

When Cassie arrived a little while later, toting a big bag of Chinese takeout, she demanded, "All right! Everyone who identifies as a man, *out*! It's girl time!"

"What if I identify as a man, but I also *like* men? Can I stay and spill tea?" Eoduun asked, having just returned from his apartment not long before.

Cassie laughed. "Nice try. No."

As Bo, Zeke, and Eoduun got up and headed out the door, Bo paused and looked back at Isaac, who continued to sit and read his book. Bo waved his hand, and Isaac looked over at him. Bo gestured toward the door.

Isaac stared flatly at him, unmoving.

Bo looked to Eve. "A little help?" he implored.

Eve signed to Isaac. *We're having girl's night.* She brushed her thumb under her chin, then formed an A-handshape and traced her jaw from her ear to her chin with her thumb, and pointed at him. *You aren't a girl.*

He signed back, circling his index finger, ending with his palm up. He then held up four fingers, touching his index finger to his nose, and arced his hand away and down, finishing by touching his chest. *Just ignore me.*

She put her hands on her hips and tilted her head at him, displeased.

He touched his chest, pointed both index fingers forward, then held one up and shook it side to side. *Where am I supposed to go?*

Eve touched her nose and flicked her hand away. *I don't care.* She signed and pointed to the boys in the doorway, *Go with them.*

He snapped his fingers together. *No.* He curled his fingers upward, then flipped them over. *Don't want to.*

"Are you two fighting? Because this gives a whole new meaning to catching hands," Cassie joked.

Eve rolled her eyes at Isaac. She touched her thumb to her chest, fingers splayed vertically, and cast it away jerkily. *Ugh, fine!* Then she signed, *If you stay, I'm painting your nails pink.*

Fine. I don't care, he signed back. *Paint them pink.*

4
Just Lick the Fucking Cupcake

"As exciting as all of this is, I think I'm gonna go now," Eoduun said blandly, turning and walking out.

"Isn't he leaving?" Bo asked, gesturing to Isaac.

"In a bit," Eve lied. Bo would make a stink if he knew Isaac had no plans to leave. "He wants to finish his chapter."

Bo narrowed his eyes at her. Walking lie detector. "Hm. Well, if you need me, you know where I'll be."

"Have fun!" Zeke called cheerfully as he followed Bo out the door. "And if you need *me*, you know where *I'll* be." He winked at Eve before closing the door behind him.

"Such a cutie," Cassie admired after Zeke closed the door. "He's the golden retriever of your little harem, isn't he?" she mused. "He probably makes *you* a sandwich after sex."

"Chicken nuggets, but, yeah," Eve laughed.

Ruth sat down at the barstool next to Eve as Cassie unloaded the takeout containers. "So, how do I get one of those?" Ruth asked enviously.

"What, a golden retriever?" Cassie asked.

"No. A harem."

Cassie snorted. "Around here? Hun, just point and pick. With looks like that," Cassie pointed a chopstick at Ruth and ran it up and down in the air, "you'll have them following you like eager puppies."

Ruth looked down at herself. "I look like shit. I need makeup and new clothes. I can fit in my brother's shirts and sweatpants, but these are the only jeans I have."

"If that's 'looking like shit,' then I must look like a damn orc," Cassie said.

"We'll take a look in my closet after we eat," Eve said. "I'm not as tall and willowy as you, but you might find some clothes that will work until we can take you shopping. It may not be your style, though, considering what I've seen you wearing before."

Ruth picked up her chopsticks and the container Cassie pushed across the counter to her. "I don't even know what my style is," she confessed.

"Glamorous. You wore lots of sparkly jewelry and expensive designer clothes," Eve informed her. She pointed to her beautifully manicured hands. "I mean, look at that nail job. You're a bougie babe."

"I would let you raid my closet too," Cassie offered, "but this bitch is *thick*. My shit's going to be way too big on you." She swiveled her curvy hips and slapped her round, firm ass. Cassie was a goddamn brick house.

"Isaac is still here," Ruth reminded her. "He's looking at us."

A devilish grin danced on Cassie's lips. "Good. Let him look." She tossed her braids and looked over her shoulder at him, then gave him a flirty little wave. Isaac got up and grabbed his jacket from the hook by the door, then left. Cassie pouted. "Why doesn't he like me? Everyone likes me. I'm likeable, aren't I?"

"Don't take it personally," Eve said. "That's just Isaac. I don't think he likes anyone."

Cassie arched a brow at Eve. "He likes *you*."

"I *need* him to like me, or I die," Eve retorted.

Cassie canted her head. "That's true. Did you fuck him yet?"

Ruth dropped a chopstick.

"No, ma'am, I did *not* fuck him." Eve then leaned in conspiratorially. "But I did heal him yesterday."

"Spill, bitch," Cassie urged. "How was it?"

"What does that mean?" Ruth asked.

"When people drink her blood, it heals them, but it's also like liquid sex." Cassie looked at Eve as she stuffed noodles in her mouth. "Was it hot?"

"Fuck yes," Eve admitted. "And I wasn't expecting it to be. It isn't usually like that with anyone but my teammates."

"What happened? What did he do?" Cassie probed.

"Nothing, really. I mean, he got hard, and he let me touch him, but he didn't engage. Just…stood there. I don't think he was expecting it to feel like that, either."

Cassie coughed up her noodles. "You touched his dick?"

"No!" Eve blurted. "His body! Like, his chest and stuff. And it was only for a few seconds. And then I stopped."

"But you didn't want to stop," Cassie deduced.

Eve took a bite of rice and sighed. "No, I definitely didn't want to. But I'm glad I did. That would've been a huge mistake."

Cassie tilted her head and hummed. "Hm, maybe not a *huge* mistake. Maybe more like an average-sized mistake."

Eve gave Cassie a pointed look. "No, Cass. A…*huge*…mistake."

Cassie gasped in delighted shock. "No fucking shit? But he's so…well, not *little*, but…average."

"I know! But he's packing some serious heat."

"Girl, get your hands on it. Just get down on your knees and say, 'Bless me father, for I have sinned!'"

"God, no, I can't do that," Eve laughed. "He's off-limits. Like you said, I can't just go around licking all the cupcakes. I have a whole box of my own."

"Fuck, I got a box too, but I'll lick that cupcake," Cassie remarked. "If I thought that cupcake might let me lick it, I would fucking lick it. I might just try to lick it anyway."

"Are you attracted to him?" Ruth asked, somewhat surprised.

"Are you *not*?" Cassie questioned.

Ruth shrugged her shoulders. "Not really. I don't think he's my type."

"'Types' are so limiting. There are too many delicious flavors out there," Cassie said. "Look at Eve's little group. She has a golden retriever, a broody emo boy, a daddy, and a charming American psycho."

Eve held up a finger to stop her. "Bo isn't part of my 'group.'"

"Not *yet*." Cassie corrected. "But that man is *begging* to be fucked."

"A cupcake begging to be licked?" Eve suggested.

Cassie and Ruth both laughed. "Yes, just lick the fucking cupcake, Eve!" Cassie said.

"I shouldn't be laughing," Ruth said with a chuckle. "That's my brother you're talking about."

"What, you never had friends thirsting after your brothers?" Cassie asked. "I find that impossible to believe."

Ruth's smile disappeared. "I don't remember."

"Shit, that's right. Sorry," Cassie apologized.

"You did," Eve supplied. "It was actually why you stopped inviting your best friend from middle school over. Her name was Amanda. You felt like she was only coming over to flirt with Bo." *And it made you jealous, because Bo was yours, and Amanda was yours, and you were terrified that they would end up dating each other and you would lose both of them. They were all you had. And then you did lose Amanda when she got into a relationship with a narcissist in high school and she stopped talking to everyone but him.*

"I'm sorry, Ruth. I promise I will find a way to put these memories back in your head." And when she did figure it out, she knew it was going to be difficult to make herself return all of these memories, knowing what they were going to do to Ruth.

Ruth pushed away her half-eaten chow mein. "Bo told me some stories about myself last night because I couldn't sleep. But they didn't feel like things that had happened to me. They were just stories. And that story about Amanda? Nothing. No connection." Ruth rested her chin on her hand. "It's disorienting."

"Or maybe it's an opportunity," Eve suggested. "You can reinvent yourself, become someone new. You have an opportunity to rebuild your relationship with your brothers, with your family."

"My parents don't want to see me. Bo told me they just needed some time, but I got the feeling he was just saying that to protect my feelings. But I don't know if I even have enough feelings about them to care right now."

Even without her memories, Ruth would soon get a sense of her relationship with her parents. Eve may be able to help rekindle Ruth's connection with Bo and Luc, but there was nothing she could do about their parents.

"Well, if it's any consolation," Eve said, "my family situation is rather fucked, too."

Cassie pulled three bottles of wine and a bottle of Jack out of one of the bags she brought in. "Let's drink about it, shall we?"

Isaac returned to the apartment a while later, and by the time he'd returned, the ladies had hit the bottles hard.

"Where were you?" Eve demanded, wagging her index finger side to side, flipping her hand over her shoulder, and pointing at Isaac. Sloppily. "That was *way* longer than it takes to smoke a cigarette."

Isaac signed back.

"Wait, slow down," Eve said, squinting her eyes at him as she ran her hand slowly up her arm.

"You're slurring your signing," he said aloud.

"Oh, he talks!" Cassie blurted in surprise.

Isaac barked, "Yes, yes, it speaks! It speaks!" He waved his hands in exaggerated annoyance.

"Why so hostile, handsome?" Cassie shot back. "It's not an attractive look. More fly honeys with honey, honey."

"I don't think that's the phrase," Eve said.

"Do I look like I care about any of that?" he asked, but he was looking at Eve, not Cassie. "Please, ignore me. Have your fun."

"But I was supposed to paint your nails pink," Eve reminded him.

"Another time. I'm going to bed." He signed to Eve. *Goodnight, Eve.*

"Did he just flip you off?" Ruth asked, scandalized.

"No. That's my name."

"Your name is the middle finger?!" Cassie laughed.

Rather than explain it, she just said, "Yep."

After Isaac emerged from the bathroom in black sweatpants and a loose white t-shirt, he stretched out on the couch and covered his face with a blanket.

"Shit, does this mean we have to be quiet?" Cassie whispered. Loudly.

"He'd *deaf*, Cassie," Ruth yelled obnoxiously. "He can't hear us."

Eve woke up with a full, aching bladder. She squinted, her vision fuzzy, and she realized she was in her bedroom with all the lights still on. She, Ruth, and Cassie were all strewn about her bed, passed out. She dizzily crawled to the edge of the bed and stood up. The room swayed.

God, she hoped no one had thrown up in her bed.

She shut the lights off in her room on her way out, bathing the rest of the apartment in darkness, and she stumbled to the bathroom to relieve herself. When she walked out of the bathroom and shut off the light, through the darkness, she saw Bo sleeping on the couch.

That was Bo, right? Of course. Who else would it be?

She shuffled over to the couch and lay down, snuggling her back up against the warm body under the blanket. She tugged at the edge of the blanket and covered herself with it, too.

"Have you been smoking, Bo? You smell like cigarettes."

Bo didn't move or speak, but she could feel his heart hammering away like woodpecker on speed against her back.

"Bo." She nudged him with her elbow. "Bo, wake up. I think you're having a bad dream." She rolled over to face him.

Terrified ebony eyes gazed back at her.

"Oh fuck!" Eve yelped, then fell off the couch in her scramble to get away.

Not Bo. Isaac. What the fuck? Why the hell did she think it was Bo?! The room was spinning as she sat up and rubbed the sore spot on the back of her head.

"Jesus, I'm sorry, Isaac," Eve slurred. "I thought Bo were you." Isaac was still frozen, his horrified gaze unfocused and distant. "Isaac?" She reached out and touched his hand, and he gasped, shrinking away from her.

"No!" he whimpered. "Don't touch me!"

Oh, god. The couch. Her drunken mind sobered up enough to realize she'd unwittingly triggered a flashback.

She had no idea what to do. She jumped up and hurried to turn the lights on, tripping over the coffee table and her own feet in the process. But once she'd flicked them on, she rushed back to Isaac, collapsing clumsily on the floor in front of him. She took his face in her hands and forced him to look at her.

"Isaac! It's Eve. It's me!" She patted her chest and signed her name. The name he'd given her. She made two S-handshapes and crossed them in front of her, twisting her fists as she drew them apart again. *You're safe.* She repeated the sign several times.

His eyes finally focused on her, and he blinked. Then he frowned, pushing her hands away and sitting up. He was panting, his chest heaving with fear and adrenaline.

She wanted to touch him, to comfort him, but she didn't want to make it worse. He was weird about being touched, and understandably so. She placed her fist in her palm and moved it toward him, like she was offering him her fist. Then, furrowing her brow, she held the backs of her fingers on each hand together, palms down, and flipped them so the palms were up. *How can I help you?*

He scowled and shooed his hand at her, not looking at her. *Go away.*

She leaned her back against the coffee table and just sat there in front of him. She wouldn't touch him, but she wasn't about to leave him like this, either.

So...she would just be here, near him.

In this stupid spinning room.

5
You're Looking at Me Like You Want to Eat Me

Eve awoke on the floor with a pillow under her head, a blanket draped over her, and a pounding headache.

She sat up and reached for her phone on the coffee table. She had a text from Luc.

Good morning, love. You sounded like you were having a good time last night. Text me when you wake up.

Eve checked her call history, and apparently, she had talked to Luc the previous night. She had no recollection of it.

I'm up. I feel like I got hit by a bus. Remind me never to mix Jack and wine again.

Luc responded almost immediately. *YOU have a hangover? Is that even possible?*

So it would seem. I just feel off.

Must be because you miss me.

Eve smirked. *Gotta be it.*

Isaac walked up and handed her a glass of water. When she took it, he touched his chin and drew his hand away, then held one arm horizontally while he raised his other arm perpendicularly toward himself. He drew a circle in the air and then splayed his fingers down from it. *Good morning, sunshine.*

Eve smiled, but it felt more like a grimace. She took a big gulp of water.

Isaac signed, *Your friend is sleeping in the bathroom.*

Eve groaned. She stood up, and was surprised to find that she still felt dizzy. She didn't get hangovers like this. She signed to Isaac. *I'll take care of it.*

Eve texted Luc, *Well, I have to go peel one of the girls off the bathroom floor. I'll talk to you later.*

Good luck. I love you. Have a good day.

A soft smile caressed her lips. *You too.*

She found Cassie sprawled out on the bathroom floor. She nudged her with her stocking foot, and Cassie groaned. "Wakey, wakey, Cass," Eve sing-songed.

"Just a few more minutes," Cassie whined.

"I have to pee."

"Go for it. I have no objections."

Eve closed the door behind her and used the bathroom while Cassie stirred reluctantly on the floor. She sat up and swiped her hair out of her face. Eve laughed at the crisscrossed patterns imprinted across Cassie's face from sleeping on her braids. "Fuck, I don't even know how I ended up in here," Cassie confessed. "My back is killing me."

Eve leaned against the counter for a moment before washing her hands. "Yeah, I'm not feeling so hot myself. Which is really strange for me. We must've *really* hit it hard last night."

Cassie stood up behind her and caught a glimpse of herself in the mirror. "Oh, good lord." She rubbed her cheek to try to dispel the

39

braid imprints. "You were going to let me walk out there like this, weren't you?"

"What? Isaac's already seen you. He was the one who told me you were in here."

"Well, there go my chances with that cupcake."

Eve laughed, even though it made her head throb.

"*Ohayou*," Bo called from the other room. "Evie?"

Something other than Eve's head throbbed at the sound of his voice. A surge of desire weakened her knees and thickened her throat. And then, it was gone.

"Are you ok?" Cassie asked.

"Mmm-hmm." What the fuck was that?

She walked out of the bathroom and closed the door behind her so Cassie could straighten herself out. Bo smiled at her behind his mask, his aquamarine and charcoal eyes twinkling in amusement as he held out a cup of coffee to her. He had a tray with three other coffees in it, and a quick, but passing, pang of jealousy smacked her.

He was only supposed to bring *her* coffee.

"You look like you had a rough night," he said, clearly holding back a chuckle.

"The night was great. It's the morning that's been rough."

Isaac stepped between her and Bo and handed her the glass of water she'd abandoned on the coffee table. He tipped curved fingers to his lips. *Drink*. Then he continued on into the kitchen.

The amusement on Bo's face vanished. "Why is he taking care of you?"

"He's not. He just brought me a glass of water."

"Did he bring the other girls a glass of water?"

Eve shrugged. "I don't think so."

"Hm."

Eve gulped down the whole glass of water. "There, now it doesn't have to bother you anymore." She took it to the kitchen and set it on the counter. Isaac swooped in behind her and refilled it with water. He slid it across the counter toward her. He made two flattened O hands with his fingertips touching, and raised his index finger. *One more.*

Bo eyed Isaac grumpily. "Hm."

Eve chugged down the second glass while Isaac stood and watched, and when she finished, she handed the empty glass back to him. He took it and stuck it in the dishwasher.

"Now, on to the main event," she chirped as she took a sip of the hot black coffee Bo had brought her.

Bo had a strange satisfaction in his eyes as he watched her sip.

Eve went into her room and woke up Ruth, who was still passed out in her bed. She checked over the bedding carefully as Ruth grumbled and rolled over. No puke. Thank the gods.

"Rise and shine, Ruthie," Bo said cheerfully. "Luc gave us permission to use the company card to get you some new outfits, so I thought maybe you and me and Eve could go do some shopping."

Ruth sat up. "That sounds fabulous. Just let me get ready."

Bo handed her a coffee. "This should help."

Cassie came out of the bathroom and joined them in Eve's bedroom. Bo handed her the third coffee cup from his tray. Then he took the last one and sipped it himself.

Eve took the empty tray from him. "I think I'm going to have to bow out on the shopping today. This hangover is ridiculous."

"Shopping? I'll go!" Cassie volunteered.

Bo looked at Eve with concern. "Are you sure, Evie? If you're not feeling well, I can stay," he offered.

"No, I'll be fine. I'm just not up to a car ride and shopping right now. I think I'm just going to Netflix and chill."

It took a lot of convincing to get Bo out the door without her. He eyed Isaac warily as Eve was seeing him off in the doorway.

"Why is he being so nice to you?" Bo wanted to know.

"Maybe because I'm nice to him."

Bo frowned. "Don't be too nice to him. I don't want him getting comfortable."

Eve patted Bo's cheek. "Aw, don't be jealous. He's not replacing you."

Bo looked taken aback. "I didn't think he was. Why would he replace *me*? He brought you water. I brought you *coffee*. I clearly win."

Eve laughed. "Clearly."

"He could never replace me...right? Why would you even say that, Evie?" Bo seemed legitimately upset.

"It was joke, Bo," Eve assured him. "You're still my one and only Daddy." When he frowned doubtfully, she slipped her arms around his waist and hugged him reassuringly, pressing her cheek against his chest.

Oh. Heat erupted between her legs as she hugged him and inhaled his scent. The memory of the dream she'd had yesterday rolled like a highlight reel in her head, and all she wanted to do was climb him like a mountain.

She *needed* him. *Now.*

She swallowed hard and forced her fingers to unfist themselves from his jacket. She took a step back. "Have fun shopping," she said, plastering a fake smile on her face to hide her burning desire.

Bo gave her a questioning look, but he didn't push. He left with Ruth and Cassie.

What the hell? Why was she responding to Bo like that all of a sudden? Was this all because of her dream?

She was just about to head to the shower when Zeke and Eoduun walked in. "How was your slumber party?" Zeke asked.

"We laughed, we drank, we blacked out, we woke up in various places around the apartment," Eve replied.

"Aw, and we missed that?!" Zeke complained.

Eoduun said, "You can tell us all about it on our hike. Get dressed, and let's go."

"Hike?"

"Yeah, there's a cool hiking trail about half an hour away," Zeke explained. "We like to go every once in a while, just to unwind. No cell service, no roads, just nature. We thought you'd like to go with us."

"Any other time, I would. But I think I'm going to sit this one out, fellas. I'm exhausted, and I'm still a little hungover."

"Poor babe. Do you want us to stay and keep you company?" Zeke offered.

"No, no. Go on your hike. We can hang out when you get back."

"You sure?" Eoduun questioned.

"Positive. Go."

Zeke bent down and kissed her chastely on her lips, but even that little bit of contact sparked inside of Eve. "We'll be back in a few hours."

Not to be left out, Eoduun pulled her to him and kissed her, too. The spark ignited and spread through her belly.

She needed to go take a shower and douse these flames before they grew into a raging, uncontrollable wildfire.

The shower didn't help. Even when she touched herself and tried different showerhead settings – the things that usually worked – nothing calmed the hungry beast in her belly.

She needed to be fucked.

That was the only way to sate it.

She sat on the couch and curled up in a blanket, and it smelled like Isaac. Jesus, even that turned her on. She looked at him as he sat in his chair, working on the last quarter of *Wuthering Heights*. Her eyes lingered on his thick-knuckled fingers. He had big hands. Big hands that she now found herself imagining all over her body.

God, she was burning up.

She cast aside the blanket. She felt like she was standing in a furnace, and the urge to peel off all her clothes was difficult to fight.

She fluttered her hand at Isaac, and he looked up at her. She signed, *Is it hot in here?*

He shook his head, then he frowned. He pointed his fingertip from one end of his forehead to the other, then pointed at her. *You're black.* He then indicated the space around her with a gesture.

Her aura was black again?

She didn't even care at the moment. All she cared about was getting out of these clothes, and getting those big hands on her bare flesh. Over her breasts. Around her throat. In her hair. Between her legs. What an opportunity she'd missed the other night when she healed him. She could've had him.

Fuck, this was wrong. Not Isaac. Anyone but Isaac. She pulled out her phone and, with trembling fingers, she texted Zeke, and then Eoduun. And then she waited. Nothing. Finally, she texted Bo.

Zeke and Eoduun went on a hike, and I can't get a hold of them. If you don't come fuck me right now, it's going to be Isaac. I can't stop it.

She set her phone on the arm of the couch.

Her eyes gravitated to Isaac. Had he always been this fucking hot? She admired the curve of his full lips as he chewed on his fingernail, his eyes focused on the words in front of him. She wanted that thumb on her lips, between her teeth. She wanted those lips on her skin. On her neck. Nibbling the shell of her ear. Claiming her mouth.

His eyes slid up from the page and met hers. He saw the need in her gaze, and she observed the subtle change in his expression. She was hyper-tuned into him, like a cat focused on the movements of a mouse, pupils blown wide. His breath quickened slightly, and his dark eyebrow twitched once.

"You're looking at me like you want to eat me," he said aloud.

"I do." The words leapt from her mouth. She couldn't stop herself as she rose from the couch and stalked over to him. He looked at her questioningly as she stood in front of him. When she climbed onto his lap, he reached for the knife at his hip. She stilled his hand with hers.

"What are you doing?" he demanded, gripping the handle. "This isn't you, is it?" he stated rather than asked.

"Does it feel like me?" she asked, grinding herself against him. The need between her legs was driving her insane.

The next thing she knew, she was crashing to the floor with Isaac, the chair overturning, and he rolled her onto her back. He sat on top of her, holding her down, his knife to her throat.

6

No One Compares to You

"Are you trying to kill me?" he growled.

"Are *you* trying to kill *me*?" she countered, a playful sneer on her lips. He had one of her hands pinned to the floor with his, so she reached the other one up and touched her fingers to his chest. She started running her hand down toward the waistband of his pants, feeling his tight abs through the fabric of his t-shirt.

He took the knife from her throat temporarily so he could intercept her roaming hand. He gathered both of her wrists into one big hand and pressed them into the hard floor above her head.

"What the fuck is this?" he demanded, looking down at her. "You're completely out of control."

"Subdue me, Isaac," Eve begged, squirming beneath him. "My monster is hungry. Feed it."

"How about I tie you up and let your team deal with it instead?" he said.

Eve gave him a sly look. "You want it. Take it. It's right here," she wiggled under him again. "Give in."

"I can't do that. It's a conflict of interest."

"It has to be you, Isaac. Zeke and Eoduun aren't answering their phones." Eve was growing desperate. She felt like she was going to lose her mind completely if he didn't fuck her soon.

"Then call Bo."

"Bo is gone with Ruth and Cassie." She swung her legs up and hooked them under his armpits, around his torso, crossing her calves over his chest, and squeezed him between her powerful thighs. She forced her legs down, pulling him off of her and bringing him to his back just long enough for her to pounce on him.

She looked down at him, but he'd suddenly stopped fighting. He was looking at her neck. She felt the sting of the knife nick, and knew there must be blood.

"Better not drink it, or I might really kill you," she warned. "Just fuck me. Just hold me down and fuck me. Subdue this thing inside of me," she pleaded. The ache in her core was becoming painful. She *needed* relief. "Just fucking do it, Isaac." She reached one hand between them and rubbed her palm against the incredible bulge in his pants.

He wanted it, even if he knew better.

He growled and rolled her off of him and onto her back beneath him. He brought the knife to her throat again. He leaned down, his face close to hers. "Or I could just kill you and never have to worry about you again."

She rolled her hips against his engorged bulge. She smiled seductively. "You and I both know which option you're going to choose." She lifted her head and bit his lip lightly. When he didn't pull away, she slipped her tongue into his mouth.

He closed his eyes and let her explore briefly before he started to take over. His tongue struggled to dominate hers, and his hand dropped the knife and slid up the side of her neck, his thumb on her cheek, his fingers slipping into the hairline behind her ear.

And then he was yanked away from her and thrown back. He was on his feet in an instant, drawing a second knife from the sheath on his belt, confused, but ready. When he saw Bo standing there, though, he lowered his guard. A strange mix of relief and irritation crossed his features.

But Bo wasn't looking at him. His blue and yellow eyes raked ravenously over Eve lying on the floor, her clothes in disarray, blood smeared on her throat. His chest heaved as he scented her blood and her desperate arousal.

"Bo…" Eve whispered. His name floated from her lips like a prayer.

Without a word, he scooped her up and threw her over his shoulder, carrying her out of her apartment like a sack of potatoes.

And she let him, like a naughty puppy whose master had come to scold her.

He brought her to his apartment, locked the door behind him, and hauled her to his room. He threw her down onto his bed and began to strip off his shirt and mask. "You have been a very bad girl, Evie," he snarled.

Oh, God, yes, I have. Eve started to pull off her shirt, but Bo stopped her. "Did I say you could take your clothes off yet?" he growled. He climbed onto the bed over top of her, shirtless and maskless, and loomed over her on all fours. He reached a rough hand up and grabbed her jaw angrily. "I warned you that he was off-limits," Bo scolded.

"But I –"

Bo crushed his lips against hers, refusing to let her finish. His tongue tangled with hers, his jaw pumping against hers. She rolled her tongue around his big canines, loving how much different it was to kiss him than it was to kiss anyone else. She whimpered into his mouth.

"You torment me every day," he panted, his lips trailing along her jaw. "You poke and poke at the beast, thinking there won't ever be any consequences." He ripped her shirt open, making Eve gasp in surprise. He swirled his tongue around her bare, pebbled nipple. "You mistakenly think I have an endless supply of patience." He skimmed his canines over the soft swell of her breast, but was careful not to draw blood. He ran his tongue over the other breast, then tilted his head to the side and looked up at her. "You've gone too far this time, Evie." He brought his face back up to hers, and wrapped his fingers around her jaw again. He ran his thumb over her lips, then slipped it between them. She rolled her tongue over the pad of his thumb.

He touched his lips to her ear, his hot breath caressing her skin as he whispered, "It's time to put you in your place." He plunged his hand into her sweatpants and under her panties. He felt the wetness in the fabric, and he ran one thick finger through her folds. He growled, "How dare you get wet for him."

"I've been wet since I heard your voice this morning," Eve placated, her hands gripping his arm.

Bo dipped his finger inside of her, and she could feel the lean muscles in his arm working as he rubbed tight circles around her clit, using her juices for lubrication. She rocked her pelvis against his hand, but she needed more.

"Beg me," Bo commanded, his voice husky in her ear.

Eve nipped at Bo's ear. "Fuck me, Daddy," she begged, panting. She felt his whole body shudder in response. God, she wanted him so fucking badly, in a way she'd never wanted anything before or ever would again. She needed him inside of her.

He yanked her sweatpants and underwear off, then ripped his pants open without bothering with the button. His cock sprang up, twitching with his heartbeat. He slipped his hand into her hair and looked down at her with those heterochrome eyes. The eyes of a wolf. A predator.

He lowered his hips to hers, the head of his cock nestling into her dripping opening. "Say it again," he demanded.

"Fuck me, Daddy," she whimpered, digging her fingers into his scarred back. She felt him shiver again, and he hummed.

"Fuck yes," he breathed, thrusting himself into Eve's tight sheath. His eyes bore into hers. "When you're with me, there is no one else. Right now, you belong to me," he growled possessively.

"I've always been yours," Eve confessed her deepest, darkest secret. She wrapped her legs around his waist. "And you've been mine since I first laid eyes on you, and I'll never let anyone else have you." She slipped one arm around his neck and buried her fingers in his silver hair, and she pulled his mouth down to hers.

Fuck, this felt so wrong and confusing, yet so right, like it made perfect sense. It was like something clicked into place, and the whole machine shifted into perfect alignment.

Bo was her key.

She wasn't sure how or why, but she was sure he *was*.

"Fuck me harder, Bo" she demanded, feeling the tension in her core intensifying, her pleasure rising.

He gripped her hip and her hair, holding her tightly, and increased the tempo and intensity of his thrusts. She fisted her hand in his hair, and with her other hand, she dug her fingernails into his back as she rolled her hips to the rhythm that her body demanded.

He slid his hand up her arm and pulled her hand from his back, intertwining his fingers with hers. They were both on the verge, and as their tongues and lips tangled deliciously, he squeezed her hand and groaned, and they pushed each other over the edge into a crashing wave of pure and utter bliss. Eve's last moan felt like it could've easily turned into a sob. It was a release that she felt from her soul, and it was as beautiful as it was terrifying.

She lay trembling beneath Bo, her face buried in his neck, holding him tightly against her. Their hearts hammered against each other, as though trying to escape their chests so they could melt into each other. Bo was a huge mistake that Eve had been absolutely desperate to make, and she was certain now that he felt the same way. But they were helpless to stop it, like two powerful magnets that had been pushed just a little too close together.

So…what now? What the fuck now?

"Are you falling for him?" Bo asked, his voice muffled in her hair. It made it sound like he was wearing his mask again.

"Falling for who?"

"Isaac." He spat the name like it tasted badly.

Eve almost laughed. "No. That…that's not what that was all about."

"But you like him."

"I do like him."

Bo huffed, and he squeezed her harder. "Well…stop."

"Stop liking him?"

"Yes. As a matter of fact, hate him, if possible," he requested petulantly.

"Why?" she laughed.

He sat up and looked down at her. His wolf eye had gone dormant again. Just blue and gray. "Because you only need one shadow, and that's me. *I* bring you your morning drink. *I'm* the one you tease. *I'm* the one you go to when you need something. And then he moves in, and suddenly you're best fucking buds, and you have your private little conversations, and he's looking at you like you're the only person in the room. And then he almost takes something he has *no fucking right to*."

"What, my body?" Eve scoffed.

"Yes, your fucking body. You're *mine*…I mean ours. And he's not one of us," Bo simmered, his wolf eye shining through again.

"Listen, *Daddy*. I had very little control over myself at the time. This *curse* inside of me needed something, and I was desperate. It was a matter of convenience, not necessarily preference. Got it?"

"You think he'll see it that way? You think he'll understand it wasn't actually *you* that wanted him?" Bo asked doubtfully.

"He already knows. He can tell when I'm not me."

"Well, add that to the list of all the things that make Isaac fucking special."

Eve sighed heavily and rolled her eyes. She grabbed Bo's face in her hands and looked up at him sweetly. "Your jealousy is adorable, but unwarranted. He's not you. He'll never be *you*. No one compares to you."

Those words that slipped so easily from her lips shook her to her core. It was true. There was no one like Bo.

Bo was special.

They had crossed an uncrossable line, and she knew that she could never go back to the way things were. She'd had a taste of him, and she knew she could never go without him. She would need him again.

Not *want*.

Need.

Fuck.

7

Do You Really Think I'm Done with You Yet?

Eve brushed Bo's hair out of his eyes as he lay on his side, looking at her. "How did you even get back to my apartment so fast?" she wondered as he absently ran his finger up the middle of her stomach, tracing the border of the large, faint birthmark that covered half of her stomach and wrapped over onto her back and up over her arm. It was the first time in a long time that she took any notice of it. She'd gotten so used to it being there, and it blended so closely to her skin tone, she rarely "saw" it on herself.

But of course he would notice it. Bo noticed everything.

"I took a page from Luc's book and teleported," Bo replied.

Her eyes shot wide. "You can teleport that far?"

"So it would seem. I'd never been able to go that far before, but when I got your message, I just...I needed to get here. I left Cassie and Ruth at the mall with the car and got here the quickest way I could think of."

Eve looked at her ripped shirt. "You were pissed," she said.

"What you were threatening to do? I wasn't about to let *that* fucking happen."

Eve leaned up on her elbow and rested her head in her hand. "So, what is Luc going to say?"

Bo sighed. "I may not survive that conversation."

"He tolerates Zeke and Eoduun," Eve pointed out, but she knew it wasn't the same.

"I'm not Zeke or Eoduun."

That was exactly it. Luc wasn't truly threatened by Zeke or Eoduun. He knew Eve would never pick them over him, if it ever came down to it.

He couldn't say the same about Bo.

"He'll have to understand," Eve said. "He told me before that you weren't *entirely* off-limits. I would think this situation qualifies as a necessary deviation from the usual arrangement."

"What would've happened if Isaac wasn't there?" Bo asked.

Eve considered it. The need she'd felt had been all-consuming. "If Isaac hadn't been right there, it would've been someone else." Ruger and Remi were just up the hall. God, Cassie would've killed her, and Eve never would've forgiven herself for such an infraction.

But this monstrous *thing* inside of her had needs that couldn't be reasoned with, and she was powerless against its influence. She'd made the mistake yesterday of not 'feeding the monster,' as Luc so eloquently put it, and today it had burst free and gone on the hunt. Was that why she felt like she had a terrible hangover this morning?

"We can't let it get to that point again," Bo said.

"I know." She felt like shit about attacking Isaac. He was the last person she should've treated like that. As someone with a history of sexual assault trauma, someone who'd just been triggered the night before, he didn't need her putting him in a position like that. She needed to apologize and find a way to make things right with him.

Eve slid her underwear up over thighs, then went to Bo's closet and grabbed a t-shirt, throwing aside her ruined crop-top and pulling his shirt over her head.

"Where are you going?" he inquired, leaning on his elbow.

She looked over her shoulder at his sexy, scarred body as he looked back at her with his beautiful mismatched eyes. His silver-white hair was mussed, his face uncovered, his expression relaxed – it was such a sweetly candid moment. She knew no one else got to see him like this. This visual was hers and hers alone.

...Fuck.

She returned to the bed and climbed on top of Bo, straddling his hips. She felt him growing hard again through the open fly on his pants. She leaned down and kissed his lips softly.

"Once was understandable," she said. "You were filling a need. But if I stay, we're going to have a lot more to explain, and I don't think Luc will be quite as understanding."

She yearned for him, but it wasn't the monster anymore. It was just *her*.

Bo looked up at her, desire stirring in his eyes as his charcoal eye flooded with golden-yellow. He raised himself up on his elbows, reaching up to tuck her hair behind her ear. Then he buried his fingers in those pink locks and pulled her roughly down, bringing her face close to his. "Do you really think I'm done with you yet?"

She gasped as he rolled her over onto her back and pressed his hard cock against her mound. "Bo..."

He kissed down the side of her neck. "What? Are you telling me to stop?" he asked in a low, threatening tone. His long canines scraped over her throat where Isaac had nicked her, and he licked the mostly-healed, raised welt. "Or do you want to see how far we can push this?"

"Don't drink from me. I might kill you."

"Do you really think you would kill *me*?"

"I almost killed Zeke and Eoduun."

"I'm not Zeke or Eoduun," he repeated. He sat up and looked down at her with aqua and scarred gold. He grinned roguishly, displaying his canines openly, and she realized that Luc had competition for the most beautiful thing she had ever seen. How could she say no to him?

He released his manhood from its fabric prison and pushed her panties aside, eager to be inside of her again. Eve whimpered as he entered her, filling her with his length. God, it felt like he belonged there.

He nuzzled into her neck, and she cried out when his fangs sank into the flesh of her trapezius. Sheer ecstasy shot straight to her core as an instant orgasm rocked her whole body, her walls clenching and spasming around Bo's cock. He moaned against her shoulder as he drank and thrust rapaciously into her. Eve panted and mewled, clinging to Bo for dear life. She tried to take control by rolling him onto his back, but he resisted.

…He resisted?

He slammed his hand into the mattress and widened his knees, stopping her from dislodging him from his position.

"Don't even think about trying to top me from the bottom," he taunted in her ear, then licked her bloody shoulder. "You'll take my power when I *give* it to you."

Yes, Daddy. Give it to me.

His pace slowed, but his intensity grew. He tightened his fist in her hair and tucked his other hand under her ass, pulling her into his deep, hard, grinding strokes. He ran his tongue up her neck and lightly nipped her jaw. Then he claimed her mouth with his, kissing her slowly, but deeply.

Fuuuuck. Bo was hitting all the right spots, stoking the fire in her belly into a raging inferno, teetering on the precipice of an explosion. She clawed into his back and gripped the nape of his neck. "Oh, god, make me come again, Bo," she whimpered.

He kissed down her jaw and clamped his mouth over her throat as he drove into her with force. He didn't bite hard enough to draw blood this time, but she felt the delicious pressure of his teeth as she arched her back, cresting into another toe-curling, earth-shattering orgasm.

She felt his power surge through her veins as he groaned and shuddered, emptying himself into her.

Her legs quivered at his sides as he lay limply on top of her, his hot breath caressing her neck. He panted, "I think you just turned me inside out."

Was it just her imagination, or did his heartbeat sound especially loud all of a sudden? And what was that other sound? Could she hear Remi and Ruger talking?

Bo pushed himself up to look at her face, and his sudden startled expression scared her.

"What?!" she panicked.

"Your eyes...they're...fuck, they're...!" He exclaimed, struggling to finish his sentence. He pointed to his scarred eye.

"What?!" She pushed him off of her and ran to look at his full-length mirror on the wall. The eyes staring back at her were not her own. They were wild, golden-yellow wolf eyes.

What. The. *Fuck.*

"Holy shit," she marveled, turning her face at different angles. "This is trippy as hell!"

Bo climbed out of bed and joined her in the mirror. "What the fuck," he mumbled, staring at their matching reflections. "Why would it show like that?!" He sounded concerned.

Eve shrugged. "I don't know, but I kind of like it. We match," she mused, nudging him with her elbow.

He looked down at her, touching her jaw to angle her head toward him. He inspected her eyes silently.

"Jesus, I can hear everything. Is this what you hear all the time?" she asked, cocking her head to listen to Ruger and Remi. They were arguing over who drank the last beer. "And smell?" She could smell someone cooking pancakes (had to be Ruger and Remi), the soap in Bo's bathroom, sex in the air, her and Bo's scents mingled.

She frowned. "How the hell did I take your power? I didn't dominate you. I didn't feel any violent urges, or hurt you, or try to kill you."

"I don't know. I was just trying to keep you under control so you didn't try to kill me."

Eve turned a sly eye toward Bo. If she'd taken his power, did that mean…? She lunged at him.

And ended up on the floor, on her back.

"Fuck! Why can't I beat you?! I took your power!" she scowled up at his amused, fanged grin. Eve touched her tongue to her teeth. "I didn't get your fangs," she noticed.

"Be glad for that," he said, then helped her to her feet.

"If I did, I wouldn't wear a mask over them. I think they're sexy," she remarked, running her finger along Bo's jaw, admiring his beautiful teeth. Her eyes slid up to his. "I love seeing you like this. Unmasked. Undressed. Unreserved."

Bo's yellow eye shifted slowly back to charcoal as he gazed at her. "I don't feel like I need to hide myself from you. You like me as I am."

"I love you as you are," she professed, realizing too late what she'd just said.

The fucking L-word.

"I mean, I'm not saying 'I love you,' or anything like that. I mean, I'm not *not* saying that, either, but it came out wrong. I just meant I love who you are, as a person."

A crooked half-smile lifted the corner of Bo's mouth. "No, I get it. I love who you are, as a person, too."

Eve heard footsteps approaching in the hall, and she saw Bo alert to it as well. She smelled tobacco smoke.

Isaac.

There was a knock at the door.

"I suppose he's probably checking to see if I killed you," Eve surmised as she quickly threw her sweatpants back on and started to walk out of the room to go answer the door.

"Maybe *I* should answer the door," Bo said as he changed into a new pair of gray cargo pants. He'd destroyed the fly of the other ones. He slipped a mask down over his head and fitted it over his nose, then gestured to Eve's eyes. "I'm not sure what he's going to make of all *that* at a first glance."

Eve followed him to the door, and Bo opened it. Isaac looked at Bo, then his eyes slid to Eve behind him. His eyebrows jumped. He pointed to his eyes.

Eve hooked her finger and twisted it at the corner of her mouth, stacked one fist on top of the other in two G-handshapes, then curled her finger in to a question mark. *Cool, right?*

He pointed at her and brushed his thumb under his chin and traced his finger across his forehead. *You're not black.* He touched the fingers of two flat O hands together, then opened his hands and spread them outward, squinting his eyes. *You're bright.* He shook his head in confusion as he touched the backs of his fingers together and flipped them, palms up. *How?*

Eve signed, *Bo cured me.* As an afterthought, she added, *Temporarily.* When he just stared at her, scrutinizing, she tapped her cheekbone with a V handshape. She pointed to herself, brushed her thumb under her chin and curled two fingers near her temple. *See? I'm not evil.*

He gave her a skeptical expression, arching a brow at her, then signed, *Sometimes you're evil.*

8

We're Done

Bo accompanied Eve and Isaac back to Eve's apartment, and Eve could feel both Bo's and Isaac's tension. Things were not obee-kaybee among the three of them.

All of that tension was warranted, and entirely her fault.

Isaac sat in what was becoming *his* chair in the living room, but Eve could feel his eyes following her as she moved through the apartment. Surveying her. Scrutinizing her. Studying her. The yellow in her eyes had since subsided, as Bo's always did, but Isaac's eyes kept flicking up to them, as though he was waiting for them to switch back at any moment.

Bo went to his spot at the kitchen island and pulled out his phone.

"Porn or texting?" Eve asked. Bo glanced at her, but didn't respond. Thinking about him reading manga online reminded her,

"Hey, I was going to borrow that wolf and bunny girl comic from you."

"Manga. And no, you weren't."

"I'm going to sneak into your apartment and steal it tonight, since I can walk through walls and shit now."

A devilish expression passed through Bo's eyes, his wolf eye making a brief appearance. "Sneak into my apartment tonight, and you may get more than you bargained for."

Eve gasped exaggeratedly. "Even with your *sister* there?!"

Bo's eyes scanned her body, but Isaac walked between them, and Bo's eyes followed him with instant irritation as he made his way into the kitchen. Eve followed behind Isaac.

"We should probably eat something," she said, tapping her index finger to her shoulder, then across to the other shoulder. She touched the fingertips of a flat O-handshape to her lips. She raised her brows and curled her hand into a C, running it down her throat to the center of her chest, then pointed at Isaac. "You hungry?" she asked him aloud.

He dipped his head in affirmation.

She looked in the fridge. "I wonder if we should wait for Zeke and Eoduun. They should be back soon, shouldn't they?" she asked Bo.

Bo looked at his watch. "They're usually gone for half the day when they go on their hikes. They could still be awhile."

"There's leftover Chinese takeout in here from last night," Eve said, pulling out the containers to inspect the contents. She held out the container in her hand. "Any takers?" she asked.

Isaac reached out and took the container from her and grabbed a fork from the drawer. He was still looking at her strangely. Eve could tell he was confused by her aura, which made her curious as to what it looked like now.

She held her palms up. *What?*

He set the container on the counter and started signing, but he was using too many signs too quickly. Ruth's ASL knowledge wasn't that advanced. She signed, *Slow down.*

He huffed in annoyance, his eyes flicking briefly to Bo. Then, reluctantly, he picked up the takeout box and said, "All of the black mist is gone. Since I got here, you've been a mix of black and light, or, like earlier today, just black. Never all light. But now you're all light. I don't understand it. You have obvious werewolf powers," he said, gesturing to her eyes, "yet not a bit of black. All monsters have some black." He looked at Bo and signed, *Even you.*

"Why the fuck does he sign at me? He knows I can't understand him," Bo complained to Eve.

"He said even you have black in your aura. From what he says, black means bad, and light means good. From what I've seen in his memories, most people are a somewhere in between, some tend more toward dark, some more toward light, but monsters are usually black or close to black. But my aura, or mist, is weird. It's straight black and straight light, swirling together."

"So, what happened to the monster in you?" Isaac asked, taking a bite of noodles. "Where did it go? Is it sleeping?" He glanced at Bo again, then back to Eve. "And what does he have to do with it?" He set the container down again with the fork in it and pointed toward Bo, brushed his thumb under his chin, then held up his index finger and acted like he was lifting it with his other hand. *He's not special.*

"What did he say?" Bo wanted to know, scowling.

Isaac acted like Bo wasn't even there, picking up his food and taking another bite.

Eve offered Bo one of the other takeout boxes, but Bo shook his head. She grabbed a pair of chopsticks from the drawer and dug into it herself. "He wants to know what makes you special," she said.

"He could've said it."

"He could've. But he didn't."

Bo's phone started ringing, and adrenaline shot through Eve's heart. She saw the color drain from Bo's face as he looked down at it. When he saw the name on the screen, however, relief washed over his features.

Cass.

Her and Bo's eyes met, and she knew he was feeling the same way. They weren't ready to face Luc yet.

Bo answered the call, then had go back to his apartment for a moment to check his fridge and cupboards and see if Cassie needed to pick up anything from the store before they came home.

When Bo was gone, Isaac commented aloud, "You looked worried."

Eve continued to look down at the lo mein in front of her, and nodded. She suddenly wasn't hungry. "I thought it was going to be Luc. He is not going to be happy about what I did with Bo."

"Knowing what I know about Luc, I'm glad it was Bo and not me."

Eve gave him an apologetic, furtive glance. "I can't even express how sorry I am about that," she said, circling her fist over her chest. "I wish I hadn't put you in that position. Now that I know how bad it can get, I'll make sure to take measures to prevent it from ever happening again. I swear, I'll never come after you like that again."

Isaac shrugged. "It wasn't *you*. I get that. But you better get that shit under control. I'm starting to like you. I don't want to have to kill you."

"Well, let's be honest. You decided not to kill me, if you recall."

Isaac gave her an unamused, flat look. "Did I make the wrong choice?"

Eve shook her head quickly. He took the last bite from the takeout container and tossed it in the garbage. He started to walk past her, but stopped next to her. "Do you remember anything from last night?" he asked.

She looked up at him. He was so close, his scent was overwhelming to her stolen senses. She could hear the breath in his lungs and his heart beating in his chest. Perfectly calm and steady.

"I'm sorry about that, too," she apologized. "I didn't mean to trigger you. My drunk ass thought you were Bo."

Isaac watched her mouth forming the words, then his eyes slid back up to meet hers. He leaned a little closer, and his voice was low when he said, "You stayed. You made sure I was ok. You cared. *That's* why I didn't kill you." He left her with that, grabbed his jacket, and walked out of the apartment.

How was she supposed to feel about that?

Eve's phone rang from the living room, but it sounded muffled. Shit. That would be Luc.

She rushed out to the living room and fumbled around, following the sound of her ringtone. Finally, she pulled her phone from between the cushions of the couch just as the ringing stopped.

She looked down at the lock screen, and was surprised to see text notifications from a strange number alongside Luc's missed call alert.

She opened the texts, and her mouth went instantly dry.

They were pictures of Luc. Compromising, *recent* pictures of Luc, obviously taken without his knowledge. They looked like security camera stills. Luc bending a red-headed beauty over a desk in a fancy-looking office. Luc tangling tongues with a busty blond. Luc from behind with long, lean, bare legs wrapped around his hips, and manicured nails on his back. The timestamps on each picture corresponded to a date when he was away from the compound.

There was even one from last night. A gorgeous tawny goddess was riding on his lap on a couch in a cushy office with his name on the giant, wooden desk.

And then she got to one with Luc and Mira in the war room, fucking on the conference table. She recognized the papers on the table and the shirt he was wearing – the day he planted the fake plan to the other Knighco members, only days ago.

He fucked Mira only days ago. Here. At the compound. *In Eve's spot at the table.*

Bile rose in her throat. She was going to vomit. She dropped the phone and ran to the bathroom just as her lo mein came back up.

Bo appeared in the doorway. "Jesus, are you ok?" he asked, worried, as she retched into the toilet.

"Don't look at me!" she shouted before retching again.

Bo ignored her and came into the bathroom. He scooped her hair up and held it back with one hand, rubbing her back with his other hand. "Was it the takeout?" he asked.

Eve began to sob. Her heart was shattered.

Luc was deceiving her.

Her phone was ringing out in the living room, but she had no desire to ever answer it again. She never wanted to see him again. Or hear his voice. Nope. She was done.

It wasn't simply that he was sleeping with other women. She was sleeping with other men, after all. *But.* They'd agreed to this arrangement. He knew who she was with. He'd *approved* who she was with. And then he'd told her he wanted only her. He told her he wasn't sleeping with anyone else.

He fucking lied.

Right to her face, he'd lied.

She was a fucking idiot for ever trusting him in the first place. She was an idiot for ever believing that a man like that would settle for her. Here it was – that other shoe she'd been waiting for. Expecting. And yet…it still hit her like a fucking gut punch.

"Evie?" Bo's voice was raised in concern. "Evie, what's going on? Your eyes are yellow again."

"He's a fucking liar!"

Bo was confused. "What?"

Eve gestured wildly at her phone out on the floor in the living room. "Go see for yourself!" She angrily ripped some toilet paper from the roll and wiped her mouth after spitting into the toilet, then she flushed away her disgust. She rinsed her mouth out in the bathroom sink as Bo looked through the photos on her phone. She glanced up at herself in the mirror, and furious, yellow wolf eyes glared back at her.

"That's his office in LA," Bo said quietly. "And that's Paris. What…there must be some explanation…" He looked up from the phone and gave Eve a pitying look. "These have to be photoshopped."

"From who? Ruth is *here*, and I have all of her memories. There's nothing in her memory bank of doing anything like this!"

"Luc has plenty of enemies who could be capable of photoshopping some pictures."

Eve stormed up to him and snatched the phone from him, hitting the "Ignore" button as Luc tried to call once again. She then scrolled to the picture of Luc and Mira in the war room. "How did they photoshop that, then? You know as well as I do that even if all of the other pictures were photoshopped, *that* picture is legit."

"Then who took it? We don't even have a security camera in that room."

"I don't know! I had cameras planted in my apartment, remember? Maybe there were more around the compound that we didn't know about."

"You can't trust this, Evie," Bo reasoned. "You should at least talk to him about it."

"Oh, I'm going to talk to him about it, and then I'm never talking to him again." She began furiously texting.

Really, Luc? She attached the picture of him and Mira, and sent it.

And this? She attached the picture dated from last night. Send.

How long have you been lying to me? She attached the rest of the pictures. Send.

Luc replied. *Where the fuck did those come from? Obviously that's not me.*

Sure. Right. Then she added, *We're done.* Send.

The phone rang, and Eve immediately denied the call. It rang again, and she denied it again.

"He won't be ignored, Evie," Bo warned her.

The little tattoo on her wrist began to tingle strangely, and she reached down and rubbed it.

Luc suddenly appeared in the room, right in front of Eve, and she shrieked in surprise.

9
No One Should Be Able to Shatter Me So Easily

"We're *done*?" he barked in disbelief. "We need to talk about this!" Then he saw her face. He slowly removed his sunglasses. "Holy shit, your eyes." He turned and looked at Bo. "What have you done?" he accused, confusion twisting his handsome face.

Eve held up her phone with the pictures of Luc and his lovers on the screen and shoved it into his hands. "What have *you* done?!" Eve seethed. She felt the hairs on her skin begin to prickle with electricity as rage clawed through her veins.

Luc scoffed. "Obviously, that's not me," he said easily. Then he caught Eve's eyes again. "You *know* that's not me, don't you?"

"Do I know that, Luc?" she growled.

Luc frowned at her. "You dare to confront me about these ludicrous, alleged indiscretions, and all the while, you're wearing my brother's shirt and glaring at me with *his* eyes?! How long has *this* been going on?"

"This," Eve gestured between herself and Bo, "wasn't going on! Something happened with my curse today, but I'm not going to explain myself to you. Not after this! You fucking *liar!"*

"You don't believe that that isn't me?" he questioned with incredulity.

She snatched the phone from him and brought up the picture of Mira. "How the fuck did someone fake this one, then?"

Luc looked at it. He shook his head. "I don't know, but they did. Eve, that's *not* me. Call Mira. She'll tell you we didn't do that."

"Like I'd believe a word out of her mouth, either. She's so desperate for your attention, she'd say anything for you."

The pressure in the room was becoming stifling. Her ears felt like they were about to pop, and there was a buzzing vibration in the air. She couldn't tell if it was coming from her or from Luc.

Maybe it was both.

Luc's nostrils flared. "I love you desperately, Eve. I would never do anything to hurt you. Don't dare to do me the cruel disservice of believing some anonymous stranger with a dark motive over *me*." His voice was threatening, and the room began to darken.

"Typical answer from a typical narcissist," Eve shot back. Static began to zap between her fingers. "'Don't believe the evidence right in front of your face, Eve. You're *crazy*,'" she mocked in a falsely deep voice.

"I never said you were crazy," Luc snarled. He stepped toward her. "But you do need to calm the fuck down so we can talk things over rationally."

"Don't fucking tell me to calm down!" Eve roared, and she heard the pop of an electric receptacle. A burning smell accosted her nose. The acrid scent of anxiety and fear permeated the air, and Eve wondered if it was coming from her. Three thunderous heartbeats drummed in her ears, like a foreboding battle drum heralding the devastation to come.

"Is this all it takes for you to turn on me?!" Luc shouted, gesturing to her phone. "Do you trust me so fucking little? Haven't you seen all the tricks, shapeshifting, spells…? God, the fact that you choose to believe I'm guilty without even *considering* that these photos were a clever trick designed to do exactly *this?!* It's *infuriating!*"

Every lightbulb in the apartment exploded, bathing the room in darkness as glass showered down, and Eve leapt back from Luc, her fists up in guard position.

The darkness was broken by a glow in the room, and when Eve looked down, she realized it was her. Blue streaks of electricity danced across her skin, like she was a living, breathing Tesla coil, focusing in her fists. She looked up at Luc.

"You don't want to fight me right now," she threatened tremulously, holding a guarded stance.

"Evie!" Bo interjected, surprised.

Luc was just as taken aback. "I don't *ever* want to fight you," he said, confusion coloring his features. "Haven't we been over this? *I won't hurt you.* Yes, I'm insulted! I'm hurt! I feel betrayed!" Luc shouted, waving his hands emphatically. "So, yeah, I'm going to yell! We're going to fight – but with our fucking *words*, Eve! Put your fucking fists down and *talk to me*, goddamn it!"

"*You're* hurt? *You* feel betrayed?!"

"Yes! Me! How could you be so quick to believe the worst of me? The only conclusion I can draw is that you were *expecting* something like this. Which means you never trusted me to begin with. And yeah, love. That fucking *hurts*," he growled, pressing his fist to his chest.

Eve suddenly smelled tobacco smoke. Isaac was coming. *Fuck.* She couldn't let him see her like this. If he saw this, he would know for certain that she was dangerous. There would be no more questioning or gray area. She was unhinged.

He would kill her.

…Or at least he would try.

When Isaac opened the door, the room went dark. Eve had quickly shut down the rage, the fury, the heartbreak – she walled it off and dissociated from it. She heard Isaac's heart rate and breathing accelerate, and he drew his knives from the sheaths on his belt. He clicked the light switch twice, but the room remained dark.

The room slowly began to light up with an ethereal glow, and Eve knew it was Luc. She'd seen him do it before. He could make the air itself glow or darken.

When Luc spoke, his voice was calm, but stern. "I'm going to go find some lightbulbs, and we'll talk when I get back."

"I don't want to talk to you again tonight," Eve snipped.

"Too fucking bad. I'm not giving you space on this."

Luc pushed past a confused Isaac and stormed from the apartment.

"*Fuck*!" Eve heard Luc shout in frustration as he made his way down the hallway, and with that one outburst, the entire apartment complex shuddered and reverberated as though the very earth had quaked, and Eve felt it all the way through her chest.

She collapsed to the floor, her knees suddenly too weak to hold her up.

Shit was royally fucked.

Was she in the wrong? She'd been so confident that she was right, but now that the dust had settled temporarily, she wasn't so sure. But who could fake those pictures? Who *would*? Dizzy, a shapeshifter, had betrayed them. He could've impersonated Luc…but *Mira*? And what about the pictures in Luc's LA office, and the one from last night, in his Paris office?

She wasn't sure of anything. There was no truth, only a thousand different possibilities.

She wanted to run away and hide.

Her phone chimed. She looked down through blurry tears, and saw that the strange number had now sent her a video. She played it, knowing she should just leave it alone, knowing it was only going to hurt.

Luc's face appeared on the screen. He was sitting at an outdoor café, leaned back with one knee casually crossed over the other, an easy smile on his face, his sunglasses on. He was facing toward the camera, but not looking at it. It looked like he was conversing with someone just outside the view of the camera.

"Eve?" he scoffed. "Don't worry about Eve. I have it under control."

An unfamiliar man's voice replied, "You sure about that?"

"Of course. She's hopelessly obsessed with me." He gave the off-camera man an arrogant smirk. "She'll stick with us. If she's as powerful as I think she is, we need her on our side, especially now that Ruth went and raised another fucking *god*. Can you imagine if I had her sleep with him and steal his powers? And if she stacked them with mine? Or Dagon's? Or *all* of them? Can you imagine?" he repeated, excitement growing in his voice. "We've never had such a devastating weapon at our disposal."

"What if she resists? She may not want to sleep with them," the strange man asked.

"She'll do what needs to be done. She'll do anything I ask."

"I'm hearing rumors that you're in love with her."

Luc laughed derisively. "Me? In *love*? Fuck no. You know me better than that. I'll have my fun, but I don't do *love*."

The video ended, but Eve just continued to stare at the screen, unable to process what she'd just seen.

"There must be an explanation," Bo said calmly from behind her. She hadn't even realized he was there. She turned around and looked up, and Isaac was there, too. They were both looking down at her. They'd seen the video.

"Whatever. I don't even care anymore," she lied, swiping burning tears from her eyes. "Him, not him…does it even matter? It's the truth, isn't it? I'm only worth something to him because of my specialty. It has nothing to do with me as a person."

"You know that's not true," Bo argued. "This is probably clever use of AI. Or Dizzy. You've seen how well he can impersonate. How completely he can steal an identity. Why aren't you even considering that possibility? That *likelihood*?"

"Because men like Luc don't pick women like me unless there's something else to be gained from it. It's as simple as that." She blackened the screen on her phone. "Even if this isn't Luc, it was the wake-up call I needed. No one should have this kind of power over me. No one should be able to shatter me so easily." She stood up and placed her phone on the counter. "I'd almost forgotten who I was. I'd started to let him shape me into something else." She looked at Bo with cold eyes. "You all did. You softened me. Molded me. Weakened my independence. Made me feel like I needed you. And it was my fault for letting it happen."

Never again. The pieces of her heart lay in splinters in the pit of her stomach, and it sickened her. Even if the man in the pictures and video wasn't Luc, it had alerted her to the danger she was in with him. If it wasn't him this time, it was only a matter of time before it was. She couldn't do this.

She went to the door and slipped her shoes on, then returned to the kitchen. She grabbed a filet knife from the drawer, and before she could overthink it or change her mind, she shallowly carved the tattoo from her wrist in one bloody swipe.

"EVIE!" Bo cried, and he and Isaac both rushed at her.

"I'm so sorry, Bo," she said, and she let the urge to be anywhere but there overwhelm her and take her wherever it would.

10

Eventually, You're Going to Need Me

Something was dragging her down as she pushed through the space around her to escape. Luc hadn't exaggerated – it was like trying to lift a Mac truck. Or push one. When she reached the destination that she already knew she would end up at, she found the reason for the drag.

Isaac was gripping her arm. She'd just warped time and space around her and Isaac *both*. Even Luc couldn't do that.

Well. Fucking kudos.

Isaac looked around at the moss-covered cedar swamp they found themselves in, then quickly diverted his attention to Eve's gushing wrist. She hadn't hit the main artery, but she was bleeding profusely, especially for her. He took his lighter from his pocket and lit it, holding it up under one of his knives. After a minute, he grabbed her wrist and touched the flat side of his knife to her injury, cauterizing the wound.

She cried out at the searing burn, the scent of burned flesh tingling in her nose. Isaac then ripped the lower part of his shirt and tied it around her wrist.

When he was done, she looked at him flatly. She touched her fingers to her head and drew away a Y-handshape. "Why the fuck do you care?" she asked ungratefully.

He looked around again, ignoring her question. He touched his finger from one side of his chest to the other, then pivoted his index finger from side to side. *Where are we?*

Eve fingerspelled *Michigan,* then *Black Lake.* She went to a fallen tree trunk and sat down, not caring if she got her sweatpants dirty.

Isaac continued to look around. *Peaceful*, he signed.

She pointed at herself and touched her fingers to her temple. *I know.*

He signed, *Why are we here?*

"*You* weren't supposed to be here," she said, not bothering to sign this time. She lay back on the log, ignoring the fear that she was going to end up with spiders in her hair. She looked up at the canopy of cedar above her.

Isaac came up and leaned over her, looking down at her. "Why are *you* here?" he amended aloud.

"Because this stupid little spot in the swamp is my happy place," she replied. "When I was a kid, I would pack up a snack and whatever book I was reading at the time and hike around the lake to get here to try to forget how much I hated the world. To me, this place looked like something from a fantasy novel. It felt so far away from the real world. It was my escape. Still is, I guess."

"So, you're running away," he concluded.

"It's what I'm good at."

"I can't let you run. You know that," Isaac informed her.

"Then kill me. I'm not sure I care anymore."

Isaac furrowed his brow. "You don't mean that."

She shifted her eyes to meet his. "Don't I? Because you know me so well, you can tell me that with confidence?"

"I only know you because you wanted me to know you. It's not a weakness, you know – connecting with people."

Eve laughed cynically.

"You know me, too, though, don't you?" Isaac continued. "As much as I threaten it, you know I won't kill you. *Can't* kill you," he admitted, looking away.

She turned her head toward him. "See? Weakness."

"Nah," Isaac shook his head. "Killing a problem is weak. Easy. Taking the effort to fix it instead? That's where real strength lies."

"Yeah. Go ahead and try to fix me. You'll just grow to hate me. Everyone eventually does."

"I don't think they do. I think it's just easier for you push them away and pretend they do."

Tears welled in Eve's eyes, and she scowled and looked away. "Shut the fuck up. Go away."

Isaac sat down on the log by her feet. He tapped a cigarette out of his pack and lit it. He took a long drag, then exhaled heavily. He pulled out his knife, picked up a stick, and started whittling it while his cigarette hung from his lips. "So, are we staying out here, or is there somewhere else you're planning to go for food and shelter?" he mumbled around the cigarette in his mouth.

"You can't stay with me. They'll track your phone."

Isaac set aside his whittling and withdrew his phone from his jacket pocket. He ejected the sim card, then held his lighter to it to melt it. Then he whipped the phone itself off into the swamp water. "Better?" he asked.

"That was stupid," she said.

"Probably."

Finally, she sat up, moss and debris sticking in her hair. "You aren't someone who makes stupid choices like that. What the fuck are you playing at?"

"I can't let a potential threat to society out of my sight. Besides, eventually, you're going to need me."

"I don't need you. I told you to go away."

"So did I," he said, resuming his whittling. She gave him a confused look, but he ignored it. "You never answered me. Are we surviving out here tonight, or are we going to make our way to civilization?" He looked at her expectantly.

She started picking debris from her hair. "The nearest town is ten miles away. And I don't have my wallet."

She hadn't really thought this through. She knew she didn't have enough juice left to jump again just yet, and even if she did, she doubted she had the control to do it again without the emotion driving it. She was completely drained and exhausted.

"You used to hike here from your house?" he asked. "Can't you just walk to your house?"

"No," she said wearily. "No, I can't."

He didn't pry. He just stood up and said, "Well. I guess we're foraging."

"No, I'm wallowing. I can't eat anyway. I'll just throw it up." Her stomach was still sick.

"You know, I'm going to run out of cigarettes soon, and then I'm going to be unbearable. We will need to get to that town at some point."

"Do you suppose my blood heals addiction?" she asked absently.

"Or maybe it just replaces it with another one."

A sudden realization struck Eve like shot to the chest. "Shit. I'm going to need...attention...at some point." She looked at Isaac with dismay.

He didn't look surprised. "Like I said: eventually, you're going to need me," he reminded her calmly, not looking at her, like he'd simply accepted his fate.

They sat in silence for a long time before Eve found a change of subject. "You don't seem to have any issues talking to me. Why don't you talk to anyone else? And don't give me that 'I don't want to' bullshit."

Isaac was thoughtful. "It's how I filter out the people who aren't worth my time." Eve looked quizzical, so he elaborated. "I don't waste my breath on people who wouldn't learn a few simple signs for me. No point in communicating with someone who doesn't care enough to make an effort. It keeps my circle small." He paused. "That's how I like it."

"You don't talk to Luc, though, and he signs for you. And Ramil knows ASL, yet you told me he wasn't trustworthy."

"Just because someone *does* sign, it doesn't automatically make me want to talk to them, either," Isaac said. "And Ramil isn't trustworthy. His aura is dark. He has ill-intent, and it gets darker when he's near you," he revealed, gesturing toward her with his knife.

Eve was reminded of her bodily response to Ramil when she sparred with him in the gym. The thing inside of her tried to attack him, like some kind of automated self-defense system. And she remembered Dagon suggesting using Ramil to draw out her monstrous powers. Did Dagon know something about Ramil? Was Dizzy not the only infiltrator?

Well, if Ramil was part of some plan against Knighco, or against Eve, Ruth didn't know about it. He was nowhere in her memories.

Isaac wandered around and collected wood, and even killed a snapping turtle, while Eve sat like a literal bump on a log. To keep her mind off of Luc and Bo and everything going on back at the compound, she tried to occupy herself by watching Isaac as he came and went and worked on building a fire and processing the turtle. As she watched him, she realized he was enjoying himself out here in the swamp.

Like a quiet little ogre.

She chuckled to herself.

Isaac glanced up at her over the fire, catching her smile. He brushed his nose twice with his first two fingers and held his palms upward. *What's funny?*

And they were back to signing again. She shook her head, touching the side of a flat O-handshape to her chin and extending it out in front of her as she opened her hand. *Nothing.*

Then she turned away from him because her face suddenly crumpled. Nothing was funny. Everything was shit. She'd lost everything. *Everything.*

What the fuck was she even doing here? She wanted to go home. But she wanted to go to the home she had the day before, not to the flaming mess she'd left behind today. If she was even able to go home now, what would she walk into? And what did ending things with Luc actually mean?

We're done. She choked on a sob. She didn't want to be done. But then she remembered what triggered the blowout in the first place, and she was heartbroken all over again. Was it him? Was it not? Would she ever know for sure? She shouldn't have blown up the way she did without finding out more. She should've listened to Bo. Her goddamn quick temper was always her downfall, and she fucking hated herself for it. Well, not just for that. In reality, she just fucking hated herself.

She hated Eve.

Eve was a stupid fucking bitch.

She unwrapped the makeshift bandage from her wrist and found that she had healed already. She rubbed the falling teardrops from the blank spot on her wrist where Luc's mark used to adorn her skin. Her stomach hollowed into a pit of despair and her chest tightened in a vice grip as she acknowledged that this spot would likely remain blank forever. Luc would never reclaim her.

And she shouldn't want him to. She needed to let him go, because this was their inevitable end. It was always going to end like this. She did this to herself. Everything about it, she did to herself. She let him in. She let him get cozy. And then at the first sign of trouble, she ripped him out like a finishing scene in *Mortal Kombat.*

It was her fault. She knew that. It always was.

Eve tucked her legs up and crossed her arms over her knees, resting her forehead on her forearms, and leaned her back against the fallen log. She felt Isaac sit next to her a few minutes later, but she didn't lift her head.

"It's been too long, princess."

Eve lifted her head from her forearms. Dagon sat across the dying fire from her, his knees angled outward with his elbows resting casually on top of them. His hands hung loosely between his legs. He tilted his head curiously at her, a lazy grin on his face as his vermillion eyes studied her. He was in his original form – with his long, dark hair, black beard, and intimidatingly huge body covered in ancient-looking tattoos. He wore dark pants, but no shirt or shoes, and his massive black wings curved over his back.

"I'm not in any kind of condition to handle your bullshit right now. Especially after you betrayed us, you piece of shit."

"Piece of shit? It wasn't like I tricked you. I told you what I was going to do, and I even gave you options. And then everyone acted all shocked when I did exactly what I said I was going to do. And then I wake up from another sealing, look through Zeke's mind to see what I missed, and hooooo boy…" Dagon whistled. "Princess. What have you done now?" He started counting off on his giant fingers as he listed, "Erased Ruth, broke Luc *and* Bo, ran off with all of Ruth's secrets, kidnapped a Vatican exorcist, cut off your tracking device with a fucking *filet knife*, and fucking poof! Disappeared with the powers you stole from Bo." Dagon raised his thick black brows and nodded. "I didn't think I could be any more impressed with you, but I was wrong. That's just…" he touched his fingers to his lips in a chef's kiss. "Beautiful."

"I forgot how much I fucking hate you," Eve spat.

Dagon's eyes flashed with unbridled rage, and in the next moment, his face was inches from hers, his arms on either side of her shoulders, his hands gripping the fallen log behind her. His wings spread wide and blocked out the light from the fire. "I warned you never to say that to me," he snarled.

"Then don't do things to make me feel that way about you," she retorted, trying to remain calm as fear gripped her heart and adrenaline shot through her. "What do you want, Dagon?"

The rage slowly faded, and his sneering expression returned. He folded his wings back. "I missed you. It's been too long. I haven't touched you in ages." He reached a hand to her face, stroking her cheek, then he slid his fingers through her hair. She hated that his touch felt so familiar on her skin. He touched his lips to hers, slipping his tongue into her mouth, and she hated how it stirred her.

He smiled against her lips and laughed low. "You're afraid to kiss me back? It's just a dream, princess. It's ok to give in."

"You're after Ruth's memories in my head," Eve blurted.

"Always straight to business with you these days. You used to be more fun," Dagon complained, trailing his lips down the column of her throat.

"I can't do anything for you without the grimoire anyway," Eve said. "And we don't have it, so there's nothing I can do for you."

"I'm patient. We'll get it, and you'll free me."

"What happens to Zeke when you're extracted? How does he die?" Eve asked as Dagon's tongue swirled over the skin just beneath her ear. Fuck, why did it have to feel so good?

"I don't know. I've never been contained to a vessel before this."

"Will his body even be in a condition that can be revived? What if he incinerates or turns to ash or something?"

"I don't know. I'm not terribly concerned about what happens to him after I leave him."

"If you ever want to leave him, you better make it your concern. Because I won't free you if I can't be guaranteed Zeke's survival," Eve told him.

Dagon suddenly stopped as his lips began to trail down the neckline of the shirt she'd taken from Bo. He gripped the neck of her shirt and tugged it down, exposing the soft mound of her breast.

"What the fuck is this?" he demanded.

She looked down, but didn't see anything. "Um, my fucking tit?"

"Someone is bound to you," Dagon seethed. His blazing red eyes leapt up to meet hers. "Who the fuck did you bind to you?!"

Eve pinched her brows. "How can you tell?"

"Who?!" he roared, furious.

"Apep! But I didn't do it! It was transferred when I erased Ruth, and then he disappeared, along with Dizzy and the grimoire!" Eve cried, suddenly terrified of Dagon's rage.

He held his hand over her chest, and it suddenly started to burn like someone had stuck a hot branding iron straight to her heart. "Fuck! Stop!" she shrieked, pushing at his hand.

Dagon growled and dropped his hand. "Fuck! I can't release it." He stared at her chest like he wanted to claw into it. Eve wasn't entirely sure that he wasn't going to.

"What does it mean?" she asked apprehensively, covering her heart with her hand.

"It means you're connected with another god. Someone who isn't *me*. How fucking *dare* he," Dagon rumbled. "I've already claimed you. You shouldn't have been able to bind another to you!"

Eve almost choked. "You already *claimed* me? What the fuck does *that* mean?!"

"It means you bear *my* mark! To other gods, you belong to *me*!" he declared, thrusting his thumb into his chest.

"Since fucking when?!"

"Since I awakened the Blood of Lilith inside of you!"

11

Dead on the Inside, the Illusion of Life on the Outside

"It appears I'm bound to you now. But…not entirely." That was what Apep had said to her. Was Dagon the reason why?

"So, what can Apep use his connection with me for?" Eve asked, hoping the question wouldn't enrage Dagon any further.

"He can find you wherever you are, like me. He can speak to you from anywhere when you call to him, like me. But this binding is more for your benefit than his. He can't harm you or intentionally set events into motion that will bring you harm.

"But since I claimed you first, and since mine was a voluntary binding, his binding to you didn't fully take. You can't tell him what to do, and you can't keep him from hurting anyone else. And if it's truly Apep you've bound to you, then he *will* hurt people. Destruction and chaos used to follow everywhere he went. He'll probably kill off everyone around you…except me and Zeke, of course, because I won't let that happen."

"How do I undo this binding?" Eve fretted.

"Kill him."

Eve sighed heavily. "Easier said than done, I'm assuming."

Dagon sat back on his haunches, pouting. He was no longer interested in molesting Eve. "Apep is a true monster. If you think I'm evil, you're going to find him absolutely intolerable. He hasn't an inkling of what you humans call a conscience."

"And you do?" Eve scoffed.

"I have scruples. They may not always align with yours, but I have them."

Eve couldn't believe she was about to ask this. "What should I do?"

Dagon stopped pouting and smirked at her. "Are you really asking 'what would Dagon do?'" he mused.

"I'll take help anywhere I can, it would seem."

"You already know what to do. It's what you were built for."

"I'm not fucking him."

Dagon arched a brow. "You can take him down with that singular power, that curse you possess, just as you did the Jötunn. No one else has to be put at risk, and hell, you'll enjoy it."

"I'm not doing that," she declared stubbornly. "What else can I do?"

Dagon rolled his eyes and sighed before answering, "You need to take the fight to him – take him by surprise. You're the only one who'll be able to get close to him and kill him, so, if I were you, I would stack as many powers as you can, including mine. Go nuclear or go home."

"That sounds…exhausting."

"Not if you can hold the powers for more than a day. And judging by the fresh state of those eyes you took from Bo, you've had some kind of breakthrough on the longevity front."

"What are you talking about? Fresh state of my eyes?"

Dagon pointed at her eyes. "I saw them flash yellow. The power behind them isn't fading as quickly as my powers faded from you. What's the trick?" he asked.

She frowned. "I have no idea."

Dagon stood up. "Better figure it out soon, princess. The clock is ticking, and you're going to need the power of your whole harem if you want to take down Apep and get that grimoire."

Eve laughed mirthlessly. "My harem? I don't think that exists anymore. Not after this."

"They're your pets. They'll be waiting eagerly at the door for your return with wagging tails and tongues lolling. You can beat them and abuse them, and they'll still come running every time you snap your fingers or call their name. That's the kind of power you have over them, because they've all drunk from the cup."

"So have you."

Dagon held his hands out in display. "And here I am, princess."

Eve's lower back was killing her when her eyes blinked open. She'd fallen asleep with her back resting against the mossy, fallen tree. The morning light was just starting to filter through the trees into her magical little sanctuary, and as she started to stir, she noticed Isaac was still next to her, his hand next to her foot. She looked down, and saw he had hooked the first three fingers of his right hand through her shoelaces.

She tried to gingerly lift his hand and untangle his fingers from her laces, but he awoke instantly. He squinted at her as he quickly pulled his hands away from her shoes. He signed, *Where are you going?*

She made a T shape and shook it side to side. *Bathroom.*

He arched his back over the log behind them and stretched, groaning.

Eve pointed at her back, then signed, *My back hurts. Does yours?*

He fixed her with a flat gaze. He made his hands into O-handshapes and pushed them away, then pointed his index fingers together. After a brief pause, he circled one index finger in the air. *Nothing hurts. Ever.*

Oh, that's right. Must be nice.

When she returned from peeing behind a tree, she signed to Isaac, *Let's go bathe in the lake.*

Isaac insisted on standing lookout while Eve undressed and jumped in the lake. She used to swim in this lake when she was a kid, but looking at it now, she wondered why. She wouldn't have jumped into it if she didn't smell like a gym bro.

When she climbed out, she used her hands to firmly swipe the excess water from her limbs. "Don't be peeking, now," Eve joked, knowing full well Isaac couldn't hear her or see her lips moving while his head was turned away. Honestly, she didn't give a fuck if he looked or not. She wasn't ashamed of her body, and she knew she was safe with him, in a manner of speaking.

As safe as one can be with one's assassin.

She didn't have a towel, and she didn't want to put her clothes on wet, so she just stood there for a while, air drying, goosebumps erupting all over her body. It wasn't cold enough to shiver, but she wasn't exactly comfortable.

Isaac turned his head slightly, checking on her without directly looking at her. "Get dressed," he said aloud, his back still to her.

She walked around in front of him, and he averted his gaze, clenching his jaw in annoyance.

"I'm still wet," she said, exaggerating her mouth movements, knowing he was still watching her out of the corner of his eye. "Why don't you go rinse off while I drip-dry."

"I'm not leaving you alone up here, vulnerable like this. Put some clothes on."

"Vulnerable?" Eve laughed. "Honey, I'm the most dangerous when I'm naked."

Isaac turned his eyes to hers, locking onto *only* her eyes. He exhaled heavily, then touched his thumb to his chest with his fingers vertically splayed and drew it away. *Fine.*

Eve watched him walk down to the lake. As he stripped off his jacket and shirt, he turned to look at her. He scowled and gestured for her to turn around.

What a prude.

She waited for him to get in the water, then walked down to the water's edge. She was *almost* dry, so she put her clothes back on. Bo's t-shirt and her moss-stained sweatpants. When Isaac was ready to come out, he saw her sitting on the dock, skimming her bare toes in the water.

"I want to get out now," he informed her.

"Then get out."

"Not with you right there, looking at me."

"It's just a body. Nothing to be ashamed of," she replied.

"I've seen the way you look at it," he retorted. He put his hands on his hips, the waterline dancing just below his bellybutton. "…And the way you're looking at it right now."

Eve chuckled and lifted her eyes from his abs. "Sorry. I won't look. I promise." She looked down at her own reflection in the water over the edge of the dock, between her feet. Bo's golden wolf eyes stared back up at her, startling her.

Homesickness stabbed her in the heart. She missed Bo. She didn't get her *"Ohayou"* and coffee this morning, and she felt incomplete without it. She felt incomplete without *Bo*.

At least she had these eyes. Maybe if she covered her left eye and stared hard enough, she could pretend it was him gazing back at her with his hungry wolf eye.

No, she couldn't. She could never look at herself the way Bo looked at her.

She knew Isaac was watching her, making sure she didn't look up at him while he dressed, his body still wet. She clapped her hand over her eyes and lifted her head toward him so he could see her lips. "Should we try to get to town today?" she asked.

"You can uncover your eyes," he said. "I have pants on." He stood there, shirtless, and withdrew his cigarette pack from his jacket. He tapped out a cigarette. "Last one," he remarked.

"So, that's a yes, then? We could try to hitchhike, or I can try to teleport us." She dreaded the thought of trying to teleport them both again. It required so much effort. "I'd rather just sit in a car and get a ride, but..." She looked down at her clothes. "I don't know who would pick us up. I look like I'm homeless."

"You are homeless," Isaac said bluntly, lighting his cigarette.

That struck Eve hard, knocking the breath from her lungs.

You are homeless.

You are homeless.

You are homeless.

The words echoed through her head on repeat.

"You're a dick," she lashed out.

He raised his palms. "What?"

Eve dropped her gaze back to the water over the edge of the dock. She bent forward until her chest was resting on her thighs, and she hung her arms down by her legs, her fingertips skimming the water alongside her toes.

She wondered what was going on back at the compound. Back *home*. What was Luc doing? What was Bo doing? What kind of uproar had she caused? Was everybody pissed? Annoyed? Were they trying to trace where the photos had come from?

The thought of those photos and that video stabbed Eve straight through the heart afresh. She'd desperately wanted to believe Luc loved her. She *had* believed it. And, as much as she tried not to, she loved him back. She loved him still. If she didn't, this wouldn't hurt so fucking much.

Alas.

She'd definitely overreacted yesterday, hadn't she? It probably wasn't even him. But even if it was, she had no right to be jealous of his conquests, did she? It wasn't like she was sitting on her hands quietly at home waiting for him every day.

But if he was sleeping around, he should've told her. He should've communicated it with her instead of trying to act like he wasn't. She'd rather be jealous and know what's going on than be lied to and caught by surprise.

No. Actually, she'd rather just shut down and not feel anything at all. It was so much easier to not care. To not love. She needed to reinforce the walls she'd allowed to crumble and fall into disrepair. She was already mixing the mortar and stacking the bricks.

She glanced up at Isaac again. He was watching her, his cigarette smoldering between his thick fingers.

The surly, deaf Vatican exorcist assassin and the unhinged, sex-crazed MMA fighter. The Angel of Death and the Abomination. What a pair they made. Maybe they should start solving crimes together.

Isaac brushed his palms past each other. *Let's go.*

"You're really worried about running out of smokes, aren't you?" she replied, looking back down at the water.

"You won't like me without them," he warned.

"Who says I like you now?" She turned and looked at him, a smirk dancing on her lips. This felt more normal. Hiding behind jokes and sarcasm. Dead on the inside, the illusion of life on the outside.

"Who says I care?" he shot back.

Good one.

She slowly unfolded herself and stood up, brushing off her dirty sweatpants. She pointed at him, splayed her fingers with the middle fingers tucked in, then tapped her middle fingers to her chest alternately. *You care.*

She walked up to him. "Put on a shirt, you exhibitionist," she teased ironically.

Eve and Isaac made their way up to the road, and after walking about a mile, an older gentleman picked them up. As he drove them to town, Eve told him that Isaac was her deaf brother, and after watching her and Isaac signing back and forth, he took pity on them. He gave them twenty dollars when he dropped them off at the gas station and wished them well.

"It's nice to know there are still some good people in the world," Eve said as they walked into the gas station.

Isaac held his fist up, palm upward, then opened his fingers as he moved his hand to the side. *Few.*

They hit the bathroom first, and Eve chugged water from the tap. She was dying of thirst at this point, and it would've taken ten dollars-worth of bottled water to quench it. It was free in the bathroom. Isaac got his cigarettes at the counter, which took damn near half of the twenty the good Samaritan had given them, and they both got a nutrition bar.

As Eve stood at the cash register, something triggered feelings of home. Familiarity. What was it? Was it just nostalgia, being back in her home town after being away for so long? She sniffed, and realized it was something faint in the air. It made her heart race strangely.

As the cashier was throwing their items into a little plastic baggie, Isaac glanced at her, then pointed to his eyes, an urgent look on his face.

Shit, her eyes had shifted from her reaction the scent in the air.

"Those are cool contacts," the female cashier said to Eve. "It's kind of weird, because just yesterday I had someone in here with these crazy, bright blue eyes. I swear they had to have been contacts, too." She added absently, "And white hair. I wonder if he was cosplaying some anime character or something."

Eve's eyes widened. "Was he super tall and handsome? Dressed nicely? Sunglasses?"

"Yes! Odd little round ones. But you could still see those beautiful eyes. I've never seen eyes quite like them. You know him?"

Isaac and Eve shared questioning glances.

12

Go Read a Book

Was it Luc? Was it Dizzy? Was it someone else impersonating Luc? And if it was an imposter, were they still here in her hometown?

"What time did he come in, would you say?" Eve asked conversationally.

"It was right before my lunch break, so probably around noon."

Luc should've been in Paris at that time. It had to be Dizzy. Or someone else.

"He was looking for someone, but it wasn't a familiar name from around here. Stacey something? He showed me a picture, but he said it was from like twenty years ago," the cashier disclosed. Then she narrowed her eyes at Eve. "Actually, she kind of looked like you."

"That was my brother," Eve lied. "He's trying to track down our birth mother. You didn't happen to have any information for him, did you? I haven't talked to him in a few days."

The cashier surveyed Eve's mildly disheveled state briefly, obviously doubting her relationship to the debonair man she met yesterday. "No, sorry. I just moved here a couple years ago, so I'm the wrong person to ask about something like that."

Eve was lost in her thoughts when she and Isaac walked out of the gas station. Who would be impersonating Luc, looking for *her* mother? Why? And what have they found?

Isaac pointed at her and slid a 90-degree angled flat hand across under his chin, then touched his head and drew away a Y-handshape. *Why did you lie?*

She replied, *I didn't lie. Stacey is my mother. She died.*

Isaac furrowed his brow and asked, *Why is Luc looking for your mother?*

I don't think it was him. She fingerspelled *Dizzy* and alternatingly raised her flattened palms. *Maybe it was Dizzy.*

Why? Isaac wondered.

Eve shrugged and shook her head. Then she signed, *If we find him, we can ask him.*

Isaac touched his finger from one shoulder to the other, stuck the index finger of one hand between the fingers of the other hand and twisted it, then pivoted his raised index finger side to side. *Where do we start?*

Eve had no idea. She was a fighter, not an investigator. But Luc was a striking man, and anywhere he or his imposter had gone, people would remember him. And if it *was* Dizzy, and he was also walking around as himself, people would remember him, too, for exactly the opposite reason. He was an unfortunately odd-looking guy.

Isaac started packing his new pack of cigarettes against the heel of his hand as they made their way slowly down the sidewalk, and Eve glanced over at his ripped shirt. Then she looked down at her clothes. They couldn't go around asking questions looking like this.

"How much cash do you have?" she asked aloud now that his hands were occupied.

"Why?"

"We're going to hit up the thrift shop. Hopefully they're still doing the 'fill a bag for two dollars' deal on clothes."

"I think I can cover that," he said sarcastically.

"I'm also going to need like a dollar to print something at the library."

Isaac lit his cigarette. "You're an expensive date."

"I'm a classy bitch. I require pampering."

He cast a sideways glance her way. "How are you feeling? Your mist is still bright."

"Are you asking if I'm feeling like a cat in heat yet? No. I feel fine still."

Isaac took a drag from his cigarette, then mused, "I think you healed my lungs. I haven't coughed since you healed me."

"Then maybe this is your sign to stop smoking while you have a clean bill of health."

"Hell no. I love smoking."

"It doesn't bother you when people give you disapproving glares, or the way the smell sticks to your clothes, or having to go outside all the time just to partake? Smoking isn't really socially acceptable anymore."

Isaac looked at her and exhaled a thick cloud. "I embrace anything that keeps people away from me. Let them disapprove."

They walked to the thrift shop, and after digging through a lot of dated and geriatric options, they were able to fill a bag with some half-decent choices. They changed into their fresh outfits at the thrift shop, Eve donning a pair of cargo pants and a baggy t-shirt, and Isaac opting for jeans and a black t-shirt, and threw their dirty clothes in the bottom of the bag.

Isaac carried the bag of clothes in one arm as they headed to the library. "That was more than two dollars," he said, signing with one hand as he spoke aloud.

"Five dollars, Isaac. Still not that bad."

"Hmph."

"And to think, I have a pair of $1200 heels in my closet at home."

Isaac scoffed, and with his free hand he signed, *Why?*

"Because Luc wanted us to match."

Isaac held his splayed hand out, palm up, then flicked it off to the side. *What a waste of money.*

"I don't know. I can think of worse ways to spend money," Eve countered. "How much do you spend a year on cigarettes?"

Isaac narrowed his eyes at her and said nothing.

When they walked into the library, Eve was struck again by that faint scent that she'd detected in the gas station. It was only then that she placed it why it was so familiar.

Luc.

It was incredibly faint, but now she was certain. It was Luc's scent.

He had been here. Not Dizzy, not an imposter, but Luc himself, looking for information on her mother.

But, why? He'd told her he was going to Paris.

Her suspicions of him were renewed. If he was lying to her about where he was, maybe it *was* him in those pictures and videos after all.

A tremor weakened her knees, and she reached out to clutch onto Isaac's arm to stop herself from collapsing to the floor. But his instinctual reaction was to dodge her hand and yank his arm away, and Eve went down.

In the next moment, Isaac quickly dropped their bag of clothes and reached out to her, just barely catching her before she hit the floor. He lifted her back to her feet, then profusely circled his fist over his chest. *Sorry!*

"Are you all right, miss?" the librarian fretted, standing from her seat behind the circulation desk. Eve brushed herself off and bit back the tremble in her lip. She approached the mousy librarian with the dated haircut standing behind the desk. "I'm fine, just tripping over my own feet," Eve faked a laugh. "Just a quick question for you, though: did a tall Swedish-looking guy come in here yesterday asking about a woman named Stacey Rose?" she asked.

Surprise crossed the woman's features. "Yes, actually." She stared questioningly at Eve. "Why?"

"Can you tell me if he found anything about her?"

"I'm not sure. He spent an hour or so looking through microfilm."

"Did he check anything out or print anything?"

The woman's expression shifted to one of suspicion. "I'm not sure that's any of your business, ma'am."

"Stacey Rose was my mother. I'm just trying to find information on her."

"Might I suggest looking through the newspaper collection on microfilm?" the librarian responded. "That's the only advice I have for you, apart from checking public records at the courthouse."

"Did he go to the courthouse, too?" Eve blurted without thinking.

"I'm sure I have no idea," the woman frowned disdainfully.

Eve nodded, chagrined. "That's fair. Ok. Thanks."

As they walked away from the desk, Eve signed, *Change of plans. It really was Luc, not an imposter.*

Isaac touched the back of his fingers together and flipped his palms upward, then touched his temple and pointed at her. *How do you know?*

"Thanks to Bo's gifts, I can recognize Luc's scent here," she whispered aloud.

Isaac signed, *What now?*

Eve pursed her lips. She signed, *We investigate my mother.* She added aloud, "Maybe we'll figure out what he was after."

Eve sat down at the one open computer in the library, and Isaac stood behind her with his arms crossed, watching the other library patrons. Eve could see their uneasy gazes flitting toward him repeatedly as he stood there looking like some kind of gangster.

He was either completely oblivious to it, or he just didn't care.

Probably the latter, because oblivious he was not.

Eve tapped his hip to get his attention, and he jerked away and glanced down at her. She pointed both fingers away from herself, pressed her palms together and then opened them like a book, then skimmed a V shape with one hand over the palm of the other. *Go read a book.*

He exhaled loudly and walked off.

Eve browsed the internet, looking for a Stacey Rose that fit the bill.

And then there she was.

"Body of Mystery Woman at Local Cemetery Identified"

The mysterious circumstances around the discovery of a body at the local Dollarville Cemetery remain, but the identity of the victim has been established as 45-year-old Stacey Rose of Grand Rapids.

The body was discovered in the early morning hours of November 5th by the groundskeeper, but police have been unable to determine a definitive cause of death. It was reported that the body was exsanguinated and in a heavily desecrated state when it was discovered. Authorities suspect an animal may be to blame, and animal control and the DNR have been recruited to assist.

No further information is available at this time in this ongoing investigation.

Eve sat back in her chair and stared at the computer screen. Her mother wasn't just dead. She'd been ripped apart and dumped like a discarded candy wrapper in the local cemetery – and from the date on the article, it had been only days after Eve's thirteenth birthday. How had she never heard of this?

Why had she been there in the first place? The Dollarville Cemetery was three hundred miles from Grand Rapids.

Eve looked for an obituary, but none of the Stacey Roses she found were her.

After fruitless hours browsing on the computer and scanning through the local paper on microfilm, Eve finally gave up. All she found in the paper was information that she'd already found online. Stacey Rose was found dead, drained of blood, and mangled on November 5th, and no one had a clue how she got that way. After a couple of blips in the paper, the case was never mentioned again.

She wandered through the stacks looking for Isaac, but he was nowhere to be found. Then, as she was walking past the children's section, she heard his voice.

He was *talking* to someone?

She slowly made her way through the stacks, and was wholly unprepared for what she found when she came to the children's reading area.

Isaac was sitting cross-legged on the floor across from a four-year old girl with a hearing aid in her ear, and he was reading a book aloud and signing it to her.

He was smiling. He was animated. And when she giggled at him, he laughed with her.

He fucking laughed.

She'd never heard him laugh.

For just a moment, Eve forgot that she was rebuilding her walls, and her heart swelled with affection.

And then the girl's mother came around the corner, looking down at her phone.

"Come on, Ari. It's time to—" and then she saw Isaac sitting near her daughter. She quickly snatched up the little girl's hand and pulled her away from Isaac's proximity, glaring at him. "Ari, I told you not to talk to strangers!" she hissed at her daughter, signing angrily. "There are all kinds of weirdos at the library."

"He deaf, Mommy," the little girl said excitedly. "He signs too! Like me!"

"He's not like you, Ari. Stay away from grown men who want to be friends with little girls."

Eve watched all of this, defensive anger rising in her chest. Isaac did nothing to defend himself, only stood up, holding his palms out placatingly, and turned away to leave, all joy erased from his face as though it were never there. Then he stopped when he saw Eve step out.

"That's my friend. He's perfectly safe," Eve assured the mother. "He's actually a priest."

The woman narrowed her eyes at Eve, and in a low voice, she sarcastically said, "Is that supposed to make me feel *better*?" Then she led the little girl away quickly.

Anger burned behind Eve's eyes. She went to Isaac's side and circled her fist over her chest. *Sorry.*

Isaac shrugged and touched the thumb of his vertically splayed fingers to his chest, then he held his fist next to his temple and flicked his index finger up. *It's fine. I understand.*

She understood, too, but it didn't make it any less heartbreaking to witness. "It might be a stupid request, but can I hug you?" she whispered, looking at Isaac imploringly.

He frowned. He signed, *Why? I'm not upset.*

She quickly swiped the stray tear that started trickle down the side of her nose. She pointed to herself. "I am."

He groaned and touched his thumb to his chest. *Fine.* He opened his arms, looking mildly annoyed.

She slipped her arms around his strong, hard body and rested her cheek against his shoulder. It was different hugging Isaac than it was to hug her teammates and Luc. She wasn't used to her head reaching any higher than their chest.

When his arms closed around her, she felt her composure failing. She hadn't realized just how close she was to falling apart until this very moment. But this was not the time, nor the place. She quickly pulled away again, touching her fingers to her chin and drawing her hand away. *Thank you.*

13

A Morbid Curiosity About the Elasticity of Morality

That night, Isaac and Eve made their way to the Dollarville Cemetery. It was only a mile or so out of town, so they just walked. Thankfully, the moon was at three-quarters and high in the sky, so the night was fairly bright as they meandered through the tombstones.

The lack of lights, however, made communication with Isaac difficult. He couldn't see her lips or hand gestures as well as he could in daylight, so they spent much of their time in silence as they ambled about, looking for a headstone that bore the name Rose. Eve had had no luck finding out what happened to Stacey's remains, so she thought it wouldn't hurt to check here.

As the night progressed, Eve tried to ignore the aching need she could feel beginning to rise within her again. Now, instead of just the tobacco smoke, her super-senses were beginning to pick up on the natural scent of Isaac's body, and his heartbeat grew louder in her ears, like her senses were honing in on him. Targeting him.

Hunting him.

She was still in possession of Bo's powers, so she'd been hoping that it meant she would be able to go longer without needing to feed the beast, too. But apparently the need for sexual energy was completely unrelated to her ability to hold on to her stolen powers.

The more she tried to suppress the need, the more her mind kept wandering back to how good he looked standing in the lake this morning.

She reached out and caught his sleeve, and as he shied away from her, as he always did, she gripped harder, not letting him pull away. She turned and gazed up at him as he looked down at her. She slid her hand down his arm and intertwined her fingers between his thick knuckles. A knowing look crossed his features, and she saw his jaw flex in the moonlight as he swallowed.

God, he was fucking hot.

She heard his heart rate accelerate, and his breath came heavy. He knew it was time. His scent shifted. A sweetness now permeated his natural musk, and she instinctually knew what it meant.

He wanted her.

She turned to him and skimmed her free hand up over his chest and slid it around the back of his neck. She gripped his nape and pulled him down to her while she rose up on her toes. He was so much easier to reach than her other boys were.

And so much more timid.

She pressed her mouth to his and ran her tongue slowly over his bottom lip, and he parted his lips to let her in. Her tongue explored and massaged his while she led his hand to her hip. His other hand followed, sliding up over her other hip and pressing into the small of her back. His heartbeat was thundering in her ears.

And then he pulled her body flush against the curve of his, his other hand sliding up to cup her face as he deepened their kiss. The hand on her lower back slid down over her round ass, and he squeezed it as he pressed his huge bulge against her belly.

He was growing less timid by the second.

He pulled away from her mouth briefly to look around. There was a bench nearby, and they made their way over toward it. When they stopped in front of it, Eve reached down and unbuttoned and unzipped Isaac's fly. Her palm and fingers curved over the enormous swelling in his boxer briefs, and as she dragged her hand upward, she found his length poking out the top. She traced her thumb over the ridge of his crown.

He was fucking huge.

She pressed on his chest, directing him to sit down on the bench behind him. *Bless me Father, for I am about to sin.* She undid her jeans and removed them, allowing the baggy t-shirt she'd had tucked into her waistband to fall around her thighs. She tossed her pants onto the bench next to Isaac, then straddled his thighs. He tugged his boxer briefs and jeans down a little, releasing his monstrous cock into the night air.

It was gorgeous. A fucking work of art. She wanted to paint that picture: his big-knuckled hand wrapped around the base, a pearl of precum glistening at the head.

But enough admiring. She needed him. Now.

Isaac held his cock in one hand and gripped her hip with the other hand, and he watched her keenly as she slowly lowered her sheath onto him. But he wasn't looking at where their bodies met. He was looking at her face, watching her eyes and lips.

She'd never seen him so focused.

Oh, good god. She had to take him slowly, inch by inch, her walls stretching and aching to accommodate him. She let her baggy shirt drape down over their connection, and she braced her hands on his shoulders for support. She knew her face must be twisted into the most unappealing grimace, but Isaac was absolutely fascinated by it. He drank in every wince, gasp, and curse with ravenous eyes, until she finally felt her inner thighs press flush against his hips.

He opened his hand and swept it in front of his face, ending with his fingers together near his chin. *Beautiful.* He then slid his fingers into the hair behind her ear, his thumb along her jawline, and pulled her face to his, kissing her sweetly as his hips flexed and pressed up into her.

She moaned and began to move with him, and his thumb slid down to her throat as they kissed. He pressed lightly against her larynx, and every time she groaned or whimpered, he rubbed his thumb slowly over it.

It was how he experienced her sounds of pleasure.

When their mouths parted, his eyes were on her face. His other hand was on her hip, guiding her movements, but he was moving too slow for her. She'd finally gotten used to his size, and her body wanted to ride that pony and put it away wet. She took his hand in hers and pressed it against the back of the bench as she rocked her hips faster.

As her rasping moans grew louder and more frequent, Isaac placed his whole hand around her throat, feeling her cry out for him through the vibrations against his hand. He watched his name roll off her lips, and he gripped her throat and pulled her into a bruising kiss as he pumped himself deeply up into her.

He was close. She could feel him swelling inside of her, and she could tell by the way he moved that he was hanging on by a thread. With a mewling cry into his mouth, her throat vibrating against his hand, she rocketed into a powerful release, her hips jerking, her core spasming and pulsing, milking Isaac's release right along with hers. He broke the kiss to watch her face as she came, and then he grunted and panted, his cock swelling and thrusting almost painfully deep, as his fingers squeezed her hand and throat.

As they came down, Isaac pulled her into a long, slow kiss, his hand sweeping up the side of her face to brush her hair back. She allowed it for a minute, but then it began to feel like they were moving into dangerous territory. Too familiar. Too intimate. She pulled away and climbed off of his lap, quickly dressing as he adjusted himself and zipped his pants back up.

He stretched out on the bench, resting one arm behind his head. "Let's get some shuteye," he said aloud. "You can sleep on me." He patted his chest, then held his hand out to her.

"That's going to be uncomfortable for you," she said.

"It's too dark to see your lips. If you're arguing, don't bother."

She signed it instead.

"It's too dark to see your hands," he said obstinately.

"Fine. Suffer," she said as she climbed on top of him. She rested her head on his chest, her forehead against the side of his neck, and let her legs drape over his. His heart beat steadily in her ear, his breath moving into and out of his lungs in slow, whooshing repetition, like the ebb and flow of ocean waves.

"A priest, princess? In a public cemetery?"

Eve opened her eyes, and Dagon was leaning his elbows on the back of the cemetery bench. He was in his natural form again, wings and all.

"Are you really here?" she asked, feeling the rise and fall of Isaac's chest beneath her.

"Of course not. Just in your head. It's the only time I ever see you anymore. When are you coming back? Your teammates are a pathetic fucking mess without you. Zeke is so fucking depressed, I've considered putting him out of his misery."

"Don't you die if he dies?"

"Exactly why I haven't. But he's made me consider it. Him and Eoduun just sit around and mope. Eoduun wants to kill Luc for driving you away."

"What's Luc doing?" Eve asked, climbing off of Isaac and standing. She kept the bench between her and Dagon.

"I don't know. He's off somewhere else."

"Do you have any idea why he would've been in Michigan, looking for my biological mother?"

"Why the fuck would I know that?"

Eve sighed. "I don't know. I was hoping maybe you'd overheard something."

"He left not long after you did. He barely spoke to anyone after he found out you ran away with the exorcist."

Eve hated to ask. She was afraid to know. But she had to. "How's Bo?"

Dagon rolled his eyes and flexed his wings. "What the fuck do you think? You abandoned your puppy. He's devastated. And cranky as fuck." Dagon stood up and rested his hands behind his head, his elbows in the air. "And once he finds out about *this?*" Dagon glanced down at Isaac. "He'll be wrecked beyond repair. You broke the code of the team. You stepped out of the circle."

Guilt thickened Eve's throat. "How do you know what I did?"

"You were dreaming about it when I popped in."

"I had no choice. If I didn't, I would've lost control over myself, over the Blood of Lilith inside me, like last time."

Dagon rested his hands on the back of the bench and leaned toward Eve. "Keep telling yourself that, princess." He pointed to her eyes. "You still have Bo's powers. You can come home whenever you want to. You had a choice."

Eve scoffed. "That's hardly a choice."

Dagon walked around the bench, stalking toward Eve, his vermillion eyes fixed on her. "I don't care what you do, princess. Fuck everybody. Whatever. But you've had your fun, and you need to come home now. We have work to do. Apep is going to be a problem sooner or later, and we need to deal with him before he comes looking for you."

"You said he can't hurt me," Eve pointed out as she backed away from him, trying to keep the bench between them.

"He can't harm you. Physically. But he can find other ways to hurt you if he decides to, and eventually, he will decide to." Dagon stopped and looked down at Isaac sleeping so peacefully on the bench. "If Apep had his hand around the priest's heart and threatened to pulverize it unless you cut off your own nose and ripped out your own tongue, what would you do?" He turned those red eyes back to her. "Or what if he said he would slit Bo's throat unless you stabbed out both of Luc's eyes? Because that's exactly the kinds of games he plays. He has a morbid curiosity about the elasticity of morality. Very *Sophie's Choice*."

Eve was sickened at the thought of actually having to make that kind of decision.

Dagon was suddenly right in front of her, and she gasped, throwing her hand against his huge, hard chest to stop herself from running into him. He clasped his hand over hers, holding it captive against his bulky pecs. "Come home, princess. You need my power to protect yourself and everyone around you. Come and take it. I'll be waiting."

14
You Can't Get Past What You Refuse to Deal With

Eve opened her eyes, her eyelashes fluttering against Isaac's neck. She pressed her hands against the bench and lifted herself up, looking around for the source of whatever awakened her. She heard a car door close, and she spotted a middle-aged man getting out of an old sedan at the front gate. At this hour, it had to be the groundskeeper. As she moved off of Isaac, she saw his arm move, and he stirred.

His thumb was hooked through her belt loop, so when she moved, it woke him up. He blinked, taking in the predawn glow in the sky, then looked over at her.

She pointed at his thumb in her belt loop, then touched her fingers to her head and drew away a Y-handshape. *Why?* "You did it with my shoelaces yesterday, too," she said.

He unhooked his thumb and signed, *I'm keeping track of you.*

She wasn't sure if it was a sweet gesture or a simple part of his job.

He looked at her. He pointed at her and signed, *You're bright again.*

Eve frowned. She pointed at herself and signed, *I was black?*

He cupped his hand over his shoulder, then dropped it down over the back of his other hand. *Last night.*

Eve pointed to the man at the front of the cemetery, unlocking the gate they had scaled last night to get in. She signed, *We need to leave.*

He held his index finger up and pivoted it side to side. *Where?*

After a minute of consideration and a heavy sigh, Eve touched her fingers to the corner of her mouth, then moved her fingertips to her cheek. *Home.* She took his hands in hers and pulled him to his feet. When he was standing in front of her, she turned, pressing her back against his chest, then took his thumbs and hooked them through her belt loops. She squeezed her fingers tightly around his wrists. She turned her head so he could see her lips and instructed, "Hold on tight."

There's no place like home. There's no place like home. There's no place like home.

Eve held onto Isaac's wrists like a lifeline and moved through condensed space. It was like stepping from one room into another, but she had to push between two freighters in molasses to get there. The world around her and Isaac compressed strangely, like the picture at the outside ring of a fish-eye lens, and in the center, she was looking at the apartment complex. She pushed toward it.

And then they were there, standing in front of the building. Isaac released her and looked around, then down at her. He nodded, impressed.

When they walked through the door, Eve saw Bo step out into the landing at the top of the stairs. He looked down at her and Isaac, his chest heaving as though he'd just sprinted there the moment he scented her, and a mix of emotions warred in his eyes. He was relieved to see her safe and well, but there was anger, too. She'd left them. Willingly. And she hadn't checked in with them to let them know she was ok.

"Evie." His voice was tight, but there was warmth to it.

As Bo gazed down at her, she heard Zeke's heavy footsteps running up the hall. "Dagon says Eve is back!" she heard him shouting. He skidded across the landing, forcing Bo to take evasive action, and as soon as his caramel eyes fell upon her, his whole face lit up like it was Christmas morning. He ran/fell down the stairs and flew to Eve, scooping her up in his bulky arms and squeezing her half to death. He spun her in a circle and nuzzled his face into her hair. "Oh my god, I missed you so fucking *much!*" he declared, his voice muffled in her hair.

"Wag, wag," Dagon's voice crept through Zeke's lips.

"Shut up, D!" Zeke said. Then he pushed Eve back at arm's length so he could look her over. "Are you ok? He didn't hurt you, did he?" Zeke cast a suspicious look at Isaac and pulled Eve to his chest once again, protectively. She was getting whiplash.

"I'm fine," Eve assured him, her face pressed into his shirt. She pushed her palms against his chest, and he relented slightly. But he kept her trapped in his arms.

Eoduun rounded the corner at the top of the stairs. He tried to look calm and cool, but Eve could see the eagerness on his face. "Took you fucking long enough," he said blandly. "But I knew you'd come running back eventually."

Bo turned his back and walked away, disappearing back into the hallway.

Daddy was pissed.

"I need to go talk to him," Eve said, trying to free herself from Zeke's embrace. He hugged her to him again, her efforts futile. "Z..." she pleaded.

When he finally freed her, she realized Isaac wasn't in the entryway with her anymore. But she could smell fresh tobacco smoke. He must've stepped outside.

Eve ascended the steps, Zeke hot on her heels, and when she got to the top step, Eoduun was waiting for her. She ran her hand down his arm. "I'm sorry I left," she apologized.

Eoduun suddenly caught her in his arms and hugged her to his chest. "You're such an asshole," he reprimanded her. "Don't fucking do that shit to me."

She smiled wryly and hugged him back. "I know. I'm sorry. It won't happen again."

"And just for the record," he added in a low voice, "those yellow eyes don't suit you. I told you not to sleep with him. It's only going to bring trouble."

"And so it has," she said, then pushed away from him. She made her way toward Bo's apartment.

"Where did you go?" Zeke asked as he and Eoduun tagged along.

"My happy place."

"I thought this was your happy place," he countered.

"I have more than one happy place."

"Why did you take Isaac with you? How did you take him with you? Luc always said that he can't jump with another person," Zeke rambled on.

"It was an accident. He grabbed my arm when I jumped. I don't know why I was able to bring him along," Eve answered. When she reached Bo's door, she turned to Zeke and Eoduun. "I need a minute. I'll meet you back at my apartment."

They reluctantly left her side after Zeke planted an enthusiastic kiss on her forehead. She took a deep, fortifying breath, and knocked. She could smell Bo's scent inside, but only him. Ruth must not be there.

"Bo, I'm coming in," she announced when he made no reply. "I know you're in there."

She turned the knob, almost expecting it to be locked, but it wasn't. She walked in. Bo was standing in his kitchen, leaned back against the counter, arms crossed, fixing her with a penetrating gaze.

"I believe you had a manga I wanted to borrow," she said brightly, trying to break the ice.

It didn't work. "You left us."

The sense of betrayal in his voice stabbed right into her heart. "I ran away. I'm sorry. It's a thing I do, apparently."

"Hunters don't run."

"It wasn't the hunter who ran. It was the girl who woke up tied to a chair in a strange bunker who ran. She'll always be in here, you know," Eve said, tapping her forehead.

"Hm." Bo looked down at his feet. "And why did you take *him*?"

"I didn't mean to. It was an accident. And I know Luc can't carry an extra person, but I did, and I have no idea how I've been able to do it."

"Hm." After a pause, he continued, "You know, I could understand if you left because you were upset and needed space. I could understand if you didn't know how to get back, or if you lost the powers and couldn't get back. I would be more understanding if you had at least let someone know that you were ok. If you were coming back or not. *Anything*." Bo's eyes finally lifted to meet hers, and they were angry. His wolf eye was shining through, piercing her with its gaze. He raised his voice, "But you gave us *nothing*, Evie. You left us fucking *hanging*! We were worried, confused, upset...Luc blamed me for letting you go, and I'm pretty sure he put a hit out on Isaac because he thinks you ran away with him, and now *Luc's* in the fucking wind..." Bo's knuckles whitened as he gripped the countertop behind him. "I don't know if you can fix this, Evie."

Hot tears welled in Eve's eyes, turning her dirty shoes into ugly white blurs as she looked down at them. She nodded, the corners of her mouth twitching downward as she fought to keep a straight face. "Understood. I fucked up." She forced a smile, because it was the only thing that could keep her face from crumpling. She couldn't stop the tears, though, and they streamed over her lips. She turned away and looked at the wall. Her throat was so tight, her words were getting stuck.

She took a deep, shaky inhale, trying to open her airways again. "Just let me know what you need me to do," she spat out quickly before her voice cracked. She swallowed and inhaled again, fighting the tightness in her throat. "I'll keep to myself. I won't cause any more trouble."

She turned around and reached for the door. As she opened it and pulled it toward her, Bo's hand suddenly slammed against it, forcing it shut again. She gasped and froze, her back to him.

"Don't you dare run away from me again," he growled from behind his mask. "You've barely begun to explain yourself. You think I'm satisfied with that? Go sit down," he commanded, pointing to his couch. "I want some fucking answers, and I'm going to fucking get them."

Eve did as she was told, and tucked herself into the corner of his couch. She felt like she was about two inches tall.

Bo stood in the middle of the room, looking down at her. "Where did you go?"

"My hometown."

"I know you left your phone, but I didn't find Isaac's anywhere. Did he have it? Could he have let us know you were ok?"

"He got rid of it because I was afraid Luc would track it."

"Where did you eat? Sleep?" He looked at her outfit. "Where did you get those clothes?"

"We camped out the first night, slept in a cemetery the next night. Hit up the thrift shop and a gas station. And Isaac ate a turtle; I almost forgot about that."

"You were gone for almost two days." He looked her over. "Yet you don't seem particularly…desperate." His eyes burned into hers, and she looked away.

She knew exactly what he was asking. "Yes," she said simply.

"Yes? Yes what?" He wanted her to say it.

"You know what," she said quietly, still not looking at him. "We did what we had to."

Bo went silent, but Eve could hear his furious heart, his enraged breathing. When he spoke, his voice was threateningly low. "You could've come home at any fucking time, it would appear. You never *had* to do anything. We were here, waiting. You *chose* this."

"I made a mistake," Eve whispered.

Bo exploded. "A fucking *mistake*, Evie? Fuck! You made *several*, each one progressively worse than the last! You wrecked the whole fucking team!" he shouted, gesturing angrily. "And Luc! He's off the reservation, Evie. I saw it – something fucking snapped when I told him you jumped. No one knows where he is, or what he's doing, because he won't answer his phone or texts. No one has seen him."

"Did anyone actually know where he was or what he was doing in the first place?" Eve shot back, anger boiling up. "You know, he was in my hometown the other day when he was supposed to be in Paris. Did anyone know that? And why was he there? Well, apparently, he was investigating my mother. Why wouldn't he tell me that? Why would he hide that from me? Pair that with the pictures of him and the video I was sent, and I'm inclined to think maybe Luc went off the reservation long before now."

Bo furrowed his brow. "What are you talking about?"

Eve's face went blank as she realized she was only digging herself deeper into the mess she'd made. If she wanted this pain to stop, she needed to just get the fuck out of the dirt. "You know what? Never mind. It doesn't even matter. Like I said, I'll keep to myself, do my job, and stay out of trouble. Scout's fucking honor."

Bo looked at her with amazement. But not the admiring kind. He snapped his fingers. "You turn it on and shut it off, just like that, don't you? We can't all flip a switch like that, you know. I can't just decide I don't care anymore."

"Is that what this is? You caring?" Eve said evenly.

"Yeah, it fucking is. You're trying to push me away and ice me out because you don't want to deal with difficult feelings – yours, mine, Luc's, the whole team's. But you need to. You need to hold them up to the light and take a good fucking look at them, because they don't just go away. This is the kind of shit that eats away at relationships, Evie. You can't get past what you refuse to deal with."

Eve just stared at Bo. "I don't know what you want me to say," she said with a shrug of her shoulders. "I just…can't right now. I'm sorry. I'm not worth caring about, Bo. How many more times will I have to fuck up before you believe it?"

Anger flared in Bo's eyes again. "Never fucking say that. You might be a little fucking asshole sometimes, but you're worth every ounce of trouble you cause me."

"I'm really not." Eve shook her head. She looked over at the door. "I should go."

"Why did you come here to talk with me?" Bo inquired.

"I came to apologize. And I did that."

Bo crossed his arms. "You wanted me to hear your apology, but you didn't want to hear my feelings on the matter?"

"I didn't realize there would be so…many," she admitted, looking down at her fingers as she picked at her nails.

"We've barely scratched the surface," Bo remarked. He stepped closer the Eve, and she looked up at him. His wolf eye had gone dormant again, and his expression was more hurt than angry. "Do you care about me?"

Her eyebrows snapped together. "Of course I care about you." She looked down at her hands again as he came closer.

Bo reached down and lifted her chin with his fingertip, forcing her to look up at him. In a measured tone, he said, "Never walk away from me again. Do you understand? Do not play with me, Evie. I am a patient man, but I have my limits, and you have tested every single fucking one of them."

His eye briefly flashed yellow.

"I'm sorry," she whispered, looking up at him.

"This team needs you," he said, his eyes softening again. "You've become so ingrained in our lives, we don't know how to function without you. I mean it, Evie: never, ever walk away again. Swear it to me."

"I'll never walk away again," she promised.

"You better fucking not." He grabbed her hands and pulled her to her feet, then enclosed her tightly in his arms. His scent surrounded her comfortingly, and his forgiveness washed over her, granting her sweet salvation. The dam broke loose, spilling all the tears she'd been choking on for two days out onto his shirt.

15

The Broken Pieces Are the Best Parts

As Bo held her while she sobbed, his fingers gently stroking her hair, one of Ruth's memories flooded through her mind. She was fourteen, and the first boy she'd ever loved had cheated on her with an older girl from his friend group. What was worse, everyone in school knew except her. Ruth couldn't understand it. She put so much effort into her looks and made sure she looked perfect every day – how could he cheat on her with that little *troll*?

Ruth stared at herself in the mirror in the hallway, heartbreak and hatred boiling inside of her. She was the prettiest freshman in school. She made sure of it. What did she need to change? Was her nose still too big? Were her eyes too close together? Maybe she needed to increase her breasts another cup size. She knew spells for body modification. They were excruciating, and not meant to be done on oneself, but she'd managed to shrink her nose and plump her lips on her own. If her mother ever found out, she'd be furious, but Ruth knew she'd never notice. She barely ever looked at her.

Bo had noticed, of course, and he'd been so disappointed in her for doing that to herself. But he was a fucking hypocrite. He had his own insecurity – his fangs. If Ruth could've fixed them for him with a spell, she would have. But curses like that were just as unalterable as the color of her eyes. She remembered when he tried to grind them down with a file one night, and they'd restored themselves within the hour. That must've been agony.

All he wanted to do was *hide*. He didn't understand the pressure she was under, the lengths she had to go to, the *longing* she had to be *noticed*. All he and Luc ever had to do was flash those beautiful blue eyes, and people were captivated.

She wasn't born with those eyes. It was one thing she yearned to change, but the one thing she couldn't. Eyes could be shifted with an illusion, but they were impossible to permanently alter with spells. And if she did change her eyes, her mother *would* notice that. She was always lamenting about how much more beautiful Ruth would've been if she'd been born with the eyes.

Those fucking eyes.

They were now reflecting back at her in the mirror as Bo approached behind her. "What's wrong, Ruthie?" he asked, concerned.

He always knew when something was bothering her. Goddamn him. "What's my worst feature?" she asked. "If you could change one thing on my face, what would it be?"

Bo scowled behind his mask. "You have a lovely face. There's nothing I would change. Why? What's happened?" His tone became dark. "Did Andy say something?"

Ruth's eyes reddened in the mirror. "He cheated on me. He took Kylie's virginity last weekend." Her lip trembled. "Meanwhile, mine remains perfectly fucking intact."

Bo's scowl deepened. "You want me to be upset about your virginity? Andy's a piece of shit. I've always hated that asshole."

"Is Kylie prettier than me?"

Bo's scowl softened. "Not a chance. He's just an idiot, and she was just willing."

"I broke up with him at lunch as soon as I found out, and they're already dating."

"Sounds like they deserve each other. Fuck 'em."

"But…" Ruth watched the tears begin to roll from her stupid green eyes, and she saw Bo's aquamarine gems turn to her with pity. She confessed, "But I still love him. Why did he choose *her?* Why couldn't he love *me*? What's so fucking unlovable about *me*?!" she shouted, throwing an angry fist into the mirror, shattering it.

Bo's arms folded around her, and he hugged her while she fell apart, like the shards of mirror scattered at her feet.

And just like he did with Ruth, he didn't let Eve go until her sobs died and the tears dried up.

Ruth had wanted so desperately to be loved, to be seen, yet she resented Bo for doing just that – because he wasn't Luc. Eve wondered if she was doing exactly the same thing. Was she selfishly taking from one brother what she was lacking in the other?

"Bo?" she asked, her voice muffled against his shirt.

"Hm?" His voice vibrated soothingly through his chest against her ear.

"Do you feel like I give Luc all the best parts of me, while you're left picking up all my broken pieces?"

Bo squeezed her tighter. "The broken pieces *are* the best parts. It means you trust me enough to let me help put you back together."

Impossibly, new tears filled Eve's eyes, but they were warm tears now, not sorrowful ones. No one had ever wanted her broken pieces before.

Bo was special. She'd cut him deep with those stupid broken pieces, and yet here he was, bandaged fingers and glue in hand, ready to put her back together again.

And where was Luc? Where was the man who broke her in the first place? An empty chair. It punched a hole right through her heart.

Bo went out to pick up some lunch while Eve returned to her apartment to shower. She desperately needed one. When she came out of the bathroom, the familiar sight of Zeke on the couch and Eoduun on the floor in front of him warmed her. Isaac had returned to the apartment as well, and he was in the kitchen, raiding cupboards. Their trip had been seriously lacking in the nutrition department, and she felt her stomach growling, too.

Eve walked into the kitchen, and when Isaac looked over at her, she signed, *Bo is bringing lunch.*

Isaac pointed to himself, made a C-handshape and dragged his finger tips down his sternum, then made a Y-shape with both hands, palms up, and lowered them. *I'm hungry now.*

Eve sniffed his shoulder as she stood next to him. She scrunched her nose and held her hand overhead, flicking her fingers down toward her, then swiped her index finger from her centerline toward the bathroom. *Go take a shower.* She pointed at him and then waved her hand in front of her nose. *You stink.*

He lifted his sleeve to his nose and sniffed it. He arched a brow. He brushed his thumb under his chin and tapped the Y handshape to his chin, then pointed at her. *You're not wrong.*

"Babe!" Zeke called from the living room. He vaulted over the back of the couch and joined her and Isaac in the kitchen. He came up behind her and snaked his arms around her waist, leaning down to rest his chin on her shoulder. "What are you doing?" he asked her.

"You're going to be like velcro today, aren't you?" Eve teased.

"You're lucky I let you shower alone," he confirmed, kissing her on the cheek.

Isaac eyed them impassively, then turned and left the kitchen, heading for the bathroom.

Eve turned to face Zeke, his hands now resting at the small of her back. She looked up into that sweet face, and those big, innocent eyes, so full of adoration for her.

"I don't think I'll ever get used to that, though," he said, raising his eyebrows as he looked down at her.

"Used to what?"

"Those yellow eyes popping up in that cute little face." He kissed her forehead. Eve blinked, not even realizing that they'd made an appearance. Zeke wondered, "Why do you still have them? I thought you only held onto our powers for a day, at most."

"I don't know." Well, that wasn't wholly true. She didn't know *why*, but she knew it was because of Bo. She'd felt it when she'd taken his power. And Isaac had commented that all of the blackness in her aura had been erased temporarily after she'd been with Bo.

Something in Bo appeased the darkness in Eve.

"Maybe you're getting better at holding onto it," Eoduun suggested from the living room. "But I wish you would just let that one go. I'm sick of the reminder."

"The reminder?" Zeke echoed.

Eoduun stood up and turned around, swaggering toward Eve and Zeke. "Every time I see those eyes, I just see you fucking someone else," he said to Eve. "And I fucking hate it."

"Bo is hardly 'someone else,'" Zeke disagreed.

"He's not you, and he's not me," Eoduun replied, walking up behind Eve. He pressed his chest against her back and reached both arms around her to Zeke, clasping his hands around the back of Zeke's neck, holding all three of them together. "There's nothing I can do about Luc, but at least Luc leaves," he continued. He leaned down to Eve's ear. "But Bo? He's going to sink his teeth into you and fight to keep you to all to himself."

"We're a team, Eoduun," Zeke countered. "He's not going to keep her from us. And even if he did try, you wouldn't let him, would you?" he asked Eve.

"The only one trying to keep me to himself is you, Eoduun," Eve pointed out.

"Not myself. Ourselves," Eoduun corrected, casting his gaze to Zeke.

Eve scented Bo just as she heard the front door to the building opening. "Bo's on his way up," she warned the boys quietly. And then the savory smell of burgers and salty fries hit her nose, and her mouth began to water.

Fuck, she was starving.

She wriggled free from between Zeke and Eoduun and met Bo at the apartment door as soon as he walked in, eagerly eyeing the greasy paper bags in his hands. She knew by the smell which one had her food in it, and she snatched it from his hands like a rabid raccoon, scampering off to the kitchen island to tear into her fare.

Ruth walked in behind Bo, and when Eve looked up at her from over her bacon burger, a mild prickle ran up the back of her neck. She didn't *want* to not like Ruth. She'd had fun with her the other night with Cassie – as far as she could remember. She'd been trying to welcome her into their circle with open arms, especially after stealing all of her memories and seeing what life was like for her growing up. But those memories also showed her just how much Ruth underappreciated Bo, and it pissed Eve off. Bo had been everything for her. He'd done his best for her when he had no obligation to do so, and she had treated him like he hardly mattered. She'd taken him for granted and given him very little in return.

And maybe, just a little bit, it pissed her off because it felt too much like looking at her own ugly reflection in a mirror.

Everyone gathered around the kitchen island to eat, and Ruth plopped down in Bo's seat next to Eve. She fought the urge to correct Ruth's minor transgression, instead asking, "So what were you up to earlier? You weren't at Bo's."

"I moved into my own apartment last night," Ruth said happily. "I'm still waiting on some appliances and some furniture, but it was mostly ready. It was so sweet of Luc to arrange that for me."

"He does it for everyone," Eve replied harshly. She caught herself. "Shit, that sounded rude as fuck. I didn't mean for it to."

Ruth cast her a curious glance. "Everything ok?" she asked.

No. "Yeah, I'm good! Just hungrier than I realized."

"I smell burgers." Ruger barged through the door. "Did you asshats get Five Guys without me?!"

Sure fucking did.

Cassie and Remi strolled in behind Ruger, Cassie announcing, "We heard Eve was back!" When they joined everyone in the kitchen, Cassie gasped, "Holy shit, Eve!" She studied Eve's face. "Did your eyes just flash yellow? I swear they just did. Like Bo's wolf eye."

When Cassie looked over at Bo, his ears reddened, and he looked down at his food.

"I borrowed his powers, and the eyes came with it," she replied simply.

"Wait. Does that mean…?" Cassie's eyes glinted mischievously.

Eve widened her eyes at Cassie. If she was close enough to kick her under the counter, she would have. Thankfully, Cassie got the message and stopped talking. But the shit-eating grin on her face said everything. Bo's face burned even redder.

Ruger eyed up everyone's food, then spotted Isaac's untouched meal. "Anyone going to eat that?" he asked hopefully.

Eve snatched it up and pulled it to her to protect it. "It's Isaac's. Not up for grabs."

The bathroom door opened and everyone turned to glance that way. Isaac stood there in a pair of black jeans, shirtless, his dark crew cut still damp from the shower. He paused, obviously not expecting to walk out into such a gathering.

"Oh, my," Cassie teased. "Is this a daily occurrence, Eve?"

"Shut up," Ruger chided. "Eyes front, soldier."

Isaac's eyes found Eve in the group, and he signed to her as he began to walk toward the laundry area at the front of the apartment. *I forgot to get a shirt from the dryer.*

Eve pivoted her first two fingers on both hands up and down quickly. *Hurry up.* She pointed to the food waiting for him.

When he appeared at her side a few moments later with a t-shirt on, she slid his lunch toward him. He watched her as she sniffed his shirt. She nodded and held her flat palm in front of her mouth, then pulled it to the side while closing her hand. *Better.*

120

He touched his fingers to his chin and drew his hand away, looking at Eve. *Thank you.* He then took his food out to the living room to sit by himself.

16

Hall Pass

After everyone had finished their meal and Ruger had devoured everyone's leftovers, talk started to shift to where Luc could be, what had happened the night of their fight, and where Eve and Isaac had been the past two days. It was the last thing Eve felt like talking about.

Eve noticed Isaac was missing, so she took the opportunity to excuse herself. She followed the smell of cigarette smoke to the front door of the building where she knew she would find him.

She leaned against the wall next to him, making sure she wasn't touching him. She kind of missed this. Just the two of them. The quiet.

"Too many people in there," he said aloud, tapping the ash from the end of his cigarette onto the ground in front of him.

"You'll get used to it."

"I won't. I don't like people."

"I used to think the same thing. But they grow on you." Then it struck Eve: Isaac was only a temporary addition to her circus. He wasn't going to have to get used to anything.

She looked over at the cigarette between his fingers. He kept tapping it, but there wasn't much ash to discard. It was barely smoldering, as though he hadn't taken a hit from it in a long time. She looked up at him, and he was staring at the trees in the distance, and a thousand miles past them.

"How long are you going to stay with us?" she asked.

Without looking at her, he replied, "I'll stay until I trust you're not a danger. Until then, I do my job."

"Are we talking weeks? Months?"

He finally looked down at her. "Are you anxious to be rid of me?"

Eve didn't lie. "Not even a little bit."

He looked back out at the trees again. "I don't know how long it will take to know for sure." He relit his cigarette and took a hit. With a deep exhale, he said, "Maybe I'll never know."

Eve looked up at him questioningly, but he still avoided her gaze.

"You can go back in," he said. "I'd hate to keep you away from your many admirers." The hint of bitterness in his tone caught Eve by surprise.

"They can wait. I wanted to hang out here with you. I thought—"

"I'm not one of your boyfriends, Eve," he interrupted curtly. "I don't need handling. Go back inside." He took a drag and leaned his head back against the wall, looking up at the sky, purposely keeping her out of his line of vision so he couldn't see her lips or hands.

She pinched her brows. What the fuck? In a petty fit, she flicked at the cigarette between his fingers, causing it to snap right at the butt, ruining it, before turning on her heel and going back inside.

Fine, brood alone, she thought...rather, signed angrily in her head.

She didn't go straight to her apartment, though. She stood in the hallway, wondering what the hell had crawled up Isaac's ass all of a sudden. He was the most impossible person she'd ever tried to understand. He didn't *want* to be understood. After his little speech in the swamp about how connecting with people was real strength, why would he now turn around and decide to ice her out?

Why couldn't everyone be as easy-going and easy to read as Zeke?

When she returned to her apartment, she snuck unnoticed past the group in the kitchen and went to her bedroom. It wasn't hard, as they were completely enraptured by one of Ruger's wild, animated stories about a rougarou hunt that went horribly wrong in Louisiana. She flopped back on her bed and looked over at the phone that someone – probably Bo – had placed on her nightstand while she was gone. The phone she'd been avoiding looking at since she got back.

She picked it up and unlocked the screen.

No notifications.

She opened her texts, and saw the last text she received was the video from the unknown number. She skipped over it and clicked on her text conversation from Luc and read back over the last message she'd sent him.

We're done.

The hand that had been fisted around her heart began to squeeze, and she realized that it had never gone away. It had been there ever since she sent that text – a heaviness in her chest that persisted through every waking moment.

Luc's hand.

Crushing her heart.

Her thumbs hovered over the keyboard. She shouldn't do anything. She should leave it alone. Stop digging. Stay out of the dirt. Give it space.

I'm home. Send.

She stared at the text. Why the fuck did she do that? She desperately wished she could undo it. She'd just opened a door that she wasn't ready to have opened yet.

But the only thing coming through was the sound of crickets. There her text sat, like forgotten, half-eaten Chinese takeout in the back of the fridge.

The longer she waited, the harder that fist squeezed, and the blurrier her eyes became.

Finally, with a shaky inhale, she exited the conversation and tossed her phone back on the nightstand. What was he playing at? He always responded immediately. No matter how busy he was, he always responded. Was he ok?

Of course he was ok. He was Luc. He was just ignoring her, like an asshole, living up to every doubt, every fear she'd ever had about him.

Zeke waltzed into her room. "There you are," he said, sounding somewhat relieved at finding her. He crawled onto the bed and dropped down next to her, snuggling his body up against hers. "Why are you hiding out in here?"

"I don't know. Still trying to sort myself out, I guess."

"Is there anything I can do?" Zeke asked sweetly, twirling a lock of her pastel pink hair around his finger.

She rolled onto her side to face him, smiling. "You're already doing it."

He looked at her hair around his finger. "Playing with your hair?"

Eve kissed his lips lightly. "No, just being my sweet Zeke is enough. You always accept me, even when I don't deserve you. It's just so easy to be with you."

He graced her with a grin. "I've been telling you all along, babe. I'm all yours. Do with me what you will."

Cassie stuck her head through the open door. "Eve? Can I talk to you for a minute?"

Zeke pouted and reluctantly rolled to the edge of the bed. He left the two ladies alone, and after he walked out to join the group in the kitchen, Cassie closed Eve's door. She flopped onto her back on the bed next to Eve.

"How are you feeling?" Cassie asked. "I heard you and Luc were on the rocks. Ruger told me that Zeke told Remi that Bo told him that you found some pictures of Luc with other women when he was supposed to be on business trips, and that was why you guys had your blowout and you ran off with Isaac. He said you even cut off the tracker tattoo Luc had on you with a butcher knife."

"Close. I didn't mean to take Isaac with me, it was a filet knife, and someone *sent* me the pictures. And there was a video of him talking shit, too."

"So it's true? You guys broke up?"

"I don't know where we stand. He swears it isn't him, and Bo is inclined to believe him, but...when I left, I found out he *is* hiding stuff from me. He lied to me, just the other day. He told me he was going to Paris, but then I found out he was in my hometown looking into my biological mother's past. And I have no idea why."

"So, just to be clear, he wasn't supposed to be sleeping with anyone else?"

"He told me he wasn't. I never told him he couldn't, but I didn't *want* him to."

Cassie chewed her lip contemplatively. "I know I didn't see the pictures, and I know I don't know all the ins and outs of your relationship, but I'm going to give you a little piece of advice anyway. You need to communicate your rules and your needs clearly. There is a lot of gray area in poly and open relationships if you don't communicate your boundaries, and misinterpretations of what's expected from each other can end up hurting everyone involved."

"It's not even just that," Eve clarified. "This isn't just about infidelity and different expectations." Eve brought up the video on her phone and showed Cassie. She plugged her ears and looked away while it was playing, because she didn't want to hear or see it ever again.

Cassie closed the video when it was over, and Eve took her fingers out of her ears. "Ok, that's fucked up," Cassie admitted. "But he swears it isn't him? And Bo believes him?"

"I don't know what he has to say about the video, because I didn't have an opportunity to show it to him before I left. But he swears the pictures aren't him. Bo thinks it's Dizzy. But how did he get to all those places where Luc was, especially without Luc ever noticing?

How did he get into his offices? I've always been a big believer that the simplest answer is usually the correct one. And what makes more sense: Dizzy coming up with an elaborate scheme to pose as Luc to do and say things to upset me for…reasons? Or that it was Luc, and he's a fucking liar? One is a conspiracy theory, and the other is the majority of the male population."

Cassie sat up and crossed her legs under her, facing Eve, who was still lying on her back. "So, what are you going to do? What happens when Luc finally shows up again?"

Eve threw her forearm over her forehead and sighed heavily. "I don't know. I guess I'll cross that bridge when I get there."

"And in the meantime?"

"I keep going back and forth between wanting to drown my shitty feelings in other kinds of feelings or wanting to have no feelings at all."

"I can understand that." Cassie inhaled deeply. "So, in the spirit of embracing 'other kinds of feelings,' I have a proposition to make. Feel free to tell me to fuck off if this is the worst timing possible. Because it's either the worst timing, or the best timing."

"…Ok…"

"Ruger and I got to talking the other night…and we came to an agreement. He and I both think it could be interesting to offer a…trade."

"A trade?" Eve echoed.

"Like, a hall pass. Or a swap, maybe? He wants to sleep with you, and I'll get to sleep with someone else. I was thinking either Bo or Isaac." Cassie scrutinized Eve's face closely, trying to read her reaction.

Eve just stared in disbelief. "I…I don't think I want to do that."

"You don't have to make any kind of decision right now. I just wanted to put it on the table, just in case you were looking for something to distract you from Luc."

"I don't really look at Ruger that way," Eve said. She didn't want Cassie to sleep with Bo, either. The thought shot fire through her veins with venomous jealousy. She clenched her teeth. "I can't tell you you *can't* sleep with Bo, but I wouldn't be comfortable with it."

"That's totally ok. I could take Isaac instead."

"Again, I can't tell you you can't sleep with him, but..." Eve looked down at her fingers. "I don't think *he's* going to be comfortable with that."

Cassie arched a brow. "Damn, Eve, you licked that cupcake too, didn't you?" She sounded impressed.

Eve tried to explain that it was necessary because of the nature of the power that cursed her, but Cassie shook her head.

"No, no need to try to justify it to me," Cassie chuckled. "You do you. But dammit, Eve. I want a bite. Just one. Don't tell me that Isaac is off the table. Now, Bo, I get. If you're claiming Bo, I'll let that go, no questions asked. But Isaac should be fair game, shouldn't he? He's not part of your team."

He should be fair game. Eve knew that, even if she felt that selfish possessiveness surging up. "But what if I don't want to sleep with Ruger? If I don't sleep with Ruger, is he even going to let you sleep with Isaac? And what about Remi?"

"Remi isn't exclusive with me like Ruger is. Like I've said, Ruger is my husband, but Remi is more like a boyfriend. He has a little more freedom. But, circling back, why wouldn't you want to sleep with Ruger? He's hot as fuck."

He was hot, in that rugged country boy way. She wasn't denying that. "I'm not saying he's not. But...I feel like it would be awkward. And my team wouldn't like it." That was an understatement. Her boys would lose their fucking minds.

Cassie held her hands up placatingly. "Just give it some thought. No pressure, no time limit. If you decide you do want to try it, let me know. We can talk it over more then."

17

Become a God

After Eve and Cassie had returned to the kitchen, and Ruger had regaled the group with a few more wild stories from the road, Bo sent everyone off to do some training. Eve's return had thrown off the morning routine, but he was determined to make up for it with afternoon training. Everyone headed to the gym.

As Eve loaded up the squat bar, she could hear Cassie talking to Ruger, thanks to Bo's lingering powers. She was telling him that she'd put the ball in Eve's court, and all they could do was wait. Eve could tell Ruger still wasn't terribly excited about Cassie showing so much interest in Isaac, but she was going to do what she was going to do, so he might as well get something he wanted out of the deal, too.

Eve didn't want to completely close the door to the possibility of one encounter with Ruger...to obtain his specialty. If she was going to have to face off with Apep, Dagon had warned her that she needed to be prepared and assemble as many powers as she could. The ability to come back from the dead might come in real fucking handy.

Bo came over to spot her on the squat rack when he noticed her approaching failure.

Always watching.

She struggled up the last rep, knowing she had nothing left in her legs after it, and racked the bar. She massaged and shook out her burning thighs. "There's something we still need to discuss," Eve told Bo as she took a drink from her water bottle and leaned her elbow on the squat rack. "And you aren't going to like it one fucking bit."

She told him about Dagon visiting her in her sleep when she was away, and how he'd seen Apep was bound to her and she needed to be prepared, because Apep was going to come for her and everyone around her sooner or later. She told him that Dagon had noticed that she was holding on to Bo's power longer, so maybe she could hold other powers longer, but she didn't tell him about Dagon wanting her to take his own powers.

Bo frowned. "He just wants that fucking grimoire, and he's betting on Apep having it."

"Apep will be a problem at some point," Eve said. "I heard him in my head that night when Luc summoned the lightning storm. He's not done with us."

Bo sighed. "It'd be fucking great if I could consult with Luc on this. I've been trying to text him all day."

Eve didn't want to talk about Luc, or even hear his name. Her gaze shifted to the view behind Bo as she caught sight of Cassie trying to chat up Isaac at the heavy bags. He had gloves on, so he couldn't sign, but he wasn't speaking, either. He was just giving her occasional bored glances as he pummeled the bag.

Ruth came up and stood next to Eve and Bo, drawing Eve's attention away from Cassie and Isaac. "I walked a mile on the treadmill. What am I supposed to do now?" Ruth wondered.

"Walked it?" Bo scoffed. "You're supposed to be working up to a jog, Ruthie."

"I hate running. But I don't want to be all muscular, so I don't want to lift weights, either. Could I do, like, a Pilates class or something? Or is there an exercise bike? Or an elliptical?" Ruth looked around.

"Do we look like we have much use for an exercise bike or an elliptical?" Bo replied. "But hey, if you want to go do some Pilates, knock yourself out."

Ruth pulled out what must have been a new phone and started looking for Pilates workout routines. "Did you want to do some Pilates with me, Eve?" Ruth invited.

"Oh, no thanks. I *do* want to be all muscular. I've got Bulgarian split squats waiting for me."

"Is that something I would like?" Ruth asked.

Eve laughed. "They're not something anyone likes."

She grabbed two heavy dumbbells and left Ruth and Bo at the squat rack. She went to an open bench and perched the top of her foot onto it. As she started to squat with the other leg, she watched Zeke at the bench across from her, doing hip thrusts. The bar was so loaded, it was bending under the weight.

He winked at her, and her heart fluttered. "Want to hop on?" he proposed.

The offer filled her head with all kinds of imagery that stirred her desire. Her eyes roved his muscular, barely-covered torso, admiring those magnificent tattoos snaking all over his body. Sweat slicked his skin, accentuating the bumps and ridges of his bulky, hard body under the gym lighting, and every time he pressed his hips up, her eyes lingered on the crotch of his gray sweatpants.

He saw her looking. She wanted him to see her looking.

Eve almost dropped her dumbbells when Isaac appeared next to her. "Jesus, you need a fucking bell," Eve complained, startled.

Isaac looked annoyed. He signed to her, *Tell your friend to stop bothering me.* His eyes darted discreetly toward Cassie, who was still over by the heavy bags.

Eve put down her dumbbells and shook her head, and she snapped her first two fingers and her thumb together. *No.* She pointed to the side, pressed her splayed hand to her chest and drew it away, touching her middle finger to her thumb, and pointed at Isaac. *She likes you.*

He mimicked the same sign, but he continued the motion by flicking his middle finger and thumb away. *I don't like her.*

Why?

He shook his head and signed, *She's not my type, and I don't need an affair with a married woman.*

Eve saw Cassie heading their way, and Isaac flared his nostrils and pursed his lips at Eve. He crossed his fists, then swung them apart, turning his palms outward. *Rescue me.* With one last look of desperation, he circled his palm over his chest. *Please.*

Eve gave him an exaggerated pouty lip, then circled her fist over her chest. *Sorry.* She signed, *You're not my boyfriend, remember?* Then, she whispered aloud, "You can handle it." If she didn't know he hated being touched, she would've given him a patronizing pat on the shoulder.

Instead, she turned her back on him and bobbed merrily over to Zeke. Zeke had started something with her that he now needed to finish.

She stood on the other side of the bench, behind him, looking down at him as he worked on finishing his set. She bent down and whispered in his ear, "Want to practice those hip thrusts in the locker room with me?"

Zeke didn't finish the set. He dropped his hips, letting the barbell hit the floor with a resonating *clang*, then rolled it off his legs. He jumped up spryly. "Fuck yes I do."

"Aren't you going to re-rack your weights?"

"It can wait," Zeke said, eyeing her curves eagerly.

As he and Eve made their way to the locker room, Eve caught Bo's gaze following them across the gym.

Always watching.

From the knowing expression in his eyes, he knew what they were doing, and for some reason, that sparked Eve's arousal even more. She wondered if he would picture it in his mind. If he was jealous. If he wished it was him that she was leading off to the locker room.

She had no idea where she and Bo stood sexually after he'd ravaged her the other day.

But she had no time to think about that right now, as Zeke lifted her onto his hips the moment they walked through the locker room doors. She wrapped her legs around his waist and flung her arms around his thick neck. He pressed her back against the wall just inside the door and took her mouth hungrily, an impatient moan rumbling in his throat as he pressed his rock-solid bulge between her legs.

He hadn't had her alone since before the wendigo hunt, and he was going to make the most of this opportunity.

Eve grinded her body against him, his sweat sliding over hers. She brought her lips to his ear and traced the tip of her tongue over the outer ridge. "Let's take this to the showers," she whispered.

Zeke carried her to one of the shower stalls, and they both quickly peeled off their workout gear and got under the hot water. When Eve tipped her head back to let the water run through her sweaty hair, Zeke took advantage of her pose to crush his lips against hers, pressing his naked body to hers. He reached past her for the body wash, then began to lather the slippery suds over her wet skin. His thick-fingered hands slowly explored every inch of her body, leaving searing heat in their wake. Eve followed suit, dripping the body wash directly onto his chest, then smoothing her hands over his firm pectorals as she spread it down to the hard bumps of his abdominals. She greedily consumed his masculine body with her eyes, appreciating every little dip and ridge between his muscles.

Eve's slippery hands traveled down below his belly button, tracing the lines of his obliques to the base of his saluting shaft. She wrapped her fingers around his girth and began to slide her hand up and down, rubbing her thumb along the head of his cock.

"God, babe, you drive me crazy," he groaned as she ran her other hand down to fondle his testicles. He slipped his hand between her legs and pressed the heel of his palm against her clit, burying two thick fingers inside of her. "Fuck, you're so hot and wet," he crooned. "Let me fuck you. I need to be inside you."

Eve turned around and pressed her ass against him. "Fuck me, big boy," she demanded playfully.

He landed a light smack of his palm on the curve of her ass, and when she yelped in surprise, he gave a low chuckle that filled her belly with butterfly wings. And then he filled her center with his long, hard cock.

Eve braced her hands on the wall in front of her and lifted up onto her tiptoes as Zeke pumped into her. One hand was hooked around her hip, pulling her against him with every thrust, but his other hand splayed over her belly, sliding up to her breasts. He pinched her nipple lightly between his fingers as he massaged the small globes. He then lifted her chest into an upright position, and she arched her back so the back of her shoulders pressed back against his chest. The hand on her hip slid down between her legs, his fingers pressing tight circles against her clit.

Zeke slid his other hand up from her breast, up over her throat, and gripped her jaw, angling it upward to grant him access to her mouth. He nipped her lip, then kissed her deeply. His soft tongue played with hers while his throbbing thickness, thrusting in and out, in and out, and nimble fingers, circling around and around, worked in tandem to draw forth the pleasure swelling inside her core.

Eve slid one hand up behind Zeke's neck, moaning into his mouth as her other hand closed around his thick forearm. She could feel the cabled muscles in his arm flexing and working as his fingers rubbed her faster, and she rolled her hips and began whimpering as her pleasure rose.

As she crested, she keened, but Zeke's mouth devoured the sound, keeping it from echoing off the shower stall walls. He swelled inside of her and moaned in response to her wild release, but he held back from coming just yet. He gave her a quick repose as she panted and shuddered with the aftershocks, but after a few moments, he turned her around and lifted her onto his hips, shoving himself up into her as she clung to him. He gripped her ass firmly with his big hands, holding her up and guiding her pace while she squeezed his waist with her powerful thighs, her arms draped over his broad shoulders.

Zeke stared into her eyes affectionately as he effortlessly maneuvered her on his cock, like she weighed nothing at all. "I want to look at your beautiful face when I come," he told her, his voice thick with desire.

Eve threaded her fingers into the hair on the back of his head, panting in his ear. Her nipples slid up and down against his tattooed pecs as he bounced her on his cock, the muscles in his arms flexing deliciously. God, he was fucking strong.

Strong as a fucking god.

And for a split second, she thought about Dagon plowing into her. For only a moment, she longed for that fucking demon.

Zeke's pace faltered, and he shoved her against the wall in the shower stall. One hand left her ass, and he tangled his fingers in her wet hair, making her cry out. It hurt, and she could tell he meant for it to hurt.

"Zeke..." she whimpered.

Then his teeth sank into her shoulder, and she cried out again, pleasure throbbing through her core as his tongue lapped up her blood. "Z, no..."

Take it. Take his power. Become a god.

His mouth left her shoulder, his teeth coming up to graze along her earlobe. "Princess..."

18

I Want My Turn

Dagon.

Eve's hand immediately clamped around his throat, pushing him back so she could look him in the face.

"Yes, princess," he choked out, grinning at her, his vermillion eyes glinting. "You know just how I like it." He tightened his grip in her hair and thrust up into her, drawing an involuntary mewl from Eve's lips.

She hated how goddamn good he felt.

He released her pink tresses from his grip and trailed the back of his finger down her jawline, his eyes fixed on her alluring lips. He leaned forward, easily pushing against the force she was putting on his throat, and overtook her mouth with his. When she resisted, pushing harder against his throat, he snatched up her hand in his and slammed it against the wall. She yanked at his hair with her free hand, pulling him away again.

He growled in frustration, but Eve was determined to speak before her monstrous desire fully possessed her.

"How did you get out?"

The frustration melted away from Dagon's features, and that devilish grin spread across his lips once again. "You summoned me." He fought against her grip in his hair and kissed her once before continuing, "You wanted this. *You* drew me out." He squeezed her ass with his other hand as he drove deeper into her, making her whimper again. He kissed the side of her neck. "Zeke just wasn't enough for you, was he?" he mumbled against her skin. She felt him smile. "You wanted to feel my power. You missed me, princess."

When she tugged at his hair again, her hand was suddenly pulled away and slammed against the wall over her head by an invisible force. Dagon slid her other hand up over her head and pressed both of her wrists together, clasping them firmly in his masculine hand. He began to fuck her rhythmically with deep, hard strokes.

Perhaps Eve was feeling lightheaded from the heat and steam in the room, but when he leaned close and commanded in a deep, firm voice, "Say my name, princess," she yielded.

"Dagon," she panted, undulating her hips against him, meeting him thrust for thrust.

A low, satisfied chuckle rumbled in his throat. His vermillion eyes bored into hers. "Someone has tamed that vicious beast inside of you. You're not trying to kill me." He looked up at her wrists submissively entrapped in his hand. "You're not even fighting me."

Eve squeezed his hips with her thighs. "Shut up and fuck me, or I *will* hurt you," she complained, annoyed with his slowing pace.

He smiled with wicked delight as he again met her pace, his breath becoming more labored as they both drew closer to their release. "Yes, princess," he purred.

As Eve's pleasure poured over yet again, her hips jerking, her core clenching, she dragged Dagon along with her. He slammed into her, crushing her against the wall as he emptied his power into her. He knew he didn't have to worry about seriously hurting her at this point, as his power was now her power, so he didn't hold back.

It was like being fucked by a freight train.

When they finished, Eve pushed Dagon away and stepped under the water to wash between her legs.

Dagon stood behind her and took her wet hair gingerly in his hands, collecting it together behind her back and letting it slide over his palms. "The yellow faded from your eyes when I poured my power into you."

"What?! They didn't turn red, did they?!" Eve fretted, yanking her hair away from Dagon's fingers.

Dagon chuckled. "No, they just returned to normal. Maybe my powers overwhelmed Bo's."

Eve paused and listened. She could still hear everyone's voices and the clang of weights out in the gym, so she still had Bo's power. She reached her hand out toward the folded-up towels on the bench by the stall door and *willed* one towel to come to her.

It flew across the room and smacked her in the face.

"You may want to practice with that particular skill," Dagon advised, amused.

Embarrassed, Eve dried her face on the towel. "I want Zeke back now," she declared in irritation. "Get back in your cage."

A brief look of surprise crossed Dagon's face, and his eyes suddenly turned brown.

Zeke blinked at her. He looked around. "What the fuck just happened?"

Eve hesitated. "You didn't see any of that?"

"Any of what?" He was confused. "One minute we were fucking, and the next, I'm just standing here."

What was she supposed to tell him? She didn't want to tell him about Dagon, but she didn't want to lie to him, either.

He looked down at her shoulder. "Shit, did I *bite* you? Is that what happened? I gave you my power?"

Eve jumped on his easy explanation. "Yes. That's what happened."

Stupid fucking liar. She felt disgusting. But she knew how he would look at her if she told him that she not only thought about Dagon while she was fucking him, but that she actually finished the job with him when he took over.

Garbage. She was steaming fucking garbage.

"Why don't I remember it?"

"I don't know. Maybe it was something I did."

Zeke looked down at himself and moved his limbs around. "I feel just fine. That's so weird." He looked up at Eve again as she wrapped her towel around herself. Then, a sudden dawning of realization washed over his features. "Oh, no, I remember now. I don't know why...what was I saying?" Zeke asked, scrunching his face and looking to the side.

"You remember what?" Eve asked tentatively.

Zeke raised his brows. "What? I remember what?" He grinned at her and slid his hands around her waist. "I remember fucking the hell out of you, li'l mama. Is there something else I should be remembering?"

"Are you ok, Z?"

"I'm perfect. Are you ok? I got a little rough there at the end. I'm sorry about that, babe. But you liked it, right?"

She gave him a reassuring smile, but in her head, she was calling on Dagon. *Did you fuck with his head?*

Dagon's voice chuckled menacingly in her mind. *I fixed the problem. You're welcome.*

What did you do?!

Easy, princess. He's fine. I just pushed pieces of my experience onto him, so he believes that was all him. No more missing time. We can't have him asking questions.

Eve didn't know whether to be grateful or unsettled. She didn't know he had the power to do such a thing. But she knew she shouldn't feel this relieved at deceiving her poor, sweet Zeke. He deserved someone so much better than her. She wished she was better than she was. She wished she was the person he thought she was. She wished she could give him that.

She closed Dagon out of her mind, unsure what to do with all of the little surprises he kept springing on her. She decided to let the issue rest, even though her guilty conscience gnawed at her stomach lining.

Zeke and Eve had left their change of clothes in their lockers, so they went out to the shared locker room to fetch them.

Eoduun walked in just as Eve was closing her locker. He greedily eyed both Zeke and Eve in their towels, but he brushed right past Zeke and went straight to Eve, shoving her against her locker roughly, bracing his hand on the locker next to her head.

He grabbed her face and tilted her head up toward him. He bent down and aggressively attacked her mouth with his. His eyes slid to the side, looking at Zeke. "Did you welcome her home properly?" he purred.

Zeke just grinned and winked at him, and Eve noticed that Eoduun swooned, ever so slightly. She wondered if Zeke saw it, too. If he did, he didn't react. He just dropped his towel and began to get dressed since no one else was in the locker room with them.

Eoduun's gaze lingered just a moment longer on Zeke, then he turned back to Eve. "I want my turn," he demanded.

Eve heard voices getting louder as the others began to head toward the locker room. "You'll have to wait," she informed him.

When she began to try to push past him, he blocked her way with his arm. He leaned closer. "When?"

"I don't know, Eoduun," she admitted. "Soon."

He wasn't satisfied with her answer, but when Ruger and Remi walked into the locker room, and their eyes immediately turned to Eve standing there in her towel, Eoduun shifted his body to put himself between them and her. "Go get dressed," Eoduun told her sternly.

Eve took her clothes and changed in the shower stall. When she came out, drying her hair in her towel, Ruger was walking through, heading to the shower stall next to hers. He smiled at her, crinkling the corners of his hazel-green eyes.

"Eve," he greeted, nodding at her.

"Cassie talked to me," she blurted.

Ruger looked around to make sure no one else was coming. "Yeah, she told me." He hesitated nervously. "I, uh…" He chuckled even more nervously.

"It wasn't your idea, was it," she stated rather than asked.

He shook his head. "No, no it was not." He looked around again. "But…you know Cass. She gets an idea in her head, and…well, that's that."

"You're not a fan of Isaac, are you?"

"No," he replied without hesitation. "But I guess if I had to choose between him and Bo, I'd rather pick him. At least he'll be leaving, and I won't have to worry about her catching feelings."

"You didn't even pick me, did you? She did, didn't she?"

Ruger laughed nervously again. "Ah, no, that…that was all me. I did pick you. I mean…" he gestured to her as if that was all the answer needed.

"Oh."

"But I get it. You don't want to. I get it, I do. It's fucking weird, right? I know," he rambled quickly. "We should just forget about it."

Eve shrugged. "It's not something I see myself doing just for kicks, but…there may come a time when I will need to borrow your abilities. And if that time comes, I will need to accept that offer."

Ruger raised his eyebrows questioningly. "My abilities?"

"Your ability to come back from the dead. I may need it in the future," Eve stated. "But to obtain that ability, I need to fuck you." She left out the part where she may hurt him, too, but that was a bridge they would cross when and if they ever got there.

Ruger nodded, "Ok. Yeah, ok. That's…yeah. Is that how that works? I've heard a little about your specialties, but I don't know much about it. So…yeah. If that needs to happen, I mean…it needs to happen, right? I can…" he paused and nodded. "I can do that."

Eve smiled at him. "Good talk. I'm glad you understand." She watched him walk into a shower stall and close the door behind him. He'd lost every ounce of his usual cocky boldness when he was confronted with that awkward conversation, and Eve was grinning to herself when she rounded the corner back into the main area of the locker room.

Bo fixed her with his wolf eye when she stepped into the room. He pointed at her, then pointed at the ground in front of him.

Uh oh.

She approached him, and he glowered down at her as he slipped a clean black t-shirt over his scarred torso. He rested his hand on the locker next to her, his other hand on his hip. "Enlighten me," he whispered harshly. His voice was too low for anyone else to hear, but she could feel the others' eyes on them. "What kind of plans were you making with Ruger? Because if I'm not mistaken, it sounded like you were planning to *fuck him*."

She looked up into those incensed mismatched eyes, and when she did, his eyes narrowed. He looked at the fading bite mark on her shoulder that was peeking out from under her shirt collar. "Was that Zeke?"

"Hm? Oh, yeah. I took his power," she lied.

…To the walking lie detector. "Hm." He continued to stare her down, waiting for more.

"Let's talk about this later," Eve whispered uncomfortably, looking down.

Bo lifted her chin to force her to look at him. "There is no need for discussion about Ruger. The answer is no," he said firmly.

When Eve began to protest, Bo gripped her jaw and repeated, more sternly, "I said *no*."

What the fuck was this deeply submissive arousal tingling in her thighs as he looked down at her? She felt it on a molecular level, in every fiber of her being – even the monster inside of her whimpered carnally. She craved his attempts to dominate her.

Maybe he could, maybe he couldn't.

Try it, Daddy.

Top me.

"Yes, Daddy," she whispered. She'd meant it to be teasing, but it came out unexpectedly obedient.

To her surprise, he didn't blush. "That's a good girl." He slid his fingers along her jaw as he withdrew his hand from her face, then turned to collect his things from his locker.

Eve's whole body was on fire.

19
It's Not Up for Debate

Eve glanced over and caught Isaac staring at her in astonishment from across the locker room. She raised her palms at him. *What?*

He signed back at her. *Your mist is...*he paused, like he was at a loss for words.

"Come on, Evie," Bo said, interrupting her conversation with Isaac. Zeke and Eoduun joined them as they headed toward the door.

Eoduun took her hand and led her along with them. Eve turned and looked back at Isaac, and she wondered just what exactly he was seeing.

She suddenly saw his thoughts, and immediately she understood his loss for words. She saw herself surrounded by an iridescent, yet oddly dark cloud, with bursts of lightning flashing throughout it. And it spanned a larger space around her than it had the first time she'd seen her aura through his eyes.

Was this what Dagon's power looked like on her?

Wait. Why the fuck was she seeing this?!

She didn't have Eoduun's power anymore...but even if she did...this wasn't Eoduun's power. She wasn't *in* Isaac's head. It was more like she was seeing his running, active thoughts in real time.

Was this part of Dagon's power?

You called? Dagon's voice filled her head.

"Eve?" Eoduun called to her, tugging on her hand. She hadn't realized she stopped, just staring off into space like an idiot. She quickly shook it off and followed Eoduun.

What are you doing in my head right now? she wondered.

You opened the connection, he supplied.

Why did I see Isaac's thoughts?

Because you wanted to see them, and you have my power to do so.

Since when can you do that? You never told me you can read minds!

Remember when I told you Ruth would be at that convention in Texas? She was thinking about it when she was fleeing after attacking us on the highway, and I saw it. That was how I knew where she would be. But I couldn't tell you that's how I knew. If told you I could read minds, you would've tried to block me out or clear your head when I was in front of you. So, I never told you. I like listening in to how much you hate how much you want me. It's one of my guilty pleasures.

Eve was mortified. *You've been able to read my thoughts this whole fucking time?!*

She heard Dagon laugh in her head. *Oh yes. But only when I'm the one in control of this body. Or when you invite me in like this and feed me your thoughts directly.*

Get out! she commanded.

And just like that, she was alone in her head again. Was it because she commanded him out? Is that what happened earlier when she told him she wanted him to go back to his cage? Was he actually *obeying* her?

When Eve reached her apartment, Eoduun tugged at her hand. "Come with me to my apartment," he implored.

Bo interjected. He stood in front of Eve's door, hands in the pockets of his black cargo pants, and looked at Eoduun with an authoritative gaze. "No. I need to talk to her."

Eoduun glowered at Bo, and for a moment, he contemplated arguing, but Eve pulled her hand from his.

"We can hang out later," Eve told Eoduun.

Eoduun scowled at them both. "Whatever," he grunted, turning on his heel and stalking away to his apartment.

Bo followed Eve into her apartment and shut the door behind him. "Tell me why you were talking to Ruger about taking his power," he said.

Eve sighed and went to the fridge. "Do you want a protein shake?" she asked, pulling out the Greek yogurt and juice. She went to her cupboard for the protein powder.

"No. I want you to explain."

Eve grabbed a shaker bottle. "I'm not sure if I should be blabbing this to you. It's kind of private."

"I'm not exactly the town gossip."

"Fine." Eve dumped the ingredients in her shake and closed the lid. She began to shake it, the little metal ball whisk inside of it rattling loudly. "Cassie and Ruger wanted to experiment a little outside of their relationship. Cassie wanted…" Eve hesitated. Should she tell Bo that Cassie wanted him? Cassie didn't seem to care about hiding it. "Cassie wanted either you or Isaac—"

It was a good thing Bo wasn't drinking a shake, because he would've spit it all over the place. He interrupted her, sputtering, "What? *Me?*"

Eve stopped shaking her bottle and walked up to him. She reached up and gripped his jaw, forcing him to look into her eyes. It was her turn. "Just to be clear: the answer is *no*. And it's not up for debate."

She could hear his heart rate accelerate as he looked down at her. His eyes slid down and lingered on her lips briefly. "I wouldn't have anyway," he commented. "And Ruger picked you. Because of course he fucking did."

"I wasn't going to take them up on it," Eve said. "But I got to thinking about this whole Apep thing, and how I should stack as many powers as I can when the time comes to face him, and I thought Ruger's Lazarus abilities would be beneficial."

"Apep can't hurt you if he's bound to you. I thought that was the whole point of Ruth binding him to herself in the first place."

"We don't know what could happen, though."

"We never know what's going to happen, Evie. But you don't need Ruger's power. You have all of Knighco on your side, willing to offer their strength to assist you and fight alongside you. You don't need to take everyone's powers to protect yourself. You need to trust that everyone will use their powers to protect you and fight for you."

Eve paused. She hadn't even considered that. Perhaps the best use of this curse wasn't to absorb as much power as she could in an effort to make herself invincible. She did have a whole team, and a whole organization of skilled hunters behind her. Perhaps she just needed to focus only on what powers she *needed*, and only when she needed them.

Less is more.

Well…*sometimes*. Wink wink.

"I just wish to hell I could get a response from Luc," Bo said.

The fist around Eve's heart squeezed mercilessly. "Don't mention his name around me," Eve grumbled, turning away from him and taking a drink of her protein shake. She went to her spot at the kitchen island, and Bo sat down next to her.

"He will come back, Evie. You will have to talk to him eventually."

"And until then, let's pretend he doesn't exist."

"I'm not going to do that."

Eve took another drink of her shake. "I am."

Bo sighed. "He loves you, Evie. He would never do anything that he thought would hurt you."

"Then why is he ignoring me?" Eve blurted. "I texted him too, and he didn't respond to me, either."

Bo shrugged. "I don't know. This has never happened before. I told you; he's going through something."

Isaac walked into the apartment. He looked at Eve, and she could tell he was staring at her aura again. From what she had seen through his thoughts, it was rather mesmerizing. And baffling.

She pointed to her shake and held both palms upward, fingers curved, and pointed at him. *You want one?*

She could see he was about to shake his head as a default response, but he reconsidered. He nodded.

As Eve started moving around the kitchen and getting out the other shaker bottle, Isaac joined them in the kitchen. He stood next to her while she mixed up his shake, and Eve caught Bo scowling at him from across the countertop.

"Does he know I know?" Bo asked Eve, still staring at Isaac. Of course, Isaac couldn't see Bo speaking from behind his mask.

Eve turned to Isaac. She pointed at Bo, then touched her fingertips to her head. She gestured between herself and Isaac using a K-handshape, then made two horizontal V handshapes and tapped one on top of the other, with the fingers pointing in opposite directions. *He knows you and I had sex.*

Isaac's apathetic expression didn't change as he looked down at Eve. He touched his fingers to his nose and then tossed his splayed fingers away from him.

"I've seen that one before," Bo said. "What does it mean? It looks rude."

"I told him you know we had sex, and he says he doesn't care," Eve filled him in.

Isaac shifted his gaze from Eve to Bo, his expression unwavering. Challenging, even.

"You're not going to start measuring dicks, are you?" Eve teased.

Isaac pointed to himself, dropped a curved-fingered hand onto his other fist, then clenched the fingers into a fist and brought it back up quickly. *I'd win.*

Eve handed Isaac his shake. "Speaking of winning, did Cassie win you over yet?" she asked him, changing the subject.

Bo frowned. "Hey, what do you mean 'speaking of winning?'" he asked, insulted.

Isaac signed to her, *Why won't she leave me alone?*

Eve bit back a grin, then signed, *She wants to measure for herself.*

"You know how much I love it when you two do this," Bo complained, looking down at his phone. "But it's fine. Ignore me. Leave me out of the conversation. I should be used to it by now."

"Isaac wants to know why Cassie won't leave him alone," Eve said to Bo. Then she turned to Isaac. "Did you know Bo was actually her first choice? Just a little fun fact, before you go and get too cocky."

Pun absolutely intended.

Isaac signed, *He can have her.*

Eve's nostrils flared and she snapped her first two fingers to her thumb. "No," she snipped.

"I get the feeling he's not keen on Cass?" Bo inferred.

"She's coming on a little too strong, I think," Eve said.

"Maybe her and Ruger just need to give it up," Bo grumbled, still looking at his phone.

Isaac left the kitchen with his shake, and Eve leaned over the counter across from Bo. She touched her finger to the top of his phone and lowered it to get his attention. "Reading porn again?" When he gave her an unamused look, she said, "I want to read that wolf boy and bunny girl story."

"Manga."

"Whatever. I'm going to your apartment to get it."

"No, it stays there. You aren't borrowing it."

"Can I read it tonight, then?" she asked sweetly, resting her chin in her hands.

Bo paused. "In my apartment?"

"Those are the stipulations, aren't they?"

He exhaled. "We'll see."

"Thanks, Daddy," she smiled.

"Don't start," he warned.

Eve suddenly felt an odd sensation, like the feeling you get when you know you aren't alone in the house. A presence. A *pressure*, almost. Then she scented strangers. No, wait. Not strangers…but she didn't know who. She stood up and went to the window. Team Beta was walking toward the apartment building from the garage.

Before Eve even opened her mouth, Bo said "I thought they weren't going to be back from Washington until tomorrow." He must've scented them, too.

She knew it was Bo's power that allowed her to scent them, but how had she *felt* them? Was that from Dagon's power? As she looked out over the team, she could tell something about Ramil was different from Veris and Mira. She looked harder, trying to place what was off, and it suddenly became clear when he turned his head. His copper-green eyes glowed strangely, similar to the way labradorite shines iridescently in the light. She'd never seen them look like that before.

She turned, intending to ask Bo if he could see it too, but when she met his eyes, she dropped the shake in her hand.

His eyes glowed in the same luminous manner.

"Evie, what the hell?" Bo asked, rushing to pick the shake up off the floor. While he wiped up the spill, Eve just stood there, dazed. She looked over at Isaac.

His eyes were normal.

She looked back down at Bo. He was looking up at her as he knelt at her feet, wiping up the last bit of the spill. "Evie?" he questioned.

She turned to the door just as Zeke and Eoduun were walking in, and when she saw the way Zeke's eyes glowed red beneath his usual caramel brown, it clicked.

This was how Dagon saw monsters.

Which begged the question…what kind of monster was Ramil?

20
Tonight Isn't for Fun

She blinked, and Zeke and Bo's luminous eyes faded back to normal. Then she heard Team Beta in the hallway, approaching the apartment door. Zeke leaned his head back out the door and waved down the hall at them.

"Hey! You guys are back!" He looked at his team. "Guys, Team Beta is back!"

Eve heard Mira mumbling out in the hallway. "Is everybody at that skank's apartment again? Never mind, I'm heading back to my place. I don't want to get her stench on me."

"Perfect, because you're not invited anyway!" Eve shouted pettily. Zeke and Eoduun looked at Eve strangely, because they had no idea what she was yelling about. They didn't hear Mira's snide comments. "Mira's a bitch," Eve explained simply.

Ramil and Veris walked into the apartment, and when Isaac saw them, he rose from his seat and casually made his way to the kitchen. He leaned against the counter near Eve, crossing his arms, looking generally unapproachable. He kept a wary eye on Ramil as Ramil made his way toward Eve.

"I heard rumors on the road that you'd taken off," he remarked in his deep, regal tone. "I'm glad to see you've returned. You are well, I trust?"

Eve stared into those strange eyes. Even without the luminosity, they were so unusual. And they deeply unsettled her.

"I'm good. You took out the Cullens?" Eve asked casually, swaying discreetly away from Ramil. She leaned closer to Bo, who had returned to his seat at the kitchen island. Out of the corner of her eye, she saw his gaze flick up to her, then to Ramil. He blackened his phone screen and placed it face down on the counter. He'd picked up on her uneasy body language.

"Oh, indeed. And as such, tonight we're due a night of celebration. You'll join us, won't you?"

As she looked at his eyes again, she felt something invasive pressing on her mind. She shoved it back – hard. Ramil blinked in surprise.

Was that him? What was that? Her curiosity activated Dagon's power, and Ramil's eyes began to glow eerily again.

Did she just repel my charm? Ramil's voice echoed thinly in her thoughts. As they stared at each other, his expression darkened, and everything suddenly went dead silent from his mind.

He'd shut her out. Which meant he either knew, or he suspected, that she could access his thoughts.

"Hell yeah!" Zeke answered, completely unaware of the sudden internal friction between Ramil and Eve. "Where're we going?"

Eve feigned ignorance, like nothing had just happened. "That would be fun, but I just got back earlier today. I'm a little tired."

"Oh, come on, babe," Zeke coaxed. He took Eve's hands in his and shimmied his shoulders at her. "Let's have a night out. Last time we tried to go out, Ruth royally fucked up our night."

The memory of that night at The Gutter when Ruth's doppelganger slit her throat on the bar popped up in Eve's head, but it wasn't just from her point of view this time. She saw Ruth's memory of it, too. Ruth had been watching the shapeshifter through its eyes using a shadowing spell. She had desperately hoped that the publicity and the coded call to arms, which only full-blooded monsters would be able to understand thanks to a spell from the grimoire, would've bolstered the numbers in her monster army. Surely they would've joined her if they thought Dagon was backing her.

But they hadn't, because Mother, Father, and Luc had effectively shut it down too quickly. Word barely spread at all. So much effort, and all it earned her was a few measly followers.

A failure, yet again.

But Ruth hoped that they got a good laugh from her walking pinata spell. Candy and razor blades. Classic. Luc would appreciate it.

Eve needed to get rid of these memories. She needed to return them to Ruth's mind somehow…but she was also hesitant to do so. What if she went right back to her old self again as soon as she remembered who she was? It could put Knighco in a very precarious position.

"We'll have to invite Team Flannel," Zeke continued when Eve was too lost in her thoughts to respond.

"Ruger's still banned from The Gutter," Eoduun reminded him.

"I refuse to go to The Gutter," Eve said firmly. It was Luc's place. She wouldn't step foot through the door. Then again, maybe she was banned, now, too.

As Ramil, Zeke, and Eoduun talked about what other options there were for a night out, Cassie popped her head in the door.

"Oh, shit, Team Beta's back? I thought I heard Ramil." She walked in with Ruth in tow.

As soon as Ruth saw Ramil, Eve swore she saw her make instant heart eyes. She sashayed up to him, suddenly reminding Eve of the old Ruth. She held out her hand to him. "Well, hello. I'm Ruth," she said smoothly.

Ramil smiled at her and took her hand. He touched the back of her fingers to his lips. "Charmed. We're fortunate that you've decided to come over to our side. I assure you, you've made the right choice."

Ruth blushed. "I'm sorry about the trouble I've caused. I don't remember any of it – not that that's an excuse. But I'm grateful to Luc and all of you for giving me a second chance, and I hope to make the most of my fresh start here."

"Absolutely. I've been in your shoes, believe it or not," Ramil disclosed. "Many years ago, I, too, was an enemy of Knighco, but have since seen the error of my ways and become a useful member of the organization. I am proof that you can earn your place here if you truly wish it."

As Eve watched Ruth and Ramil getting along so well, she felt uneasy about these two former enemies of Knighco forming an alliance. Was that wrong of her? She knew hardly anything about Ramil, other than the fact that he had gone toe-to-toe with Luc in the past. She didn't know anything regarding the circumstances around that conflict.

Had he been at odds with Knighco because he was a monster? Why hadn't anyone told her Ramil was a monster? They'd been upfront about Bo being half werewolf, about Dizzy being a shifter, and about Kai being a skinwalker. So why the silence about Ramil?

Goddammit. She needed to know.

Yes, princess?

What the hell is Ramil?

Dagon chuckled in her head. *So you learned how to see monsters already, too? Well, I wish I could tell you. I have no idea. His shine is strange, which leads me to believe he's some kind of hybrid.*

Hybrid? Like what Ruth was creating with the grimoire? Eve wondered.

Not like that. A born hybrid. The shine is deeper in a born hybrid, as though it comes from below the surface of the eye. Ruth's hybrids had a more superficial shine.

Does Knighco know what he is?

I don't know if they even suspect he is a monster. He's been passing off his abilities as a specialty rather than a curse.

You never said anything to them? Eve accused.

Why would I? I'm not on their payroll. I'm their prisoner.

Eve couldn't exactly fault him for that reasoning.

Wait a minute…*You wanted me to try using him to activate my powers! You wanted me to sleep with him without telling me he was a monster?!* Eve fumed.

I was curious what would happen, Dagon said simply. *I was certain his monstrous power would trigger your defenses. I've never seen the extent of his full powers, and I wanted to know what they were. And you would've been fine – you killed a Jötunn.*

Eve was disgruntled. *For every morsel of information you give me, there are like five things you keep to yourself. I'm not a fan of that, Dagon,* she chastised.

Maybe if you spent more time with me, I'd have more time to divulge my secrets to you, princess.

Eve pushed him out of her mind without another word.

Eve glanced back at Isaac. Did he know that Ramil was a monster? He'd mentioned him having ill-intent and a dark aura, but he'd never mentioned him being a monster. She would have to ask him later.

In the meantime, she'd better make sure to keep some kind of walls up in her mind. Ramil had already tried to infiltrate her mind – to what ends, she wasn't certain.

Eve noticed Ruth and Cassie were both looking expectantly at her. "What?"

"You're going to get ready with us, right?" Cassie asked. "Ruth got some super cute outfits the other day, and we're going to need your help picking one out."

She glanced at Bo. He just shrugged at her.

"Are you going?" she asked him.

His eyes met hers, and she already knew the answer before he said it. "I go where you go."

If she wanted to learn more about Ramil, she didn't have much choice but to spend some time around him. Tonight isn't for fun – she was on a mission.

Eve and Cassie brought some outfits to Ruth's new apartment, and as they all tried on their different choices, Ruth kept bringing up Ramil.

"Ramil is quite handsome, isn't he?" she said with a smile, turning in front of the mirror on the back of her bedroom door to admire her backside in the little black dress she had picked out.

"He's good-looking," Cass said, "but he's also kind of scary, like Mads Mikkelsen in *Hannibal*. All cultured and debonair, but he might decide to cut off your tit in your sleep and cook it for breakfast."

"Ew!" Ruth twisted her face in disgust. "I don't think he gives off that vibe at all!" She looked to Eve. "What do you think of him?"

Eve hesitated as she carefully squeezed into the tight pink crop top she was pairing with her dressy sage-green joggers. Dagon's superstrength wasn't as difficult to control as Zeke's was, but she still needed to be careful. "I think there's more to him than meets the eye," she answered truthfully.

"In a good way, or in a bad way?" Ruth asked.

"I'm still not sure."

"Well, I think I like him," Ruth said. "As soon as I laid eyes on him, I felt it. On a visceral level. It's like, for the first time since my memory was stolen, I felt my powers tingling. Like my powers were reacting to his."

Eve didn't like that. And though it wasn't *untrue*, she didn't love how Ruth worded the part about her memory being *stolen*. "We will find a way to return those memories to you, Ruth. I swear."

"Well, I've been thinking about that," Ruth said as she eyed the outfit Eve had chosen. "I still have my powers. I just don't remember how to command them. If I train, I may be able to just pluck my memories right back out of your head. Getting into people's heads was something I used to be able to do, right? Bo mentioned it."

Eve liked that even less. She didn't want Ruth in her head. She didn't know if she fully trusted Ruth to just pop in, only take her own memories, and then pop back out without messing with anything else. But was that fair for her to feel that way?

"That...that's a possibility, too," Eve conceded reluctantly. "Like I said, we'll get them back to you one way or another."

"I know you say that, but I feel like it's been a low priority." Ruth glanced at Eve again, then turned up her eyebrows. "Oh, but I understand! I'm not saying it's your fault. You've had a lot going on. I just feel like I could be, and *should* be, putting more effort into it myself. I can't just put it all on you to find a solution. It's time I started rediscovering my own powers, my own independence. I should be able to fix my own problems."

A tight smile pursed Eve's lips and she nodded.

"What do you guys think?" Cassie asked, doing a little flourish and a turn for them to show off her burnt-orange mini cocktail dress. It complemented her dark skin tone beautifully.

"Oh, that's gorgeous, Cass," Eve gushed.

"Think Isaac will appreciate it?" she asked with a wink.

"Well, he's deaf, not blind, so yeah, I'd say," Eve joked, but the fist around her heart clenched at the memory of Luc saying similar words to her.

Where was Luc, anyway? What was he doing?

"You two look so cute," Ruth said. "Now I feel overdone. Should I change?" she asked, looking down at her stunning black dress, running her hands over the dips of her waist. It was dressier than what Eve was wearing, but it was comparable to Cassie's dress.

"I don't see the problem," Eve replied.

"Yeah, there's no such thing as too sexy, right?" Cassie added. "Especially if you're trying to impress Ramil. That looks like the kind of outfit he would be into...or, that he would want to see you get out of." Cassie waggled her brows.

Ruth grinned, admiring her long legs in the mirror. "You think so?"

"What are you worried about? You could show up in a paper bag and still look fantastic," Eve assured her, looking at herself next to Ruth in the mirror.

Both of their eyes began to glow strangely, as Dagon's powers revealed both of their monstrous natures. Ruth's witchy eyes shined a more brilliant green than they already were, but Eve's brown eyes took on a subtle, deep amethyst sheen in the layers beneath. It was a different kind of shine than she'd seen in the others.

And it was so much less striking, she thought as she stared at Ruth's reflection next to her.

She felt incredibly inadequate next to that gorgeous, willowy blonde, and she was very, very glad that Ruth was Bo and Luc's sister. She couldn't compete with all those supermodel attributes. Ruth looked like a Victoria's Secret Angel, and Eve looked like she was due back for her shift at the chocolate factory in the morning.

She was definitely going to have to wear the tallest heels she owned tonight. Power heels.

Oh…but not those ones. Not the red bottoms.

Eve rubbed the heel of her hand over her chest, trying to soothe away that persistent ache.

21
You're a Pain in My Ass

The hunters all met up at a new club that night – everyone except Mira, who refused to have anything to do with Eve, as she blamed her for Luc going AWOL. Mira insisted someone needed to stay behind to watch over the compound.

The club wasn't as expansive as The Gutter, and not nearly as nice, but the music was loud and the drinks were cheap. As Cassie, Eve, and Ruth strutted up to the bar, their handsome entourage in tow, Eve felt a deep satisfaction at the eyes that turned to watch them pass.

Yes, they're ours. Hands off, ladies.

But seriously, Eve was going to fight anyone who touched any of her boys. She almost wished someone would try it, because she was itching for a good fight, but, looking around at the other patrons, she doubted it would be a fun or fair fight. She'd just end up ruining someone's face.

Ruger ordered the ladies a double shot, then immediately called for another. Eve turned her back to the bar and looked out at the dance floor as she downed the second shot. The mass of bodies writhing against each other and bouncing around reminded her of boiling water. She could feel the music thumping through her whole body, and she felt the urge to jump right into the middle of that boiling chaos.

She did a quick headcount of her boys: Bo had taken a seat at the bar with his fruity sex on the beach, looking down at his phone; Eoduun and Zeke were standing near her, looking out at the dance floor, their heads close together as they tried to converse over the music; and Isaac…where was Isaac?

Finally, after scanning the room several times over, she spotted him back in the corner, leaning against a speaker with his arms crossed. He looked like a bouncer in his black slacks and shirt. Even from across the room, she could tell his eyes were fixed on her.

She started to walk away from the bar to go check on him, but an unfamiliar hand closed around her wrist. She yanked her arm away and whipped around so quickly, Ramil's eyes rounded.

"My apologies! I only wanted to ask if you wanted to join me out there," Ramil said, dipping his head toward the dance floor. But it was odd how clearly she could hear him over the music. He wasn't even shouting.

Were his words spilling straight into her mind?

The skin prickled on the back of her neck, and she turned her head to find Ruth glaring at her.

Great.

"I was just going to go check on Isaac. But I think Ruth wants to dance," she said, drawing his attention to the witch.

In a flash, Ruth's glare shifted into a pleasant smile as Ramil's eyes turned to her. He smiled back at Ruth, then returned his attention to Eve. "Perhaps later, then?"

Eve gestured to her boys. "I think my dance card is pretty full. Maybe another time."

Before he could ask anything else, she escaped across the dance floor toward Isaac. When she reached him, however, the music from the speaker was uncomfortably loud. She pointed to her ear, then shook both fists alternately. *It's loud!*

Isaac touched his ear and shrugged. He signed, *You looked like you were dancing.* He then signed "loud" again, but continued the hand shaking longer than necessary. It did look like a dance move.

Eve made a sarcastic face and brushed her first two fingers down her nose. *Funny.* She then signed, *Why are you over here?*

He replied, *Cover your ears. Come here.*

Eve stuck her fingers in her ears and walked closer to him. He reached out and pulled her toward him, switching places with her so she could stand with her back against the speaker.

The music reverberated straight through to her bones. She looked up at him as the music vibrated her eyeballs. As she took in the borderline pleasant expression on his face, with the corner of his lip tipped up, she imagined how it would feel if he took her right now against this thumping speaker.

No. That wasn't allowed. She didn't need to be thinking about him like that. She stepped forward and switched places with Isaac so he was against the speaker again.

His gaze shifted to something behind her, and annoyance spread over his features. He quickly grabbed her hand and led her away from the speaker, straight into the mass of people on the dance floor. He weaved through the crowd and led her out the other side. As soon as they were clear, he released her hand.

What was that all about? She signed. She didn't realize how convenient knowing ASL was in such a noisy environment. She wished everybody would utilize it.

He fingerspelled *Cassie.*

Oh. *She just wants a night with you. She and Ruger agreed to a trade.*

Isaac frowned, then eyed her suspiciously. *What did Ruger get? Don't look at me like that.*

Did he get you?

Eve crossed her arms over her chest momentarily, then rolled her eyes and snapped her first two fingers to her thumb. *No.* She added, *He wanted me, but it's not going to happen.* She looked back at the bar. Ramil was talking with Remi, and Ruth was standing next to him, having her own conversation with Cassie. Eve turned back to Isaac and signed, *Did you know Ramil is a monster?*

He nodded.

What kind of monster is he? Eve asked.

Isaac shrugged, touching his fingers to his temple and twisting his palm outward as he drew it away. *I don't know.* He added, *He's very black. But Dizzy was black. Bo is black. Kai is black. You're sometimes black. Dagon is red and black.*

So, all he could tell was whether someone was a monster or had propensity for evil. He couldn't tell what they were.

Isaac's eyes again shifted to someone behind her. She turned just in time to see Zeke and Eoduun coming up behind her. Zeke's hands slipped around her waist as he slid up behind her, and Eoduun's fingers intertwined with hers as he sidled up next to her.

"Come dance with us, babe," Zeke begged, his lips close to her ear.

Eve turned her head back to Isaac, but he was already gone.

She allowed Eoduun and Zeke to lead her out onto the dance floor, and as the music thumped through her, she swiveled her hips and draped one arm over Eoduun's neck, one arm back behind her around Zeke's neck, while Zeke grinded behind her, both of their hands all over her body. Moving so sensually between them like this, bodies sliding against each other, their hips swaying with hers, awakened the need between Eve's thighs.

Using Dagon's power, Eve took in Zeke and Eoduun's thoughts, and, just as she suspected, they were as horny as she was. Eoduun was imagining the three of them dancing together naked, except he was in the middle, Zeke and Eve's hands all over him. Zeke was thinking about bending Eve over while she sucked Eoduun's cock, and he was wondering if she was going to let them share her tonight.

Eve looked into Eoduun's dark, smoldering eyes and melded his imaginings with her own, taking them over and shaping them into her own fantasy. As she imagined both of her hands clasped together, stroking both him and Zeke at the same time, their cocks pressed together, she saw a shadow of confusion pass through Eoduun's eyes.

What the fuck...why was I just fantasizing from Eve's POV? Eoduun wondered.

Eve mentally pulled back, surprised. He *saw* what she had done to his thoughts? She only meant to play off of it for her own personal amusement, not realizing she could influence his thoughts as he saw and felt them. That was meant for her mind only, not his.

Is this how Dagon filled the missing memory in Zeke's mind from the gym showers? How much power did Dagon have? Could she speak telepathically to Eoduun? She wanted to try it, but she didn't want to reveal to anyone that she had Dagon's powers, because if she did...they would know how she got them, and she wasn't ready for everyone to be pissed about her fucking Dagon. Again. And Zeke would know that she lied to him about what had happened in the showers.

She would have to try it on a stranger. She glanced over at the tall, thin woman with the cute bob haircut next to her who was dancing a little stiffly. Eve listened to her thoughts, and was doused with self-doubt.

I probably look so stupid. I should've worn the other shirt – this one shows too much of my bloated belly. I should've skipped dinner. Connor probably thinks I suck at dancing. I do suck at dancing.

Eve conjured a feeling of confidence, and pushed it into those intrusive thoughts. *You look fabulous, and you're here to have fun. You don't suck at dancing. Everyone is too busy worrying about themselves to even worry about your dancing, anyway. You got this.*

The woman's eyes darted around as she danced, confusion filling her mind. It quickly faded, however, and a fresh sense of determination trickled through to Eve from the woman.

That's true, the woman thought. *No one is even paying attention to me. No one cares if I suck at dancing, do they? Just have fun, Sloane. Just have fun. You can do that.*

Eve pulled back again, a little thrill of excitement at her discovery tickling in her throat. With Dagon's powers, she could influence other people's thoughts and speak directly into their minds. She wondered if the woman heard it as her own thoughts, or if she heard it in Eve's mental voice. Was Eve forcing her target to manifest the thought, or was she speaking it directly to them?

Ruth's white-blonde hair caught Eve's eye, and Eve saw that she had finally lured Ramil out onto the dance floor with her. Ruth's long, lithe body was rolling and gyrating beautifully against his tall, lean form. They made a handsome pair, if a dangerous one.

At least Ruth was less dangerous without her memories. But Eve realized that if she could use Dagon's power to push thoughts into other people's minds, it might be possible for her to use it to feed Ruth her memories. Did she want to do that, even if she could?

Eve watched the pair dancing, and she prodded once again into Ramil's mind, even though she was a little afraid of intruding on some more private thoughts. With the way Ruth was undulating on him, she couldn't blame him.

But when she was finally able to push carefully past his barriers, the thoughts that came through weren't remotely passionate. He was calculating. Ramil was considering Ruth's strengths. Her usefulness to him. *She still has all of her power. I can feel it. She just needs to be reminded how to use it. She could be beneficial to have at my side.* Eve saw herself in Ramil's mind, and realized he was watching her through the crowd. *But Eve...she's the one I need.*

Eve's curiosity was so intense, she had to pull out of his mind before she accidentally blurted something into his thoughts. She couldn't alert him to her presence.

She didn't like the dark, obsessive turn his emotions took when he regarded her. *She's the one I need*. Needed for what? It felt like something sinister. Something of immense importance to him.

Eve needed another drink, so she led the boys off the dance floor, back to the bar. She found Bo still sitting in his same seat next to Remi, nursing the same drink he had when she'd left him. She weaseled in between him and Remi and hugged both arms around his solid bicep, looking down at his phone.

"*'Webtoons'*?" she said questioningly, reading the address bar across the top of his browser.

He blackened his screen. "Can I help you?" he asked, annoyed.

"Aw, don't be mad. I just needed a dose of Daddy pheromones." She squeezed his arm tighter and rested her head against his shoulder. His scent wasn't as strong as it had been, and she couldn't hear his heartbeat. The powers she stole from him must finally be starting to fade.

"You need another drink," he surmised flatly.

"That too."

Bo got the bartender's attention and ordered Eve a sex on the beach. When the bartender handed it to her, Bo paid for it. "There. Don't say I never did anything for you," he said.

"Thanks, Daddy," she said sweetly. "Now, scoot over. I want to sit with you."

Bo looked incredulous. "No. This is a one-ass seat, and there's already an ass in it." He glanced down the bar at Zeke and Eoduun, who were also ordering drinks. "What happened to your entertainment?"

"We took a break. Now you're my entertainment."

"Lucky me."

Eve pouted. "Fine. I'll go find Isaac."

As she began to walk away, Bo's arm caught her around the waist and pulled her back. "No. Stay."

His arm lingered around her for a few moments longer than it needed to, and he turned his seat obliquely to the bar so he was partially facing her, putting his knee outside her thigh, blocking her from escaping again.

Eve leaned against the open space in his seat between his legs and propped one buttcheek up onto it. "This'll do," she said cheerfully.

"You're a pain in my ass," he said, his voice low and close to her ear.

She gave him a sly grin. "And you love it."

He sighed heavily, but she saw the hint of a smile in his eyes. Bo glanced down at his blank phone screen and said, "Should I assume that you aren't coming to my apartment to read manga tonight?"

"Why do you say that?"

"I saw the way you were dancing with the boys, and the scent of your arousal filling my nostrils is hard to ignore." Bo's scarred eye started to swirl into yellow, but he suppressed it. "I just assumed you'd be going home with them."

Heat flushed over Eve's skin. "What, you'd rather we blow this joint and go sit in your room and read manga together? Is that what you're trying to tell me?"

Bo arched a contemplative brow. "It's not the worst idea."

Eve leaned her shoulder into Bo's chest. "I bet I can think of a better one," she teased wryly.

Bo made a sound low in his throat. "Playing with fire, Evie."

Eve tossed her head back onto Bo's shoulder and looked up at him. "Burn me."

22

Dance With Me

Bo couldn't stop his wolf eye from fully shifting this time. He closed his eye and rubbed it, trying to get it under control before any normies noticed.

"Don't do this to me in public," he scolded, blinking his eye open again. Cool charcoal gray.

"Why would I stop? I'm just getting started. You make this way too much fun."

Bo's hand slid up around Eve's throat, his palm stretched across her trachea. His masked lips came close to her ear, and he rasped, "I am not above carrying you out over my shoulder. Keep pushing."

White hot desire seared through Eve's belly. *Punish me.* She remembered the way he'd hoisted her over his shoulder and carried her to his bed the day she'd lost control over the Blood of Lilith inside of her, and the memory only stoked her need further…

Until she was hurtled back down into the dirt at the memory of what happened later that same day.

The pictures.

The video.

The fight.

Luc was everywhere in her head, seeping into memories where he didn't belong. She couldn't escape him. He was souring everything good that she still had because he'd made sure to have his fingers in every aspect of her life in some way or another.

Everything reminded her of him.

She'd been trying her best to distract herself from the gaping pit in her stomach, the fissure through her heart, with pleasures of the flesh. With mysteries. With new powers to play with. With anything and everything that would keep her mind and body too busy to dwell on the pain, because she knew what was going to happen the moment she found herself alone in stillness.

She would shatter into a thousand pieces.

She hailed the bartender. "Three shots of Cuervo, please. No chaser."

"Oh, this can't be a good thing," Bo remarked.

When the bartender brought the shots, she set two in front of Eve, one in front of Bo. Eve snatched up the one she put in front of Bo. "Nope, that's mine, too," she clarified as she tossed some money on the bar. Then she took all three shots, chasing them with a big gulp of what was left of her cocktail. She turned to Bo. "Dance with me."

"I don't dance. You know this."

"If you don't dance with me out there, I'm going to dance on you right here," she threatened.

"Classy," Bo retorted.

Eve laughed. "When have I ever given you the impression of class?"

"Maybe I should just take you home. I don't see things getting better from here."

"Just dance with me," she cajoled. "You don't even have to do anything wild, just move your shoulders." She slid off the seat and took his hands in hers, tugging at them alternately to make his shoulders shimmy.

"Evie..." Bo protested, tipping his head back in exasperation.

Eve intertwined her fingers in his and started dancing in front of him, waving their arms around to the music. "Come on, Bo," she begged.

She saw his eyes drift down to her swiveling hips, then quickly dart back up to her face. He groaned. "I'll dance for one song, if you let me take you home afterward," he bartered.

Eve waggled her eyebrows. "You want to take me *home* with you?" she teased, dancing closer to him.

"I want to take you home before you get sloppy," he said, rising from his chair. "I have no intention of babysitting you when you're incoherent."

"Fine. If that's what you have to tell yourself," she sing-songed. She backed up to the dance floor, dragging him along with her.

Once they were in the middle of the crowd, Bo pulled Eve closer and guided their intertwined hands behind his neck, then freed his fingers from hers. He put one hand on the small of her back and moved his body with hers, his hard thigh rubbing up between her legs.

Eve looked up at him, mild surprise in her eyes. "Oh, shit, you can dance."

He leaned close to her ear to be heard over the music. "I said I don't dance. I never said I can't."

As they moved to the rhythm, her body against his, she couldn't help but remember the way his body had felt grinding against hers when he was inside of her, in his bed. She wanted him, but she had no idea if that door was open or not. He'd tamed the beast within her when she'd needed it, but it had been a matter of necessity. Sure, he'd then given her his power in a second romp, which was completely unnecessary, but it was still in the realm of "gray area."

But if she fucked him tonight, that was something else entirely. It wasn't a matter of circumstance. It was a choice, and if she made that choice, it may mean that she was closing the door on Luc.

And, even though she talked a big game, she knew she wasn't ready to close that door.

The song ended entirely too soon, and Eve groaned when Bo began to lead her from the dance floor. As she followed along behind him, pouting, she noticed the tequila was beginning to make her world sway just a little. But she also noticed it was beginning to make her problems matter a little less, too.

When Bo told Zeke and Eoduun he was taking Eve home, they both insisted they were ready to head out as well. As the boys settled their tab, Isaac stepped up beside Eve. He looked down at her.

Are you drunk?

Eve seesawed her hand. She signed, *We're going home. Do you want to leave with us?*

Isaac glanced surreptitiously over at Cassie, who was at the bar, smiling at him. She gave him a little wave. He turned back to Eve, then nodded his fist and circled his hand over his chest. *Yes, please.*

On the car ride home, Eve sat in the backseat between Zeke and Eoduun. Eoduun ran his hand up Eve's thigh, leaning close to her to whisper in her ear, "I want to fuck you so fucking bad." His eyes flitted over to Zeke. "We can invite Z, too. He might be a little more adventurous after all the shots he downed tonight. We could have some real fun."

Eve glanced up at the rearview mirror, and her eyes briefly met Bo's before he returned his attention to the road. He'd obviously heard.

"Evie already made plans with me tonight," Bo stated firmly.

A heated look of resentment crossed Eoduun's features. His hand clenched Eve's thigh tightly. "You promised me time with you," he reminded her.

Bo answered for her. "She made me fucking dance. In public. I think I earned my time with her."

When they arrived at the compound, and Eve headed past her apartment toward Bo's, Isaac grabbed her arm. She cast a questioning glance back at him.

Where are you going? he signed.

Bo's place. She pointed to herself, then pushed her raised index finger out to arm's length and brought it back to herself. *I'll be right back.*

Isaac threw Bo a disparaging glance.

Bo frowned behind his mask. "What?"

Isaac turned and walked into Eve's apartment and shut the door.

"I'm not going to miss him one fucking bit when he leaves," Bo grumbled.

"I will," Eve admitted. "I like Isaac."

"Don't remind me."

Zeke and Eoduun walked with Bo and Eve as far as Eoduun's apartment. Zeke caught Eve and hugged her.

"Goodnight, babe. I'm going to hang out with Eoduun for a while, so if you decide to stop over before you go back to your apartment, we'll be here for a bit."

"She's not going back to her apartment," Eoduun said curtly. He glared at Bo, and knowingly added, "...Is she?" Before Bo could answer, Eoduun snatched Eve into his arms, raking one hand into her hair, and claimed her mouth aggressively. Possessively. It made her head spin. When he finally released her, he smirked at Bo. "There. I hope she tastes like me."

Eve licked her lips. "I probably already do, because you taste like tequila."

Eoduun rolled his eyes, but there was the tiniest hint of amusement cracking his annoyed façade. He and Zeke went into his apartment, leaving Eve and Bo alone in the hallway.

Eve followed Bo into his apartment, kicking her shoes off at the door. "When in Rome," she announced as she left them where they landed instead of lining them up nicely under the coat rack like she normally would have.

She flounced into his kitchen, and he sauntered along behind her, his hands casually in his pockets. "What do you have for snacks?" she asked as she started opening cupboards.

"Sorry, not much of a snacker," Bo apologized, watching her rummage through his kitchen.

She opened the fridge. "What the fuck do you eat?" she wondered as she scanned the mostly empty shelves.

"How do you think I manage to maintain my girlish figure?" he teased.

"Man cannot live on pumpkin spice lattes alone," she chastised. She closed the fridge and went back to the cupboards. She pulled out a box of saltines. "How old are these?"

Bo pulled his mask off and dropped it onto the counter. "I don't remember ever buying those," he answered, crossing his arms and leaning back against the counter.

Eve's eyes lingered on his freshly exposed lips, then dropped down to appreciate the way his biceps pushed his pectorals together beneath his tight, white v-neck t-shirt. Man cleavage. "Why are you so fucking hot?" she blurted. "Do you even *try*, or does it just happen?"

Bo's face flushed, and he looked at the floor. "For fuck's sake," he mumbled. He pushed off from the counter. "There's a stash of pretzel chips in the cupboard next to the stove. Eat some. Please."

Eve tossed the box of saltines behind her onto the counter and started toward Bo. "Why would I want those when there's a snack right here?" she grinned, pinching her fingers at him.

"Evie, no," Bo protested, holding his hands out to stop her. "I'm not a fucking snack."

"You're not just *a* snack. You're *the* snack." She bit her lip and waggled her brows at him.

Bo caught her by the wrists before she could molest him, and he looked down at her. "Behave, Evie. You're drunk."

Eve twisted her mouth contemplatively. "Hm…you sure about that?"

"Let's just take it easy, all right? I thought you wanted to read that manga. I'll go get it for you, and you can sit quietly and read it, ok?"

Eve dropped her hands, and Bo let go of her wrists. "Fine, wolf boy," she said disappointedly.

Eve followed Bo into his room and flopped onto his bed, watching him look through his giant manga collection.

"Nerd," Eve teased.

Bo turned and raised his eyebrow at her, holding the wolf boy and bunny girl manga. "Nerd? Do you want to read this or not?"

Eve held her hand out for it. "Sorry. Yes."

Bo strolled over to the side of the bed and slowly lowered the book toward her, but as soon as she reached for it, he snatched it out of her reach. "What do you say?"

"Please?"

"Please what?" He gazed down at her expectantly.

"Please..." Eve racked her brain. Please what? "Please...Daddy?"

Bo dropped the manga onto her lap, a crooked grin revealing those glorious fangs briefly before he turned away from her to return to the bookshelf.

"Such a fucking tease," she complained after him. She opened the book and found where she left off last time. A few minutes later, Bo placed a small stack of manga on the floor next to her side of the bed, then took his own stack to his side of the bed and reclined back against the pillow next to her. She glanced down, and saw that he'd brought her the next books in the series.

She scooted over and nestled into his side, resting her head on his shoulder. She glanced over at what he was reading. It was a historical fantasy story, with a pretty young girl and a handsome, ancient fox spirit.

"Is that one smutty too?" Eve asked.

"I don't know. I just started it."

"Tell me if you get to a good part," she advised him, then returned her attention to her own manga. She was having a hard time focusing on the words on the pages, though. The alcohol in her system was in full effect on her senses. She fumbled through several pages, but she found herself concentrating more on the way Bo's body felt next to her than she was on the manga.

She finally gave up and closed the book with an annoyed groan. "I can't focus. My eyes are all wonky."

Bo chuckled next to her. "You finally get your manga, and you can't read it? That's unfortunate."

She propped it in front of the manga he was currently reading. "Read it to me."

Bo scoffed. "How am I supposed to read this to you?"

Eve opened it and pointed at the page. "See these letters here? You sound them out, and they make words. You say the words with your mouth."

Bo dropped his head back against the headboard. "Oh, thank you. I'm so glad you clarified that for me."

"Just read the words. I can see the pictures," Eve said. She hugged his arm, then looked up at him and booped his nose. "Please, Daddy?"

Bo exhaled deeply. "You're the fucking worst."

"Thanks. I try." Eve flipped the manga open to where she left off. "Ok, go." She snuggled in and waited for him to start reading.

So he did.

But Eve stopped him. "No, you're making everyone sound the same. You need to do a different voice for the bunny girl."

"I draw the line at doing voices."

"You mean like you draw the line at dancing?" she egged.

"You can coerce me into doing a lot of things, Evie, but you will not make me do voices."

"What if I pinch your nipple when you read the bunny girl parts?"

"Then I'll stop reading. Leave my nipples alone."

Eve ran her hand over Bo's firm chest, teasing the pad of her thumb over his nipple. She felt it pebble under the thin fabric of his shirt.

"Don't you dare."

"I'm not doing anything," she said innocently. She rubbed her thumb in slow circles around his nipple. "Just read. You don't have to do the voices."

Bo pressed on, and Eve found her hand sliding down over his abs. Slowly, she trailed it further down to run her finger along the V at the waistline of his pants. He stopped reading again. "What are you doing, Evie?" he asked accusingly.

"Nothing."

"It doesn't feel like nothing."

"What does it feel like?"

"Something."

"You're going to have to be more specific," she said in a low voice as she ran her hand back up his chest, up the side of his neck, and cupped her palm along his bare jawline.

"If you want *that*, maybe you should head across the hall to Eoduun's," Bo said.

Eve pushed her way onto Bo's lap, straddling his hips, forcing him to set the manga aside. "Is that really what you want me to do? Go jump into Eoduun's bed?" She felt Bo hardening between her legs, his swelling cock pressing up against her. "It doesn't *feel* like you want me to go anywhere."

"I don't think we should go there again, Evie. Not until…not until you and Luc settle things."

Eve gazed into his aqua blue and golden-yellow eyes, and she saw her own burning desire reflected there. Reflected in that aqua orb that looked exactly like Luc's, where she'd seen *his* burning desire for her, too. Eve combed her fingers into Bo's silver-white hair, the color so similar to Luc's. Even here, in her safe space, Luc haunted her through his brother's face.

Eve slid her arms around Bo's neck and dropped her forehead to his shoulder, her own shoulders slumping. Bo wrapped his arms around her and hugged her against him, and she hugged his neck tighter.

"Don't you want me?" she murmured.

"You know I do. But if we start something, I can't just turn it back off again. I don't want to start something until I know where things stand with Luc. I don't want to complicate things."

"I hate him," she whispered.

"No, you don't," Bo replied quietly.

Hot tears were overflowing from Eve's eyes before she even realized she was crying. "What am I supposed to do when he comes back?"

"Talk to him. Don't yell. Don't jump to conclusions. Don't accuse. Just…talk it out."

"He doesn't love me anymore."

"Yes, he does."

"You don't fucking know that," Eve sobbed into Bo's neck.

"I do know. I know Luc. If he didn't love you, he'd be here, business as usual, completely unaffected," Bo assured her. "It takes a lot to shake him, and you do it so effortlessly. It's because he loves you."

"I'm fucking pathetic. I shouldn't have run. I shouldn't have lost my cool. I should've just stayed and talked so we could've figured this all out then and there. Now he won't even call me, or text me back, and I feel like I'm waiting in fucking limbo for him to come back and crush the rest of my heart."

Bo ran his hand over her hair gently while he continued to hold her. "Regardless of how things went, and regardless of how they go when Luc returns, just remember that you are so incredibly loved, by all of us, and we'll be here for you no matter what happens. *I* will be here for you, *always*."

If Eve knew nothing else, she knew *that* with all her heart. He'd been cleaning up Luc's messes since he was a kid, and here he was, holding her together with all his might, making sure she didn't crumble under the weight of Luc's betrayal.

Bo would always be there for her.

Eve caressed the side of Bo's face. She had so much she wanted to say to him. How special he was to her. How much she needed him.

How she felt like she could handle just about anything with him by her side. How he was her best friend. Her forbidden desire. Her favorite person in the whole entire world. Her safe space.

But she didn't. It would only complicate his feelings, and hers. She just kissed him on the cheek and said, "I know. Thank you."

After a while, when the tears dried up, Eve climbed off of Bo's lap and picked up the wolf boy manga again. She handed it to him. "I'll behave this time."

Bo read to her, and it wasn't long before her puffy eyelids started to get heavy.

A knock on the door startled Eve awake. She pushed off of Bo's arm and sat up, looking around. She saw Bo must've switched to the fox spirit manga after Eve had fallen asleep, but he now set it on the nightstand next to the bed. The clock on the nightstand showed it was well after midnight. "What the fuck?" Bo muttered.

"What? Who is it?" Eve asked, alarmed at Bo's tensing. "I don't have your powers anymore. I can't smell them."

"Blood. Dizzy's blood."

23

Please Love Me Again

Bo climbed out of bed, and when Eve followed behind him toward the door, he motioned for her to stay back. As he drew closer to the door, however, he paused. "Luc?"

Eve's heart leapt into her throat. She pushed past Bo and threw the door open.

And immediately took a step back.

Luc stood in the doorway, all six-foot-five inches of him splattered in blood, some of it dry, some of it still wet. His blue button-up oxford shirt was absolutely drenched in it. From his blood-soaked hands hung Dizzy's severed head, Luc's fingers tangled in the bloody mop of hair. No, not just severed – *ripped*. Tendons and arteries hung jaggedly from the torn flesh, dripping blood gruesomely onto the carpet in the hallway.

But it was Luc's eyes that startled Eve the most. He wasn't wearing his signature sunglasses, so she could clearly see his eyes were wild and wide, the bright aquamarine blue clashing horrifically with the dark, dried blood all over his face. These were not the eyes of a man in full possession of his faculties.

Luc dropped Dizzy's head, and it rolled to a stop at Eve's feet, Dizzy's lifeless, milky eyes staring up at her. "I fixed it," Luc announced darkly. He stepped toward her into the apartment, and Eve took an instinctive step back. He thrust a blood-spattered folder toward her. "It wasn't me. I can prove it wasn't me."

Eve stared at the folder, afraid to touch it.

Luc didn't wait. He opened it and started quickly explaining the receipts, photos, and forms inside, getting bloody fingerprints all over everything. "Look at the time stamp on this receipt. I couldn't have been in my office because I was out to lunch. And I have a security camera photo, too. See? That's me leaving the restaurant." He went through the entire folder, rambling like a madman, showing every shred of evidence he'd gathered that it wasn't him in the pictures she'd been sent. "I hunted down Dizzy, and I got him to confess. He was using Ruth's traveling stones and portals to follow me around. Look." Luc dropped the folder in his hands, papers and photos and receipts scattering all over the floor, and dug his phone out of his pocket, holding it out to Eve.

A battered and beaten Dizzy was on the screen, chained to a chair, obviously at the end of a long session of horrific torture. His voice came out choked and raspy. "It was me, Eve. I just liked pretending to be Luc. I liked the perks. All of those women thought I was him. Even Mira thought I was him. But I didn't send you those pictures. I don't know who did that, or why." Dizzy's blackened eyes focused on the man behind the phone as he continued, "There, happy now? I won't do it ever again, I swear! Hey, I'll even give you the grimoire! I'm tired of trying to hide it from that crazy guy Ruth summoned!" Dizzy broke down in tears. "I just wanted to be something more than the screwup that everyone hated…"

The video ended and Luc just let his phone drop onto the floor rather than putting it in his pocket. "See?" His aquamarine eyes blazed. "It wasn't me. I would never hurt you like that, Eve. I love you so fucking much." He collapsed to his knees in front of her, his expression beseeching. "Please…please love me again."

Eve looked at him, then down at Dizzy's head on the floor between them. She opened her mouth to speak, but she couldn't make words come out.

Luc filled the silence with more pleading. "If you still don't believe me, steal Eoduun's powers and go through my head. All of it. Everything. I won't hide anything from you, because there's nothing to hide."

Bo spoke up from the sidelines. "Is this what you've been doing the whole time you've been gone? Is this why you weren't answering my calls or texts?"

While still gazing up at Eve, Luc answered, "I wasn't coming back empty-handed. I had to fix it. So I did. I fixed it."

Eve finally opened her mouth. "Why were you in Newbury? Why were you in my hometown when you were supposed to be in Paris? Why were you investigating my mother without telling me?"

Confusion clouded Luc's face.

"I know it wasn't Dizzy," she added. "I scented hints of your presence there, because that's where I went when I disappeared."

Recognition cleared his eyes. "Oh! Yes! I was there. I finished in Paris early, so I thought I would start looking into your birth mother for you."

"Why?"

Luc furrowed his brow. "Because you asked me to. You said you wanted to know more about her. I told you I would look into it."

Oh. Fuck. Eve was an absolute fucking asshole.

"You should've checked in, Luc," Bo interjected. "You had no reason to ignore us like that."

"I was busy," Luc reasoned.

"Our father has been up my ass wanting to know why he can't get a hold of you. You missed three important meetings and lost a vendor. Or so he tells me."

"I was *busy*," Luc repeated, his tone more threatening this time, his wild eyes turning toward Bo, but not quite meeting with Bo. He looked back up at Eve. "I've proven my innocence, have I not?"

Eve nodded. She couldn't deny everything he'd shown her, and it was making guilt churn her stomach. She should be the one on the floor on her knees.

"Then you're not mad anymore, right?"

She shook her head.

Luc stood up and looked down at her. "Then tell me you love me again. Say it. Please." His tone was part begging, part demanding. He *needed* her to say it.

Eve looked down at Dizzy's head at her feet, then used her foot to nudge it aside as she stepped closer to Luc. She interlaced her fingers with his giant, blood-stained hands. As gross as he was right now, she felt that irresistible magnetism toward him. Being near him made her heart finally stop hurting. She looked up at him, and with a tremble in her voice, she confessed, "I never stopped loving you."

The wildness in Luc's eyes melted away, and a smile spread across his face. "And we're not 'done,' right?"

Eve shook her head. "No, we're not done. I'm so sorry."

Luc scooped her up and hugged her against his blood-soaked chest, completely ruining her outfit. But she didn't care. She wrapped her legs around his waist and threw her arms around his neck and hugged him back.

But with the relief of having her beautiful psychopath back came the remorse of having knocked down the domino that started this whole chain of events in the first place. She really was hell-bent on sabotaging her own relationships and happiness. If she kept this shit up, she was going to have to face the day when she succeeded.

She was such a fucking asshole, and she couldn't figure out why these guys gave even half a shit about her. She should be soaking up every bit of their love that she could, not throwing temper tantrums and kicking them in the teeth.

Bo interrupted, "This is all very touching, and I'm truly glad it all worked out, but, Luc, can you please remove Dizzy's head from my floor? He's getting blood everywhere."

"I'll pay to have it cleaned," Luc assured him, but he wasn't looking at Bo. His gaze had dipped down to Eve's lips.

But as soon as he started to move in for a kiss, Eve clapped her hand over his mouth. His striking blue eyes met hers questioningly.

"Your face is covered in blood," she said. "Is any of this yours?"

Luc made a muffled sound behind her hand to indicate it wasn't.

"I'm not kissing you and getting Dizzy's blood in my mouth. That's disgusting," she asserted. He made a pitiful muffled sound and looked at her pathetically, but she held firm. "No."

He reluctantly conceded. But as soon as she moved her hand away, he plunged his hand into her hair and pulled her face to his, claiming her mouth hungrily before she could resist him. He wasn't letting her go without a blood-stained kiss.

Eve growled in annoyance for only a moment, but it gave way to a desperate sigh. Fuck, she'd missed him so much.

When he finally lowered her to her own feet, Bo approached them with a garbage bag, and he thrust it into Luc's hand. He pointed at Dizzy's head. "That doesn't stay here."

"Chill, brother. You're acting like I tracked dog shit in here or something." Luc bent over and picked up Dizzy's head by the hair. "It's just a little blood." While he was down there, he picked up the phone he dropped as well.

"It's a whole fucking *head*, Luc," Bo said flatly. "You dropped a *head* on my goddamn floor."

"And you're being such a baby about it. It's just a head." Luc held up Dizzy's head for emphasis. "It's not like it's rotten or anything. It doesn't even really stink yet," he added, giving it a tentative sniff before dropping it into the garbage bag.

"Just get it out of here." Bo looked over at the clock on the wall. "We'll get caught up on everything tomorrow. I need to get to bed." Bo walked up to Eve and grabbed her face, kissing her on the forehead. He looked her in the eye meaningfully. "See? All's well that ends well. Goodnight, Evie." He then returned to his bedroom and shut the door.

When Eve and Luc stepped out of Bo's apartment, Eve saw a trail of blood from her apartment door to Bo's. Luc must've teleported to her door first, then gone to Bo's. They followed the blood trail to her door.

"I'll be right back," Luc said, stopping in front of her door. He raised the garbage bag. "I need to drop this off to the incinerator."

"Maybe you should change your clothes while you're at it," Eve suggested as she opened her door and stepped into her apartment. "Or take a shower."

Isaac was sitting in his chair in the living room, and when he saw Eve walk in, his eyes immediately dropped to her bloody clothes. He rushed to her. *What happened?!* he signed, looking her over.

Luc's hand was suddenly around Isaac's throat. "*You...*" Luc snarled accusingly as he slammed Isaac against the wall. He raised his other hand, and Eve saw it begin to flicker with flashes of electricity.

What the fuck just happened?

She jumped into action, throwing herself at the two of them, wedging herself between Luc and Isaac, using herself as a human shield. "No! Luc, stop!"

The electricity in Luc's hand sparked out, but he didn't release Isaac just yet. "Why did you take him with you? He should be dead already," Luc growled, still glaring at Isaac.

"It was an accident! Luc, stop! I didn't mean to take him, but he grabbed me when I jumped, and I pulled him along."

Luc paused, and his eyes shifted to Eve's. "He did it on purpose. He wanted to be alone with you. That's all he ever seems to want."

"No, he didn't do it on purpose. It was purely accidental. He came running to me because I took a filet knife to your tattoo on my wrist so you couldn't track me."

Isaac suddenly shoved Eve away so she was no longer between him and Luc. "I don't need your protection," he said aloud. Then he quickly maneuvered out of Luc's grasp and pulled both knives from his belt.

Luc laughed mirthlessly. "You brought a knife to a gun fight, padre," Luc spoke and signed now that both hands were free.

"If you touch him, I won't forgive you," Eve warned Luc.

Luc stiffened. He turned his head to Eve. "But he touched *you*, didn't he? He's going to pay for it."

"How would you even know that?"

"Because I know how long you were gone, and I know he wouldn't have passed up his opportunity to take advantage of your needs."

Luc disappeared and popped up behind Isaac, kicking him in the back of the knees, dropping Isaac to the floor. But Isaac quickly swung his knife around, and if he had been striking at anyone but Luc, he would've carved a brutal, gaping wound into their thigh. But Isaac's tactical knife compressed and warped and passed around Luc's thigh without causing so much as a scratch. Luc cocked his fist back, prepared to land a devastating blow to the side of Isaac's face.

But it never landed, because Eve hurtled herself across the apartment with lightning speed and tackled Luc to the floor with Dagon's immense strength surging through her. He never saw it coming, so he didn't have time to bend space around him to dodge her. She sat on top of his stomach, glowering down at him, her hand on his chest to hold him down. "I told you to stop," she seethed. "So fucking *stop*."

Luc's intense eyes burned into hers as they narrowed. "Where did you get that speed?"

A moment of panic surged through her like acid. "I stole powers from Zeke."

"Zeke's not that fast."

"Maybe I've improved on his specialty. I've been known to do that, you know," she reasoned, then quickly returned to the issue at hand. "Now, are you going to stop attacking Isaac, or am I going to have to use Zeke's superstrength to kick your ass?"

"Stop protecting him," Luc growled.

"You're being a bully!"

Luc scoffed. "Bully?! Hardly."

"Let's get something straight, Luc. When he and I..." She didn't finish that sentence because Luc's nostrils flared with fury. "I thought you'd been running around on me with strangers. I thought you and I were over. And it isn't something that's happened since. It was a one-off, just to keep the beast at bay." And then, somewhat untruthfully, she added, "You have nothing to be jealous of."

Luc gritted his teeth as Eve continued to glare down at him. Reluctantly, he said, "Tell me he's not trying to replace me, and I'll let him live."

Eve was taken aback. "He's *not* trying to replace you!" Eve huffed. "Jesus, Bo said the same fucking thing. You all act like I'm in love with Isaac."

"Are you?" Luc's eyes seemed suddenly darker.

Eve glanced up, keenly aware of Isaac standing there, watching them. When her eyes met his, he didn't look away or pretend he wasn't paying attention. He wanted to know her answer just as much as Luc did.

Eve looked down at Luc. "Isaac is my friend. I care about him as a friend. I'm not in love with him. You're the one I love, Luc. You know that."

Luc reached up and fisted his hand in the front of her shirt, lifting his head from the floor. "Then you won't mind telling him to leave so you can prove it to me."

But Eve didn't need to tell him, because Isaac was already grabbing his jacket and pulling the apartment door closed behind him. Eve looked after him at the closed door.

Luc pushed up onto his hands and bent his long legs, raising his knees, and Eve's ass slid down his stomach and came to an abrupt stop in his lap, bumping against his thighs. He pointed at the closed door. "You may not love him, but he obviously has feelings for you." His expression darkened. "He's not allowed to love you. He does not get that privilege. He's an outsider."

"He doesn't love me, Luc. Maybe he cares about me, maybe he has a little crush, or maybe he doesn't even think twice about me. Who knows with him. But he certainly doesn't *love* me. He wouldn't bring me the severed head of our enemy just to get back into my good graces."

A proud smile washed away the darkness in Luc's bloody face. "I'd kill anyone for you. For any reason, or any lack of reason."

Not exactly where she was going with that, but she'd take it. "See? Who else could love me like that?"

Luc cupped the side of her face in his enormous bloody hand and pressed his lips to hers. She didn't even care about Dizzy's blood anymore.

Speaking of Dizzy...Eve pulled back momentarily. "What did you do with Dizzy's head?"

Luc's eyes looked past her, and Eve turned to look at the garbage bag on the floor by the door. "I'll take care of it after," Luc said, then pulled her in for another searing kiss.

Eve didn't have to ask after what.

24
Beautiful Chaos

Luc's hand slid down the back of her pants and gripped her ass, pulling her into a rhythmic grind on his lap while his other hand cupped her face. Eve ran her hands down the sides of his corded neck as she kissed him, their mouths moving more urgently, their tongues more fervent. Luc groaned, the sound vibrating through Eve's whole body, making her insides hum with need.

"I love you, Eve," he whispered against her lips. He leaned back and gazed at her with mesmerizing, greedy eyes. "You're *mine*. I may share you when I have to, but that doesn't change the fact the you belong to *me*. And I will never belong to anyone but *you*." He ran his thumb along her bottom lip, his eyes watching the way her lips parted. "Even if you try to throw me away, I'll do anything to get you back." His eyes met hers again. "*Anything*."

Eve bit his thumb lightly, tasting Dizzy's blood on his skin. "You wouldn't respect my decision and let me move on, like a normal, sane person?" she asked tauntingly.

Luc flipped her over onto her back, his arm protecting her from hitting the floor too hard as he pressed his body between her legs. His thick shaft pressed against her through his slacks, and he rocked his hips, rubbing it against her. His hand pressed into the floor next to her head. He leaned down, his face close to hers. "Sane? You know I'd never be something so boring. You're mine, and I plan to keep you. If you ever want to leave me, you're going to have to kill me first." He crushed his lips against hers in a bruising kiss.

As Luc kissed along her jaw, Eve began to unbutton his disgustingly bloody shirt. "You are a huge, walking red flag, you know that? I should run while I still can," she teased.

Luc hummed a low chuckle against the crook of her neck and jaw. "Oh, it's far too late for that."

Far too late. Eve ran her palms over Luc's firm, bare chest, his shirt hanging open, heavy with Dizzy's blood. "Please take off this gross shirt," Eve begged.

"It's just a little blood," he said nonchalantly as he kissed down her neck. "You already have it all over you." He licked the hollow between her collarbones. "I can taste it on you."

Eve pulled her ruined shirt off, and Luc reached behind her and easily unsnapped her bra, casting it aside. His mouth devoured one soft mound, his tongue laving over her nipple while his palm massaged the other. Eve buried her fingers in his hair while he worshipped her breasts. Her core was flooded with heat and need, but the inside of her chest was overflowing with emotion. She'd missed him even more than she'd realized, and her throat was thick with the feelings welling up inside of her.

"I want you inside me, Luc. Please," she begged, rocking her pelvis against the solid ridge in his pants. "I need you."

Luc slid his body along hers as he brought his lips back up to her mouth. "God, you're so fucking sexy," he whispered, then kissed her deeply, pressing his hips against her. She ran her hands up around his sides, under the back of his shirt, digging her nails into the flesh of his muscular shoulder blades. He growled into her mouth.

She dragged her nails down his back, then reached for his zipper. Luc's hand stilled hers, and he sat back on his haunches, looking ravenously down at her with blood still smeared over his face, his bloody shirt hanging open around his fit abs and firm pecs, his platinum white hair in disarray. Beautiful chaos. He reached down and unbuckled his belt, then yanked it smoothly from his belt loops. He folded it in half, then leaned forward, dragging the cool leather over Eve's bare neck and chest, down her belly, and over her pants.

"What are you going to do with that?" Eve asked, eyeing the belt as his knuckles tightened around it.

Luc hooked his other hand around the back of her knee, raising her leg to expose the curve of her ass. He suddenly smacked the belt across her ass cheek, making her yelp in surprise. He bit his lip and chuckled. He tossed the belt and rubbed his hand soothingly over her bottom, then leaned forward and kissed below her ear. In a low tone, he said, "That's for all the trouble you've caused."

"Only one? I got off easy," she teased.

"Oh, you'll get off easy. More than once," he promised.

Eve gazed up at him as he leaned over her, his eyes roving her bare flesh, his body supported by one hand on the floor near her head, the other hand next to her ribs. He looked like a predator standing over his prey, ready to devour her.

And then her apartment door burst open. "Eve! There's blood..." Cassie's voice trailed off as she saw Luc and Eve on the floor.

Eve quickly crossed her arms over her bare chest and looked around Luc. Cassie, Ruger, Remi, Veris, Ramil, and Ruth all stood looking through her doorway, mouths agape. They must've been returning from the club.

Luc had his back to the door, and he made no move to maintain modesty. He didn't even flinch, or look toward the door. "The zoo's closed. Come back tomorrow," he called coolly, looking down at Eve with unwavering intensity.

Cassie hesitated, then backed out the door, the latch clicking closed quietly.

"I think everybody just saw my boobs," Eve whispered.

"I think you mean everybody just saw *my* boobs," Luc corrected possessively, his voice husky as he palmed her breast and brought his lips to her neck again. He trailed hot kisses down the column of her neck, down over her breasts, and down the long, vertical division between her abdominal muscles, which also marked the border of her birth mark. He hooked his fingers in her waistband, tugging off her pants and underwear. His hands gripped behind her thighs, spreading her legs wide as his mouth ventured over her mound, his hot breath caressing her as his tongue stroked over sex.

Eve gasped and arched her back off the floor, the back of her forearm falling across her eyes, her other hand sliding up over her own breast. Her legs trembled as Luc found her sweet spot and assaulted it ruthlessly with quick flicks of his tongue, two thick fingers thrusting into her. He moaned with her in his mouth, sensing her impending orgasm, and it sent her over the edge, wave after blissful wave cascading over her.

"Hands and knees, love," Luc commanded huskily, unfastening and dropping his pants. "I'm going to fuck you like a goddamn animal."

Eve rolled onto her belly on the hard floor, but Luc was already scooping her hips up, bringing her to her knees. She looked back at him as she felt the head of his cock pressing into her slickened slit. He had one knee on the floor, the other leg bent with his foot planted on the floor by her knee, like he was in position to propose, giving him more freedom of movement. The intensity in his eyes as he gazed at her revved her core, and he stretched her walls and slid into her with a satisfied groan, his teeth catching his lower lip alluringly.

"Fuck, Eve, you feel so goddamn good," he praised. He leaned forward and grabbed her arms, pulling them back, his fingers gripping her forearms. He then used them to pull her body back against him with each powerful thrust.

As her eyes glanced down at the floor, Eve realized she was completely at his mercy in this position. If he suddenly let go of her arms, she wasn't sure she'd be able to catch herself before she faceplanted. She tensed her legs and widened her knees.

Luc leaned over her, still holding her arms back, and whispered in a teasing tone, "What's the matter? Don't you trust me?" His lips grazed the back of her shoulder in light kisses as he rocked his hips into her, his pace falling into a slow, deep, decadent rhythm. His fingers flexed around her forearms.

Eve turned her head to look behind her. She smirked at him. "Don't forget that I'm stronger than you right now."

Luc pulled Eve up, raising her back to his chest and releasing her arms. He held her body against his as he continued to drive into her from behind, one hand on her belly, one hand snaking up her neck. His mouth dropped to her ear, the tip of his tongue tracing the ridge. His voice was low and husky when he whispered, "Take my power."

Eve's breath caught in her throat. She pushed away from him and whirled around to face him. "No," she replied bluntly.

"Yes," Luc argued, scooping her up and carrying her to the bedroom. He lowered her onto the bed, and, after shucking off the bloody clothes still clinging to his body, he climbed on top of her. He nestled his hips between her legs and pressed himself inside of her again. "Take it, Eve," he begged. He brought her hand to his mouth and kissed her palm as he slowly rocked against her. "Just give me a little blood, and take my power."

"Why?"

"Why not?"

"Because I could kill you, Luc."

"You haven't killed anyone you didn't mean to yet," he countered.

"I've been *stopped* from killing both Zeke and Eoduun. I don't trust myself not to hurt you."

He kissed the inside of her wrist where his tattoo used to grace her skin, and his eyes slowly slid up to meet hers. "You didn't kill Bo."

She didn't. And she didn't even want to, which was completely unexpected. And then Dagon…she hadn't wanted to kill him this last time, either. What was it he'd said to her? *"Someone has tamed that vicious beast inside of you. You're not trying to kill me."*

Was it possible that the homicidal urge had somehow been cured?

"Just take it," he persisted. "I want you to have it. I'm willing to take the risk."

"Why?" Eve searched Luc's eyes. "Why do you want me to do this so badly?"

Luc leaned down and kissed her collarbone. "Because I never again want to see the look of fear in your eyes that I saw the night you ran away from me, or the look of horror on your face when you saw me standing outside Bo's door. I want you to *maintain* power over me, so you *never* feel threatened by me. You've never had and never will have a reason to fear me, but you do. I've seen it. You love me, but you still don't fully trust me. This way, you hold all the power. I don't want you to be afraid of me ever again." He lifted his head again and looked down at her with sincerity.

Eve opened her mouth to reply, but her lips pressed closed again. She couldn't deny that he did strike fear into her when he lost his temper. He was so powerful, it was terrifying when he put it on display. He'd never used it to hurt her, nor had he ever threatened to, though. And in moments like this, when her rational brain was in control, she knew she had nothing to fear from him.

But when things got heated and tempers flared, the past trauma took over her mind, her body, her emotions. It was involuntary. She went into defense mode, because anger could never be trusted. Anger compelled gentle hands to cause harm, and she'd seen the kind of harm Luc could cause to those who'd crossed him. The evidence was out in her entryway in a plastic garbage bag, and splashed all over that face that was gazing so endearingly at her.

Eve met his eyes. "And what if I try to kill you? Who will stop me?"

"You'll just have to exercise some restraint. I trust you."

Eve pinched her eyebrows together. "You shouldn't. This thing inside me can't be trusted."

Luc raised his brows, then thrust his hips against her, making her inhale sharply as he buried his cock further into her. "Oh, this thing inside you absolutely can be trusted," he teased. "It's completely under your spell."

Eve rolled her eyes. "You know what I mean. The Blood of Lilith. My curse."

"I'm not trusting your curse. I'm trusting *you* to control it." He kissed the side of her neck, then up along her jaw. When he reached her lips, he kissed her softly – then bit into her plump lower lip.

25

If You're the Death of Me, So Be It

Her blood welled to the surface and seeped into his mouth, and as his tongue ran over the puncture, lapping and sucking it up, a surge of euphoria rushed through her. She felt Luc's cock pulse inside of her, and a low moan rumbled in his throat.

"Oh, god, Eve," he murmured against her bloody lip as he thrust into her with renewed vigor.

And then she felt it - the rage, tingling in the roots of her teeth and the base of her tongue, and it vibrated down through her throat and belly, straight to her core. It felt so goddamn good and so fucking awful at the same time.

Her feelings became tangled and knotted, like strands of Christmas lights. Love was intertwined with hate, ecstasy with rage, compassion with bloodlust. Her reaction to the curse had never been this intense before, and she was both exhilarated and terrified.

There was only one thing of which she was certain.

She was going to kill him.

Devour him.

Enjoy every last drop of him, and wring him out like a used fucking rag, because he was *hers*, and she would eat this cake before it could ever fall into the mouth of another.

Mine. MINE. MINE.

She pushed Luc over and rolled on top of him. She gazed down at him ravenously, a wicked grin on her lips. "You shouldn't have let me do that."

"You're not going to kill me, love," Luc assured her confidently, thrusting up into her.

Eve threw her head back, eyes closed, and rolled her hips on top of him, reveling in the way his thickness filled her. "Mmm," she hummed. When Luc's hands came up to caress her breasts, she ran her fingers up his forearms and held the backs of his hands in hers, intertwining her fingers with his as he massaged her soft globes. She guided one of his hands down her belly, and she pressed his thumb against her clit while she rode him, slow and steady. She was already teetering on the verge of ecstasy, her violent rage and carnal pleasure twisting in her core, like blood red and sunny yellow swirling together into a brilliant blaze of orange oblivion.

She released his hand when his thumb began to rub tight circles at her apex, and she ran her palm up his hard stomach, between his pecs, and wrapped her fingers around his throat. When she began to squeeze, the pressure in her fingers tightening as the pressure between her legs grew, Luc's hand abandoned its task at her clit and reached up to grip her wrist.

"Eve."

She squeezed tighter, and his brows dropped in concern. She leaned forward, gazing into his beautifully apprehensive eyes, and whispered, "Did I say you could stop?" She crushed her lips against his and rocked her hips, drawing a moan from Luc's throat. She felt the vibration against her palm, and she squeezed harder.

It only made Luc moan more.

He was enjoying this.

Her mouth charted a path down over his jaw to his neck as her hips worked against his, feeling his hot cock throbbing between her clenched walls. She flexed, squeezing around him, and he gasped raggedly for air.

"Fuck, Eve…"

"I can't control it, Luc," Eve whispered against the tender skin over his carotid artery. Her teeth tingled and ached in unison with the ache low in her belly. She *needed* to tear into his flesh. Her pleasure rose, and her body gyrated against his as his shallow breath caressed her ear with quickening, staccato pants.

A deep, animalistic grunt tore from Luc's throat as his power erupted and poured hotly into Eve. Eve's teeth sank into his throat, her self-control dissolving as a flood of primal pleasure overtook her.

In one final, last-ditch effort to save Luc from herself, she mentally pleaded, *Dagon, stop me,* as Luc's blood washed over her tongue.

And suddenly there were two thick fingers in her mouth, stopping her teeth from closing any further. She felt a tug at her hair, and her head came up, Luc's blood running down the side of her mouth.

"You called, princess?" Dagon purred into Eve's ear. "Does this mean it's my turn now?" He was kneeling on the bed behind her, his fingers still clamped between her teeth, his other hand tangled in her mane. For the briefest moment, she craved exactly that. But the moment passed quickly, and she came to her senses and pushed Dagon away.

She looked down at Luc, his hand over the bleeding bite on his neck, his eyes gazing up at her with a strange mix of awe, fear, and…delight. "You tried to kill me, you little rascal," he remarked breathlessly, a grin lifting his lips. He made it sound as though it were no more serious than her cheating at Monopoly. His eyes flicked to Dagon. "But I knew you'd find a way not to. Points for resourcefulness, love." He sat up and captured her mouth in a searing kiss, his blood still sharp on her tongue. He broke the kiss and touched his forehead to hers, his fingers sliding into her hair. "That was so fucking hot."

Eve pushed against his chest, keeping him at bay. She frowned at him. "I would have killed you if I hadn't called to Dagon to save you."

"If you're the death of me, so be it," Luc said, smiling sweetly at her, blood trickling down his neck. "I can think of worse ways to go."

Eve reached around Luc and snatched up the knife she'd been keeping inside her pillowcase, then used it to cut the fleshy side of her hand. She brought it to Luc's mouth, and as his tongue laved at it, Eve felt her desire rekindling. She felt Luc hardening inside of her again.

No. She pulled her hand away, allowing him only enough to heal his neck. He licked his lips, grinning at her, then turned his attention to Dagon, as though he only just remembered he was there.

Luc pulled Eve's body tight against his as though to hide her from Dagon's eyes. "You can go away now," he told Dagon. "Show's over."

Dagon sneered. "You act like I don't know every inch of her body already." When Luc's gaze grew lethal, Dagon added, "Or exactly how it tastes."

Luc's hand shot out, electricity arcing over his skin as he prepared to electrocute Dagon, but Eve's reflexes were faster. She caught his arm with her hand, and the electricity died instantly.

Luc scowled at his arm, then at Eve. "Are you going to let me have *any* fun?"

"You've had plenty," Eve countered. She then pulled away from him and stood up, snatching an oversized pajama shirt from her dresser and slipping into it. She looked at Dagon.

Thank you. But you should probably go now, she said mentally.

I expect a reward for this, Dagon replied, his eyes sliding indiscreetly over her body.

We'll discuss it later. Now go back to Zeke's room before he wakes up.

Dagon sucked his teeth and raised a brow at Eve. "As you wish, princess," Dagon said, bowing low, his tone dripping with sarcasm. He turned and walked out the door.

Luc rose from the bed and picked up his boxers from the floor. As he stepped into them, he looked at Eve. "I'm going to need an explanation for that."

"I can speak with Dagon mentally. You know I can do that. I did it when Ruth abducted me, and he gets in my dreams…" Dreams. She dropped down and looked at the bowl under her bed that held the dreamcatcher concoction.

Bone dry.

Luc came up behind her. "Do you even need that now? You two seem awfully chummy all of a sudden."

Eve stood back up and turned to face Luc. "He came to me in my dreams when I was…away." She told him about Dagon revealing that he bound himself to her when he awakened her, and she told him everything Dagon told her about Apep. "So, yeah, I guess you could say we've gotten 'chummy.' For the time being, he's on our side."

"I don't like it, Eve. Dagon can't be trusted, bound or not. He's already tried to betray us. You should let me deal with him."

"I can handle Dagon. Especially now, right? I have the same powers you do," Eve smirked.

Luc flashed a smile at her, then stepped up to her and wrapped his arms around her. "You know, of the eight billion or so people on this planet, you're quite possibly the only one who I know for *certain* can kill me. And it is so fucking hot. You have no idea."

"You're insane. What's hot about that?"

"I don't know. Just knowing I'm completely at your mercy, at your *whim*…I've never felt anything like it before."

"Well, I hate to burst your bubble, and I hate to bring up Bo right now, but—"

"Then don't."

Eve looked up into Luc's eyes, and jealousy burned in those impossibly bright, aquamarine depths. She sighed and pressed on anyway. "It didn't work with him. He wasn't powerless against me."

Luc furrowed his brow. "What? How?"

"I don't know. But I held on to his powers a lot longer, too."

"Hit me," Luc commanded, taking a step back. "I'll try to bend you, and we'll see if you can override it."

Eve cocked her fist back and launched a right hook at his torso. She was fully prepared to catch her balance if she moved straight through him, but her fist landed right in his ribs...hard.

Luc grunted in surprise and doubled over at the strike point. "Ow, fuck! Didn't hold back, did you?"

"Honestly, I didn't think it would work," Eve said, trying to stifle a giggle. "Sorry."

"My turn."

Eve gasped as Luc's hand shot toward her. She reacted as though he was throwing a punch, even though she soon realized he was only jabbing his fingers at her. She felt a shift in the energy around her as his fingers compressed and bent in front of her chest, not making contact.

"You thought I was going to strike you?" he teased.

"This is so much easier to control than Bo's version."

"Can we stop comparing with Bo, please?" Luc requested, an edge to his voice.

"Calm down, I'm comparing notes to try to understand these powers, not to try to make you jealous."

Luc sat down on the edge of the bed, still only in his boxers. "I know, I know. It's just...I have concerns when it comes to Bo. You're different with Bo."

"Then you're really not going to like this," Eve ventured apprehensively.

Luc fixed her with an uneasy stare.

She looked down at her hands. "I think Bo may be the key to controlling this curse."

When he didn't reply, Eve met his questioning eyes. He finally asked, "What makes you think that?"

"Because I kept his powers longer, and I didn't try to kill him when I took them. Even Isaac commented that my aura lost all of its monstrous darkness and wanted to know how Bo did that. And then when I took D—" Eve sputtered, almost dropping a truth she wasn't ready to drop. "—Zeke's powers while I still had Bo's, I had no desire to kill Zeke. But now that Bo's powers have faded, I'm back to feeling murdery again."

Luc leaned back, resting his weight on his hands behind him, and sighed. "And what does Bo think of all this?"

"I didn't tell him yet. All he knows is that my aura changed. But I'm still not one hundred percent certain that I'm right. So far, it jibes, but I could be missing something."

Eve watched Luc's face, and even covered in Dizzy's blood, she could see the conflicting emotions in his features. He turned to survey her briefly before responding.

"I don't want to lie to you, Eve. I hate it. But...If there's a way to tame this curse, I guess I'd rather it be Bo than someone like Dagon."

Eve nodded her head, agreeing silently.

Luc sat up again and leaned forward, resting his elbows on his knees. "Why Bo, though? Why not, say, *me*, for instance? What the fuck makes Bo special?"

Eve shook her head. "I don't have an answer for you." *Bo is my safe space. My happy place. My harbor.* She wouldn't say it out loud, but she suspected it wasn't necessarily that *Bo* was special, but that her *relationship* with Bo was special. Bo was her lighthouse.

She loved Luc with an intensity she'd never felt for anyone else, but she understood that her relationship with Luc had the potential to unleash devastation on her heart like nothing she'd ever seen.

Luc was an atomic bomb in her hands.

Luc rose from the bed and held his hand out to Eve. "Come on, love. Let's go wash all this blood off."

26
Anything But That

After a shower that took entirely too long, Eve and Luc stepped out of the bathroom and found Isaac had returned. He was in the kitchen, sitting in Bo's spot.

Eve felt a strangely primal, carnal response between her thighs when she saw him sitting there, and it caught her by surprise. It felt like when her curse was acting up, but she knew that couldn't be the case. Luc had just fucked her soundly on the floor, in her bed, and in the shower.

She brushed it off and went to the fridge, her back turned away from Isaac to avoid looking at him while she waited for that surge of arousal to fully dissipate. She heard a sharp inhale behind her, and the legs of the barstool scraped harshly against the hard floor as Isaac quickly shifted off of it. Eve whipped around, and Isaac was leaned back against the counter behind him, staring at her, his eyes wide.

Luc moved to Eve's side, looking at Isaac, and Eve heated at the brush of Luc's arm against hers, his clean scent filling her nostrils with his proximity. Luc signed and spoke, "What the fuck, padre?"

Isaac didn't even cast a glance at Luc, his eyes fixed on Eve. He signed to her, *What did he do to you? Your mist is...* He hesitated, then brought his hands to his ribs, palms facing himself, and raised them up quickly, forming his fingers into claws. *Angry.*

Eve did a quick dive into Isaac's head, curious to see what he was freaking out about.

A gasp caught in her throat when she saw herself through his perspective. She was trapped in a roiling storm of Dagon's reddish iridescence and Luc's lightning, black clouds swirling, churning, raging – and not a single ray of redeeming light shining through anywhere. The expanse of her aura had spread, as well. It was massive.

While she was in his head, she happened to notice Luc's aura as he stood next to her. It was as striking as his eyes – aquamarine blue, streaked with arcs of electricity. But there was a strange thin layer around her whole body, about an inch thick, of nothing. Not black, per se, but *absence* of light.

Like a black hole.

She realized Luc and Isaac were both watching her. She released her white-knuckled grip on the fridge door behind her and signed to Isaac, *What does it mean?*

Isaac shrugged his broad shoulders and shook his head. He signed, *Nothing good.*

Luc scowled and signed, "What, are you suggesting my powers are bad for her or something?"

Isaac tipped his head and raised his palms alternatingly. *Maybe.*

"Can't be," Luc scoffed. He spoke and signed, "Bo and I have most of the same powers, essentially. If he alleviates her curse, why would I exacerbate it?"

"We don't know if that's the case," Eve pointed out. "I don't feel any differ...ent..." Oh, but she did, didn't she? She felt it even then, as she fought to keep her eyes from scanning Isaac's tight form and her hands from groping Luc right here in this kitchen in front of Isaac.

Her curse was on the prowl.

"Fuck," she uttered under her breath. Luc cast her a questioning look, and she looked up at him, admiring the sharp, chiseled features of his gorgeous face. "The monster is starving."

"Still?!" Luc asked incredulously.

"I think Isaac is right. Something is definitely off. I shouldn't still be this...hungry." She gave Luc a coquettish look. "I think you're going to have to keep me up *allll night.*"

A devious smirk curled Luc's lip. "Oh, I think I can do that."

After several long rounds in the bedroom, however, it became apparent that it wasn't enough. As the sun started to rise, glowing pink through Eve's curtains, she flew apart in yet another wave of pleasure as Luc breathlessly slammed into her, yet her body only felt hotter, less fulfilled, hungrier.

Starving.

She was starting to feel that tingle in her teeth, that sense of violent rage simmering just below the surface. She needed to get this under control before she started delving into more depraved appetites. She was on fire, and nothing was quenching this insatiable thirst.

But she knew what would. She could feel it in her gut, the one thing that could subdue this raging monster, slake this need, but she was afraid to admit it to Luc. She'd been hoping that the problem would pass, but it was only getting worse.

It was time.

She needed Bo.

"Luc," Eve whispered as he slowly deflated inside of her, spent once again.

He rolled off of her and wiped the sweat from his brow, looking up at the ceiling. "It's still not enough, is it?" he surmised with a long exhale.

"I think it might be time to test a theory," she said timidly. She watched his throat bob as he swallowed, her fingers itching to wrap around it and squeeze. She balled her fist into the sheets instead.

Luc turned to face her, and she could see just how exhausted he was. "By all means, do share your thoughts with the rest of the class. I'm running out of fluids."

Eve scrunched her nose. "Ew."

"Don't 'ew' me. You're the one wearing all my fluids."

"Ok, double fucking ew. Stop saying 'fluids.'" Then her eyes shifted from his and she focused on his beautifully sculpted chest, covered in a sheen of sweat, rising and falling with every breath. An unwelcome urge to shred that beautiful flesh with her fingernails tickled in her bones, making her shudder. "I think we should find out if Bo can…fix this."

Luc sighed as though he knew that suggestion was coming, and any ounce of amusement on his face vanished. Now he just looked defeated.

"Luc?" she pressed when he didn't reply.

A muscle in his jaw ticked. "I heard you," he said quietly. "I'm just…processing."

The need between Eve's legs was becoming more urgent with each passing moment, and she could feel her control slipping. She began to absently grind herself against Luc's thigh, her fingers gliding over his hard stomach. "I'm going to go wash your *fluids* off of me while you process." She needed to move away from him before her dark desires took over.

She started to climb off the bed, but Luc trapped her hand in his and stopped her retreat. He dragged her into his arms and pressed his lips sweetly to hers, then gazed into her eyes. "Do you love me, Eve?"

Her heart faltered when she saw the distress in his eyes. Fear. She gave him a reassuring smile. "Desperately."

"You know I would do anything for you, including handing you over to my brother, apparently. But I need you to do something for me. Something simple," he beseeched.

"Anything."

"Promise me you won't fall in love with Bo."

Anything but that.

"Luc, this isn't for love. This has nothing to do with love." She started to sing, "*What's love got to do, got to do with it...*"

But Luc wasn't letting it go that easily. "Then give me peace of mind. Just promise me."

Eve kissed him lightly, resisting the desire to bite into his lip. "This isn't going to make me fall in love with Bo. I promise." He searched her eyes for signs of deception, and Eve fought the urge to avert her gaze. She broke the tension with, "Keep looking at me like that and I'm going to start thinking you have more fluids to give me."

Luc narrowed his eyes and grinned. "I'd give it my best fucking shot, love, but I believe you were going to go hop in the shower." Then, reluctantly, he said, "I'm going to call Bo. I'm sure this conversation won't be awkward at all."

Eve strolled toward her bedroom door, but as she began to open it, Luc called to her. "Hey, put on some clothes. Isaac is out there."

Eve ignored his request. "It's too fucking hot for clothes. My whole body is on fire."

Luc was suddenly in front of her, his hands spread across the doorway, blocking her exit. He tilted his head toward the oversized t-shirt she'd cast aside earlier. "Put. Something. On."

With an exasperated huff, Eve did as he asked, then accepted the slap on the ass she'd earned as she walked past him out of the bedroom.

It took every ounce of her self-control to walk straight to the bathroom and not allow her eyes to wander to Isaac sleeping on the couch. She trusted herself less and less as time ticked by, and she knew the beast inside of her wasn't above tackling Isaac to the floor.

Luc joined her in the bathroom when she was stepping out of the shower, a pair of her pajama shorts and a tank top in his hands.

"Did you go to your apartment?" she asked. He was wearing a clean pair of casual slacks and a white fitted t-shirt.

"I had to take care of Dizzy's gourd, remember? Figured I'd grab some clean clothes for myself on my way." He handed her the clothes in his hand, and she began to slip into them. "Bo is waiting for you in his apartment," he informed her in an even tone while he watched her keenly. "Is it wrong that part of me really fucking hopes this doesn't work?"

"You don't want to lock the monster back in its cage?" Eve rebutted.

"I do. But... I wish there was another way." Luc narrowed his eyes contemplatively. "I wonder if there's anything in Lilith's grimoire that would be helpful."

"Not that it would do us any good right now anyway," Eve pointed out. "We don't have it."

Luc looked at her blankly. "I have it."

For a moment, Eve reigned in the powerful hunger low in her belly as she was overtaken with shock. "You have the grimoire?!"

"I got if from Dizzy. I can't read it, though. Every page is blank to me, so there must be some kind of spell to reveal its writing." He gave Eve a sly look. "I think you can help me unlock it."

Ruth's memories. She had everything she needed to be able to read the grimoire, but nothing about blank pages immediately came to mind. "Does that mean I can use it to do spells?" Eve whispered in awe.

Luc shook his head. "You can read the spells and incantations, but you can't perform spells, because you're not a witch." After a slight pause, realization dawned on Luc. His eyes widened, and a grin spread over his face. "Except you are. Right now, in a way, you are."

Eve frowned. A witch? She looked at herself in the mirror behind him, trying to summon Dagon's powers to see the monster in her eyes, to see if anything had changed, but she couldn't draw them out. The god-like powers she'd been trying to hide must have faded already. Without Bo's boost, she was back to losing stolen powers within a day or so.

Luc elaborated, his eyes gleaming, completely absorbed in his own revelation. "My skills are nothing compared to Ru's, but I do possess the powers of a sorcerer. Which means you do too, for now."

She was having a hard time focusing on his words when she couldn't take her eyes off of his perfectly kissable lips; when he was leaning so casually against the bathroom counter, looking like he needed some help out of those clothes. She was pulsing with need at this point.

She wanted to chain him up and make him beg for mercy.

Eve ran her hands down Luc's chest. "I can't even think about that right now," she purred. "All I can think about is wringing every drop from you, over and over again." She reached for the fly of his slacks, but he caught her hand.

He leaned down and whispered in her ear. "It goes against my very nature to have to stop you, love, but you're expected elsewhere, remember?"

There was a knock at the apartment door, and Luc rolled his eyes. Eve followed him out of the bathroom, and when Luc opened the door, he greeted Bo with, "A little too eager, maybe?"

Bo stood in the hallway in gray joggers and a white t-shirt, his hands in his pockets, his mask over his nose and mouth. He looked past Luc at Eve. "Come on, Evie. Let's see what we can do about your little problem," he said nonchalantly.

Eve's feet began carrying her toward him of their own volition. At that moment, she wanted nothing more in the world than to be close to Bo, to do anything he wanted. It was as though his voice suddenly held some unbreakable command over her.

Before she walked out the door, however, Luc grabbed her around the bicep and pulled her back to him. His mouth was on her neck in the next instant, her flesh beginning to tingle and burn where his tongue and teeth made contact. A low whimper escaped her throat.

When he was finished, he kissed the love bite lightly, and his eyes slid up to meet Bo's. "Just so you don't forget who she belongs to."

"Luc!" Eve chastised, rubbing her hand over the mark.

Bo's expression was unchanging. "Do you still write your name in your mittens, too, little brother?" When Luc narrowed his eyes at him, Bo took a step back and angled away from him, looking bored. "Don't worry, I'm fully aware." His gaze shifted back to Eve. "Come on, Evie. I'll get you coffee afterward."

Eve looked up at Luc. "I love you," she said, then slipped from his hands and followed Bo back to his apartment.

27
All Mine

As soon as Eve was through the door, she reached behind her and locked it. Her eyes roved Bo's sexy form as he sauntered to the middle of the room, pulling off his mask and tossing it onto the back of the couch. He turned his suddenly wolfish gaze to her, fixing her with wild gold and bright blue, and her insides melted into a pool of molten desire.

Holy fuck, did she need him. Now.

She lunged toward him, and as she fell into him, he caught one hand in her mane, the fingers of his other hand gripping her jaw as his mouth descended hungrily on hers. He kissed her like he'd thought of nothing else since the last time he kissed her. Like a man possessed.

Yes. This. This is what I need, she thought blissfully as she melted into him, her body contouring to his, her hands cupping the sides of his thick neck, just below his ears.

"Fuck, Evie," Bo growled against her lips. "You'll be my undoing." He suddenly tightened his fist in her hair and pulled her back, holding her face inches away from his. His fierce, mismatched eyes burned into hers. "Say it," he commanded.

She didn't need to ask. "Fuck me, Daddy," she begged breathily.

He arched a brow at her, waiting for the rest.

"Please," she whimpered.

A slow smile revealed his delicious fangs. "That's my good girl," he crooned. He scooped his arm around her and hoisted her over his shoulder, hauling her to his bedroom.

Bo deposited Eve onto the bed. She shimmied out of her shorts and rose to her knees at the edge of the bed, then stripped out of her shirt while he watched her intently. She reached for him, fisting her hand in his shirt and tugging him toward her until his thighs bumped against the side of the mattress. She trailed heated kisses up the side of his neck, but as she began to kiss along the rough stubble on his jaw that he hadn't had time to shave yet, his hand caught her by the throat and stopped her from reaching his lips. She looked up into his eyes questioningly.

He leaned forward and whispered low in her ear, "Not until I can taste myself on your tongue, little rabbit."

Fuuuck... Those words sent shivers through Eve's whole body, making her core pulse. She dropped to her hands and knees on the bed and began to eagerly tug at Bo's joggers. He pulled his shirt off and dropped it on the floor next to him, then gazed down at Eve in front of him, his cock in her hand, her eyes turned up to his.

Bo buried his hand in her hair as she ran her tongue along the underside of his thick shaft, and his head tipped back momentarily when she took him into her eager mouth. He looked down at her again and thrust his hips forward, gripping her hair tighter. Eve swallowed the gag as he pushed beyond her natural limits, her throat milking his cock with each reflexive swallow, and he groaned appreciatively. Her eyes began to water.

"That's it, Evie. Take the whole fucking thing." He began to pump into her, fucking her mouth like he owned her. His other hand slid under her chin. "Eyes on me," he commanded, and Eve's eyes shot open. She hadn't even realized she'd closed them. She looked up at him, watery tears beginning to stream from the corners of her eyes.

His wolf eye blazed, and he flashed his dangerous canines in a sultry smile as he took in the sight before him. "Fucking gorgeous."

He bit his lip as he watched her, his thrusts coming quicker and harder, and she felt him swell in her mouth, her jaw stretching to accommodate the extra girth. With a gasping groan, Bo spasmed and spilled over down her throat in hot, brackish spurts.

Eve gasped for air when Bo pulled away. He hooked a finger under her chin and tilted her face up to look at him. He ran his thumb over the tears running down her cheeks. "Now kiss me," he demanded, his voice low and husky.

Eve rose up on her knees once again, her hands gliding up over the beautifully scarred muscles of his torso. She loved his scars. They were as beautiful to her as his eyes and fangs were. She reached up and cupped his handsome face in her hands, grazing her thumb along the long vertical scar over his golden wolf eye.

"Your body is my favorite work of art," she whispered against his lips.

Bo silenced her with a deep, dominating kiss, his tongue seeking the proof on hers that he had claimed her mouth as his own, a pleased moan rumbling in his throat when he tasted himself there.

Bo kicked off his sweatpants and boxers, then climbed onto the bed, forcing Eve onto her back beneath him. His eyes roved her round curves and tight, feminine muscles, but his appraisal faltered when his gaze fell upon the mark that Luc had left on her neck, and he scowled.

"That just won't do," he simmered.

Eve felt Bo's sharp teeth sink into the tender flesh of her neck directly over Luc's love bite. She keened as an explosion of euphoria crashed over her like a tidal wave, ravaging every nerve in her body as she dug her nails into Bo's shoulders and clenched her thighs around him. She jerked her hips up as the orgasm tore through her, rubbing her dewy petals against his reinvigorated erection, urging him to push inside.

Bo's tongue lapped up the blood spilling from his bite, an animalistic purr rumbling low in his throat. "Do you want me, Evie?" he asked, his tone soft, yet dangerous.

"I *need* you. Give it to me, Bo," she begged.

She felt his cock twitch against her. "If I do, are you going to be a good girl?" he crooned, his teeth nipping her earlobe.

"I'll be anything you want me to be," she breathed.

"Then be mine. All mine. Wipe everyone else from your mind, and think only of me."

Eve slid her fingers into Bo's silvery-white hair. There was a dangerous thundering in her heart as she looked up into his eyes and whispered, "I'm always yours."

Bo's eyes filled with red-hot desire, but there was something else behind it. Something…possessive. He smoothed his hands up her arms, then guided them up over her head. He gathered both of her wrists in one hand, freeing his other hand to trace his fingers over her jawline.

"Don't ever forget it, Evie," he warned, squeezing her wrists, his weight pinning them down. He trailed his other hand down the length of her body, up the side of her thigh, and hooked his hand under her knee. He pinned her thigh down to the mattress, opening her hips, and she clung to him with her other leg hooked around his waist.

With a powerful thrust of his hips, Bo plunged into her, making her whimper as he staked his claim. "That's it, baby," he praised, thrusting into her again. He whispered in her ear, "Cry out for me. Let the whole compound know what I'm doing to you."

Submit. Surrender. Obey.

Eve didn't hold back. She moaned his name as he pumped into her, and Bo's cock pulsed. "Yes, Evie," he urged. "Say my fucking name."

"God, Bo, I'm going to come…" Eve panted, rocking her hips harder against him, her wrists straining against his grip.

"Don't you dare," he warned. "You don't come until I say."

Eve whined, "Please…I'm right there, Bo." She chewed her lip and moaned in protest. But something deep inside of her longed to obey, longed to do anything he said. Longed to please him.

Longed to belong to him, utterly and completely.

She fought to tamp down on the rising pleasure that threatened to erupt and rip her apart, but every thrust and roll of Bo's hips tipped her closer and closer, the pressure building to a boiling point she couldn't resist any longer.

"Bo," she agonized, looking up at him pleadingly.

His heterochrome eyes flared with an incinerating heat. "Beg me properly."

"Please, Bo," she mewled. "Please let me come."

Bo's cock began to pulse inside of her, and his breath hitched in his throat. He smiled alluringly at her. "Good girl. Come all over my cock, Evie," he rasped, fucking her hard and deep. "Scream for me."

She flew apart, his name riding on her cries of ecstasy as she writhed beneath him, her tight core clenching and wringing him dry as he poured himself into her, spasm after spasm, thrust after thrust, until they both lay limply, breathless, and satisfied to their very souls.

Beautiful oblivion.

Eve could hear Bo's heart hammering in his chest as she curled up against him, inhaling the scent of his body, their sex on the sheets, and…the soap in the bathroom. She'd taken in his powers again, but her pleasure had been so consuming that she hadn't even noticed it happening.

The only thing she'd been able to focus on was Bo. His body against hers, his commands driving her every move, his very presence dominating her senses. She'd even forgotten the real reason she was here until just now. Her curse. Her dark needs.

She immediately knew the Blood of Lilith inside her had been subdued. She knew it the moment Bo's lips had crushed against hers. There was no longer any room for doubt – Bo was her cure.

And Luc's power was gasoline on the fire.

Bo wrapped his arms around her and hugged her against his hard chest, kissing her forehead. He rested his cheek against her head. "Better?" he asked.

"Better." She reached up and touched his cheek, pulling back so she could look at his handsome face. "Bo?"

"Hm?" he hummed, his eyes half closed as though he could fall asleep at any moment.

"The things we say to each other…during…" She hesitated, afraid to have this conversation, but unable to stop herself from bringing it up.

His eyes blinked open and he gazed back at her. "Heat of the moment, I know," he replied in a flat, unreadable tone. Then he pulled her back to him and pressed her face to his chest, and she knew that he wasn't ready to face this conversation or its consequences yet either.

28
It Was You

Eve sat at her usual spot in her kitchen, a black coffee in front of her, while Bo was in his spot next to her, looking down at his phone like he wished he could be anywhere but there at that moment. Luc leaned against the counter across from them, his arms crossed, his round sunglasses hiding his eyes. Isaac watched them from the other end of the kitchen, his eyes focused hard on Eve. She couldn't see into his head anymore, but she knew her aura must have changed again, and he was fascinated by it.

Luc rubbed his temples with one hand. "So, let me get this straight: I piss off your curse, and Bo brings it to heel. Is that the gist of it?"

"Not *you*. It's your power," Eve replied. "I think maybe it's just too much on its own, or maybe it was too much when it was combined with—" Dagon's name almost popped out of her mouth, but she caught it, "...Zeke's power. I think Bo provides a buffer. Maybe."

Luc asked, "But you still have it, right? My power."

"I don't know. I don't know how to tell apart yours from Bo's."

Luc placed a napkin on the counter in front of Eve. "Bo and I don't have *all* the same specialties. We both have the eyes, but like I said, I inherited sorcerer specialties from my mother's side, whereas he inherited the werewolf curse from his."

Eve paused. "Wait. Does that mean you have the Blood of Lilith, too? As a witch?" She remembered seeing Ruth's emerald eyes shining with the telltale iridescence of a monster when she had Dagon's powers.

Luc shook his head. "Sorcery is different. It isn't a derivative of Lilith's Blood. It's an aptitude for metaphysical manipulation of the world around you. But it can be bolstered by the Blood of Lilith, through a rather nasty sacrificial ritual – one that Ruth surely performed the moment she left our household. It's the only way she could ever be as powerful as she is. ...Was."

The memory of Ruth slitting the throat of a handsome young kitsune she'd lured out into the woods and incapacitated with spells crept into Eve's mind. She could taste the coppery blood Ruth sipped from the chalice he'd bled into. She wasn't even out of high school when she'd performed it, but she'd kept it a secret from the family. Like they would ever notice her sudden surge of power, anyway.

Ruthlys was such a fitting name.

Luc pulled her from the gruesome memory. "You have my aptitude, the Blood of Lilith, *and* Ruth's memories, so you should be able to do anything Ruth could do." He gestured to the napkin on the counter. "Use Ruth's memories. I know she had plenty of spells memorized. Light this napkin on fire, or make it float, or fold it into an origami crane. Anything. Dealer's choice."

Eve stared at the napkin and summoned Ruth's memories to the forefront of her mind, and when she dug for spells, she was overwhelmed with the wealth of knowledge Ruth had accumulated. She had so many powerful spells fully committed to memory.

No wonder Ruth had been such a formidable foe.

She smirked when she stumbled upon an illusion spell. It was intended to temporarily make an object appear as another. She began to whisper the spell in a language she didn't understand, and she could feel an energy flowing from her chest toward the napkin. She imagined the object she wanted the napkin to turn into as she uttered the last few words.

A hot pink dildo sat on the kitchen island where the napkin had been moments ago. Eve erupted into laughter. She slapped the counter with her palm as she laughed, and the impact of her hand made the dildo wobble. She threw her head back and laughed even harder.

Luc sucked his lips between his teeth, a snort escaping him.

Isaac left the kitchen.

Bo shook his head and stared at his phone. "Birds of a fucking feather."

Luc leaned forward and poked the dildo with his finger, and it tipped over with a light thud. An amused grin lit his face as he looked at Eve. "All joking aside, this is actually really fucking impressive."

Eve narrowed her eyes contemplatively. "I don't know. I've seen bigger."

Luc held his palms up. "Well, obviously." He picked up the transformed object and gave it a light shake. "It's even got a believable heft to it," he remarked. "When I was trying to learn illusions, I always had a hard time getting the perceived weight to change. And you did it, just like that," he marveled, snapping the fingers of his other hand.

Eoduun and Zeke walked into Eve's apartment, and when they came into the kitchen, they both stopped to stare at Luc holding a hot pink dildo.

Zeke furrowed his brow. "Luc, you're back! But...why are you...?"

Luc raised the sex toy at them. "You boys ready for today's training? Might want to do a few extra stretches."

Zeke looked genuinely concerned. He looked between Eve and Bo, then back to Luc. "You're not...we aren't really..."

Luc tossed the dildo to Zeke, and Zeke didn't know whether to catch it or dodge it as it flew at him. At the last minute, he cupped his hands and caught it as it bounced off of his broad chest. Then he hot-potatoed it to Eoduun.

"Seems real, doesn't it?" Luc mused as Eoduun watched it fall to the floor with a thwack, making no attempt to catch it.

"And why are we playing with sex toys in the kitchen?" Eoduun asked blandly.

"It's not a sex toy," Eve said, still giggling immaturely.

Eoduun looked down at it, then slid his gaze back up to Eve. "Trust me. I know a sex toy when I see one."

"Look, Eoduun," Zeke said as he bent down and picked up the dildo off the floor. He held it up like he was holding a gun and spoke in an imitated voice, referencing a line from the *Boondock Saints* sequel. "Does this make me look gay?"

Eoduun raised a dark eyebrow at him and appraised him, clearly playing his part, and replied, "'You look like you might'a seen one up close.'"

"Sex toys *and* role playing? What have you started, Eve?" Luc teased, smirking at Eve.

The sex toy suddenly returned to its original form, and the napkin slipped from Zeke's fingers. "What the fuck?"

"Better think twice before you dab your mouth with a napkin around me," Eve teased.

"*You* did that?" Zeke asked, amazed. "How?"

"Gather around, children," Luc said, gesturing for Zeke and Eoduun to join them around the kitchen island. "Let me tell you a tale."

Luc filled the team in on catching up with and killing Dizzy, obtaining the grimoire, Eve taking his powers and using them to turn

218

a napkin into a dildo, and then reluctantly went on to inform them about the latest developments regarding Eve's curse.

Eoduun's expression darkened. "If Bo can tame Eve's curse, what the fuck does that mean for Zeke and me? Are we out?"

Eve shook her head adamantly. "No, of course not! I still need regular *attention*. But with Bo, I can take specialties without the murderous urges and I can keep them longer. Something about his powers keep my curse from raging."

Eoduun crossed his arms. "Maybe it isn't him. Maybe it's just you."

Eve frowned. "What do you mean?"

Eoduun stared at her, then shook his head. "Nothing. Never mind." He looked at Bo. "You're awfully quiet about all of this."

"Is there something you'd like me to say?" Bo challenged, finally looking up from his phone. Then, as his gaze slipped past Eoduun and fell on Isaac out in the living room, he turned his attention to Luc, ignoring Eoduun altogether. "We have a way to control Eve's curse now. Does the Vatican really need the exorcist here anymore?"

Luc sighed. He gripped his hands on the edge of the counter and leaned forward against it. With his back to Isaac, he said, "I hate it as much as you do. Unfortunately, that is not my call to make. They won't call him off until *he* decides Eve is no longer a threat. I can try to appeal to Sister Fiona, but I'm not sure what good it will do me." Luc tilted his head thoughtfully and added, "But I think I'll move him to another apartment, effective today."

Eve set her jaw, but she fought the urge to argue. It would only further their distaste for Isaac if she said she didn't want him to leave Knighco yet, and make her team even more suspicious about her feelings for him. But she'd grown attached to Isaac, whether they liked it or not. She didn't want to push him to leave.

Luc's phone chimed in his pocket, and Eve noticed it had been chiming fairly regularly this morning. But he hadn't looked at it once.

"Are you ever going to check your notifications?" she asked him.

"I'm avoiding responsibilities for as long as I can." He looked down at his expensive watch. "Which means I have about an hour."

Eve raised her brow, encouraging him to elaborate.

"I have to leave in an hour," he revealed hesitantly.

Eve's heart dropped into her stomach. "I just got you back," she quarreled.

"I know, love, and I know we still have shit to work out. And I promise we will," he placated.

She swallowed the anger and disappointment that tried to compel her to argue. She had no right to be angry. He had an empire to run, responsibilities she knew nothing about, and a heaping plate that required his constant attention. She demanded enough of his time and had caused him enough grief. Now was not the time to push it.

However, there was one thing that had been nagging at the back of her mind ever since he returned. One little thing that he somehow failed to address with the expansive compilation of exonerating evidence he'd presented to her.

She didn't want to bring it up, especially in front of everyone, but she needed an answer before he left her again. "We do still have shit to work out. And there is one thing I'd like you to clear up before you go. I was waiting for a good time to bring it up, but I guess it's now."

Luc gave her his full attention.

She swallowed hard. Her throat didn't want to form the sounds. "The video."

Confusion colored Luc's features. "Video?"

"The video I was sent, along with the photos. I know you must have gone through my phone after I ran. I know you must have seen it," Eve said. Luc's expression shifted to one of comprehension. "You proved that it wasn't you in the pictures, but what about that video?"

He lowered his voice. "We should talk about this in private."

Every inch of Eve's skin prickled with betrayal. "It was you."

"It was an act, love. I was saying what he needed to hear," Luc explained.

"Who?"

Luc hesitated. Shame drooped his features in a way Eve didn't realize was possible. "My father."

Eve's head whipped around to give Bo an accusatory stare. "You saw the video. You heard that man's voice. It didn't occur to you to mention that it was your *father*?!"

Bo leaned away from her as though she were about to attack him. "I didn't think it was real, so I didn't think it mattered."

Eve turned her wrathful gaze back to Luc. "How could you say those things about me? To your *father*?!"

"You don't know my father, Eve. He needs to believe you mean nothing to me."

"You said horrible things! Why the fuck would he need to think that? Why would you need to take it that far?"

"Because he has his fingers in everything, and if he thinks I'm compromised in any way, he will find a way to replace me or remove the compromising element. Even here. He will do anything to avoid scandal and sullying the family name. Anything to prevent any hint of failure associated with *his* name. He can't find out that you mean something to me. He can't know he can use you against me, to control me. He can't see weakness in me." There was true concern in Luc's eyes when he quietly added, "He can't know I have feelings."

The anger was shocked clear out of Eve's system. "He can't know you have *feelings*?" she echoed.

Luc suddenly looked embarrassed, like he hadn't meant to say that part out loud. "None of what I said was ever to reach your ears, because none of it is even remotely true. It was an act, a straw man version of myself to keep my father happy and maintain his confidence in my abilities as a leader."

Eve looked to Bo again, and Bo dipped his head in agreement. Luc wasn't lying.

"That's fucked up," Eve spat in disgust.

"That's just how it is." Luc rested his hands on his hips. "And now you understand. Yes, it was me. No, I didn't mean it. I am sorry you had to hear it, but we can discuss it further in private. For now, I would like to move past it and worry about *who* was recording me and taking pictures of Dizzy and sending it all to you, and why."

"Is Celeste working on it?" Bo asked.

"She will be as soon as Team Delta returns. Oh, which reminds me," Luc pulled his phone out. "She sent me a lead. I can send Team Flannel, but I wanted to give you guys first dibs."

Eve watched as Luc handed Bo his phone and the rest of the team discussed the possible case without any further mention of the video or Luc and Bo's father.

29
The Burden of Choice

Eve left the rest of the team to strategize amongst themselves in the kitchen and joined Isaac out in the living room, irritated with the feeling of being disregarded. She knew Luc felt that he had settled the issue for now, but she felt anything but settled. Luc had presented his father with a sullied, tarnished image of her. He'd painted her in a painfully unflattering light. Maybe he didn't need to know that Luc had feelings for her, but did his father really need to think he respected her so little?

...*Did* he respect her so little?

Isaac lifted his gaze from the book in front of him and watched Eve sit on the couch adjacent to him. Eve noticed he was now reading *Moby Dick*.

She signed, *I think you'll be getting your own apartment soon.* Then, after a brief pause, she added, *Unless you've decided I'm not a threat, and you want to go home.*

Isaac dog-eared the page he was on and closed the book, setting it in his lap. He hooked his index finger and pivoted his wrist down, touched the fingertips of two flat O-handshapes together, then tapped his wrist and indicated himself. *I need more time.* He added, *Your mist has been very strange. I don't understand it.*

No one does. Maybe we'll never understand, Eve signed. Then she remembered the grimoire. Was there something in it that would help her understand her powers? Ruth had mentioned reading about the Abomination, but the memories Eve pulled up only covered what Ruth had already told Eve – information that had already been confirmed when Luc told her her father had been a son of Cain.

There could be more, though. She needed to get her hands on that grimoire.

"Eve," Zeke called out. "You want to go on a hunt?"

Cassie suddenly popped her head into the apartment. "Did I hear you say hunt?" She walked in, her eyes immediately seeking out Isaac. She smiled flirtatiously at him.

Isaac signed to Eve, using a sideways K handshape that he rocked back and forth between them, then made two pistol fingers pointed to the side. *Let's hunt.* He gave Cassie an uncomfortable glance, then added, *I need to get away from her.*

Eve gave him a knowing smile, then rose from the couch, catching Cassie's arm when Cassie began to head into the living room. Eve redirected her out to the kitchen to join the rest of her team.

"You're coming on a little strong, Cass," Eve whispered.

"It's the only way I know how to come on to a guy," Cassie whispered back. "Usually, they're into that."

"Isaac isn't your typical guy," Eve pointed out.

Eve hopped onto the barstool next to Bo at the island, and Cassie wedged herself between them, resting her elbows on the counter.

"So, where are we going?" Eve asked. "And we're taking Isaac, right?"

Cassie shot her a look of utter betrayal.

Sorry, Cass.

Luc shoved his phone in his pocket. "Isaac answers to the Vatican, not me, but I doubt your bestie would let you leave him behind," he said in a mildly spiteful tone. "And you're heading back to Newbury. Could be a coincidence, or you or I may have caught someone or something's attention when we were there. Two women were found dead, which isn't strange in and of itself, but the manner of their deaths was strange. It was as though their bodies just instantly decayed. Pair that with the fact that a cornfield nearby inexplicably rotted overnight, and we have ourselves a case."

Eve scrunched her nose. "What the hell can make an entire cornfield rot overnight?"

"There are several creatures and so-called gods associated with decay and rot," Bo said. "Or it could even be a pissed off witch. We won't know until we dig in and investigate."

"Is Team Flannel providing an assist on this one?" Cassie asked hopefully.

"Sorry, Cass," Luc addressed her. "I'll need you here until Team Delta returns. You can keep an eye on Ruth for me while I'm gone."

Eve suddenly felt that old, familiar pang of worry she remembered from high school, and wondered if Cassie and Ruth were going to talk about her while she was away.

She's such a slut.

She uses that curse as an excuse. Gotta fuck 'em all!

What do they all see in her, anyway?

She's always causing problems.

She's so annoying.

She's not even that pretty.

You're so much more elegant and classy, Ruth.

Oh, but you're so much prettier and curvier, Cassie.

Eve ain't shit.

Eve sucks.

We shouldn't be friends with her.

"Oh, speaking of Ruth," Cassie said, interrupting Eve's dark thoughts, "she was talking about wanting to start relearning how to use her powers, at least until she can get her memories back."

Ruth's imagined voice infiltrated Eve's thoughts. *Eve won't give me my memories back. What a bitch. She's not even trying. She erased me and made me lose everything I knew, everything I was, and she doesn't even care.*

"I was hoping it would be all right if I helped her," Cassie continued. "I'm not a witch, but I can be there for moral support."

Luc waved his hand dismissively. "Sure, fine. But keep me apprised of her progress. She was our enemy not so long ago, so I'd rather she take her sweet time rediscovering her skills."

"You don't trust her?" Cassie asked.

"No. And you shouldn't, either," Luc said bluntly.

Cassie looked curiously between Eve and Luc. "Are you *purposely* keeping Ruth's memories from her?" she wondered.

A defensive anger rose in Eve's chest. "Of course not!" she blurted. "I don't know *how* to give them back, or even if I can."

Eve imagined Cassie telling Ruth, *Your memories allow Eve to speak to Isaac with sign language, so that's probably why she doesn't want to give them back. She wants to get close to Isaac so he'll want her, not me.*

Cassie held her hands up defensively. "Oh, no, I wasn't accusing, hon. Honestly, it'd be the smart thing to do, considering. I don't know if she really *should* ever get her memories back. I prefer her the way she is now."

"I'm not sure she likes me all that much," Eve replied.

"What?" Cassie scoffed. "Nonsense. But I'll kick the ass of anyone who doesn't like you, so if it comes to it, so be it. One insult, and I'll throw down on your behalf."

Eve gave a short chuckle. "I don't think that'll be necessary, but I appreciate it."

Eve suddenly felt a strange tingle in her chest, like ants were crawling around under her skin. She pressed her palm to her sternum and rubbed it, but the itch was too deep.

Then it began to burn, and she grimaced, digging the heel of her hand into her chest.

"Evie?" Bo worried.

"Apep." Dagon's voice slipped past Zeke's lips, warning them only moments before the ancient demon god appeared in Eve's kitchen, standing right next to her. The burn in her chest instantly disappeared.

Then Eve was looking at Zeke's broad back, and Apep was stumbling back, away from Eve. Her eyes ran up Zeke's neck, and she saw the gill slits behind his ears. Not Zeke.

"Dagon," Apep greeted casually as he straightened his tall, slender form and brushed off his fine, tailored black suit. He ran his hand through his striking burgundy hair, his bronze eyes shining strangely against his deep-golden skin. As he moved his head, Eve noticed the faint illusion of scales on his skin when the light hit him at certain angles.

He was a lot more stunning in the full light of day.

But the soulless evil lurking behind those eyes froze Eve to her core. Dagon scared Eve sometimes, but he never made her feel like *this*. Compared to Apep, Dagon was downright cuddly.

Eve could hear the chirp and buzz of electricity emanating from both Luc and Bo as they faced Apep.

Cassie stood next to Eve, her stance ready, but Eve could feel Cassie's arm trembling against her own. Cassie was terrified.

Eoduun flanked her and Cassie, and Eve heard Isaac's knives slipping from their sheaths as he stalked into the kitchen.

Apep appraised them all coolly. "Relax, I didn't come to wreak havoc. If I had, you'd all be dead already." Apep tilted his head so he could make eye contact with Eve around Dagon. "Except you, of course, little devil. I can't kill you. But I could make you wish you were dead." His eyes widened with wild delight as he took Eve in.

"Simply *pulsating* with power right now, aren't you, little devil?" Eve could see the gears turning in his head as he assessed her. "I wonder how much we can squeeze into that mortal vessel before you just…" He opened both hands quickly. "*Pop.*"

A gruesome, bloody image of herself flitted through her head, and she was certain she wasn't the one who put it there. She pushed up a wall in her mind.

"How did you get in here?" Luc demanded. "This whole place is warded."

Apep twirled his finger in the air. "Loophole," he sing-songed, then gracefully directed his twirling finger toward Eve. "She let me in." A mirthless smile stretched across his face and he pressed his hands over his chest in mock adoration. "I'm imprinted upon her heart." He tilted his head to the side. "She carries me with her everywhere."

"Why are you here?" Dagon growled threateningly.

"A little birdie told me that someone tore apart that idiotic shapeshifter who ran away with my grimoire. And now the grimoire is missing. Again. And frankly, I'm growing weary of this little game of keep away." Apep leveled an intense gaze at Luc. "Hand it over. You have no idea what you're harboring. The power in that book was never intended to be wielded by mere mortals."

"It's not here," Luc replied.

Apep became slightly distracted, turning his head as though he was suddenly sensing something. Eve could hear the footsteps approaching from the hallway.

"Oh, now *that's* interesting." His eyes focused past the group in front of him as Ramil entered the room. He narrowed his eyes and ran his tongue along his back teeth. "You don't see that every day."

"What's going on here?" Ramil asked cautiously. "Who is this?"

"Just a stray who followed Eve home," Luc said smoothly. "He was just leaving."

Apep reevaluated the situation, looking from Dagon, to Luc, to Ramil, and he dipped his head. "Perhaps I was." He regarded Luc with an arrogant air. "The longer you withhold what I want, the more problems I will make for you." Apep held up seven fingers and looked at Eve. "Oh, but I can't go without bestowing a parting gift. Pick a finger, little devil."

Eve's voice caught in her throat, and she looked to Bo, then Luc, hoping for some kind of guidance.

"Don't play his game, Evie," Bo advised.

"Pick one, or you pick all," Apep grinned, an evil spark in his bronze eyes. "She who hesitates…"

Dagon and Luc both stepped forward, Luc raising his hand as electricity zinged between his fingers, but Apep stepped back and said, "Uh-unh, unwise. Make a move against me, and it's 'ashes, ashes, they all fall down' before you even land a blow." Apep looked back to Eve and wiggled his fingers. "Tick tock."

Seven fingers. Seven hunters in the room, aside from her. She had to pick. She had to pick *now*. But which fingers correlated to whom?

Apep watched her keenly as she quickly tried to figure out which finger was Ramil's. Finally, she spat, "Right index."

The evil gleam intensified. "Oh, but *your* right, or *mine*?"

No.

Apep folded down the index finger on *his* right hand, then mused, "You actually *chose* someone here, didn't you? And now you get to wonder whether you decided this fate, or whether I was going to pick whomever I wanted anyway. Which is worse – the illusion of choice, or the burden of choice?"

Apep snapped his fingers, and when he instantly disappeared, Bo collapsed to the floor, landing in a heap next to Eve.

30
Eve Holds My Leash

"Bo!" she shrieked and dropped to her knees next to him. Luc, Cassie, and Eoduun all rushed to join her at his side, and Dagon, Isaac, and Ramil stood over them. Eve turned Bo's face to her and pulled his mask down. He wasn't breathing. She lifted his eyelids, but through her blurry tears, she could only see a lifeless stare in those beautiful mismatched eyes.

Apep had just obliterated her heart in her chest.

No. NO. FIX IT. FIX IT NOW.

In a frenzied panic, Eve reached across and snatched one of Isaac's knives from his hand and slashed it deeply across her palm. She opened Bo's mouth with one hand and held her other hand over it, blood pouring from the gash onto his tongue and down his throat.

"Come back, Bo. You have to come back," she pleaded, sobbing. "I can't lose you. I can't ever lose you. Don't leave me. Don't leave me. Don't leave me."

Luc took Eve's hand and tried to press a kitchen towel to the cut. His voice was thick as he said, "That's enough, love. You're losing too much blood too quickly."

Eve shoved him away. "Not until he wakes up!" she cried. "I will bleed for him until he wakes up!"

And if he didn't wake up, she didn't want to stop bleeding anyway. A world without Bo wasn't one worth living in.

Dagon warned, "I will not let you sacrifice yourself for him, princess."

Eve ignored him.

Isaac stepped forward and crouched down next to Eve. He grabbed her face and forced her to look into his eyes. "He'll wake up," he said aloud. "His mist is coming back. You've given enough." He took the towel from Luc and wrapped it around Eve's hand, then held it against his chest. When relieved sobs shook her, Isaac pulled her to him and hugged her tightly, and Cassie rubbed her back soothingly from behind her.

Bo groaned, and Eve tore herself from Isaac's embrace. She leaned over Bo and looked down at him as he opened his eyes. "Evie," he croaked.

Eve cupped his face and peppered kisses all over him. "Oh my god, I hate you so fucking much," she cried breathlessly, laughing with relief as tears streamed down her face. She threw her arms around him and squeezed him to her, burying her face in his neck. "Don't ever try to fucking die on me again, you asshole."

"You're so sweet," he grumbled sarcastically. He propped himself up on his elbows, and Eve sat back on her ankles. Bo looked around at the group, then lifted his mask back over his face. "So, I take it I was the lucky index finger?"

"I didn't pick you, Bo. You must know that."

There was a brief pause in the room as everyone's minds jumped to the next logical question. *Who* did *she pick?*

"You picked me," Ramil said, looking down at her and Bo. But his expression was understanding, not hurt or vindictive. "It's ok," he said before she could deny or explain. "Of everyone here, I mean the least to you, and I fully understand. But I do hope we can change that someday, Eve. I would consider myself incredibly fortunate to be able to count myself among your friends."

"I'm sorry," Eve apologized anyway. She didn't trust Ramil, but she still felt terrible. "I shouldn't have picked. I shouldn't have played his stupid fucking game."

"You had to," Dagon chimed in. "It would've been more than just Bo if you hadn't. Apep may play games, but he doesn't make idle threats."

Zeke's brown eyes suddenly overtook the vermillion, and he scowled. "Jesus, Dagon, stop fighting me when I say I want to come back out," he complained. Then he looked down at Bo, and his expression crumpled to concern. "Are you ok, Bo?"

"Getting there."

Zeke crouched down and looked over at Eve. "Dagon's right, babe. You had to choose. Don't beat yourself up over that."

Luc helped Bo to his feet, and everyone stood up with him. "Are you going to be up for a hunt?" Luc asked him, looking him over.

"What kind of hunter would I be if I allowed a brief brush with death to hold me back?" Bo joked.

"That's the spirit," Luc grinned, clapping him on the back.

After Luc sent Cassie and Ramil on their way, tasking them with informing their teams that they need to ramp up their efforts in looking into Apep's possible weaknesses, he turned to Eve. He held his arms out. "Come here, love."

Eve fell into Luc's arms and pressed her cheek against his chest as his arms encircled her tightly. "You're still leaving," she surmised.

"And so are you. We can't sit on our hands and let Apep push us into a corner while we come up with a way to kill or seal him. We can't let every threat paralyze us."

"Obviously, I need to leave," Eve pointed out. "I'm the reason he got in here in the first place. If I'm not here, he can't get past the warding, and the grimoire will be safe." Then it dawned on her. "I can't be in the same place as the grimoire. I'll never be able to even look at it, will I? He'll know the second I get my hands on it."

Zeke interrupted. "Dagon said he thinks he knows a way around that."

Luc sighed. "Out with it, then."

Dagon's vermillion eyes overtook Zeke's. "Through me."

Eve turned away from Luc and crossed her arms, facing Dagon. "Through you?" she repeated dubiously.

Dagon stepped forward. "You and I share a psychic connection that you can open at any time. You could view the grimoire through my eyes, even if you're a thousand miles away, and decipher to me in real-time."

Bo barked a humorless laugh. "Well, that sounds like a supremely terrible idea."

Eoduun grunted in agreement. "Like we'd let you get anywhere near that thing."

"I only want one thing from that stupid book," Dagon pointed out. "My freedom. And I can't accomplish it without a witch who can use it. So what good does it do me to run off with it when I have everything I need right here?"

"No one ever agreed to grant you that freedom," Luc said.

"Eve will. Eventually, she will," Dagon replied confidently. "It's in everyone's best interest to do so, isn't it? Think about it. Extract me, and Eve can bring Zeke back to life. He gets his autonomy back. I get mine. You'd then have the option to try to take me on if you wish without risking Zeke. It's a win-win."

"That's not a win-win," Luc argued. "The contract you hold with Zeke is the best leash we could ever ask for. If we set you free, we lose that balance of power."

"Not true. Eve holds my leash. It's the price I pay to keep her branded to me."

Luc's brow furrowed. "The fuck did you just say?" He turned to Eve. "The fuck did he just say?" He looked back to Dagon. "I thought you were bound to *her*."

"I am. And in return, she belongs to me. It's a binding not to be taken lightly."

Eve became indignant. "I don't *belong* to you! You said I bore your mark in the eyes of other 'gods.' Fine. But that doesn't make me *yours*."

"If you say so, princess."

Eve narrowed her eyes. "What are you not telling me?"

Dagon grinned impishly at her. "Wouldn't it be nice if I could walk freely among you so I would have all kinds of time to divulge my secrets?" His eyes lingered on Eve's lips as he took a step toward her. "Just imagine how much I could share if I wasn't restricted to these narrow windows of yard time."

Luc moved between them, looking down on Dagon. "She isn't yours, and you can forget about your freedom. It's not up for discussion."

Dagon laughed. "Enjoy looking down on me now, because my true form has a good two or three inches on you." After a brief pause, he added, "And I'm taller, too."

Luc touched two fingers to Dagon's forehead, and his red eyes flashed brilliant blue before Zeke clenched his eyelids closed in anguish.

"Fuck! God, I fucking hate that!" Zeke complained, rubbing his forehead.

"But it's so convenient," Luc said. "Imagine if I couldn't do that anymore, and I just had to *deal with him* when I wanted to end a conversation." Luc grimaced and made a disgusted sound. "I don't even want to think about it."

"Do you think that could work, though, what Dagon suggested with the grimoire?" Eve wondered.

"I don't know. But we'll find another way."

"If Ruth used the grimoire to summon Apep, there's probably a spell in there to put him back," Eve suggested.

"I'm aware. And that's probably why he wants it so badly, so it can't be used against him."

"Then I think we should give it a shot, Luc," Eve said. "We need to know what kind of weapon we have."

"You are far too trusting, love," Luc sighed. "Dagon will find a way to fuck us over for his own benefit. It's what he does." He gave Eve a sideways glance. "And I'm not particularly pleased about your new connection to him. No good can come of it. We need to find a way to break that binding."

"What? No."

Luc paused. "What do you mean 'no'?"

"I mean I'm keeping him bound to me. Like it or not, I need him right now. You saw how he put himself between me and Apep. Maybe he doesn't play nice with everyone else, but I don't need him to be nice. I just need his power."

"You have my power," Luc countered.

Eve gave him a knowing look and lowered her voice. "I do. And Apep didn't seem even remotely concerned. We need to face the possibility...probability...that he's a lot more powerful than we thought."

Luc chewed the inside of his lip uneasily. He leaned close to Eve so no one else could hear him and whispered, "And how do we know that Dagon won't suddenly decide to join Apep in his mission to obtain the grimoire? Hm? He's got a spotty track record in the loyalty department."

Eve whispered back, "Then maybe we need to give him a reason to be loyal to us."

Luc's jaw flexed. "Granting Dagon freedom would be a mistake. I will not bend on this."

A black, viscous gob of guilt balled in Eve's guts as she whispered, "We don't have to mention how long he would be free. If the grimoire has a spell to reseal Apep, the same could be done for Dagon. Promise him freedom if he helps seal Apep, then…turn the same spell on him."

Eve felt sick at her own treachery. What sickened her the most, though, was that she knew she had the power to persuade Dagon to go along with this plan. She knew he would believe she had good intentions. And as long as she could keep him from discovering this planned betrayal in her thoughts, he would never see it coming from her.

Human garbage.

Luc raised a brow and smiled, and she wanted to throw up.

She still felt like her insides were coated in filth as she sat in the backseat of the Toyota, wedged between Zeke and Eoduun. Luc had taken off for California, and her team and Isaac were headed in the opposite direction, back to Eve's hometown.

Before they left, however, Eve had taken advantage of her new powers of sorcery and Ruth's knowledge in her head, and she had cast a cloaking spell over Luc, Isaac, and the rest of her team. She didn't know how effective it would be against Apep, or if it would even work on herself since he was bound to her, but she hoped that for at least the next two days, they would all be relatively hidden from any efforts Apep might make to locate them.

And now that she was away from the compound, Team Flannel would once again be safe within its warded walls.

Eve looked over as Eoduun flipped through the file folder in his lap. "Anything interesting?" she asked.

"More disgusting than anything," he replied. "Both women were found in their backyards, in full decomposition, as though they had been out there for weeks. But one woman had reportedly been working at the library just the evening prior to her body being found, and the other woman had been out with her sister only two days before."

As Eoduun flipped past a page, Eve caught a glimpse of a familiar face. She reached out and flipped the page back.

"Holy shit. That's the librarian I talked to when I was in town." She flipped through to the next victim's file, and her face blanched. "And that's the gas station attendant I talked to." She looked up and met Bo's eyes in the rearview mirror. "I brought up Luc and mentioned my birth mother's name to both of these victims." Eve yanked the file from Eoduun and began to shuffle through it. "Where was the cornfield that rotted? Is there a map?"

Eoduun pointed it out to her, and her blood turned to sludge. "That's the field across the road from the lake where Isaac and I spent our first night in town."

Isaac signed at Eve from the passenger seat, *Do you have any family around we should check on?*

Eve shook her head. "No, I don't have any family there anymore. My mom and step-father moved away years ago. But we may want to check on whoever is living in my old house. It's not far from that rotted corn field – it's just on the other side of the lake." Then, with a slight blazing of her cheeks, she added, "And we may want to check out the cemetery."

"The cemetery?" Zeke echoed.

"We slept there the second night after looking for my birth mother's grave stone. If this thing is following my tracks, like it seems to be, it could make a stop there. I'll text Luc and see where he went when he was in town and who he talked to. That should give us a good starting point."

"You're starting to sound like a true hunter," Bo praised her. The way he glanced at her in the mirror, she could almost hear the implied "*good girl*" in his tone, and it made her inner thighs tingle.

"Thanks, Daddy," she teased, and noticed Bo's ears redden. "Want me to teleport ahead and get started? It could save us a few hours," she offered.

"No, we stay together until we know what we're dealing with," Bo replied.

Eve closed the file and handed it up to Isaac so he could return it to the laptop case by his feet. As soon as she leaned back again, Eoduun enclosed his hand around hers and used his other hand to brush her hair away from her ear.

He leaned close and whispered, "Just so we're clear, I'm calling dibs. Tonight, that pussy is mine."

31

We Don't Hunt the Same Monsters

They were still three or four hours away from Newbury when Bo pulled into a roadside motel for the night. They'd been on the road all day, and everyone was ready to call it a night. Eoduun was quick to get the credit card from Bo and run into the front office to secure two rooms. He wasn't taking any chances.

The rooms were across the parking lot from each other, and Eve couldn't help but wonder if that was by design. When everyone began to unload their luggage from the trunk, Zeke looked back and forth between the two doors.

"Who is staying where?" he wondered.

"You, Eoduun, and Isaac can room together. Eve is with me," Bo replied.

Eoduun shot him an incredulous glare. "No, Eve is with *me*."

Bo's wolf eye flashed with anger as he quickly turned on Eoduun. "Know your place, boy. I'm your captain, and I call the shots. Eve is with *me*. She can *visit* you, but she will be sleeping in *my* room."

Eoduun clenched his teeth, but held his tongue. "Whatever. But I don't want Isaac in my room. Zeke can stay and play, but Ears is all yours." Then he narrowed his eyes and smirked. "Unless you want me to let him stay and watch," he taunted.

Eve intervened. "Call him Ears one more time and I won't go anywhere near your room tonight," she hissed defensively. She yanked one of the keys from Eoduun's hand and looked at the room number on it. She pointed to the corresponding door. "I'm taking this one, and Isaac is coming with me. So you boys can hash out the rest amongst yourselves."

Isaac tossed his duffle bag over his shoulder, shrugged at the team, then turned his back on them and sauntered after Eve.

Eve threw her bag on the bed furthest from the door. She pointed at the other bed, then signed, *You can sleep there. If someone breaks in, they'll murder you first.*

Isaac gave her an annoyed expression and touched the fingers of his flat hand near his mouth and extended it outward. *Thanks.*

Bo walked in, an air of irritability rolling in with him. He closed the door behind him and looked over at Isaac, reclined casually on the bed Eve had assigned him, a book in his hand. He then stalked over to the bed Eve had claimed, shoved her suitcase to the side, and flopped down on his back.

"Fuck, that car has the most uncomfortable seats," he groaned.

Eve moved her suitcase to the shitty little desk in the corner, then crawled over the bed to lie next to Bo. He opened his arm to her without a second thought, and she snuggled into his side, resting her head on his bicep. He reached up for his mask, about to pull it off, but the rustling of the bedding when Isaac shifted on the other bed reminded Bo that they weren't alone. He dropped his hand, leaving the mask in place.

"You're grumpy," Eve remarked.

"I'm tired."

"I'm sorry about Eoduun. He's just feeling left out."

"Hm."

"I should probably head over there, actually," Eve said, and she started to lift herself off the bed.

Bo pulled her back to his side. "Mnh-Mnh."

Eve pushed on his chest. "I can't just lay here."

"Sure you can."

"I'll fall asleep."

"So be it."

"Bo," Eve chuckled as she tried to pry herself away from his side. When she finally succeeded, she swung her legs over the side of the bed and stood up, stretching her arms over her head. God, it felt good to be out of that cramped little car.

She used the bathroom and freshened up, and when she came out, Bo was no longer on the bed, but rather digging through his bag for a change of clothes. When she walked past, he dropped his clothes on the bed and followed her to the door. He rested his forearm high on the door before she could open it, leaning over her. She turned and looked up at him.

He gazed down at her with crystal and charcoal. In a low, stern tone, he ordered, "You will come back to me tonight, understand?"

"Of course," she replied, discreetly inhaling his scent as he stood over her. She suddenly had no desire to leave this room.

He didn't budge. His eyes remained fixed on hers. He tilted his ear toward her as though he hadn't heard her. "Hm?"

Eve smirked at him, her cheeks growing hot. "Yes, Daddy."

Bo grunted in approval, then touched a masked kiss to her forehead. He pushed off of the door and turned his back to her, grabbing his clothes off the bed and heading into the bathroom.

Eve stepped outside, the cool night air whisking away the traces of Bo's scent on her clothes and the heat from her skin. She heard the door open again behind her, and she glanced back.

Isaac. He had an unlit cigarette hanging from his lips. He stepped out of the room and pulled the lighter from his pocket, flicking the flint as he cupped his hand around the flame. He inhaled deeply, then looked over at Eve as he exhaled a thick cloud of smoke. He looked like he had something to express, but he kept it to himself.

She held her palms up. *What?*

He shook his head and pushed an O handshape away from his chest. *Nothing.*

She wondered if he was judging her. Her *boyfriends*. But this little visit to Eoduun wasn't only for pleasure. She wanted to test her curse, to see if she could steal Eoduun's mindsight without any homicidal urges. If this went off without a hitch, any shadow of a doubt would be dispelled.

This was the final bit of proof she needed to *know* Bo was the key to controlling her curse.

Eve signed, *If I don't try to kill Eoduun, it will prove we can control my curse.*

Isaac shrugged. *Maybe.*

If I can control it, are you going to leave?

Isaac raised a brow as he took another drag of his cigarette. As he exhaled, he asked, "Should I?"

"No. You should join Knighco instead," she said aloud, but she fingerspelled *Knighco*.

Isaac coughed and choked on the smoke in his throat at the unexpected suggestion. "I don't think that's an option."

"If it were, would you?"

Isaac chewed the inside of his cheek and looked out over the dimly lit parking lot. He brushed his thumb under his chin and shook a Y-handshape left and right, his palm facing her. *Unlikely.*

Eve frowned. She touched her temple and drew away a Y-handshape, then brushed her thumb under her chin. *Why not?*

Isaac turned his dark, sleepy eyes to hers. "We don't hunt the same monsters."

"You know, spoiler alert, but that white whale kills Ahab at the end of *Moby Dick*, right?" Eve remarked. "Obsession with revenge doesn't often end well for those consumed by it."

"It took a piece of him that he couldn't ever get back." Isaac tapped the ashes from the end of his cigarette and leaned back against the side of the building, crossing one ankle over the other and shoving one hand in his pocket. "His quest for revenge was the only thing keeping him from being consumed by something darker."

Eve rolled her lips between her teeth. "Well…It was worth a shot," she relented. She glanced over at Eoduun and Zeke's door. "I'll be back later. Don't lock me out."

I'll wait here, Isaac signed.

"You don't need to wait up."

"There could be creeps lurking."

Eve eyed him up and down exaggeratedly, and she laughed when he narrowed his eyes at her, unamused.

"Oh, please," Eve said, drawing visible arcs of electricity to her fingertips and allowing Bo's yellow wolf eyes to shine through. She whispered an incantation under her breath and felt a release of energy from her chest as an empty fast-food bag lying on the ground near them suddenly ignited. "I'm scarier than any creeps in a motel parking lot."

Isaac watched the paper bag burn with a bored expression on his face. He turned his gaze back to Eve. "I'll wait here," he repeated aloud, unfazed.

When Eve walked into Eoduun and Zeke's room, she interrupted Eoduun's impatient pacing. He turned eagerly toward her, then wrinkled his nose. "You smell like cigarettes."

"I was outside talking to Isaac," she explained.

Eoduun stalked up to her, but he didn't slow as he approached. He wrapped his palm around her throat and walked her backward until her back hit the door. He pressed his body against hers, looking down at her with parted lips and hooded eyes.

"I'm not going to taste his bad habit on your tongue, am I?" he asked suspiciously.

Eve lifted her chin defiantly, reaching up to run her hand along his sharp jawline. She slid her thumb over his lower lip. "Only one way to find out."

She barely had the last word out before Eoduun's mouth was on hers in an aggressive, demanding kiss. He moaned as their tongues tangled, and he released her throat to slide his hands down to her ass. He gripped her tightly and lifted her onto his hips, and she threw her arms around his neck.

"I can't wait to feel you coming around my cock," Eoduun rasped against her lips. "And then I'm going to let Z fuck that tight pussy when I'm done with it. And then I'm going to hold you down and destroy you again. You're going to be so full of our fucking cum."

Eve nipped his lip. "You're fucking filthy."

"Not as filthy as you're going to be."

Eoduun carried her to the bed where Zeke was sitting with his shoulders leaned back against the headboard. Eoduun stood at the foot of the bed and lowered her, her body sliding down his until her ass hit the mattress. He ripped her shirt off over her head, then reached down and yanked her pants from her as she leaned back on her elbows. Eoduun hooked his arm behind her bent knee and flipped her over roughly onto her stomach, then pushed her knees out wide, her ass in the air, spread wide open for him. Eve looked up at Zeke, sitting at the head of the bed, while Eoduun unfastened his pants behind her. Zeke had his lower lip between his teeth, his hand in his gym shorts, stroking himself as he gazed at her.

"Let me see it," Eve urged Zeke.

Eoduun smacked his palm smartly against Eve's ass, making her yelp. She felt his hard cock slide vertically up against her wet slit, saturating himself in her desire. The way his hot length rubbed against her clit and both sensitive holes at the same time made her pulse against him.

"You fucking heard her, Z. Let us see it," Eoduun demanded smoothly.

Zeke lowered his shorts, revealing his rigid cock to Eve and Eoduun's greedy eyes. As they watched him pleasure himself, Eoduun hummed in appreciation and sank his length into Eve. He splayed his hand over her lower back and ass, his thumb rubbing slow circles around her asshole. Eve moaned as he began to pump his cock in and out with the same cadence as his stroking thumb, his other hand sliding up her back and tangling in her loose pink locks.

"You like that, you nasty little slut?" Eoduun hissed as he yanked on her hair, forcing her head up.

She rocked her hips back, slamming her ass into him. "If you have to ask..." she sassed, earning her another smack on the ass.

"You know what? We have a better use for that mouth." Eoduun leaned over her back and reached up over her shoulder, pulling on Zeke's ankle and dragging him over the comforter toward them. He didn't stop until Eve's face was hovering right above Zeke's throbbing erection.

Eoduun squeezed one hand on Zeke's muscular thigh and held Eve's head in place over Zeke's cock with the other. "Open wide, nasty girl." Eve parted her lips, and Eoduun shoved her face down onto Zeke. She took him deep, gagging, and Zeke pulled his hips back into the mattress, backing off to help accommodate her.

"Suck him at the pace I fuck you," Eoduun ordered, using his hand in her hair to assist her as he thrust into her, harder and harder.

God, she loved having them both at the same time.

She looked up at Zeke, who was propped up on his elbows, alternating between watching her head bob on his cock and watching Eoduun pummel her from behind. She pulled up when Eoduun slid out, and she swallowed Zeke deep when Eoduun buried himself into her. Up and down, in and out, like the rhythm of an erotic song.

Eoduun returned one hand to her ass, and this time, he slid his thumb into her tight hole. Eve whimpered at the strange sensation, clenching around his digit.

"Relax," he commanded. He spit on her asshole and alternated between slowly circling his thumb in a circle, then in and out, loosening her up, and Eve couldn't believe how fucking *good* it felt. She heard him spit again, the warm saliva sliding down over her hole, and he replaced his thumb with two fingers, stretching her further. She whimpered around Zeke's cock again as the dull ache building inside of her suddenly and unexpectedly exploded into a toe-curling orgasm. Her whole core clenched and pulsed around Eoduun's cock, her asshole squeezing his fingers, and it started a chain reaction. She heard him moan as her response to him pushed him over the edge, and he jerked and slammed into her as hard as he could. Zeke followed immediately behind them, spilling over onto Eve's tongue and into her throat with a deep, desperate groan.

Eoduun pulled Eve's body up, her back still to him, and turned her head toward him. He leaned over her shoulder and kissed her voraciously, emitting a low moan as he tasted Zeke on her tongue.

"Fuck, that's fucking hot," he mumbled against her lips. "My filthy little whore." He turned his gaze to Zeke, then amended, "*Our* filthy little whore."

Zeke raised himself up onto his knees in front of Eve. He touched her chin and guided her lips away from Eoduun's to his own, kissing her slowly, deeply. "She's our sexy little goddess," Zeke said sweetly, smiling against Eve's mouth as his hands explored her breasts, brushing a thumb over her nipple. He kissed down the side of her neck, and Eve could feel his cock thickening against her again. "She should be worshipped."

Eoduun tugged at her hair, pulling her head back against his shoulder as he kissed down the other side of her neck. "Then worship her, Z," he challenged, untangling his fingers from Eve's tresses, relinquishing control.

32
Take Us Both

Eve pushed on Zeke's chest, and as he leaned back onto the bed, she crawled over him, settling her hips over the length of his swelling manhood, letting it press down against his stomach instead of taking it inside of herself just yet. Eoduun came up behind her and brushed her hair aside, touching light kisses to the hollow of her shoulder before surprising her with his teeth.

Shit, she'd been immediately distracted when she came into this room and had forgotten she wanted to test her control over the monster inside her. She hadn't given these boys a drop of her blood yet.

Eve reached back and buried her fingers in Eoduun's hair. She turned her head and whispered in his ear, "Make me bleed."

"For fun, or to feed the monster?" Eoduun asked as he climbed off the bed and reached for the knife sitting on his duffle bag.

Eve looked down at Zeke and kneaded her fingers into his bulky pecs, swirling her thumb over his nipples. "Both," she replied to Eoduun. "Let's see how much power I can hold."

Zeke gazed up at her as his hands smoothed up her thighs and slid around to squeeze her ass. He rolled his hips against her, rubbing his hardness between her legs. "Is that a good idea?" he asked. He ran one hand up her back, all the way to the nape of her neck, then gripped it and pulled her face down to his, her breasts flattening against his chest. "Shouldn't one of us keep our specialty from you, just in case something happens?"

Eve's hands glided up the side of Zekes' neck. "You mean, who's going to stop me if I lose control and try to kill someone?" She kissed his jaw.

"It's not like it hasn't happened before," Eoduun said as he joined them on the bed again, the cold carbon fiber of the knife handle touching Eve's spine. He slowly ran it up between her shoulder blades.

"If I get out of control, call for Bo. He'll stop me."

Eve felt the sharp steel sear across her skin, and she drew a sharp inhale between clenched teeth.

Eoduun's mouth hovered over the gash on her shoulder, his breath hot on her flesh as he snarled, "I don't want to hear another man's name from your mouth when you're in our bed." Eve opened her mouth to protest, but in the next instant, Eoduun's tongue ran the length of the gash, eliciting a moan from her lips instead.

Zeke covered her mouth with his own, swallowing her moans of pleasure. He couldn't stand to wait any longer, and he lifted her hips and shoved his cock inside of her.

As Zeke filled her, Eoduun reached around, and she felt the cold steel of his knife against her throat. With a light flick, he produced a shallow nick at the base of her neck.

"Drink, Z," he commanded.

Zeke didn't hesitate, his soft tongue stroking over the cut, his lips sucking around it. Eve gasped and moaned as Eoduun resumed his attack on the gash along her shoulder, and she began to move her hips, riding Zeke's cock.

Eoduun once again spit behind her, but instead of his fingers, Eve felt the knife handle pushing into her asshole. He inserted the handle an inch or two, then withdrew it slowly. As he slowly worked it in and out, Eve moaned. Eoduun whispered in her ear, "You're nice and relaxed. You want more, don't you? Take us both. Let me fuck your ass. I promise I'll go easy on you…this time."

Eve was lost in the pleasure coursing through every nerve in her body, and fuck yes, she wanted more. She *wanted* them both at the same time. "Do it," she begged.

The knife was quickly replaced with Eoduun's warm fingers when he swiped up the juices from her and Zeke's union and rubbed them around and into her asshole. And then the head of his cock was at her hole. It was hot and slick as he rubbed it against her, stimulating those sensitive nerve endings, sparking her desire into an inferno of need.

Eve slowed her pace on Zeke, only gently rocking her hips, as Eoduun slowly entered her from behind. His arms dropped down on either side of her, supporting himself on his hands near Zeke's shoulders, and he began to move. Slowly. Carefully. Sensually.

Fuuuuuck.

They were both inside of her, and she'd never felt so *full*. The pleasure from the front and the mix of pain and pleasure from the back worked in maddening tandem to drive her to a fever pitch.

Eoduun licked the wound on her shoulder once again, sending a jolt of pleasure through her, and he whispered, "I feel like I'm fucking you both right now." He moved his hand from the mattress near Zeke's shoulder and grazed it over the base of Zeke's thick neck, then wrapped his fingers around Zeke's throat. "I could fucking get used to this," he added.

Gazing down at Eoduun's hand around Zeke's throat sent another thrill through Eve's core, putting her right at the tipping point. She buried her hand in Zeke's hair and crushed her mouth against his, moaning against his tongue as her breath came harder and faster, the pressure building, the pleasure rising, until the coil inside her burst into an explosion of euphoria. She pulsed and rocked and keened, not even sure which part between her legs initiated the reaction. Everything was clenching and spasming as she cried out in pure bliss.

The boys again were right behind her, grunting and moaning, both pushed over the edge by the way her body was reacting to the things they were doing to her. Their power surged through her as they both released inside of her.

Utter elation.

As they lay in a tangle of limbs on the bed together afterward, panting and breathless, she looked at the two of them, so beautifully satisfied.

And she hadn't felt any desire to hurt them.

Bo was, without a doubt, the key to controlling her curse.

Eve untangled herself from the boys. "I'm going to take a quick shower, and then I need to get back," she said.

"Just stay," Eoduun mumbled, his eyes closed, his face buried in the pillow.

"Bo wants me back tonight." In truth, she *wanted* to get back to Bo. She was looking forward to crawling into bed next to him.

"Fuck Bo," Eoduun grumbled irritably.

"Isaac is probably waiting outside for me, too," Eve added.

"Fuck Isaac," he retorted. "What the fuck does Isaac care? He shouldn't even be here anymore. You obviously have your powers under control."

"Maybe, for now. But maybe Isaac should join us at Knighco," she suggested. "He could be a huge asset."

"You think he would join us?" Zeke asked, intrigued by the idea.

Eoduun suddenly sat up, wide awake now. "No. Fuck that. We don't need him. We don't want him."

"Why not?" Zeke asked. "Dude's got mad skills."

"He wants Eve. That's the only reason he's still here, and if he stays, he'll be up her ass all the time, *forever*," Eoduun argued.

"He doesn't *want* me," Eve dismissed. "We just get along well. We're friends."

"Don't give me the 'he's just a friend' bullshit," Eoduun countered. "He's had his cock inside of you. God, it makes me want to gag just saying it."

"Don't be such a drama queen," Eve said with a roll of her eyes. "It was a one-time thing."

Eoduun cast a knowing look at her. "Once is all it takes. If he stays, it'll happen again. He's too close to you to be able to resist forever."

Zeke turned his head to Eve. "He's got a point, babe."

"He doesn't want me," Eve repeated. "End of story." Eve was absolutely certain Isaac wanted no part of this polyamorous situation she was in. He didn't want to be another one of her boyfriends. He did what he needed to when they were alone in Newbury, but that…that was different.

Eve left the conversation at that and took a quick shower. When she came out of the bathroom, Zeke was passed out, and Eoduun was sitting at the foot of Zeke's bed in his boxers, brooding. He stood up and pulled Eve into his arms.

"I will kill anyone who tries to take you from us," he whispered darkly. "I share with Luc because I have to. I share with Bo because *you* have to. But Isaac? He has no place in our circle. I don't trust him. He wants more than you think he does."

Eve pressed her hand to Eoduun's chest and looked up at him. "No one is taking me from you, especially not Isaac. Trust me, he wants no part of *this*," she said, drawing a wide, horizontal circle with her finger. She cupped his jaw with her hand and pulled him down to kiss him lightly on the lips. "You're being such a jealous boyfriend. Enough. Goodnight."

When Eve opened the motel room door, Isaac was leaned against the wall next to it, his chin on his chest, his arms crossed. He lifted his head when he saw her come out.

You didn't have to wait, she signed.

He pushed off the wall and followed behind her as she headed back to their room without replying.

Bo was lying in bed staring at his phone when Eve and Isaac came in. He was under the covers, but he still had his mask on. "I trust all went well," he said evenly without lifting his eyes from his phone screen.

"You want a detailed report?"

Bo gave her a sideways glance. "Not necessary. I have ears."

Eve felt a blush burning in her cheeks. He heard her even from across the lot?

Isaac took his bag and went into the bathroom, so Eve grabbed her pajamas from her suitcase and started to change into them next to Bo's bed.

When she pulled her bra off, Bo exhaled loudly. "Hurry up," he grumbled, turning his head away.

Eve propped her hands on her hips. "Do my boobs offend you?"

"Get dressed."

"It's nothing you haven't seen before."

"I don't need to see them right now."

Eve rolled her eyes and slid her oversized t-shirt on over her pajama shorts. And just in time. Isaac came out of the bathroom a moment later. Eve watched him drop his bag next to the other bed. He raised his eyebrows and held his hands up, fingers spread and palms down, then closed his fingers. *Lights off?*

Eve nodded.

He signed, *Goodnight, Eve,* using the unique sign he'd assigned to her, and he clicked off the light and climbed into the bed by the door. The lights from the parking lot still managed to illuminate the room dimly.

"So…where am I sleeping?" Eve asked.

Bo threw the covers aside, inviting her into bed beside him. "You know where you're sleeping."

She did know. She just wanted the invitation. She slid under the covers and flopped her head back onto her pillow, staring at the ceiling. In the stillness, she could practically feel the power humming through her body.

Bo put his phone on the stand between the beds, then took his mask off and placed it next to his phone. After he settled in on his side of the bed, he waited a few beats before saying, "I don't bite."

"That's a lie."

"Why are you a mile away?" he wondered.

Eve rolled onto her side and looked at him across the expanse of bed between them. He was on his back, his head turned toward her, one arm up behind his head.

"Why are *you* a mile away?" she retorted.

"I was here first."

"So you're glued to that spot, then?"

Bo sighed. "Never mind. Goodnight, Evie." He closed his eyes.

Eve looked at his handsome profile in the dim light seeping around the curtains. Damn it. He'd called her bluff. She grumbled and scooted over, throwing her leg over his and wrapping her arms around his arm. She nuzzled her face into the side of his neck.

She heard him sigh contentedly, and he intertwined his fingers with hers. "Ah, that's the stuff," he teased.

"Goodnight, Bo. No biting," she warned.

"Same goes for you," he shot back.

33
Death

That night, Eve dreamt she went to Newbury again. She found herself standing on the dock at Black Lake, near her old home. At least, that was where she felt she was, though everything looked different, as it always does in dreams. She walked to the end of the dock and looked down at her reflection.

She recoiled at the gaunt, corpse-like face gazing back up at her, and she scuttled backwards away from the edge of the dock. Was that her reflection?! But the face began to rise up out of the water, and Eve slowly backed away as it rose higher, revealing a zombie-like creature. As it rose higher yet, she saw the head of a pale, deformed horse, all the soft tissue around the snout and eyes decayed away. And then the rest of the pallid horse's body rose from the waters.

A zombie on a horse?

The horse clip-clopped onto the dock and stood in front of her, icy water dripping onto her feet. She and the zombie stared at each other silently, and, inexplicably, she wasn't afraid.

Until she looked down, and saw rot and decay slowly blooming from the horse's hooves. The wood of the dock was withering and rotting before her eyes, and as it spread toward her, she realized she couldn't direct her feet to flee. As it crept closer, closer, she began to scream. She was going to rot.

At the last moment, however, the spreading rot diverged around her, leaving her unscathed. She turned to watch the path of the scourge, and that was when her heart stopped.

Bo was standing on the shore, looking down at his phone.

"Run! Bo! Run!" she screamed at him, but no sound came out. She couldn't run to him, as the rot had closed around her, leaving only a small circle of safety for her to stand in.

He turned his head and looked at her, but it was as though he couldn't see the danger creeping toward him. She waved her arms, she signed at him, screamed soundlessly, but it was useless. He just stared at her while the rot spread across the water, turning it oily, and reached the shore.

Not Bo. Please, don't take Bo, she pleaded in her heart. She watched helplessly as the rot touched Bo's boots, and as he stared at her, his eyes widened with fear.

He knew death had come for him.

"Bo! No!" Eve sobbed as his body began to wither, his eyes sinking back into his skull, his skin sloughing from his bones and plopping wetly to the ground.

Eve choked in horror at the mound of disgusting flesh that used to be Bo.

In her unbearable grief, she stepped out into the rot. She wanted to rot, too. She couldn't live without Bo.

But nothing happened. She looked down, and took another step into the spreading rot.

She was immune. She could've saved him. If she'd been brave enough, she could've saved him. And now...she couldn't bring a pile of clothes and rotted flesh back to life with her blood.

This was forever.

She dropped to her knees and sobbed as the zombie's horse stepped over her and walked away, spreading its death and rot as it went.

"Evie!"

Eve thrashed at the hands touching her, sobs tearing her throat raw, until she opened her eyes and saw Bo and Isaac's worried faces gazing down at her. The sobs continued to hitch her breath as she slowly sat up, realizing that it had all been a dream. With renewed tears, borne of relief, Eve clutched at Bo and pulled him into a suffocating bear hug.

"Evie," he rasped. "Evie, I can't breathe."

"Shit, sorry," she apologized. She'd forgotten about Zeke's preternatural strength coursing through her body. She quickly loosened her grip, but she didn't fully release Bo. She sniffled and rested her head on Bo's shoulder, pressing her forehead against his neck, and he enfolded her in his comforting embrace. His fingers traced languid circles on her back.

"Must've been a hell of a nightmare," Bo surmised.

Eve only nodded against his shoulder.

It wasn't until they were in the car on the way to Newbury that she felt composed enough to share the nightmare she'd conjured.

Eoduun was contemplative. "Do you think it was some kind of vision? Premonition? Or just a bad dream?"

"Jesus, I hope it wasn't a premonition," Zeke said, looking across Eve at Eoduun. "I don't think I can handle zombies that ride zombie horses. That's a little too 'winter is coming' for me."

Isaac signed to Eve from the passenger seat. *Four Horsemen.* He held his hands out, one palm up and one down, then flipped them. *Death.*

Everyone looked to Eve, hoping for a translation. She sat forward in her seat. "Wait, are you suggesting the Four Horsemen are *real?* You think we're going to run into the 'pale rider' in Newbury?"

Isaac shrugged.

"Let's hope it was just a bad dream," Bo remarked from behind the wheel, glancing at Eve in the rearview mirror.

But when the team rolled into Newbury a few hours later, Eve felt an ominous uneasiness settle in her chest like the dark clouds overhead. They had pulled over to take a look at the rotted corn field, despite the light drizzle, as it was on the road that led into town. As Eve's gaze swept over the blackened, stinking, collapsed stalks, she couldn't deny the parallels of her dream.

I only dreamed that because I read the reports, she told herself as she covered her nose. *It means nothing.*

Zeke gagged and pulled his shirt up over his nose. "I wasn't expecting it to smell this horrible."

Bo took a few steps into the field and crouched down, using a stick to poke at a rotted stalk on the ground. "This is more than just the smell of death. It shouldn't smell *this* fucking bad."

Isaac wafted his hand in front of his nose and pinched it, then made air quotes near his temples. *Stinks of evil.*

Bo's eyes zeroed in on something on the ground, and he leaned in as close as he dared. He leaned back again and pointed at it. "What does that look like to you?" he asked the team.

They all leaned in, covering their noses and mouths.

Adrenaline zinged through Eve's limbs. "A hoof print," she replied, barely above a whisper.

Zeke took a step back. "Don't love that," he commented.

Eve turned to look at the lake behind them, across the highway.

…Just in time to see a lumpy, round object dip down below the water's surface, barely making a noticeable ripple in the drizzle-pocked surface.

"Look!" she cried, jutting her finger toward the lake. "There's something in the water!"

Everyone turned to look, but it was gone. And so was Eve. She'd used Luc's powers to teleport to the dock, and she stood at the edge, staring out at the water. If it was an animal, it would surface again. She'd seen beavers, birds, turtles, even river otters in this lake, but nothing that even remotely resembled what she'd just seen. It was like a big, misshapen pumpkin, but it had been too far away to see any detail.

The team pulled into the boat launch behind her, but her eyes were fixed on the water.

"What the fuck, Evie?" Bo chastised as he slammed the car door. "You can't just go running off on your own like that when we're on a case!"

"But I saw something," she reasoned.

"Especially if you've seen something!" Bo argued as he approached her. "You could be running straight into a trap. Straight into danger!" She still stood with her back to him as he came up behind her, so he reached around and grabbed her jaw, turning her head to face him. She gazed up at his wolfish eye, full of anger, tiny water droplets collecting on his pale eyelashes. But there was something else shining through, and if Eve wasn't mistaken, it was a tinge of fear. "You follow *my* lead, Evie," he said in a low, commanding voice. "I can't keep you safe if you don't stick with me."

Eve sighed. "Yes, Daddy," she said demurely.

Eoduun interrupted, calling out from the shore, "Shit, guys. I think these are hoof prints, too."

The team gathered around the crescent-shaped impressions in the dirt next to the paved boat launch area. They led right up to and disappeared into the water, and they looked fairly fresh, not yet washed away by the rain.

"Ok, this is just getting creepy," Zeke said.

Eve looked out over the water again. "Whatever I saw in the water hasn't resurfaced."

"I'm not sure I want it to," Zeke replied uneasily.

They searched for any further evidence, but the rain was beginning to pick up intensity. Bo recalled everyone to the car, as they still had to check into the motel, and they had an appointment that afternoon with local authorities. They would return later tonight when the skies cleared.

"So, what authority are we posing as today?" Eve wondered as they began unpacking their luggage at the motel.

"CDC," Bo answered.

"This is feeling too much like a zombie apocalypse movie," Zeke said as he unlocked the door to his and Eoduun's room directly next door to Eve's. "I hate zombies. They're so fucking gross."

"We don't know that Eve's dream about the zombie on a horse was a true vision," Bo pointed out. "We may be reading too much into the hoof prints. There's an Amish community in this area, so it isn't like there aren't horses around."

"Or," Eve chimed in, "it's a little more biblical than zombies. What if Isaac was onto something?"

"We need more information before we can even begin to guess. Evie, I need you and Isaac to meet with the owner of the corn field. Eoduun and Zeke, you'll meet with neighbors of the victims. I'll talk with the police and the medical examiner."

Eve followed Bo into their room and sarcastically remarked, "Oh, you'll let me go off without you now?"

Bo glanced over at Isaac, who had his back to them as he dropped his duffle bag on the bed closest to the door and began to rifle through it, and said, "As much as I don't like Isaac, I admit he is skilled. I don't fully trust him, but I trust he's not going to let a monster kill you."

"Pretty sure I wouldn't let a monster kill me, either. Don't forget, I still have Luc's powers."

"Powers that are still new to you. Powers you've never been trained to control. Powers that are temporary."

Eve smirked at Bo as she dropped her luggage on the floor next to the bed. "You sound like you want to test my temporary powers. Want to wrestle?" she challenged.

Bo ignored her goading. He pulled a stack of laminated cards from his pack and tossed them across the bed to her. "These are your fake IDs. Don't lose them."

As Eve picked them up and shuffled through them, looking for the CDC one, she heard her phone chime. She pulled her phone from her pocket and looked down at it.

Sexiest Man Alive.

How is my love today?

Eve replied, *We've arrived at the motel. Not sure what we're dealing with here, but something's definitely fucky.*

Her phone notified her of an incoming video call. She went into the bathroom for some privacy and accepted the call. When Luc's perfect face popped up on her screen, she smiled. "I definitely prefer this to regular phone calls," she informed him.

"I'm inclined to agree," he said, grinning back at her. In the background, Eve heard a woman telling 'Mr. Fagerberg' that they are ready for him. Luc glanced away from the screen. "In a moment," he said dismissively, presumably to the woman. When his attention returned to Eve, he said, "Now, love. Tell me what's fucky."

Eve gave him the abridged version of her dream, then told him about the hoof prints and whatever she thought she saw in the lake. "I'm afraid my dream was more than just a dream," Eve confessed.

Luc slid his sunglasses off of his face and stuck the temple tip between his teeth, biting it contemplatively as he looked away from the screen. After a moment, his brilliant aquamarine eyes turned back to her. "You said it was raining when you arrived?"

Eve scrunched her brow. "Is that relevant?"

"Maybe." Luc's face contorted in uncertainty as he looked away again. "No, probably not."

"What is it?"

"Mr. Fagerberg, this way please."

Luc gave Eve an apologetic smile. "I'm not sure, love, but I'll do a little digging for you. I love you, gorgeous, I have to go. I just needed to see your beautiful face."

When the call ended, Eve frowned at herself in the mirror. Luc seemed to have some kind of idea what was going on. A clue, at least. Why wouldn't he tell her?

34

A Waste of Fucking Space

Eve picked at the scratchy tag under her collar that she forgot to cut off of her suit jacket as she and Isaac bumped along in the old Silverado of local farmer, Jay Tremble, out to his ruined field of corn. The ripped bench seat did nothing to offset the lack of suspension in the old rig as Mr. Tremble steered them down the rough path behind his house that led to the field, the windshield wipers squeaking noisily on a setting just a little too aggressive for the light rain.

"I know it's muggy in here. Sorry about that," Mr. Tremble apologized. "The old gal doesn't have AC. But once we reach the field, you'll see why I don't have any windows cracked. I hope you have a strong stomach." Then, almost as an afterthought, he leaned forward and looked at Isaac, loudly and slowly articulating, "Sorry it's so hot in here!"

Isaac regarded Mr. Tremble impassively.

"Must be hard for him," Mr. Tremble said to Eve. "Shouldn't he be on, like, disability or something?"

Eve arched a brow at the farmer. "No. He's perfectly competent." She glanced over at Isaac, but he just stared straight ahead, his countenance unchanging.

Thankfully, they pulled up to the field and ended the awkward conversation. The horrid stench infiltrated the cab of the truck before it even came to a complete stop.

"Cover your nose and brace yourself, guys," Mr. Tremble advised. He turned to face Isaac and repeated himself loudly, miming covering his nose.

Isaac gave a curt nod and stepped down out of the truck, not bothering to heed Mr. Tremble's advice. Eve covered her nose with her jacket and followed him.

They walked out into the field, stepping carefully and occasionally slipping on a slimy corn stalk. Mr. Tremble led the way and explained, his voice muffled by the cloth over his face, "This field was fine just a few days ago. Then, I woke up to this. There wasn't frost or excessive rain or flooding or anything overnight or in the days leading up to it. I don't know who or how, but somebody killed my whole field." He stopped Eve and Isaac, looking down at the ground. "Oh, yeah, there's one more thing. I think my horses got into this shit, too. You can't really tell now from the rain, but there were hoof prints all around here, and now my horses are all sick. The damnedest thing is, they were all in the pasture when I went to bed, and they were still there when I got up."

"Are you suggesting someone let them out and put them back in?" Eve asked.

"I can't think of another way to explain it. They obviously got into the corn. The vet thinks so, too."

"So someone killed your corn *and* sickened your horses?"

"That's what I told the cops. I don't know who hates me enough to have done it, though. I try to get along with everybody."

Eve collected samples from the rotted corn plants, though she wasn't sure if they would actually be tested at Knighco or not. That wasn't her department. Let *Mira* worry about that.

When they'd concluded their business at the farm, Eve and Isaac took the rental car down the road. Eve wanted to make a quick stop at her old house to see if the current owners had seen or heard anything strange.

Eve turned the car into her old driveway, and the weeds scraped along the bottom of the car as she pulled up to the deserted house. From the state of it, it was clear it had been abandoned some time ago. Even though she had fled this house as a teenager and moved in with her then-boyfriend, it still saddened a small part of her to see the place she grew up in fallen into such disrepair.

Empty.

Broken.

Forgotten.

She and Isaac stepped out of the car and looked at the house. She signed, *Maybe it's best no one lives here. We know we won't find any rotted bodies.*

Isaac leaned against the bumper and plucked a cigarette from the pack in his front pocket. He lit it, took a drag, then signed, *You sure? Might find a meth lab.*

He wasn't wrong. Eve stepped cautiously along a safe perimeter of the house, and Isaac pushed off the car and ambled along behind her. She went around the side of the house, then crept up to a window. She gestured to Isaac to come to her and give her a boost. He grunted, then put his cigarette between his lips and crouched over, folding his hands into a stirrup for her.

Eve was a little surprised at how effortlessly Isaac hoisted her up to the window. She signed at him, *Were you a cheerleader?*

His lip curled, lifting his cigarette in an unamused sneer.

Eve peered through the cobwebby glass. Last time she'd laid eyes on that dining room, she'd stormed out of it with her boyfriend, Grant. She was seventeen, and he was twenty-three, and her step-father had just told her that if she left with "that pedophile," she'd better not come back.

So she never did.

She suddenly wondered what would've happened if she hadn't left with him, if she'd never moved in with Grant. Life had been hell with her step-father, and her mother just stood aside and let him berate her and smack her around. But Grant had turned out to be worse.

And then came Adam.

Would life have turned out differently if she'd just stayed?

...Probably not.

The room looked so much different without furniture and appliances, yet so much the same. A shell of a nightmare.

When Isaac lowered her back to the ground, she held her palm up and swiped her middle finger across it. *Empty.* She held her palms up, fingers curled, then pointed at the house and swooped one hand under the other. *Want to go inside?*

Isaac discarded his cigarette and shrugged.

Eve went back around to the front porch and tried the door, but it was locked. Isaac tried the kitchen window next to it, but again, locked. Lucky for her, Eve knew that the window in her old bedroom had a faulty lock. It would turn as though it was locking, but the lock was broken off, so even though it looked like it was locked, it wasn't.

Eve led Isaac around the back of the house, but as she rounded the corner, she stopped abruptly. Isaac came up on her and almost bumped into her, but he caught himself. The smoke lingering on his clothes wafted over her, and she felt the brush of his arm against the back of hers.

Then he saw what had given her pause.

"It was here," he announced aloud, stepping around her to investigate the hoof prints trampling the ground around one window.

"That was my room," Eve said, pointing to her window when Isaac looked back at her.

He looked back down at the prints, then at the window. He signed, *Death came looking for you.*

"Cute," Eve replied sarcastically. "Let's just see if there's anything else in here it may have been after." She pointed up at the window, then rested her vertical fist in her other palm and pulled it toward herself. *Help me up there.*

After pulling the screen and jimmying the broken lock, Eve raised the window and climbed in. She turned around and held her hand out to Isaac to help him up. He shook his head and gestured for her to back up. He then parkoured himself up and through the window.

Eve bumped her thumbs alternately against her sides. *Showoff.* She turned and surveyed the room. It felt strange to be inside this house again. Even stranger, some of her posters were still clinging to the walls. She fingered the curling corner of the faded, glossy paper, admiring the bulky physique of Dwayne "The Rock" Johnson. She'd been obsessed with him as a teenager. He still had some hair on his head in this poster.

Was her family the last family to live in this house? She'd heard her mom and step-dad had moved out after her younger brothers moved out, but she didn't know exactly when that was or what had happened to the house after that.

She was surprised they hadn't repurposed her room when she left. Were they expecting her to come back someday?

She took in the familiar space. The furniture was gone and the dust was thick, but the smell of the house was the same as she remembered. She didn't even know she remembered that scent until it hit her like a sock full of doorknobs. Memories she'd worked so hard to suppress now flooded her brain, tightening her chest with anxiety and regret. She'd sat in this room with the door closed, in silence, hours upon hours of her young life, listening fearfully for the approach of heavy, angry footsteps. Dreading having to leave the safety of her room to use the bathroom because *he* might need to use it when she was in there, and he hated when she inconvenienced him like that. Hoping to avoid *him* when she went to the kitchen to get a snack, but knowing she had to walk past the living room where he sat, and sometimes the mere sight of her was all it took to provoke his wrath. She did nothing right. She was a burden. An annoyance. A waste of fucking space.

He hated her.

He made sure she knew it.

I don't want to be here.

Isaac leaned into her line of view, his deep brown eyes fixed on hers, breaking the dark reverie she'd fallen into. She blinked, tears spilling onto her cheeks. "Oh, shit," she mumbled, swiping the heels of her hands over her cheeks. "I'm not crying, I swear," she said.

He moved toward her and stood close to her, his hands folded behind his back – not touching her, but close enough to be of comfort. "I understand," he said simply.

"No, it's nothing like what you've been through. I'm just being stupid," she chastised herself. She turned to walk out of the room, away from Isaac, but a large hand closed around her wrist, stopping her.

"It's not a competition," he murmured in his unique articulation. "You're entitled to feel your pain."

Eve brushed his hand away. "I'm fine. Let's keep looking."

Isaac didn't push the issue.

The house was empty of furniture, appliances, and any evidence that any monsters had been there. All that remained were a few wall hangings and some old DVDs and books. There was nothing for them here.

Eve returned to her room to take one last look. She plucked a book from the shelf against the wall, rubbing her thumb over the edge of the worn pages. *Anne of Avonlea.* She couldn't remember where she'd gotten this book, but she'd read this several times in the summer before fifth grade. She'd had no idea at the time that it was part of a series, and she'd never read the rest of them, but this book...oh, how she'd loved it. She'd idolized and wanted to be Anne. A small grin tugged at the corner of her mouth as she remembered putting extra butter on her bread, even though she didn't actually like it that way, because there had been a scene where Anne was putting a thick layer of butter or lard on bread and the author made it sound so appealing.

She grabbed another book. *Pride and Prejudice.* The weight of it felt good in her hands. This had been her favorite book for ages. She'd read it in sixth grade, and she'd only understood about half of it, but when Mr. Darcy confessed his feelings for Elizabeth, it had rocked her world. She read it again in high school a few times, and each time she read it, she picked up more that she had missed or had forgotten the last time.

Some stories just never get old.

Isaac reached up and pulled a book from her shelf. *White Fang.* Oh god, she'd loved that book. She'd become obsessed with wolves and huskies and anything Jack London wrote after she'd read that in middle school, especially *The Call of the Wild.*

My favorite book, Isaac signed.

You can have it if you want it, Eve replied.

Isaac raised his brows in surprise and gestured to the books on the shelf. *Are these your books?*

Eve nodded. "All of this shit was mine. I guess no one else lived here after us," she said aloud. She was having a hard time signing with books in her arms.

What's your favorite? Isaac wondered.

"Hard to choose," she admitted, her eyes wandering over the titles on the spines. *Good Omens. The Hitchhiker's Guide to the Galaxy.* The *Twilight* series. All of the *Harry Potter* books. Some Stephen King and Dean Koontz. Some random romance and YA stories. Some classics. Even a Brian Greene book, *The Fabric of the Cosmos*, had made its way onto her shelf. Her tastes were all over the place. "Gun to my head, I guess this," she said, holding up *Pride and Prejudice.*

And then she saw a tattered old book that she'd completely forgotten about; a book she'd read over and over and over as a girl. *The Black Stallion.* She had been absolutely enamored with that story. She pulled it from the shelf. "But when I was little, it was this. I was *obsessed* with horses in elementary school." She chuckled to herself.

"I used to pretend the Black Stallion was running along the roadside next to the bus every day on the way to and from school. I pretended my bike was the Black Stallion, too."

Isaac gave her an amused smirk.

"Yeah, I was a fucking dork. I know. But goddamn, did I love horses."

Eve and Isaac crawled back out the window, books in their arms, and gave the hoof-prints one last inspection. There was a clear path beaten down through the woods behind the house, as though whatever had left the hoof-prints had traversed it heavily, leaving and returning multiple times. Eve and Isaac followed the path, even though Eve already knew where it led.

Straight to the lake.

She hugged her books close to her chest to keep the drizzle from damaging them as she looked out over the lake again. "Something is in that water. I'm sure of it," she declared. She looked at Isaac, a sudden thought disturbing her. "What if it was in there when we were bathing in the lake that morning after I teleported us here?"

Isaac became pensive, but whatever was on his mind, he kept it to himself. He grunted, then turned and headed back toward the car.

She walked in front of him. "What is it?" she asked, scrunching her brow.

He gestured back toward the hoof prints behind them, then tapped *The Black Stallion* in her hand. He signed, *Maybe a horse is obsessed with* you.

35
Tell Me I Can Kill Him

When the team reconvened later that afternoon at Eve's favorite local restaurant, Eve shared what she and Isaac had found at her old house.

"I think if we want to find this thing, the house is our best bet. I think it's been looking for me."

"Why would it be looking for you?" Eoduun wondered.

"Maybe Apep sent it," Zeke guessed.

"I don't think so," Bo countered. "Apep seemed more interested in the grimoire than in Eve."

Eoduun's phone chimed. "Oh, that neighbor sent me the doorbell camera footage," he announced.

Zeke explained to the rest of the table, "The next-door neighbor of the dead librarian said he caught something weird on his doorbell camera, but he was having a hard time finding it when we were there." He saw Eoduun's eyes widen as he stared down at his phone. "What is it?" Zeke asked, leaning over to look. A look of disgust and confusion contorted his features. "What the fuck is that?!"

"I've never seen anything like that in my life," Eoduun said. He placed the phone in the middle of the table so all could see, and restarted the video.

The video showed a front porch and a paved driveway at night, the darkness partially lit up by a porch light. From the left side of the screen, two horse legs stepped into the illuminated portion of the driveway, but the upper part of the creature was hidden by the darkness. As it progressed, it appeared that there were two more appendages dangling near the ground, hanging down from the middle of the creature, and then the back legs came into view.

"What the fuck are those things dangling there?" Eve asked, leaning her face closer to the phone to get a better look. "And is it just me, or does it look like it doesn't have any skin?"

A single, huge, glowing red eye suddenly flashed higher up on the screen, and Eve gasped and jumped back in her seat.

The eye disappeared as soon as it had appeared, and the legs walked off the screen.

Isaac shook his head and scowled. He tapped a Y-handshape to the palm of his other hand. *Impossible.*

Eve frowned at him, touching her head and drawing away a Y-handshape. *Why? What is it?*

Isaac took Eoduun's phone and started typing on it. When he returned it to the table, the browser was open to a cryptid page about a Scottish creature Eve had never heard of: the nuckelavee.

These creatures were known for causing plagues and illness, wilting crops, and sickening livestock with their toxic breath. Eve looked down at the artist renderings of the creature and shuddered. It was a disgusting, skinless horse with black veins snaking all over its body, and one huge red eye set above its gaping jaws. In the middle of the horse's back, a similarly skinless human torso rose up, like a grotesque variation of a centaur. The human head, if you could even call it that, was deformed, shockingly enormous, and canted oddly, as though the neck wasn't strong enough to hold it up.

"Gross," Zeke blurted. Then he pointed out, "Hey, that's kind of like the zombie on a horse in your dream, Eve."

That fact hadn't eluded her.

Isaac pointed to the description, then signed to Eve, *They can't tolerate fresh water and rain. It can't live in Black Lake.*

Bo was of the same sentiment without knowing what Isaac had disclosed. "No, it can't be. Nuckelavee can't live here. They need salt water."

"Dagon says it's not impossible," Zeke announced. "But it takes a powerful curse to summon and bind a nuckelavee to a fresh body of water. Oh, and it can't live there forever, so if it's been there long, it'll be weak."

Bo scoffed. "Suddenly Dagon wants to help?"

Zeke shrugged. "He says it's for Eve."

"Why, though?" Eve asked. "Why would anyone go to the trouble of putting this disgusting thing in Black Lake? And what's it got to do with *me*?"

Everyone looked at Zeke. "What? I don't know," he said. "Dagon doesn't either."

"There's only one way to find out," Eoduun said, snatching up his phone and sticking it in his pocket. "We'll hunt it tonight, and I'll read it."

The waiter brought the team their food, and Eve looked down at her burger. The lumpy hunk of meat smothered in ketchup never looked so unappetizing.

"I need to hit the ladies' room," she said, nudging Bo so he could move aside and let her slide out of the booth.

She stared at herself in the bathroom mirror as she washed her hands, but she wasn't actually seeing herself. She was lost in her thoughts, remembering her dream from this morning. While the nuckelavee wasn't an exact match to the zombie on a horse in her nightmare, it was damn close enough. Which meant it wasn't just a nightmare, and Bo was in danger.

She needed to keep Bo away from this thing, at all costs. But how? How could she keep him safe?

She was still stuck in her own head, pushing the door open to walk out of the bathroom, when she felt her scalp crawl. Her eyes shot up and she stopped abruptly, only inches from a monster she thought she'd never have to see again.

Adam.

Fucking *Adam*. The man who taught her to fight. The man she *had* to fight to survive.

Her mouth went dry.

He walked toward her, and she backed into the ladies' room. He followed, the door swinging closed behind him. He looked down at her, his cruel blue eyes quickly assessing her. "Well, look what the cat dragged in."

Eve couldn't tear her eyes from his as her heart thundered in her fucking knees. Last time she'd found herself face to face with this man, he'd sworn to her that he'd kill her if she left him. And then he'd tried to.

She had the full abilities of her team at her fingertips – Zeke's strength, Eoduun's mindsight, Bo's wolfish senses, and Luc's immense power. She could crush this sorry excuse of a man with a snap of her fingers, if she so desired, yet here she was, folding into flight mode. But as much as she wished to flee, her legs wouldn't move. She just stood rigidly, staring. Immobilized. Malfunctioning. Stuck in a place she thought she'd escaped.

"What, you're too stuck up to talk to me? Grow the fuck up. It's been almost four years since we broke up. You can be civil, you know." When Eve couldn't make her mouth form words, Adam laughed humorlessly. "Fuck, why do I even bother with you? I guess once a slut, always a slut. I saw you sitting with all those guys over there. Real classy, Evrys."

Eve and Adam were just inside the ladies' room, out of sight of the booth where her team was, but as soon as Adam said her name, Bo appeared in the doorway and stalked up behind him like a man singularly possessed. He must've heard the confrontation.

He grabbed Adam by the back of his shirt collar and yanked him backward, simultaneously kicking the back of his knees, dropping Adam to the floor before he even knew Bo was there.

But Adam was the one who trained Eve. He was an experienced fighter, so he wasn't down long. He leapt up and whirled to face Bo. When Adam saw Bo's wild, fire and ice eyes, though, he hesitated. Bo closed the distance between them in an instant, his hand around Adam's throat, and slammed him against the wall.

Bo yanked his mask down, baring his sharp canines as he leaned close to Adam's face. He snarled, "I will fucking murder you. Stay the fuck away from my Evie."

The shock on Adam's face shifted to defiance. "Try it. You think your colored contacts and fake vampire fangs scare me, weirdo? I'm a champion MMA fighter. Fighting is what I *do*."

Bo grinned, his canines gleaming. "And killing is what *I* do." In a flash, he drew a blade and pressed it under Adam's chin.

Shit.

"Bo!" Eve protested, rushing to his side, gripping his arm to stay his hand. "Bo, that's enough. He's not worth it."

"No, but you are," Bo replied through clenched teeth, his eyes never leaving Adam's.

The door swung open as a mother and her little girl walked in. They paused, the mother extending a protective arm across in front of her daughter. Bo pushed away from Adam and quickly pulled up his mask and sheathed his knife, keeping his eyes on Adam.

"Apologies, ma'am. We were just leaving," Bo said.

Adam rolled his shoulders and brushed his hand under his nose as he smirked at Bo. "This isn't over," he declared. "You'll regret laying hands on me, freak." He glanced at Eve. "I think I'm going to enjoy the next time we meet," he said ominously before turning and stalking out of the bathroom.

Eve and Bo followed him out, then lingered outside the bathroom door as they watched Adam saunter to the counter to pick up his to-go order. He turned and blew them a kiss before he left the restaurant.

"You're shaking," Bo noticed when he finally looked down at Eve. He slid his hand over her shoulder and gently pulled her head against his chest. He kissed the top of her head through his mask. "Who the fuck was that?" he murmured, his face still in her hair.

The biggest piece of shit on Earth. The worst thing that had ever happened to her. The monster that broke her over and over again until she didn't recognize herself anymore. The reason she flinched and cowered away from Luc every time he raised his voice.

"An old boyfriend," she said.

Bo looked up, his eyes scanning the windows to the parking lot. "The reason you got into MMA," he said knowingly.

"That's the one." Eve pulled away from Bo. "Adam Larson. I thought he left town. I didn't know he would be here, or I would've been more careful. I'm sorry I dragged you into that."

"Evie—"

"Please don't tell the others about this, ok? About him. They don't need to know. It's embarrassing. I have all this power inside me, and I just fucking stood there. I fucking *froze*. Pathetic." Eve started to walk away, but he grabbed her arm and pulled her back to him.

In a low, dangerous tone, Bo said, "Tell me I can kill him."

Eve scoffed and brushed it off. "You're acting like Luc."

"I'm not sure if you've noticed, but we *are* related." He leaned closer to her, his eyes burning into hers. "I will kill him. Tell me it's what you want."

Eve's heart fluttered at this dark act of service he was offering her. He wanted to protect her. This was Bo's love language. But right now, she needed to focus on how to keep him safe, not put him in the path of danger. "For now, let's just forget about him and focus on the case."

"Hm," Bo grunted with dissatisfaction. "Don't you wish him dead?"

Eve sighed. "Yeah, I fucking wish he was dead. But I don't want to worry about him right now."

Bo was silent as he followed her back to their booth.

"What the hell were you guys doing?" Eoduun demanded, eyeing Bo suspiciously when they returned to their seat.

Bo responded, "Eve ran into an old acquaintance. Nothing to get your panties in a wad about." Under the table, he squeezed Eve's knee.

When the team returned to the motel, Zeke and Eoduun followed Eve into the room she shared with Bo and Isaac. Isaac and Bo followed behind, and Isaac went straight to his bed and stretched out with the copy of *White Fang* Eve had given him. Zeke plopped down on the other bed, and Eoduun dropped down next to him. Eoduun winked at Eve and patted the bed between them.

Bo kicked his boots off and said, "Don't mind if I do," and pushed Zeke over into Eoduun, then reclined back against the pillow with his hands folded behind his head. "We should rest up before we get prepped for tonight," he remarked. "We want to be sharp for the hunt. Maybe you boys should retire to your own room for a bit."

Eve chimed in, "Oh, but you boys look so cozy all snuggled up together." She sat down on the edge of Isaac's bed. She turned to look at him, and he glanced back at her with boredom in his sleepy, dark eyes. He slid over to give her room, granting permission for her to lie next to him.

Why did that make her feel special?

She flopped back onto the pillow and sighed. She had a knot in her guts that had been twisting itself up since she'd run into Adam. She felt Isaac's gaze on her for a few moments before his elbow bumped into hers. She turned her face toward him.

He furrowed his brows and tapped a Y-handshape to his chin twice. *What's wrong?*

Eve touched a flat O-handshape to her chin and cast it away. *Nothing.*

Isaac raised a brow. *Don't lie to a priest,* he signed, his expression sarcastically disapproving.

Eve smirked. *I fucked a priest,* she signed back. *Lying to one is the least of my sins.*

Isaac dipped his head in concession.

"They're doing it again," Eoduun said in exasperation.

Eoduun hates when we sign, Eve signed with an amused smirk. *He feels left out.*

Isaac made a dismissive expression. He swiped his hand across his forehead and jutted his thumb toward the boys. *Forget him.* He pointed at the books she'd brought in from the car and signed, *Stay and read with me.*

Eve reached over and picked up *Pride and Prejudice.* When she opened it and started reading, Eoduun sighed heavily.

"I really wish he would go back to Rome," he grumbled.

Eve read a few pages to the background din of the boys' conversation, but it wasn't long before the book dropped down onto her chest and she closed her heavy eyelids for a quick nap.

36

Crawl to Me

Eve stared out the window of an apartment she'd never seen before, yet it seemed so familiar, like she'd been here a million times. There was a large, wooden desk behind her, and an old green couch in the middle of the room. She somehow knew it was Isaac and Bo's apartment. The second-floor window she was standing in front of overlooked a dirty back alley, and she watched a couple of shady-looking miscreants walk by.

Two strong arms came around either side of her, caging her from behind, and two heavy-knuckled hands rested on the windowsill next to hers. She smelled the tobacco lingering on his clothes and felt his body heat behind her before his firm chest pressed against her back. She tilted her head to the side, and his lips immediately swooped in to taste the hollow of her shoulder. His hand slid up her arm, his fingers gracing over the delicate column of her neck as she hummed to let him know she liked the way his lips felt on her skin.

She reached up and pressed her palm to the side of his neck, then turned around to face him.

Isaac grinned at her, standing there in an old white tank top, his lean muscles flexing as he shifted his weight into his hands to lean into her. His lips crushed against hers, and she could taste the smoke from his morning cigarette on his tongue. Some people say it's like kissing an ashtray, but it didn't bother her. It was just how Isaac tasted.

Isaac lifted her ass onto the windowsill and pressed his hips between her legs. She hooked her ankles together behind his thighs and slid her hands up under the back of his tank top, enjoying every bump and bulge in his tight muscles. He kissed her more deeply, his thumb pressing lightly against her larynx. She hummed for him.

This felt so natural. So normal. So *good.*

Isaac gripped her ass and lifted her from the window sill, turning to deposit her onto the desk. He pressed his hand against her chest, guiding her to lie back, so she leaned back onto her elbows, looking up into those hooded, dark walnut-colored eyes.

When Isaac began to unfasten Eve's jeans and slide them down over her thighs, she suddenly became aware of Bo standing in his bedroom doorway, watching them, his wolf eye ablaze. She opened her mouth to say his name in surprise, but at that moment, Isaac dropped to his knees between her legs, hooking her knees over his shoulders. His tongue delved into her folds, and Bo's name came out as a gasp.

"Bo…!"

Eve closed her eyes and dropped her head back, reveling in the sensations of Isaac's hot tongue massaging her clit. She grabbed his hand from her thigh and dragged it up to hold it against her chest. "Oh, fuck, Isaac," she moaned.

Bo approached the desk, sauntering around the opposite side of the desk from Isaac, near Eve's head. He tugged his mask down around his neck and buried his hand in Eve's hair, leaning down to take possession of her mouth. The tongue in her mouth and the one between her legs worked in unison to drive her pleasure to new heights, and she moaned into Bo's mouth. He smiled against her lips, then leaned close to her ear.

"Does his tongue feel good, Evie?"

Eve made a breathless sound of affirmation.

Bo tightened his grip in her hair, making her cry out with pleasureful pain, as Isaac cupped her breast, tweaking her nipple between his fingers. She burst over that blissful edge. Bo devoured her cries as she rocked herself against Isaac's face, her core throbbing with each wave of pleasure.

As she lay, panting, Isaac stood between her trembling legs, unfastening his pants. She looked up at Bo, and he was doing the same. She looked back to Isaac just as his huge cock bobbed free from his boxer briefs. He stroked it a few times, rubbing his thumb slowly over the head, and Eve admired just how fucking gorgeous that monstrosity was. She'd almost forgotten how goddamn perfect it was.

Her head was suddenly jerked back, and she was forced onto her back on the hard wooden desktop, looking up at Bo, her head hanging off the edge of the desk.

"Enough staring. Don't make me jealous, sweetheart," Bo warned.

Eve grinned up at him. "Wouldn't dream of it, Daddy. You know you're my favorite."

"That's a good girl." Bo pressed the silky head of his cock against her lips. She'd never taken someone in her mouth from this angle, with her head tilted back like this, upside down. "Open wide, baby," he urged.

When she parted her lips to take Bo into her mouth, Isaac speared into the dripping heat between her legs, stretching her to her limits. Bo pushed into her mouth, muffling the moans Isaac was eliciting from the other side of the desk. Isaac gripped Eve's hips as he pumped into her with hard, deep strokes, as Bo wrapped his hands around her neck and fucked her mouth with her head tipped back over the side of the desk.

Eve's own moan awakened her. She was wrapped like an octopus around a warm, hard body, her face nuzzled in his neck. The light scent of smoke surrounded her.

Isaac.

She leaned her head back and looked up at him, hoping to high heaven he wasn't awake.

No such luck. He gazed down at her with mild amusement on his face. He arched a brow and signed, *Pleasant dream?* Then his eyes were drawn to the foot of the bed.

Eve followed his gaze, and found Bo standing there, looking down at them, his arms crossed, his wolf eye an inferno of rage. He pointed at Isaac, then pointed to the door.

"Get the fuck out," Bo seethed behind his mask.

Eve untangled her limbs from Isaac and said, "He can't understand you with your mask on, Bo. And he didn't do anything."

Bo raised a silver eyebrow at her, the fury in his eyes only burning brighter. "Oh, don't misunderstand, Evie. It's *you* who's in trouble." He pointed to his vacant bed. The boys must have returned to their room when she was asleep. "Go sit on my bed."

Heat burned her cheeks and unfurled in her belly. "Yes, sir," she said demurely. She took the two steps between the beds and perched on the edge of the other bed.

Isaac regarded Bo with bland annoyance, then looked over at Eve. He signed, *Do you want me to leave?*

Eve nodded. *Go have a smoke. I'll sort this out.*

Isaac swung his legs over the side of the bed and pushed up off of it, stretching as he stood, clearly taking his sweet ass time. He maintained defiant eye contact with Bo as he collected his jacket from the chair in the corner and made his way to the door. Before closing it behind him, he glanced at Eve, touching his chin and fingerspelling. *Good luck.*

"You're determined to push your luck with Isaac, aren't you?" Bo reprimanded her, crossing his arms and leaning back against the dresser with the television on it. "You know he's off-fucking-limits."

"It was a dream. I wasn't doing it on purpose."

"Was it *him* you were dreaming about?"

She looked away and chewed her lip guiltily. "Again, I didn't do it on purpose." She looked up at him. "It's not like I can control who I dream about. And you were there too, by the way."

Bo's brows shot up.

Eve elaborated, "You and Isaac were sharing me. On a desk. But it was just a dream, Bo. You can't get mad about a dream."

"Watch me."

Eve dropped her head back and sighed. "I'm sorry, ok? I don't know why you're so pissed."

Bo pointed his finger accusingly at Isaac's bed and blurted, "You were wrapped around him the way..." His voice trailed off, and he looked down at his feet, a deep scowl furrowing his features.

"The way what?"

He looked over at the window as he answered sharply, "The way you wrap yourself around *me* when we sleep." He turned his gaze back to her. "And contrary to your little fantasy, I *will not* share you with him. You are *mine.*"

It was Eve's turn to be surprised. "Careful, Bo. It's one thing to say that kind of thing in the heat of the moment—"

"I don't give a fuck, Evie. It's true, even if it isn't supposed to be. Even though we dance around it, you and I both know it."

"Stop talking, Bo. Please," Eve begged. She wasn't ready to air this. She didn't want to have this conversation. "I said I was sorry, ok? Let's just forget about it."

Bo sighed and dragged his hand down his face, pulling his mask down around his neck. He fixed Eve with an indecisive gaze, his head tilted slightly. He ran his tongue over his teeth, shifting his weight on his feet as he stood up straighter. A darkness fell over him, and he pointed to the floor in front of him. "Crawl to me."

Do it. "Excuse me?" *Crawl to him. Beg him. You're his.*

"You heard me." When Eve continued to hesitate, he took a small step forward and lowered his voice. "I want your apology on your hands and knees, Evie. Show me how sorry you really are. Now. Crawl. To. Me."

Desire pooled between Eve's thighs as she dropped to her hands and knees on that grungy motel floor. She gazed up at him from across the room.

"Come to me," he commanded.

Eve crawled on her hands and knees to him, and when she stopped in front of him, she rose up to her knees. She ran her hands up his muscular thighs, her hand traveling up over the bulge in his pants. His knuckles whitened, gripping the dresser behind him as Eve unzipped his pants and withdrew his swollen cock. She leaned forward, looking up at him, pausing with her lips just barely touching the head of it. "I'm sorry, Bo," she whispered, looking up at him innocently, then took him into her mouth without breaking eye contact.

"Oh, fuck…" Bo moaned, closing his eyes and lolling his head back briefly.

He looked back down at her, and his lips parted as he began to pant. He tangled his fingers in her hair and urged her to pick up the pace. She followed his lead, right up until she felt him swelling in her mouth and was sure he was about to burst.

At that point, she released suction and opened her mouth as wide as it would go, pulling back from him, putting an instant end to his pleasuring. He growled in frustration and tried to thrust his hips forward, his cock twitching. "Evie, please! Fuck!"

She grabbed his wrist, and he let go of her hair. Eve stood up, dragging her body against Bo's as she rose in front of him. She whirled him around and pushed him back, and he dropped down onto the edge of his bed. He watched her like a starving wolf as she shimmied out of her pants and underwear, then she climbed onto his lap, impaling herself slowly down onto him, feeling him throb as he penetrated deeper inside of her. His fingers found their way into her hair again, and his lips caressed the underside of her jaw.

Eve touched her lips to his ear, whispering, "Do you forgive me?"

He groaned. "You know I never stay mad at you, Evie." Then, after a few heavy breaths, he kissed her deeply and, panting, made a startling request. "Tell me you love me."

Eve stopped abruptly, and she could feel him throbbing inside her, just on the brink of spilling over. She leaned back so she could see his face, searching his eyes. "What did you just say?"

"I don't care if you don't mean it. I just want to hear you say it," he confessed.

"That's crossing a line," Eve whispered.

"*This* is crossing a line. I don't give a fuck anymore," he said breathlessly. He pushed on her hips, urging her into motion. She moved her hips to the rhythm he set.

"Why do you want me to say *that*?"

Bo growled in frustration. "God, just say it! Please. Tell me you love me," he begged.

Against her better judgement, Eve took his face in her hands, his mismatched eyes piercing hers as she turned her eyebrows up and gazed at his handsome face. "Bo…you know I love you." She leaned into him and kissed him sweetly as he was finally allowed the release he'd been edging. He wrapped his arms around her and held her tightly as he emptied himself inside of her with a deep, satisfied moan.

When he was finished, she draped her arms around his neck and held him to her. His breath puffed lightly over her shoulder as she stroked his hair. "Why did you want me to say that?" she softly asked again.

"I just did," he replied elusively. He placed his hand on the side of her face and kissed her tenderly. It made her stupid heart flutter.

"I feel like you should say it back. It seems only fair, since you made me say it. Don't you love me, Daddy?" she teased. She started to climb off of him, but he pulled her back to him and kissed her voraciously. He was hardening inside her again.

He maneuvered her onto her back and stripped his shirt off, then his lips descended upon her again, kissing down her neck. She pressed her hands to his bare chest and pushed against him, but he didn't budge. "Bo, stop," she whispered. "Isaac could walk back in any time now."

"I don't care. You haven't come yet." Bo grabbed her wrists and yanked her hands away from his chest, forcing them down onto the bed above her head. He held them there as his lips crushed down onto hers again. She whimpered against his mouth as he grinded his hips against hers, thrusting himself into her. He was rock-hard already, and his enthusiasm was intoxicating. Eve forgot her protests.

"Say it again," he whispered against her lips.

She knew what he was asking. "I love you, Bo."

He smiled and sighed, and she felt him pulse inside of her. His tongue explored her mouth and moved sensually with hers, sending little zings of pleasure from her tongue to her core. He released her wrists and instead intertwined his fingers with hers, squeezing her hands as he plunged into her harder, his firm abdominals and chest sliding against her body. She wrapped one leg around his waist as she rocked her hips with his, her pleasure quickly rising.

Bo's lips grazed her ear, his breath hot on her neck, and he whispered breathlessly, "I know I'm not allowed to, but I love you, Evie. I love you so fucking much."

His confession sent a shockwave straight to Eve's core. She buried her face in his shoulder and sank her teeth into his flesh to muffle her moans as her body convulsed with pleasure. She cried out Bo's name.

The feeling of her body writhing beneath him and the pain from her teeth in his shoulder pushed Bo over the edge once again, and he shuddered and tried to subdue his groan as he came. After a few final pumps, he relaxed his body on top of hers, his full weight melting into her. His face was next to hers, turned toward her, and he slid his hand down her arm and brought it to the side of her face, running his thumb slowly over her cheek as he gazed softly at her.

"Now *I'm* in trouble," he whispered, more to himself than to Eve.

37
Night Mare

As Eve quickly dressed, she was realizing just how much she and Bo had fucked up.

They hadn't just crossed a line. Or multiple lines. They'd crossed *THE* line. Fuck, they were so far over it that they couldn't even see the line anymore.

Eve looked at Bo sitting on the bed, his mask up over his face again, a distant look in his eyes. She could think of only one way to fix this, one way to reinforce the cracked dam and stop the floodwaters from catastrophic overflow. "Heat of the moment, right?" she ventured cautiously.

Bo's charcoal and aqua eyes turned to hers, and he studied her for a spell. "Yeah. Heat of the moment," he nodded. But his eyes said something different.

He wanted to blast down the dam.

Eve needed to change the subject. They needed to put this L-word nonsense behind them, and she knew exactly how to do that: start a fight. "I don't want you to come hunting with us tonight," she disclosed.

Bo shot her a surprised look. "Why?"

"My zombie horse dream wasn't just a dream – that much is obvious now. And I saw you die. I don't want you anywhere near that nuckelavee thing."

Bo stood up. "I appreciate your concern, but that's not your call to make, Evie."

"Then you make it."

Bo shook his head as he picked up the weapon bag and dropped it onto the bed. "I'm not sitting this out. You know I'm not going to do that." He began to check over the contents.

"You know it would destroy me if anything ever happened to you, don't you?" Eve said.

"You know I feel the same way about you, but I don't lock you away from danger, as much as I would love to. We have a job to do, and I intend to do it." Bo checked the magazine on one of the handguns, then looked down at his watch.

Eve was desperate. "What would it take?"

He looked up at her. "To keep me from the hunt?"

"I'll do anything," she swore.

Bo frowned at her from behind his mask, then returned the gun to the bag. He zipped up the bag and hoisted it over his shoulder. "If I don't go, no one goes. You know I would never sacrifice someone else to save myself."

Fuck. She knew he was going to say something like that. "What if *I* stay here with you?"

Bo turned away from her. "Give it a rest, Evie. It's not up for negotiation. I'm going."

"I'll let you kill Adam!" she blurted.

He paused with his back to her. He turned his head toward her, but not enough to face her, his eyes not rising to meet hers. His voice was low and dark when he said, "What makes you think I haven't done that already?"

Eve froze. "Did you?"

Bo ignored her question. "We're going hunting tonight. If you want to stay behind, be my guest, but *I'm* not passing up the opportunity to kill the creature that's stalking you." Bo walked out the door to begin packing the car.

Isaac was waiting outside, and when he saw Bo walk out, he walked in. He signed, *He's still angry.*

She knew that, but she didn't know why. Was it because she asked him to sit this one out? Or was he still mad about her dream, and about Isaac? Or was it more complicated than just that?

Eve signed back to Isaac, *We need to keep an eye on Bo tonight. If my zombie horse nightmare is right, he's in danger.*

Isaac arched a brow. *You want me to protect the guy who hates me?*

Eve gave him a beseeching expression and pointed to her head, then her chest. *For me?*

He rolled his eyes, then tapped his thumb to his chest with his hand splayed vertically. *Fine.* He gave her a meaningful look. *For* you. *Not him.*

When the team pulled up to Eve's old house, darkness was just beginning to creep in. The rain had ceased, but the sky was still overcast, obscuring the moon. Eve and Eoduun took a spotlight with them when they went into the house so they would be ready to shine a light on the nuckelavee when it came in. Bo, Isaac, and Zeke went around the back of the house.

Eve led Eoduun to her old room, hoping the nuckelavee would come to her window again like it had been.

"'*Come to my window*,'" Eve sang quietly as she stood looking out her bedroom window, watching the boys lay out a wide ring of fire accelerant around the area she and Isaac had found the hoof prints earlier. She felt Eoduun saunter up behind her, and a flashback of her fantasy dream from this afternoon played in her head. Isaac and Bo. A fantasy that would never come to fruition.

Isaac could never happen again. That realization filled her with such a deep sense of loss. She had a connection with Isaac that felt special. Unique. And, after being in his head and seeing his past, she was fairly confident that this was a special friendship for him, too. But their sexual connection had deepened their relationship, and though she knew it had been a necessary and one-time arrangement, she longed for more.

Greedy fucking whore.

"We probably have some time to kill before the action starts," Eoduun whispered into Eve's ear as he came up behind her and snaked his arms around her waist.

"Not now, Eoduun," Eve whispered.

"Later, then?" he asked hopefully.

"I don't know. Maybe."

Eoduun stiffened. "Maybe? What, you have other plans or something?" he snipped.

"I have other things on my mind right now, that's all."

Eoduun's arms dropped to his sides and he stepped away from Eve. "Bo did something, didn't he?" he postulated reproachfully. "Did you guys fight or something? Is that why I saw him leaving the motel earlier after Z and I went back to our room?"

Eve's head jerked in Eoduun's direction. "What do you mean he left?"

"Did you fuck Isaac again or something?" Eoduun accused.

"What? No! I fell asleep! That's all! But what do you mean Bo left? Where did he go? How long was he gone?" Eve demanded.

"I don't fucking know. I didn't see when he came back."

Jesus. Maybe he really did kill Adam. Eve assumed he was just being cryptic and trying to push her buttons when he'd suggested he'd already done it, but...

She didn't know how she felt about that. She watched Bo out the window, wondering what the hell had gotten into him lately. He was…different. Something was off.

Had she broken Bo?

Tell me you love me.

Luc had warned her about Bo right from the beginning. *He doesn't share. He is possessive. If you start fucking him, even just for training, he will need you to be his, and it will eat him alive if you aren't.*

Was she destroying her favorite person in the whole entire world because she couldn't love him the way he needed to be loved? The way he *deserved* to be loved?

God, she ruined everything she touched with her filthy hands.

Eoduun dragged her from her own head. "What gives, Eve? You're being standoffish. What happened?"

She shook her head. "Nothing happened. I don't mean to be standoffish. I'm just exhausted."

Eoduun sighed and crossed his arms. "Whatever."

"Whatever," she mocked teasingly. "You know, you don't have to end every conversation that way."

"I don't."

Eve hummed contemplatively. "Hm…ninety percent of the time you do."

Eoduun rolled his eyes. "Whatever." A tiny smirk quirked the corner of his mouth.

Eve rested her temple against Eoduun's shoulder and watched out the window with him. Zeke, Bo, and Isaac were nowhere to be seen now, effectively hidden in the darkness, awaiting the arrival of their gnarly quarry. But somehow she knew where Bo was. She could *feel* him out there. She focused her eyes on the spot where she was sure he was hiding, and a slight shift of form in the darkness confirmed her hunch.

She couldn't let anything happen to that man. She would protect him with a ferocity heretofore unseen in this world if anything or anyone dared threaten his life. She would rain down a thousand deaths and devour the offender's soul.

Bo was special.

Eoduun's sharp inhale snapped Eve's attention to the clearing. An enormous shadow picked carefully through the trees, following the worn path from the water's edge. A single red orb bobbed behind the branches as the creature made its approach to the house, and as it stepped out of the wood line, the grotesquely enormous head on the human torso lolled to the side. The milky white eyes sunk into the gourd were somehow both dead and raging.

The nuckelavee paused and snorted, a thick vapor spewing from the wide, rotted nostrils of the horse head. It pawed the ground, causing the garishly long, dangling human arms to swing at its sides, its fingertips brushing in the dirt.

It was on high alert.

Flames erupted and formed a circle around the beast, bathing the abhorrent thing in enough light to see it clearly.

Eve wished she could turn her eyes away. Bile rose in her throat. Nothing could've prepared her for how repulsive this thing would be in the flesh. Without any skin, she saw veins pumping black blood, and muscle fibers, tendons, and sinew glistening under a yellowish ooze that bubbled up from below. The monster reared up in a rage, whinnying in the most frightful way, like a mutilated steam whistle, and gnashing its half-rotted horse teeth.

The wide mouth on the giant human head gaped open, and an unexpectedly wheezy, feminine voice called out, "Evrys..."

Was it...a *she*?

"I can't fucking read it," Eoduun whispered in surprise, staring intently out the window at the nuckelavee, his purple irises spinning.

Zeke, Bo, and Isaac surrounded the creature, giving it a wide birth, standing well outside the ring of flames, guns aimed at it.

The disgusting human head suddenly lolled and turned its white eyes toward Bo, the bulging red eye on the horse head following suit.

The feminine voice was suddenly furious. "Evrys!" it wheezed as it charged straight through the wall of flames at Bo.

In the blink of an eye, Eve pushed through time and space and threw herself in front of Bo, shoving him back with Zeke's strength, lightning already arcing from her fingertips as she squared off with the horrific nightmare baring down on her.

Truly a night mare.

Eve braced for impact, ready to light this bitch up like the Fourth of July.

The impact never came. The nuckelavee pulled up short, skidding its Clydesdale-sized hooves in the dirt in front of her.

"Evrys."

The voice was soft and relieved. Affectionate. Motherly.

Eve looked up with wide, disbelieving eyes. The nuckelavee stood calmly before her. The horse head lowered down, the glowing red eye level with her face. The rotting horse muzzle pushed forward and nuzzled her shoulder affectionately.

What. The. Fuck.

She looked up past the horse head, which was now dropping down to nibble at her shoelaces, and gazed into those milky white orbs set deeply in the big, wobbly head. The mouth opened and said her name again. It was as though she wanted to tell Eve something.

"Why are you here?" Eve asked tremulously. Her attention was fully fixed on the nuckelavee, but she was suddenly aware of her boys around her, ready to fight at the drop of a hat. She was grateful that they were there, but she instinctively knew that there would be no fight.

The nuckelavee's mouth worked for a moment, trying to form words with obvious difficulty while the muzzle of the horse head began to curiously investigate Zeke's shirt while he cringed away from it, trying not to gag at the putrid smell it exuded.

"Sa...afe..." the nuckelavee wheezed.

Safe? Eve looked to Eoduun. "Did you get a read on it?"

He shook his head with furrowed brows. "It isn't working. I can't get anything from it."

Eve looked up at the nuckelavee. "I'm going to try to look at your memories, ok? I want to know what happened to you, and how you got here. Will you let me into your mind?"

The horse head swung around, turning the cycloptic red eye to Eve. It stared straight into her eyes, an overt invitation.

Eve opened the tunnel and, instead of pouring herself in like she did with a possession, she only dipped a toe in, so to speak. She didn't want to accidentally put herself inside of this gigantic, necrotized beast of burden.

Memories flooded in. Eve saw craggy cliffs and lush green hilltops, sandy beaches and roiling ocean waves, and clouds of smoke in the air with rotted fields and dying livestock. There were centuries of these memories flashing through Eve's mind in quick succession, like a flipbook.

Until the scene changed. Eve grasped at that different image. The nuckelavee was standing in the dark, having just risen from waters that weren't her own. She looked around with all three eyes at a small lake and trees she didn't recognize. She didn't like this water. It burned, but she felt tethered to it, the way she was supposed to be tethered to the ocean.

Where was she?

Her eyes were drawn to two human women standing in the reeds on the bank. She hated humans. She charged through the water at them, prepared to unleash her pestilent vapors into their lungs as she stomped their bodies with her heavy hooves. But as she approached, a deep and unyielding compulsion stopped her. She couldn't hurt them. She *wanted* to, but she couldn't.

"Come to us, Mòrag," the woman with the flowing, fiery red hair commanded. Eve was aware of a Scottish accent, but in Mòrag's memory, it sounded natural.

She was compelled to obey. She approached the women, and without knowing why she felt the need to do so, her forelegs dropped to kneel in front of them. She raged against the urge, but it was irresistible.

There was a short blonde woman with the witch, and Eve couldn't help but notice a strong resemblance to herself. Her birth mother. The blonde woman held out a small tuft of hair, and Mòrag could smell that it was saturated with blood. The red-haired witch recited a spell, and Mòrag opened her mouth. The blonde woman dropped the hair into Mòrag's mouth and clasped her hands around her muzzle to close it and hold it closed. The witch murmured an incantation, and suddenly Mòrag was filled with overwhelming purpose.

Protect the child, the source of this hair and blood. She was close by. Mòrag could feel her, smell her. She would endure these burning new waters, as she must, because she needed to stay close to watch over the child.

Evrys was never to be harmed.

38
Her Girl

Eve saw memories of Mòrag watching her as a child. Sometimes she watched through the trees from the forest path as Eve played in the back yard of her home, or watched her sitting in her room through the window, especially at night. Sometimes she watched from the water as Eve walked along the banks, and many memories were of Eve sitting in her little swamp, reading a book quietly.

In those early memories of Eve's childhood, annoyance and hatred for Eve pervaded Mòrag's thoughts. She resented that she was compelled to protect this child from the shadows. She hated humans. She hated these waters that burned her and turned to ice that she had to break through in the winter. But as time went on, the feelings shifted. She supposed the little girl wasn't *so* bad. Sometimes she was even kind of funny to watch, even if she was an ugly little thing. Humans and their weird skin.

That tolerance slowly turned to mild affection. Mòrag would snort to herself when she saw Eve dancing like a fool in her room. She worried for her when she saw her sneaking out of her window in the middle of the night and left the boundaries of Mòrag's domain. She felt at ease when Eve was near the water, reading in her favorite place. She felt for Eve when she saw her crying and upset. She hated the father-figure who was so often the source of those tears, but as much as she wanted to stomp him into a bloody pulp, she knew that wasn't her purpose. *He* wasn't the one she was supposed to be protecting Evrys from.

Those creatures came later, when Evrys turned thirteen. She suddenly fell ill and was away for weeks, and Mòrag fretted. The longer Evrys was gone, the more the waters burned, and the weaker she felt. Her mind grew fuzzy, and confusion overtook her with increasing frequency. She had an impending sense of doom, and she knew a storm of some kind was blowing in.

And then Eve returned after a long battle with her illness, and just like that, Mòrag felt restored.

A few short nights after Eve came home, Mòrag stood outside her window, relieved to have her girl back home where she could see she was safe, when she sensed something sinister. A man crept around the corner of the house, his eyes glowing yellow.

Werewolf.

Mòrag winded him and stomped her massive hoof. He had no business lurking around Evrys's home. The glowing yellow eyes cast her a brief, assessing glance.

"Well, you're something new," the wolf-man remarked.

Mòrag focused her energy into her rarely-used larynx to voice a reply. "…Old." Hundreds of years old. This pup had nothing on her. She took a challenging step toward him. "Leave."

"Not without my prize. I'll just grab the girl and go."

Mòrag charged him, and he backed away from the house, confusion swirling in his yellow eyes. "I don't know what you are or why you're here," he said, irritation tinging his voice, "but you need to butt out. You have no idea what you're interfering with."

"Leave," Mòrag repeated, stomping for emphasis.

The wolf-man shook his head and pulled his shirt off over his head, tossing it onto the ground. "Are you some kind of guardian?" he asked. Mòrag bobbed her horse head in affirmation. The man kicked his shoes off. "Just know, even if I fail, there will be more after me. We'll never stop coming for her."

With that, he shifted into his wolf form and lunged at Mòrag. He was the first of many to die trying to capture Eve. Memories of Mòrag's numerous battles spun through Eve's mind, yet none of these creatures ever revealed anything to explain why they were after Eve. Mòrag always attacked without question after that first werewolf. If she sensed a monster in her territory, she dispatched them immediately.

Then Eve saw herself storming from the house with Grant, and she felt the anxiety Mòrag experienced. That anxiety grew into dread and loneliness as the weeks dragged on without bringing Eve's return. When weeks turned to months, Mòrag's despair became unbearable. She again weakened with Eve's absence, and one night, when she couldn't bear it anymore, Mòrag slipped into hibernation deep in the waters of Black Lake.

The next memory hit Eve like a shockwave. Mòrag was jolted from her hibernation as Eve's presence rippled all around her in the water. She was here! She was home! But the years of hibernation in these inland waters without Eve nearby had severely weakened her, and her mind was murky, her body engulfed in an inferno of agony. The only clear thing she could focus on was the overwhelming sense that Eve was in grave danger. Mòrag's aching body and muddy mind carried her to the surface of the water, and she dragged her heavy hooves onto the bank and up through the wooded path to Eve's window.

The girl wasn't there. No one was there. Confused, Mòrag returned to the bank and looked out across the lake. There, at the public access, she saw Eve walking toward the road with a man, and then she disappeared from view. By the time Mòrag made her way to the public access, Eve was gone.

Mòrag waited for Eve's return, slowly pacing the woods behind her house and repeatedly checking the public access and Eve's favorite spot in the swamp. The next day, Mòrag felt the pang of loss once again as Eve's presence was snuffed out in an instant.

Mòrag's cloudy mind became agitated, and she was sure that something disastrous had befallen her girl. In a rage, she vented her pestilent vapors in the corn field and barn across from Black Lake, a warning to whatever may have harmed Evrys. She knew she wasn't going to live long without Eve at this point, so she was desperate. She had nothing to lose. She went after any hint of Eve's essence she could follow, which led her to the librarian and the gas station attendant. Mòrag's confusion led her to believe those women had harmed Eve, so she killed them.

Eve then saw the memories of today. Mòrag sensed her proximity when the team stopped at the cornfield on the way into town, and it was her that Eve saw bob under the water. Mòrag longed to follow her, to watch over her, relieved that she was alive, but the rain trapped her in the lake. Her tolerance of freshwater only extended to Black Lake. Rain, rivers, and any other body of freshwater would still burn her like acid.

So, she bided her time, until tonight. She felt Eve was close again, so she came to check the house, following her scent. She was suddenly surrounded by flames. Was Eve under attack?! She caught a strong scent of her girl, but it wasn't her. It was a man. He'd been close to Eve. He must have hurt her!

Kill him! Kill him! Die!

As she bore down on the man, however, rage surging through every fiber of her enormous body, Evrys appeared.

Her girl.

She was here. She was safe.

A deep serenity washed over Mòrag, calming the rage and confusion.

She was never letting her out of her sight again.

Eve withdrew from Mòrag's mind. "I had no idea," Eve marveled. "I'm safe, Mòrag. Thank you for protecting me all this time, but you don't need to worry about me anymore," she relayed softly. "I have a whole group of protectors now. You can return to your native waters and rest easy. You're going to die if you stay here."

"No...You stay," Mòrag wheezed.

"I can't stay here. This isn't my home anymore."

Eoduun shifted uneasily from one foot to the other. "So...I take it we aren't killing it?"

Mòrag huffed and stomped at him, but Eve reached out and stroked the poor, disgusting creature's thick horse neck, calming her. She wondered if the mucus would wash off easily like snot, or if it was going to be more difficult, like slug slime.

"No. She was just trying to protect me." She looked up between Mòrag's white, humanish eyes, and her cycloptic red one. "How do I break this spell my mother put you under? How do we free you from Black Lake and get you home?"

Mòrag didn't have an answer. But Eve suddenly realized that *she* knew. Rather, Ruth knew, and those memories were still in her head. But she needed materials and a spell book that Ruth left in Montana – with Apep.

Fuck.

Eve sighed. "I'm going to need you to hang in there, Mòrag. I have a plan, but I need to get some things. I'll stay close tonight so hopefully you can build up your strength."

Eve convinced Mòrag to return to the lake for the night, but as soon as she was out of sight, Bo was on Eve, demanding answers.

"That was the most foolish thing you've ever done. I should bench you for life, you know that?" He crossed his arms and leveled a lethal gaze at her. She knew he would be furious with her for putting herself in harm's way again, but she didn't regret it. She'd gladly do it again to protect him. "What the fuck, Evie?"

"I did what I had to do. You'd do exactly the same thing, so don't look at me like that." Eve tried to shift away from an argument by filling them in on what she saw in Mòrag's mind – how her mother and a Scottish witch summoned Mòrag to protect her, and how monsters started coming for her once she turned thirteen, but Mòrag killed them.

"Why were monsters coming for me?" Eve wondered. "And how did my mother and that witch know that they would come for me?"

"Panacea Blood is rare. Valuable," Bo offered. "If anyone knew what you were, and they thought you were unprotected, they would have no qualms about taking you and keeping you as an unwilling cure-all. Your mother must have known that you would become a blood healer, or she at least suspected it."

"Except I'm not just a blood healer. I'm a fucking Abomination."

"Maybe she knew that, too."

Eve informed them that she knew how to free Mòrag from the spell placed on her. What she didn't share, however, was what she needed to perform the spell and where she needed to go to get those things. They'd insist on finding another way, but there wasn't time. She could sense from Mòrag's mind just how weak she was. She wouldn't survive much longer like that.

Eve might have to do something stupid and reckless.

"Why do we care about saving that thing? Just let it die," Eoduun suggested coldly. "We came here to kill it. It killed two women, and we can't trust it won't hurt anyone else."

Bo rubbed his forehead. "He's not wrong, Evie."

Zeke came to her defense. "But it protected Eve for all these years. Doesn't that count for something?"

"It was compelled to protect her, Z," Bo corrected. "As soon as that spell is broken, who knows how the nuckelavee will react? It might try to kill all of us, Evie included. And even if it didn't, what happens when we send it back to Scotland? It's going to follow its nature, and its nature is to kill and spread rot and disease. There are no redeeming qualities in a nuckelavee."

"Mòrag is different," Eve argued. "I've been in her head. I've felt what she feels. She's not just a mindless killing machine. She *cares* about me."

"That may be," Bo conceded, "but that does nothing to prove that it won't hurt anyone else. We can't let it go, Evie. We need to put it down."

Eve scowled and lifted her chin defiantly. "I won't let you kill her."

Bo regarded her with sympathy, but he replied, "You don't have a choice. It's our job to protect people, to hunt the things that would hurt them. Your nuckelavee has already proven to be dangerous. It's already killed. This isn't up for debate. You need to put your feelings aside and do what you know needs to be done."

Eve's nostrils flared. She leaned close. "Is that what you do, Bo? You just push your feelings aside, huh?"

Bo held her gaze. "All the fucking time."

In a voice only Bo could hear, she challenged, "Is that what you were doing when you went off and killed Adam? Pushing your feelings aside?"

Bo took a step closer. "I could've made it so much messier than I did. So, yeah. You could say so."

So, it was true: Bo killed Adam. Eve finally broke eye contact with him as she reflected on his confession.

Zeke took Eve's hand, his bulky shoulder brushing against hers. "Maybe we should talk to Luc about it before we do anything. We can go back to the motel and worry about the nuckelavee tomorrow."

Eve didn't budge when Zeke pulled on her hand as the group began to move back toward where the car was parked. He turned and looked at her questioningly.

"I need to stay here," she said. "I told Mòrag I would stay close so she could regain some of her strength."

Eoduun sighed. "If we're going to kill it, I think I'd rather not let its HP bar slide back to full."

"Let's stop talking about killing it," Zeke advised quietly.

Isaac pressed down two Y-handshapes, palms downward, then touched his fists together vertically and indicated her and himself. *I'll stay with you.*

"If you're camping out, so am I," Zeke offered Eve as well, without understanding Isaac's signs.

"Well, I guess I don't have much of a choice, do I?" Eoduun complained.

Bo threw his hands up and dropped his head back in exasperation, looking up at the night sky. "Sure, why the fuck not?"

39
For a Price

As Eve lay on the hard floor of her old bedroom between Zeke and Eoduun, she watched the shadowy outline of Bo's form sitting with his back against the door, his elbows resting on his knees. His blue eye cut through the dark, much like his brother's, scanning the room and windows. She sat up and wrapped her arms around her knees.

"You need to rest," Bo informed her, his voice only audible to the temporarily hypersensitive ears she'd stolen from him. Eoduun and Zeke didn't stir.

"I told you not to kill Adam," she whispered back, equally quiet.

"You never told me I couldn't kill him. You just refused to tell me *to* kill him. But you wanted him dead."

"I said we'd worry about it later."

"I dealt with it now so we never have to worry about him again."

Eve couldn't deny the tinge of relief that the knowledge of Adam's death brought. No one else needed to suffer at his hands the way she had. But... "You should've told me you were going to kill him."

Bo stretched one long leg out in front of him. "You knew I was going to kill him. I won't apologize for it, and I'd do it again in a heartbeat. He was an easily fixable problem."

"Just like Mòrag is an easily fixable problem? We just kill everything that poses a problem for us?"

"The nuckelavee has to die, Evie. You can't just free it and then send it off to be someone else's problem. Everyone it hurts or kills from this point forward is blood on our hands. We have a responsibility to make the hard choices, to do the difficult things we don't always want to do. Sometimes doing the right thing doesn't feel like the right thing. Sometimes it hurts like fucking hell. I wish it could be any other way, because I hate anything that hurts you, but it's the way it has to be."

Eve sat with Bo's words, digesting. She understood his sentiment, but he hadn't *felt* the affection she'd felt from Mòrag. At the same time, she'd also felt the hatred Mòrag harbored toward other humans. She hadn't seen much of the memories from before Black Lake, but in the memories of Mòrag killing the librarian and the gas station attendant, there was a distinct sense that she was not new to killing humans.

In every likelihood, she would kill again.

That admission settled like a rock in Eve's guts.

Tears welled in her eyes. She took a deep, shuddering breath. "She spent all these years watching over me and waiting for me, protecting me from whatever was after me. She cares about me. How can I repay her by condoning her murder?"

She felt sick. She could free Mòrag, if she wanted to. She had all the power inside of her to accomplish that. She could teleport to Montana to fetch the spell book and then perform the ritual to break the enchantment with the witchy powers she stole from Luc. This was a viable option for her, and it felt like the right thing to do.

But as soon as she thought about Mòrag hurting anyone else – hurting Bo, for instance – it ripped her insides out. There was no right answer. There was no perfect choice. There was only what was best for the good of humanity.

...But humanity sucked and didn't always deserve what was best for them.

Eve stood, impulsive determination driving her heart. "Don't do anything until I get back. Bear with me."

"Evie! Where are you going? Wait! Don't you dare!" Bo shouted as he leapt to his feet.

She was already gone.

She was in a darkened room, standing in front of a picture window. Mountains jutted up hazily along the moonlit horizon, and a wide expanse of rangelands stretched as far as she could see. She turned and looked around, and as her eyes adjusted to the dark, she saw she was in an expansive bedroom with a Western hunting lodge aesthetic. She didn't scent anyone else in the room, but a bouquet of strange scents wafted to her from all over the house. She needed to hurry.

If Ruth's memories served her, the spell books would be in the nightstand drawer. She had transfigured them into dark romance novels. Eve quickly and quietly stole across the room to the bedside tables. As soon as she saw *His Deadly Touch*, *Under His Mask*, and *Monsters in Her Bed*, she yanked them from the drawer and stuffed them in the waistband of her joggers.

Mission accomplished. She focused her energy on trying to warp space to get the hell out of this place to get back to her team...but it was like trying to push up one last rep after already hitting failure. She just couldn't muster the energy to make it happen.

She was stuck in Montana until her energy could build.

...*If* she managed to hold onto Bo and Luc's powers long enough, that is. Goddamn it.

She wished she had the grimoire. She could've cast a spell and used traveling stones, which is what Eve just now realized Ruth called the strange sigils she used to jump from one place to another. It was a traveling stone that Varghrir had used to take Eve to Scotland. If she had the grimoire, she could be back in Michigan already.

Eve heard heavy footsteps and voices in the hallway outside the open door, so she quickly dropped down and rolled under the bed next to her. As she lay silently, her heartbeat thumping in her ears, she sifted through Ruth's memories of the Montana ranch. There had been an army of monsters here before Ruth and Apep's attack at the paper mill, but she had no idea how many were left after Luc's thunderous annihilation. She knew this place was cloaked, and no one would find it unless they'd already been there. The only reason she was there now was because of Ruth's memories.

Which meant no one would be coming to her rescue. She patted the pocket of her joggers, but she already knew her phone wasn't there. She'd left it in the car in front of her old house because it was almost dead anyway. She glanced down at her wrist with regret. She should've had Luc put his tracker back on her skin.

Well. This was a fucking pickle. Damn her stupid, impulsive decisions.

Maybe she could just hide out until she had enough juice to get the hell out of here. Yes, that's what she would do. A long, elaborate game of hide and seek that only she knew she was playing.

How hard could that be?

"I hate when he's here. He scares the shit out of me," A panicky whisper drifted to Eve's hypersensitive ears from the hallway.

"Just stay out of his way, and you'll be fine," a calmer voice reassured the first.

"You saw what he did to Julie. She was just pouring a cup of coffee, minding her own business!" the first voice pointed out as the voices drifted away from the door.

"She took the last cup. I mean…I kinda get it," the first voice reasoned.

They were obviously talking about Apep. He was here. Shit. She'd hoped he would be out wreaking havoc somewhere else since he was no longer bound to Ruth. Eve needed to let someone know where she was, just in case she didn't come back.

No, fuck that. She would make it back. At any cost, she would make it back to her boys. But if it started to get dicey, she would open her connection with Dagon and tell him where she was. Until then, they didn't need to know, or they would worry unnecessarily. Bo was going to worry either way, of course, but if he knew she'd jumped right into the viper's den, he'd have a coronary. She wondered if he'd immediately called Luc to tattle on her.

She just needed to sit quietly under this bed until she had enough power to jump back to Newbury. Easy peasy.

And the universe laughed and threw her a big middle finger.

Eve caught a frighteningly familiar scent as she heard a jaunty whistle approaching from the hallway, and footsteps entered the bedroom. She froze, barely breathing. The overhead light clicked on, and Eve saw a pair of snakeskin shoes and black pantlegs stroll in. The door closed, and the feet crossed the room to the closet. Black slacks dropped and pooled around the snakeskin shoes, and the closet door opened as the shoes stepped out of the slacks. Women's clothing began littering the floor all around the bare ankles in the snakeskin shoes as the jaunty whistle continued.

There was some unseen activity when the clothing stopped hitting the floor, and Eve could only surmise that he was putting something on.

The bed suddenly shook, and Eve had to clap a hand over her mouth to stifle the gasp. Wham! Wham! Wham!

Was he jumping on the bed?!

She heard the unmistakable sound of a metal blade sliding across a sheath, and a moment later, a carbon steel katana plunged through the bottom of the box springs and sank into the floor only inches from her head.

A startled squeak sprang from her throat, but it was drowned out by the creaking and groaning of the bed as he jumped some more.

The sword wiggled, then was yanked back up out of the bed. Eve slid herself over as far to the edge as she dared.

And then everything went still and silent. Only the sound of Eve's hammering heartbeat and shaky breaths filled the room. She waited, tears of overwhelming anxiety filling her eyes. Her chest was about to burst.

"Hi." A sinisterly cheerful voice was in Eve's ear, and Apep was on the floor under the bed next to her, his face inches from hers. Shining bronze eyes pierced hers. "Cozy under here."

Eve gulped down a strangled yelp as she tried to scramble away, but Apep grabbed her hand. With Zeke's superstrength, she ended up just dragging him along behind her because he wouldn't let go.

"What's wrong?" he asked as he dragged behind her like a ragdoll, his dark burgundy hair flopping around in his face. "I thought we were having a lovely Queen Charlotte, King George moment there."

When Eve was clear of the bed, she jumped up and shook her hand violently, finally freeing herself from Apep's grasp. He stood up, and Eve got a good look at what he was wearing.

"You're in a dress," she blurted, gaping at the sparkly beige cocktail dress.

He turned around, exposing the back. "Zip me up?" he implored, shimmying his tattooed shoulders. When Eve made no move to assist, he shrugged and faced her again. She heard the dress zip up behind him. "Clothing styles change so much from century to century, millennia to millennia. I'm told this is for women, but it's quite close to something I would've worn back in my heyday, and it would've been considered incredibly masculine. Yet you gawk at me as though I'm a sideshow. You humans are so funny."

Eve wrapped her arms protectively around herself, mostly to keep Ruth's spell books secured under her shirt, tucked in her waistband. It was time to phone home.

Dagon, are you there? I'm at Ruth's Montana ranch, and Apep found me. Just, you know, fyi.

Dagon's furious voice filled her mind. *Why would you go there?!*

Yeah, yeah. I know. I'll jump back to you guys as soon as I can. I'm just trying to entertain Apep until then so he doesn't kill me. If you don't hear back from me in an hour or so, tell Bo. Otherwise, keep this to yourself.

You're like those infected creatures that run straight for the things that will eat them instead of away from them, Dagon chided. *Are you sure you don't have a parasite?*

I had a good fucking reason, ok?

Apep's voice suddenly invaded the conversation in her head. *I'd love to hear it.*

"Hey!" Eve shouted out loud, instantly slamming down and boarding up the walls in her mind, even from Dagon.

"Your reinforcements will never find us. No one can find this place unless they've already been here." Apep began to pace around the room, fidgeting with trinkets on the shelves. He took his finger and slid a glass figurine all the way to the edge of the shelf and left it teetering. "But even if they did, they wouldn't get past our defenses. I'm not even sure how you found this place, but I must assume it has something to do with you stealing Ruth's soul." He walked past a painting on the wall and casually nudged it so it was slightly crooked.

"I didn't take her soul. I took her memories."

"Is there a difference?" In an instant, Apep was in her face, all traces of joviality vanished from the angular planes of his golden-toned features. The bronze of his eyes no longer sparkled with mischief. "Why *are* you here, little devil? Did you decide to end the suspense and bring me the grimoire?"

Well, maybe it was a good thing she *didn't* have the grimoire after all.

"I didn't come to see you. It was an accident."

"You didn't stumble across this place by accident."

"It was Ruth's memories that pulled me here. I meant to go somewhere else," she lied.

"Oh? Where? I'll take you there." A wicked gleam sparked in his eye briefly. "For a price."

"A price I can guarantee I'm not willing to pay. No, I'm good. I'll just walk." Eve backed away from him.

Apep tilted his head thoughtfully, the overhead light catching the faint scale-like pattern on his skin. If he wasn't so goddamn terrifying, he'd be pretty fucking hot, and Eve was disgusted with herself for thinking so. He stepped aside and gestured widely toward the bedroom door. Eve couldn't decide if the sparkly dress made him less terrifying, or a thousand-fold more.

"What's this?" she asked cautiously.

"Go ahead. Walk right out the front door if you'd like. I won't stop you."

Eve narrowed her eyes. "What's the catch? Am I going to be blown to bits by landmines if I do?"

Apep only grinned at her, his eyes suddenly wild with unhinged delight. It was the most unsettling smile she'd ever seen.

"I can't actually leave, can I?"

"I get the feeling you do all kinds of stuff you can't."

Shattering porcelain startled Eve, and she whipped her head to the side just in time to see the scattered, jagged pieces of the broken figurine from the shelf settling to a rest on the floor.

When she turned back, Apep was gone.

40
Don't Blink

Shit. Eve took little comfort from his absence, because it only begged the question: where had he gone? What was he up to?

His scent had faded, and she couldn't tell if he was still in the house or if it was only a remnant of his presence. She adjusted the books in her waistband to secure them more snugly, then moved quietly toward the closed bedroom door. She didn't hear anyone outside it, so she slowly opened it and peeked out. No one was around, so she stepped out of the room. To the right, she cast her gaze down a narrow hallway that turned to the left at the end, and to her left, a hallway that opened to the right. There were a couple of closed doors on each side of the hallway. Straight in front of her, there were two enclosed staircases; one leading to a lower level and one next to it leading upstairs.

Maybe it would just be safer to sneak out the window in the bedroom.

She turned around and ran face-first into a solid wall. "What the fuck?" She pressed her hands against the wall where a door had been only moments before. "What...what the *fuck*?!" she repeated.

She looked up and down the halls, then quietly hurried to the nearest door. She turned the knob and opened it slowly, hoping no one was inside. It was a closet.

Eve heard voices coming down the hall from around the corner, so she stepped into the cramped closet and closed the door. She stood in the dark and listened, waiting until the footsteps passed and receded. She heard a door close down the hall.

When she was certain the coast was clear, she slipped out of the closet...and gasped.

She was in a kitchen. She turned and looked behind her, and found she was standing in a pantry.

"What. The. Fuck," she whispered in bewilderment.

Apep appeared, sitting on the counter with his legs crossed. He was now wearing a flowing black robe and black work boots. "Lost, little devil?" he taunted, twirling a large buck knife in his hand.

"What is this?" Eve demanded.

"This is fun. Let's play a game." He grinned and bit his lip, his deep burgundy hair falling into his face as he leapt off the counter. He brushed it back out of his eyes and fixed Eve with a psychotic stare. "I've been sealed away a long time, so I've been absorbing everything I can about your 'modern' world. And you know what I just can't get enough of? Your horror films. The fear, the torture, the psychological trauma, the blood and guts...and there's nothing I love more than a good plot twist." He slid a Ghostface mask over his head. "So tell me..." He cocked his head to the side and altered his voice. "What's your favorite scary movie?"

Eve took a step back into the pantry. "No, I'm not playing this game."

Apep suddenly lunged at her, and Eve slammed the door closed between them. The knife plunged through the wood, and Eve shrieked.

And then nothing. Eve glanced behind her, and realized she wasn't in a pantry anymore. She was in an ugly green bathroom with a green tub and sink. Whispers drifted up from the sink drain.

"I'm not playing!" she shouted, covering her ears.

Shit, she'd seen this movie. She knew what came next, and she wanted absolutely no part of *It*. As soon as blood began to erupt from the sink, she burst back out the door.

Except she wasn't in a kitchen now. "Goddamn it! Stop!" she cried, her gaze spanning a darkened living room. The television clicked on, but there was only static on the screen. "Yeah, yeah. 'They're heeeeeere,'" Eve called out. But then, through the static, an illuminated circle formed. Or, more accurately, a *ring*. A white, ghoulish hand pressed forth out of the screen, followed by a head curtained in long, stringy black hair.

"Nope." Eve turned to see what was behind the next door, but the door was gone. A long, dark hallway stretched before her. She had no choice but to run. She was either going to find an exit, or she was going to stay on the move until she could perform a teleportation back to Newbury.

But first things first, she needed to do something else with these damn books in her joggers. They started to slip down as she ran down the hallway, so she pulled them out and carried them in her arms. But when she looked back up, she saw that the carpet was a weird geometric pattern of orange, brown, and red, and the walls were lined with doors, like a hotel corridor. She stopped and looked behind her, but it was just an empty hotel corridor.

When she turned back, two Apeps were standing in front of her, wearing frilly blue dresses. "The only way out is to win the game," both Apeps said simultaneously.

She looked past the twin Apeps and saw an elevator. "I don't even know the rules! How the fuck do I win?"

Eve heard the squeak of wheels, and a tricycle came burning around the corner in front of the elevator doors, driven by a demented little Jigsaw doll. As it rolled toward her and the Apep twins, a tsunami of blood burst from the elevator doors.

Eve turned and ran the other way, but again, the scene had changed. She was in a dark bedroom. A man in blue coveralls stepped out from behind the open closet door. He was holding a butcher knife and wearing a modified Captain Kirk mask, like Michael Myers.

"Haven't you ever watched a scary movie?" Apep said from behind the mask. "The only way to win is to defeat the monster."

Eve glanced down at the books in her arms. "Or break the curse," she whispered.

"Oh, this isn't a curse. I've just brought you into the quantum realm. The domain of the gods. Infinite possibilities all at once, but reality only exists when it's being actively measured or observed. Some call it Heaven, some call it Hell. It's a very individual experience. I've tweaked our little slice of paradise to fit a theme, as you can tell."

"Reality exists when it's observed...so, what, don't blink?" Eve surmised. But she blinked as she said it, without a thought.

Apep was suddenly right in front of her again, butcher knife raised. "Blink and you're dead," he replied in a low, threatening voice. Eve raised one hand and sent surges of energy to her fingertips. Lightning flew from her hand and knocked Apep back into the wall. She hoped it didn't use up too much of the energy she was trying to reserve.

Then she bolted. She didn't know how to kill a god. Or a demon. Or whatever the hell Apep was.

Well...she knew *one* way. But that did her little good in this particular situation. She tried to call out to Dagon in her mind, but she felt a strange interference, like her call was being blocked.

Fuck.

As Eve ran down the dark corridor, she saw an open door ahead on the right. She slowed and looked in as she ran by it. Inside, a malamute lay on the hay-covered floor, shaking violently and unnaturally. Its face began to split open.

"Oh, fuck that!" Eve screeched as her legs pumped like pistons, carrying her away from *The Thing*.

She rounded a corner, and slammed into Apep. It felt like hitting a brick wall, but Eve was surprised to see him fall back onto his ass. Even from behind his Michael Myers mask, she could tell he was just as shocked as she was.

"Thanks, Zeke," she mumbled under her breath, grateful for his strength.

Apep was on his feet instantly. "You're full of surprises. I love surprises. But I have surprises for you, too."

"You can't hurt me!" she blurted. "Dagon told me you can't hurt me! You're bound to me!"

Apep chuckled with malevolent delight. "But you fear me, all the same. I chase, you run. You can't help it."

Eve clenched her eyes closed. "No! No more surprises, no more running!" She clutched the disguised spell books tightly to her chest, keeping her eyes closed. "You said things only become real when they're observed, right? So if I don't look, none of this will be real!"

Apep laughed, his voice ringing in her head. "That's almost clever. But you use more than your eyes to observe the world around you. And if you somehow do manage to deprive all of your senses and pass out of my quantum realm, you land right back in my den of monsters." She felt his breath on the back of her neck. "And unlike me, they *can* harm you. So, if you're looking to survive, you're better off if you just stay and play in my little labyrinth of horrors."

Fuck. He was right. At least for now, her odds were better here. But when she opened her eyes, a tiny smirk quirked the corner of her lips, because she realized something.

She was a monster, too.

She looked at the books in her hand, and using Ruth's knowledge and Luc's powers, she transfigured them into hair ties. She rolled her neck side to side, then pulled her hair back into a ponytail and twisted the ties into her hair. Before turning to face Apep, who she could hear breathing behind her, she conjured an image in her head and mentally fortified it to match her will. If reality in his realm revolved around her ability to perceive it, to observe it, then she would draw forth the reality she wanted.

Game on.

When she turned, she smiled. "My turn."

Apep looked over at the red balloon hovering in the air next to his head, the string gripped tightly in his own hand. He gazed down at himself, mystified. He was in a yellow raincoat, wearing a pair of rainboots. "What the…"

"Welcome to *my* illusion, Peppy." Electricity skittered over the skin on Eve's forearms and hands. "Time to float."

Apep looked at her with wild delight. "A twist!" he declared gleefully. "You know how to play. That's good. It'll make your time here pass so much more smoothly until I get that grimoire."

Eve's brows pinched. "What?"

"You haven't figured it out? You may have learned how to change the scenery, but that doesn't change the fact that this is a prison, and you've been given a life sentence."

"You said I could leave."

"Absolutely! If you can find the exit. But you won't, unless you can deliver me the grimoire. Tell me where it is, and I'll give you a juicy hint on how to get out."

"You're never getting that grimoire," Eve hissed.

Apep pressed his hand to his chest. "You enjoy my company that much? I'm flattered."

"I'll just kill you."

Apep released the red balloon, allowing it to float up and away. "Kill me? Good luck." He shrugged out of the yellow raincoat, and Eve noticed he wasn't wearing a shirt beneath it. His golden skin shone with iridescent, almost imperceptible reptilian scales, and beneath them, he was covered in tattoos. He was lean, but his muscles were finely developed, and they pushed out in round bunches beneath his strangely beautiful canvas.

Stop looking at him like that.

He kept the black jeans and dark rain boots, but he pulled a grimy, bloodied hockey goalie mask from thin air and settled it over his face. His hand shot out, and Eve was startled when his fingers gripped her neck. He pulled her close to his face.

"But you can't touch me!" Eve choked out, sudden fear muddling her senses.

"Surprise! In this place, the rules don't *always* apply. I get to draw out realities where I'm not bound to you. That's my favorite part about the god's domain." Eve could hear the hidden smile in his voice. "It's absolute, delicious chaos."

Eve drew a surge of electricity up through her body and concentrated it at her neck, channeling it right to Apep's hand, shocking him. He quickly withdrew, shaking his hand and hissing through his teeth.

"Feisty!" Apep praised, heavily accentuating the F. "Good. You'll need it for the next phase of this game, now that I've found a reality where I can manhandle you."

Eve eyed him warily. "And what game is that?"

"Tag, and I'm 'it.'"

"What, like murder tag? You catch me, you kill me?"

Apep laughed darkly. He stepped close to her, and in a low, dangerous tone, he said, "Where's your sense of creativity? No. How about...I catch you, I fuck you."

Eve's eyes widened as she looked up at his hockey mask. "Are you serious? You fuck me, I'll kill you."

Apep tilted his head. "Or will you? Do you think you'll have the power to kill me here?" He took a step back. "Let's find out, shall we? A fuck to the death." When Eve didn't move, he placed one hand over his eyes, covering them. He held up three fingers. "Three...two...one...*ready or not, here I come.*"

41

The Poisoned Apple

Eve spun on her heel and took off like a bat out of hell. She noticed they were in a dark, creepy forest now, and branches grabbed and tore at her clothes while tree roots reached up and caught at her feet.

She needed a moment to think, to come up with a plan. She thought she'd gained the upper hand for a moment, but he'd turned the tables yet again, knocking her off-balance, keeping her in a state of reaction rather than action. She felt like the stupid babysitter scrambling away from the serial killer, tripping and stumbling over everything.

She took a quick glance behind her, and a little yelp of surprise sprang from her throat. Apep was right on her heels, racing after her, leaping effortlessly over logs and dodging limbs, his whitish goalie mask almost glowing in the darkness as it bobbed through the trees behind her.

Fuck fuck fuck.

Adrenaline surged through her veins, and her legs pushed harder. He'd rattled her confidence. If he caught her, would she be able to kill him? Would her curse take over and allow her to do what she needed to do to finally rid the world of him, or had this stupid domain stripped her of her ultimate power? She had no idea.

She glanced back again, and he was gone. She veered to the right and ran to a thick-trunked tree, pressing her back up against it. She gulped air and swiveled her head, scanning the darkness for that creepy mask, but she saw nothing but trees and shadows. She tried to slow her breath so she could hear better, but her pounding heart thundered away in her ears.

A fuck to the death. Did that mean he intended to kill her if she didn't kill him?

She suddenly scented him, and a hand crept from around the tree trunk behind her and brushed her ponytail from her shoulder. Eve yelped and took off at a dead run. She could hear Apep laughing sinisterly, but she couldn't be sure if his voice was resonating through the forest or straight into her brain.

One moment Eve was running, and the next, she was being lifted off her feet, Apep's hand around her throat, and she came down hard, slamming onto her back on the ground. Sticks and rocks jutted up, painfully cutting into her back as Apep sat on top of her.

She scrunched her whole face as she clamped her eyes shut, trying to change the situation with her mind. She'd done it once; she could do it again. Right?

But Apep's weight on top of her didn't disappear, and his hand on her throat didn't relent. He stroked a finger down her cheek with his other hand. "Nice try, little devil, but I'm already touching you. You're too entangled in this environment. You can't change this reality."

The beast inside of her stirred, finally awakening to the situation at hand. It coiled, and her body reacted much in the way it had when she'd tried to spar with Ramil: violent, murderous desire. *Dominate him. Devour him. Utterly annihilate him.* Her chest heaved as she opened her eyes and looked up at Apep's shirtless, tattooed body looming over her. He pulled the mask off, his hair spilling over his bronze eyes like sweet red wine as he sneered down at her.

"Wolf eyes," he remarked, looking back and forth between the altered golden orbs she was currently sporting. They didn't show through nearly as often when she had multiple specialties under her possession, but she could tell when they did shine through. "They suit you."

"More than you know," she replied, boldly dragging her gaze down to his lips, his neck, and his tattooed chest and shoulders. The sinewy cables of his inked forearms flexed as he squeezed her neck a little tighter, and she grinned up at him. "Just wait until the wolf who gave them to me finds out what you're doing to me."

He cocked a dark brow. "I killed the wolf."

"And I resurrected him." Eve ran her hands up Apep's thighs. "I should bring him your head," she threatened confidently. Her curse had slipped seamlessly into the control room and was running the show. Her blood ran hot with equal parts rage and desire. Neither fear nor reason were part of the equation any longer.

Take him. Own him. Destroy him.

Apep's eyes glittered darkly as he leaned down, his lips hovering a hair's breadth above hers, and he whispered, "Try it."

In one swift motion, she pressed one hand up against his chest and locked her other arm around the elbow of the arm he was squeezing her neck with, then thrust her hip up and knocked his elbow to the side, breaking his hold on her throat and sending him tumbling over in the leaves and forest floor debris. She rolled with him and landed on top of him, straddling his hard stomach.

She dug her fingers into his heavily tattooed bare chest and rolled her hips against him. He grabbed her wrists, then jerked her arms out wide, forcing her to fall forward, her face right next to his. They panted and stared at each other for a moment, sizing each other up. Eve bit her lip hard enough to draw blood, then whispered, "Just don't die before I get off, demon boy." Her lips crashed against his, and her blood hit his tongue.

An erotic, euphoric rage roared through her body, shooting tingles from her teeth to her toenails. It rippled through her core like the echoing report of a long-range rifle. She arched her back and cried out into his mouth, and he responded in kind, his fingers squeezing her wrists painfully, his hips bucking up against her. She clenched her muscular thighs to his sides, refusing to be unsaddled from her throne.

"So that's the power of the Abomination's venom," Apep marveled breathlessly. He released her wrists and raked both hands into her hair, pulling her back in for another searing, bloody kiss. He bit her lip sharply, lusting for more of her potent venom.

As desire raged between her thighs like an untamable wildfire, Eve reached between them, the palm of her hand sliding over the bulge in his pants. She needed his power. She *craved* it.

"Oh, you don't get that just yet, little devil." Apep pulled her hand away and sat up, his chest bumping against hers as she straddled his lap. His eyes danced with a menacing glee. "I want a taste of the poison between your legs."

Before she realized what was happening, Apep had flipped her around, shoving her face and chest down into the dirt with her ass in the air. He pulled her arms back and held her wrists tightly at the small of her back, and he wrapped his legs across the back of her shoulders, pressing her down into the ground. She struggled against him, but quickly realized that, even with Zeke's strength, Apep was still more powerful.

Shit.

She felt the fingers of Apep's free hand in the back of the waistband of her pants, and he roughly dragged her joggers and underwear over her embarrassingly exposed round ass and down her thighs.

And then she felt his hot breath dance over her sensitive flesh, and a thrill snaked up her spine and sent tendrils of heat simmering through her belly. He flattened his long, velvet tongue over her sex, and Eve parted her lips in an involuntary gasp, not caring about the dirt that pushed into her mouth.

Apep's lips brushed against her petals as he hummed and praised, "That's the sweetest peach I've ever tasted." He gave her another slow swipe of his tongue before he buried it deep into her center. He flexed and wiggled it inside of her, and she squirmed against his face at the sensation. Jesus, how long was his tongue? It filled her better than some of her old boyfriends had.

His tongue slowly slipped out of her, and he immediately returned that godly appendage to her clit, where he attacked with vigor.

"Oh, Jesus," Eve mewled, eating dirt as she panted and writhed against him, the ache in her core swelling to the point of bursting.

And just as she was about to climax, he stopped.

Oh, hell no. He wasn't going to edge *her*. The power of her curse reared its head, and Eve broke free from Apep's hold. She kicked one leg out of her joggers and tackled Apep onto his back. She slammed his wrists onto the ground and pressed her knees down onto his arms, his head between her thighs, and she lowered herself onto his face. She gazed ravenously down at the devilish eyes looking up at her. She fisted one hand into his hair and commanded, "Finish it."

He took her clit into his mouth and sucked, wriggling his tongue against her at a strong, steady pace.

Fuuuuuuck.

Eve's hips jerked as a powerful release tore through her, and her thighs clenched around Apep's head. She grinded on his face as she throbbed and pulsed against his tongue, riding out every last ripple of that decadent shockwave.

But as she wound down, her legs trembling, Apep took the opportunity to slip his arm free and reach up to grab her neck. He pushed her back as he sat up, and Eve hit the ground on her back with an unflattering grunt. Apep was on top of her, his hips between her thighs, the bulge under his jeans pressing uncomfortably against her over-sensitive, bare core.

"I'd love to fucking tear you apart, but this feels dangerous, little devil," he confessed as he hooked his hands under her knees and pushed her thighs wide open. He traced a finger up her bare skin, charting a slow, meandering path toward her greedy core. "There's an immense power simmering just below the surface, and it's tethered right between your legs." He plunged two fingers inside of her slick heat, cupping her mound with his palm. "What happens when it's unleashed?" he wondered suspiciously. "You taste like a sweet, innocent peach, but you are, in fact, the poisoned apple."

Eve bucked against his hand, her lip rolling between her teeth. "Why don't you try a bite? Don't tell me you're *scared*," she taunted.

Apep paused, his face betraying a sense of trepidation. "Scared? Never." He withdrew his fingers, looking down at the way her arousal glistened on them, and he narrowed his eyes. "But I'm not stupid, either."

And just like that, he vanished.

Eve sat up, startled. Her eyes swept the dark forest, but she was alone. Her curse screamed at her, hungry for the power it was promised, the power it had been denied. The crushing weight of her failure held her in place for a few moments as she came to terms with the fact that she had Apep centered in her sights, ready to take the kill shot, and she'd let him slip right through her fingers.

"Bitch!" Eve bellowed into the dark woods. "Get back here and finish what you started!"

Silence.

She'd fucked up. As she stood up and pulled her clothes back on, she felt the overpowering need aching between her legs.

Feed me.

Eve had released the beast into the pit, then denied her an opponent to devour. And she was having none of it. She demanded her hunger be sated.

Eve needed to get back to Bo. He could handle this. She drew her power to her eyes and tried to warp the space around her to get back to him, but the view that opened before her stopped her in her tracks.

Instead of seeing where she wanted to go, like she usually did, she saw flashes of different scenery flickering quickly before her eyes, like the world was a giant slot machine and she'd just pulled the lever.

She pulled back, not willing to take the risk. This quantum realm she was in must've been like riding a bullet train, and she wasn't about to try to jump out of it at full speed. She needed to figure out how to get out of this place.

She drew on what she'd learned from Apep: as long as she was observing her environment, she was stuck in whatever reality was before her. But if she could manage to close it out, deprive all her senses of the world around her, she could escape this labyrinth of possibilities and drop back into her own reality. Eve needed to create an environment that would be conducive to closing out everything around her.

The first thing that popped into her head fit perfectly into Apep's theme of horror for his quantum labyrinth: *Stranger Things*. Eve closed her eyes and imagined the sensory deprivation tank that was used to hone Eleven's psychic powers, and she imagined herself in the same float suit that Eleven wore. When she opened her eyes, her surroundings had changed. She was in a sanitized, white clinical setting, and she looked down at the large, cylindrical tank of water before her. There were noise-cancelling ear plugs in her hand, so she stuck them in. Her world went silent, and she was reminded of when she dived into Isaac's head.

There was a heavy, space-age looking helmet on the floor next to her, so she lifted it and placed it over her head. She climbed down the ladder into the tank, and she felt the float suit doing its job as she went deeper into the pitch black depths of the tank. The water was at just the right temperature that it felt neither hot nor cold. She reached up and pulled the lid down over her head and let go of the ladder.

She was bathed in complete darkness, silence, and floating in an abyss. Panic flared in her chest. Her eyes widened, but she saw nothing, as though she were blind. She suddenly couldn't tell up from down, and she felt like she was spinning out of control. She threw her hands out to grab for the ladder, but it was gone. She flailed and gulped air from the helmet, but after a few moments, she began to mentally talk herself down.

This is the way out. Calm. Nothing will hurt you. Calm. Breathe in, two, three, four. Hold, two, three, four, five, six, seven. Out, two, three, four, five, six, seven, eight. Again...

After a few of these measured breaths, Eve began to feel her heart rate return to normal, and the tingling in her scalp and limbs subsided. A serenity seeped through her as she floated in this silent nothingness, and for a moment, she wondered if this was what it felt like to be dead.

If so, it wasn't so bad.

Eve slowly became aware of a hardness against her back. She blinked her eyes open and found herself lying supine on the floor in the bedroom at the Montana ranch. The sky out the window was already starting to brighten, heralding the looming dawn, which meant Eve had been gone for hours. Her sense of urgency returned, crushing the calm of the moment before, and with it, a flood of need cascaded over her.

She needed to get back to her boys. *Now.* She went to the closet and quickly grabbed the antique-looking physician's bag she knew Ruth kept her unique supplies in, then she summoned the energy to warp and compress the space between herself and the place she wanted to be – the place she would find relief from this deep, incessant aching between her thighs.

She was no longer in Montana, but again staring at the front porch of her old home. Golden light splashed across the treetops around the lake, the morning sun already hanging low in the east. Eve noticed the Toyota was gone, but the voracious curse inside of her was drawn to something...someone...still inside the house. Her feet carried her up the steps and through the door, her nose already hot on his scent.

He was alone.

Vulnerable.

An easy target.

She dropped the physician's bag at the door, tearing the hair ties from her ponytail and tossing them onto the bag, allowing them to return to their original spell book form, before stalking back to the bedroom where she knew she would find him.

42

Exorcise Me, Priest

When she pushed through the door, Isaac looked up from his book, his back leaned casually against the wall, his elbows resting on his knees. He didn't look surprised to see her, as though he already sensed her presence, but then he caught a glimpse of her aura. He swiftly stood, his hand reflexively tracing the sign of the cross as he faced her, his eyes taking in the air around her.

"You're alone," Eve said aloud as she pointed at him and held her hand at chest height and tightly circled a D-handshape.

Bo and the boys went to check the hotel. He thought you might be there, Isaac signed. Then he indicated her aura. He raised flat palms upward, then flipped two D-handshapes from palm up to palm down. *What happened?*

Eve closed the distance between her and Isaac, and he held his ground, stiffening at her approach. He held his hands ready to fend off whatever she threw at him, not sure what to expect. Eve reached for his face, but Isaac captured her wrists in his heavy-knuckled hands and held them tightly. She barely noticed as she slammed her body against his, looking up at him with fire in her eyes. She pressed a light kiss to the base of his neck, then dragged her tongue up over his Adam's apple, then under his jaw. She lifted onto her toes and touched her lips to the corner of his mouth, giving his lower lip a nibble.

He didn't shy away from her. She could feel his heavy breaths caressing her skin, his chest rising and falling against hers. She was losing grasp of her last thread of control, and his lack of resistance only fanned those flames. It felt an awful lot like submission.

"You know what I need," she said, leaning back a little so he could see her mouth.

"I don't think I can fix this," he worried aloud, his hands still occupied with confining her wrists. "You're too far gone. You need Bo."

Eve smirked at Isaac and sing-songed, "Bo isn't heeeere." Her eyes dropped to his lips, and she licked hers hungrily. "But you are." She looked back up into his deep brown eyes. "Exorcise me, priest."

Isaac's eyes darkened, and he set his jaw. He flipped Eve around and slammed her back against the wall, pressing her wrists over her head. "Fine. But first – confess. What did you do? How did you get this way?"

Fury seeped into Eve's expression. "I had him. I was close enough to kill him. But as soon as I let the monster out to play, he ran."

"Who?"

"Apep. He started this demolition machine and just left it running." Eve rubbed herself against the enormous bulge growing in Isaac's pants and watched the pulse point on his neck jump quickly. "I need you to shut this thing down before I do some real damage."

"I don't think an exorcism is going to work for this," he admitted, his breath heavy.

"Come on, Isaac. Bless me from the inside," she begged. Desperation soaked her underwear, her potent venom silently beckoning to Isaac.

He didn't ignore that call. She knew he wanted this. He's been wanting this again ever since the cemetery. He just needed a reason.

Any reason.

He released her wrists, and her hands flew to unfasten and lower his pants. He made no attempt to stop her, nor did he hesitate after she kicked her joggers off and hooked a leg around his hip. He buried the head of his massive cock between her legs and thrust up into her, slamming her back against the wall forcefully. One hand gripped her thigh, holding it in place over his hip, while his other hand slid up to her neck.

Oh god, the way he filled her. She winced a little as he stretched her to her limits and pushed deeper inside of her than anyone else ever had. It was like he was trying to touch her soul with his cock. She whimpered as he drove into her, slow and deep at first. She clung to him, both arms over his shoulders, needing more. *More.* She rocked her hips faster, urging him on.

He grunted, dropping his hand from her neck as he reached down and gripped her other thigh. He lifted her off the ground, settling her weight on his hips as he pressed her harder into the wall. His cock sank even deeper, and she cried out.

But still, she needed *more.* The monster inside of her had been promised blood. Power. A sacrifice. *Kill him.*

She began to twist her fingers into his hair and clench her thighs around him, and the rising rage began to creep up her spine. She took her heel and kicked it into the back of his knee while she pushed off the wall, torquing her body to throw him down. He swore at her as they hit the ground and she tried to roll on top of him. But he wasn't having it. He forced her onto her back and thrust into her, hard, making her whimper.

He began to chant something she didn't understand, and the sharp, violent urge suddenly began to dull. He spoke quickly, though breathlessly, as if he were reciting something from memory as he fucked her on the floor.

"*...omnis satanica potestas, omnis incursion infernalis adversarii, omnis legio, omnis congragatio et secta diabolica...*"

His words, spoken in a firm, heated tone, pushed down and subdued the darkness inside of her as one hand held both of her wrists to the floor and the other hand held a fistful of her hair, keeping her face focused on him. She gazed up at the inferno in his eyes, mesmerized, as he finished with, "*...Ab insidiis diaboli, libera nos, Domine. Ut Ecclesiam tuam secura tibi facias libertate servire, te rogamus, audi nos.*"

The savage instinct that thirsted for blood took a knee, bowing instead to the hunger for pleasure.

Eve's lip quirked up at the corner. "That was so fucking hot," she confessed.

Isaac looked down at her, and for a split second, Eve saw something in those dark eyes that made her heart flutter. But before she had time to study his face, he crushed his lips to hers, kissing her deeply. He released his grip on her hair and brought his palm back to her throat, and she moaned for him as his tongue danced with hers. He moved his hips in deep, rolling thrusts, and the way he felt inside her drew a wild sound from Eve that she'd never heard rise from her own throat before. The orgasm hit her like Mike Tyson in his prime, and might've even taken a chunk of her ear while it was at it. She keened and clung to Isaac for dear life as she rode the crest for so long it almost became painful.

A priest shouldn't fuck like this.

As she lay beneath him, shaking, still pulsing around his monstrous cock, she realized he hadn't finished yet. He looked down at her and breathed, "I want to see that one more time. It's like seeing the face of God. It's fucking beautiful." He sat back, kneeling, and pulled her onto his lap. He wrapped one arm around her waist and splayed his other hand over her upper back as he guided her into a slow, easy pace.

Eve gazed into his eyes as he grazed his hand up her back and cupped it around the nape of her neck, and he glanced at the air around her. An uncharacteristic grin of pride lit up his face.

"What?" Eve asked.

"You're bright again," Isaac revealed. He pulled her to him, pressing a searing kiss to her lips as she rode him slowly.

Eve wrapped her arms around his neck and gyrated her hips, feeling every inch of him inside of her. The desire burning in her core had nothing to do with her curse any longer. No, this was all her.

Not the Abomination and the Angel of Death. Just Eve and Isaac, too lost in each other to heed the fact that this was forbidden between them.

Isaac gripped her tightly as he met her gyrations with long, deep strokes. She felt that sweet heat unfurling in her core again, and she rocked her hips faster. "Harder," she begged, her cheek pressed against his as her body melded against his. She knew Isaac couldn't hear her or see her lips moving, but he didn't need to. He read her body, knowing exactly what she was asking for. He jerked his hips up, driving into her with force, carrying Eve closer to the precipice of bliss.

Isaac felt the way she began to pulse around him, her walls gripping him tighter. He grabbed her around the throat and pulled her mouth to his, a low groan rumbling in his chest as he kissed her like he owned her. He brought his lips to her ear and stroked his thumb over her throat. "Come for me," he commanded.

She was already there, a moan erupting from her as she came undone once again, her head thrown back in wild abandon as she reveled in the explosion of euphoria. She felt him swell and spasm inside of her, on the heels of her release, and the room was filled with the erotic exultations of their pleasure.

As they came down from that ultimate high, panting and sweaty, Eve heard a car pull into the driveway. She shot to attention. "Shit," she blurted, leaping up and snatching her pants off the floor. She quickly signed to Isaac, *Get dressed!*

She paused and listened once she was dressed. She should be able to hear them talking. She should hear better than this. She inhaled, and quickly realized her wolfish sense of smell was gone.

Oh no.

Oh no.

She whispered a simple incantation to ignite a scrap of paper on the floor, but it didn't burst into flame. Nothing happened.

No!

She turned on Isaac, who was brushing his palms over the wrinkles on his shirt. He glanced up at her, and the lazy, content expression on his face shifted to one of concern. He tapped a Y-handshape to his chin twice. *What's wrong?*

Eve frantically signed, *Did you exorcise my stolen powers?!*

Isaac furrowed his brow and shrugged. He tapped his temple with his fingers and turned his palm outward as he drew it away. *I don't know. They're gone?*

Bo and the boys walked into the house. Eve heard Bo call out to her, his tone urgent, but she didn't respond. She was lost in her own mind, in her realization that she couldn't save Mòrag. Those spell books she risked so much to collect were useless to her if she didn't have Luc's powers of sorcery.

She sank to her knees on the floor in utter defeat.

43

We Kill Monsters

Bo stepped into the room with Zeke and Eoduun hot on his heels. He had his phone up to his ear, and Eve suspected he was talking to Luc. "She's here. She's safe. We'll talk later." He shoved the phone into his pocket and, the next moment, he was in Isaac's face. He audibly sniffed the air around him, his scarred wolf eye flashing gold. He fixed Isaac with a murderous stare as Zeke and Eoduun came to Eve's side to make sure she was ok.

For the first time ever, Bo slipped his mask down so Isaac could read his lips. In a low, threatening tone, he seethed, "Touch what's mine again, and I'll cut you into pieces and send you back to Vatican City in a barrel of acid."

"Bo!" Eve expostulated.

Isaac met Bo's threat with an unwavering gaze, his expression as dismissively bored as ever.

"What happened?" Eoduun wanted to know, narrowing his eyes at Isaac. He took a confrontational step forward, but Bo held his hand up to stop him.

"Nothing," Bo said, still looking at Isaac. He pulled his mask back up and turned his mismatched eyes to Eve, who was still sitting on the floor. "How many fucking times do I need to tell you to stop running off on your own?! Montana? Really?!" he demanded. "And if you're going to do stupid shit, at least bring a goddamn phone with you, and stop using Dagon as a fucking telegraph!"

Anger rose in Eve's chest, but she knew she deserved every bit of Bo's wrath. She tried to remain calm as she stood up and explained, "I went to get Ruth's spell books so I could send Mòrag back to Scotland. I had no problem getting there, but I had to wait a while to build up the power to make the jump back, and…well…I ran into a little hiccup."

"Yeah, Apep. We fucking heard that, too. Jesus Christ, Evie," Bo exhaled, running his hand down his face. "You're going to put me into an early grave, you know that? And probably yourself while you're at it. This has to *stop*." He glanced back at Isaac, and added, "All of it."

Eve lowered her gaze to the floor. "I know. But I couldn't just sit by and let you kill Mòrag when I had the power to save her. If I told you what I had planned, you would've tried to stop me."

"Fucking right I would have! It was a shit plan, Evie!"

She looked toward the door where the spell books and Ruth's supply bag sat. "It almost worked," she said regretfully. "I can't work a spell now, but maybe if we come back—"

"The nuckelavee's dead, Eve," Eoduun interrupted.

Lead filled Eve's stomach as her head jerked toward him. "What the fuck do you mean she's dead?"

"I mean exactly what I said," he replied, exhausted irritation in his tone.

Eve looked around at her team. "Did you kill her?" She shot Bo an accusatory scowl. "I told you to wait!"

"You don't call the shots, Evie!" Bo shouted, and there was a sad desperation in his voice. "I told you, sometimes you have to make the hard choice. But sometimes the hard choice is made for you, and you just have to accept it. I'm sorry, and I know you hate me right now, but you need to accept that this is part of the gig. We kill monsters."

Eve's nostrils burned, signaling the beginning of angry tears. "You *are* monsters." She pushed past Zeke and Eoduun and shoulder-checked Bo on her way out. She grabbed Ruth's stuff and went to the car, dropping into the passenger seat and slamming the door. She couldn't stand to be touched by any of them right now, so there was no way she was squeezing in the backseat with anyone. Let them figure out how to fit back there.

The ride back to Nebraska was almost as quiet as it was long, because Bo drove all the way through instead of stopping at a motel. Eve stared out the window the whole ride back, ignoring all calls and texts from Luc, as well. She knew he had a hand in the decision to kill Mòrag. Other than Sister Fiona, he was the top shot-caller. He could've put a stop to the hunt. He could've given Mòrag a second chance.

But, by his own admission, he didn't believe in second chances.

Well, Eve did. And it was that moment that she finally made the decision to give Ruth a second chance. If Ruth had been there, part of the team, with all of her memories and knowledge of sorcery, *she* could've saved Mòrag.

It was time to give Ruth her memories back, and Eve had a vague idea of how she might be able to do it.

But she would need Dagon's powers to be able to feed the memories back into Ruth's mind, and that posed a whole new dilemma to figure out.

By the time they arrived at the compound, it was already late, and darkness had fallen. Eve stormed ahead of the team with her luggage bag as she headed to her apartment. She'd ignored Zeke's offer to carry her bags for her, and wordlessly wrenched her arm from Eoduun's grip when he tried to confront her about her persisting grudge, not bothering to argue with him. The endless hours in the car had done nothing to dampen her resentment.

Bo and Isaac gave her a wide berth, though Eve frequently felt their eyes upon her.

She just wanted to be alone.

When she stepped into her apartment, however, her gaze was immediately drawn to the ridiculously handsome, fair-haired psychopath asleep on her couch.

Goddamn it, Luc.

She cursed the way her heart swelled at the mere sight of him, despite her lingering anger. She heard the boys coming down the hall behind her, so she quietly stepped in and closed the door behind her. She kicked her shoes off and left her luggage by the door, silently moving toward the couch in her stocking feet. She rested her elbows on the back of the couch and looked down at Luc.

His pale eyelashes fanned out over his flawless cheekbones, and his white hair fell in beautiful disarray over his forehead. His arms were stoically crossed over his chest, his ankles crossed and propped on the far arm of the couch. His breath came slow and even, and Eve subconsciously matched her breathing with the rise and fall of his chest. He was still dressed in a three-piece suit with his sunglasses tucked into his breast pocket, which made her wonder if he'd come straight here from wherever he'd been.

He looked so sweet and innocent when he was asleep.

As angry as she was, she couldn't stop herself from climbing over the back of the couch and sliding down onto him. She slipped his sunglasses from his pocket and deposited them safely on the coffee table before draping herself over him like a weighted blanket and nestling her forehead against his neck. A deep, contented rumble sounded in his chest, and his arms unfolded from under her and wrapped around her, engulfing her.

"Mmm, my baby's home," he sighed in a soft, husky voice. He stroked one big hand soothingly over her hair. "I missed you like crazy, love," he confessed.

Eve blinked her misty eyes and inhaled deeply. "I missed you, too." She didn't even realize the truth to those words until right now.

"You were ghosting me," he pointed out.

"I can miss you *and* be mad at you."

Luc lifted his head. "What did I do now?"

Eve pushed up off of him reluctantly. She sat on his stomach with her palms on his chest and looked down at those mesmerizing aquamarine eyes, and she almost forgot what she was mad about. Almost.

"Did you tell Bo and the boys to kill the nuckelavee?"

Luc stared back at her, confused. "Did *I* tell them to? They didn't have a choice. Bo said it attacked them when you took off to Montana. What were they supposed to do?"

Eve tucked her chin, furrowing her brow. "What do you mean it attacked them? No one told me that." Eve's heart sank with guilt.

Luc gave her a knowing smirk. "Did you give them a chance to tell you before jumping to conclusions?"

Eve closed her eyes and tilted her head back, sighing heavily. "Fuck." She shook her head. "They should've said something. We had the whole ride home, and no one explained the situation to me."

"Did you *ask* what the situation was?"

Eve stood up, feeling like a total twat. She didn't answer the question he already knew the answer to. "They should've told me."

Luc sat up and swung his legs off the couch, caging her legs between his thighs. He took her hands in his and arched a brow at her. "Maybe they were mad at you, too," he reasoned. He lifted her hand and brought it to his lips, kissing her knuckles. "Why did you want to spare the beast, anyway? Nasty things, nuckelavees."

"She watched over me and protected me when I was growing up."

"So I heard. But am I also to understand that its protective disposition was prompted by an enchantment?"

Eve frowned. "Her feelings were real. I felt them through her memories."

"Were they?" Luc doubted. "It takes powerful sorcery to bind a nuckelavee to a body of freshwater. I mean, I understand *why* they used that particular creature to protect you – it's an absolute unit, and vicious as they come. Someone with that kind of power would have no issue making an enchantment feel like genuine sentiment. Enchantment hinges on the ability to manipulate the target's emotions. Alter emotions, and you can make anyone do anything."

Eve's certainty faltered. "But...I went to all that effort to try to save her. All of it...it was for nothing? The second I released her from her enchantment, she would've gone right back to hating me?" Eve shook her head. "No. No! Because she *did* hate me at first. She resented that she had to protect me, so the enchantment didn't make her *like* me. She *grew* to like me. That was genuine. I know it, Luc."

Luc sighed. "Deliberating the sincerity of her feelings isn't going to bring her back. And I'm going to be honest with you, love. The boys made the right call. The only call."

Bring her back. "Wait. I could bring her back to life, couldn't I?" Eve said hopefully. "Maybe it's not too late!"

Luc gripped her hands tighter and held her gaze. "No, love," he said softly. "You know what we do with a body when we kill a monster. That nuckelavee is nothing but ash and bone by now. You know this." He rose to his feet and hugged Eve, cradling her head against his chest.

She sagged into him. "I'm just so fucking mad," she grumbled against his chest. "I'm mad at Bo and the team for killing her. I'm mad at you for agreeing with their decision to do it. I'm mad at Mòrag for attacking them and forcing their hand. I'm mad at Isaac for exorcising my powers, rendering me absolutely fucking useless with the spell books I stole. But most of all, I'm mad at myself - for taking such a stupid risk, for disappointing everyone, for *wanting* to save Mòrag, for not being *able* to save her..."

Luc took her by the shoulders and pushed her back a step so he could look at her face. "Whoa, whoa, skip back a bit. What do you mean Isaac exorcised your powers?"

Shit. Eve hesitated. She looked up at the ceiling and chewed on her lip. When her eyes returned to his, she could see the jealousy fracturing those aqua pools, reading her like a book.

His voice darkened. "What did he do, Eve?"

"It was my fault. When I came back from Montana, my curse was activated after being attacked by Apep, and Isaac was the only one around to handle it. But when he tried to get it under control, he said some Latin shit, and *poof*! All of my stolen powers were gone."

Confusion and disbelief settled onto the planes of his handsome face. "So…he just wiped the whole fucking slate?"

"He shook the Etch A Sketch."

"With an exorcism prayer?"

"I assume so. Well, I mean, the prayer and—"

Luc scrunched his face and waved his hand, interrupting her. "Yeah, yeah, I get the fucking picture." He propped his hands on his hips. "Well, shit. You can't make a jump with me. I guess we'll have to take the jet tomorrow morning."

It was Eve's turn to be confused. "Did you plan for us to jump somewhere?"

"I found Stacey Rose's daughter."

44

Let Me Tell You About My Nuckelavee

"Well, not her real daughter," he amended. "The child you were switched with. It appears she raised her as her own. Her name is Emma."

"Where is she?"

"Michigan. Just outside of Grand Rapids."

"And what, you were just going to drop in on her? And say what, exactly?"

"That we're cold case detectives investigating her mother's death, and we wanted to interview her. Seems the obvious choice."

Eve's apartment door opened, and Isaac strolled in. It startled her because she hadn't heard him approaching. She had gotten too used to having Bo's hypersensitive hearing and olfactories. She couldn't even smell the cigarette smoke on him from here. He dropped his duffle bag on the floor next to Eve's luggage, gave Luc a curt nod to acknowledge him, then headed toward the kitchen.

"First things first," Luc said, watching Isaac in the kitchen with a steel gaze. "I need to show Isaac his new apartment. He can't stay with you anymore, love. I'll end up murdering him." He picked up his sunglasses from the coffee table and slid them onto his face.

Eve knew the change in accommodations was coming, but she still felt a small pang of disappointment. She liked having Isaac with her. But she also liked him being alive.

Eve followed along as Luc walked Isaac down the hall to his new flat. He showed him to the door between Cassie and Ruger's and Ramil's apartments. It was a little further down the hall than Eve hoped for, but at least he was still on her floor.

Luc swung the door open and held it wide. "Home sweet home," he said and signed to Isaac. Then added, "Until you go back to Rome, anyway."

Isaac sauntered into the apartment, Luc and Eve trailing behind him. He looked around at the familiar setup. It was nearly identical to Eve's apartment. He disappeared into the bedroom with his duffle bag, and Eve flopped down on his couch.

"This is just like my couch," she remarked, lying back and stretching out.

"They had a sale," Luc replied, resting his hands on the back of the couch, looking down at her. "I have four more just like it."

Isaac came back from the bedroom wearing a clean shirt and a book in his hand. He sat on the couch near Eve's feet, crossed one ankle over his knee, and started reading. Eve toed the cover of his book to get a better look at it, and he glanced over at her.

Still working on Moby Dick? she signed.

It's a long book, he signed back.

"Sister Fiona tells me you have a video conference with her tomorrow night," Luc spoke and signed at Isaac, interrupting. "What are you going to tell her?"

Isaac shrugged.

Luc leaned forward, as though he were expecting more, but it never came. "Fascinating. More specifically, do you think you'll be gracing us with your presence much longer?"

Isaac's eyes met Eve's briefly before answering. He shrugged again, then held his palms up, lifting them alternately. *Maybe.*

"You're just a fountain of information. Maybe I should sit in on this meeting, too," Luc said and signed. He adjusted his collar. "I think I'll make arrangements to do so. I trust you don't mind."

"I thought you wanted to go interrogate that Emma lady," Eve pointed out.

"I can Zoom from anywhere. Besides, the Vatican might be interested to know what kind of activities their Angel of Death has been up to."

Isaac signed, *I've kept Eve's curse under control when needed. They only care that I do my job. They don't care how I get it done.*

"We'll see about that." Luc reached down for Eve's hand, and when she took it, he helped her to her feet from the couch. "I think I almost preferred it when I was afraid he was going to *kill* you."

Eve cast him a surprised look.

"I said *almost*." He led her to the door, then turned back to Isaac and signed and said, "Enjoy the apartment. Don't feel obligated to leave it. Feel free to be a stranger."

"Luc," Eve chastised, shoving his towering frame out the door. She turned back to Isaac and signed, *You're always welcome at the zoo. Come see me any time.* She could feel movement behind her, and she turned to look at Luc.

He quickly dropped his hands and smiled innocently at her.

"Don't threaten him behind my back," she reprimanded him.

"I would never," he promised saccharinely.

"Right," Eve shot back sarcastically. "Never."

"I threaten him in *front* of you. I *insult* him behind your back," he corrected.

Eve sighed, stepping out into the hallway and shutting Isaac's door behind her. "You're impossible."

"But in an endearing, hopelessly adorable way, right?" he said brightly as he fell into step next to her.

"No. None of that."

A door opened behind them, and Eve heard Cassie's excited squeal. "Eve! I thought I heard you out here!" She barely had time to brace herself before Cassie plowed into her, hopping onto her back and hugging her arms around Eve's neck. "I've missed you, girl!" She planted a lip-glossed kiss on Eve's cheek.

Eve laughed and patted Cassie's arm. "I missed you too, Cass. I hope you and Ruth didn't have too much fun without me."

Cassie released Eve and walked alongside her, and she made a disgusted sound. "Ugh. Definitely not. All she wanted to do was talk about *Ramil*, and see what *Ramil* was doing, and hang out with *Ramil*. I am so ready to talk about something else. *Anything* else."

"Let me tell you about my nuckelavee."

Cassie glanced over at Luc, then leaned in to whisper in Eve's ear. "Is that like a sex thing?"

If Eve wasn't still upset about the whole situation with Mòrag, she would've laughed hysterically. Instead, she just smirked. "No. Not a sex thing."

"So, is Isaac back, too, then?" Cassie inquired casually.

"He is. And he has his own apartment now, too. Right next door to you."

Cassie's eyes lit up. "Well, isn't that convenient?"

As they approached Eve's apartment door, Zeke opened his door and stepped into the hallway, carrying a plate of chicken nuggets. When he saw Eve, a contrite smile graced his features. He held out the paper plate to Eve. "Peace offering? I heated them to perfection. And look! They're shaped like dinosaurs. I made them just for you."

Eve smiled softly as she took the plate from Zeke. "Thanks, Z. They're perfect."

"I'm sorry we killed your zombie horse," he apologized quietly.

Eve exhaled. "I know." She lifted onto her toes and pressed a kiss to his cheek.

Luc cleared his throat behind her.

Eve rolled her eyes. She tilted her head toward her apartment door and told Zeke, "You may enter."

Eve sat at the kitchen island with Cassie sitting next to her, eating nuggets and regaling her with the events of the previous few days, while Zeke provided supporting details. Luc stood with his hands gripping the edge of the counter by the fridge, leaned back, watching Eve from behind his sunglasses as she orated. She knew Bo kept him updated when they were on the road, but now he could hear her whole side of the story.

Well, the parts she wanted to share, anyway.

As she was telling Cassie about the nuckelavee's memories, Eoduun walked into the kitchen. He held up a jar of pickles.

"I found an extra jar in my fridge. Thought I'd put it in your fridge…in case you wanted any."

Another peace offering.

"Thanks."

He stuck them in the fridge, but not before opening them and taking one out with his fingers. As he snapped a bite out of it, he said, "You know, we wouldn't have killed that fucking thing if it hadn't attacked us first."

"I know. I mean, I *didn't* know then, but I do now."

Eoduun looked at the pickle in his hands. "I won't apologize for it, but I don't like that it upset you."

Eve rested her chin in her hand. That was as close to an apology as Eoduun was capable of. "I know." She regarded both him and Zeke. "I should've listened to the whole story. I'm still upset she had to die, but I understand, and I don't blame you guys for it. I'm sorry I was such an asshole about it."

"You were a huge asshole about it," Eoduun agreed.

Eve pressed her eyes closed for a moment and flared her nostrils, taking a beat before responding. "Let's just say we're good, ok?"

He shrugged and stuck the rest of the pickle in his mouth. "We're good."

Ruger's voice sprang up loudly from the doorway. "Rumor has it, you fucks took down a *nuckelavee*," he called out, obviously impressed with such news. Moments later, he and Remi appeared in the kitchen. "Please tell me it's true. Was it fucking disgusting? I've always wanted to see one."

Everyone looked at Eve, gauging her reaction before speaking, so she spoke first. "It's true, and, yes, it was pretty nasty. And I hope we never run into another one ever again."

"I'd never heard of a nuckelavee before today," Cassie said. "It never came up in any of my training."

"We're not supposed to have them here," Ruger replied. "How did it get here?"

"I was just getting to that part," Eve said, then continued telling them about what she saw in the nuckelavee's memories.

Just as Eve was getting to the part where she made the jump to Montana, she heard a deep, male voice in the hallway, and something about it made her skin prickle. Then she heard Ruth say, "Oh, Eve must be back." Moments later, Ramil and Ruth walked into the already crowded kitchen.

Cassie pointed a finger between the two of them. "You two have been connected at the hip."

Ruth smiled up at Ramil. "He's been helping me try to relearn how to use my powers." She cast her eyes over the faces in the room, then settled on Luc, and excitedly informed him, "Today I was able to cast a spell on a rat that compelled it attack anything we marked with a laser pointer. And then, I was able to revoke the spell. I've been having trouble revoking."

"She's making wonderful strides," Ramil praised. He looked over at Eve. "How was your hunt? Are we toasting to success tonight?"

Eve shook her head somberly. "This wasn't a kill to be celebrated." Then she looked from Ruth to Ramil, and asked, "You're helping Ruth train? Are you a sorcerer?"

He shrugged. "I've been known to dabble. I can work a spell in a pinch."

Eve glanced at Luc, and with the way his head was turned toward Ruth and Ramil, she could see his eyes behind his sunglasses. His gaze was ice-cold as he regarded Ramil. Something wasn't sitting right with him, but he didn't speak up.

Eve turned her attention to Ruth. "Speaking of your powers, I think I may have figured out a way to return your memories to you." Everyone's attention snapped to Eve, including Luc's. "I just need to obtain the powers I need, and maybe we can try it."

Ruth's eyes widened. "That would be amazing!"

Luc pushed off the counter. "Well, sounds like we need to strategize. If you'll all excuse us, Eve and I have business to attend to."

"Sure, *business*," Eoduun said spitefully as he rolled his eyes and pushed away from the kitchen island.

As Luc began to usher everyone else toward the door, Ramil approached Eve. She fought the urge to slide from the barstool to put space between them. He bent down and whispered in her ear, "If you think my powers would be useful, I am happy to offer them to you."

Eve's eyes rounded. She leaned away from him. "Do you even know what has to happen for me to take them?"

A low chuckle bobbed in his throat. "Everyone in Knighco knows." He stood up straight and grinned down at her. "I've heard you don't tolerate Luc's sorcery powers well, so I thought maybe mine would suit you better. That's all." As he turned to leave, he added, "Give it some thought."

Luc returned to the kitchen just as Ramil was walking out, and he looked to Eve questioningly. "Did I miss something?"

Once Ramil was out the door, she blurted, "Do you know Ramil is a monster?"

Luc removed his sunglasses and stuck them in the breast pocket of his shirt. His beautiful eyes narrowed thoughtfully. "Well...sort of." Then he arched a brow at her. "But no one else knows aside from Sister Fiona and Mira. How did you find out?"

Skipping over his question, Eve asked, "What do you mean sort of?" she asked, crossing her arms.

"Tell me how you found out. Was it Isaac?" He seemed more curious than suspicious.

But he should be suspicious, because she found out using Dagon's stolen powers that she shouldn't have had, and never told anyone she'd taken. He'd be livid if he knew.

"Isaac said he had a dark energy, but it was through Dagon I found out he was some kind of monster." Not a lie. "So why do you say he's 'sort of' a monster?"

"Because we can't pinpoint *what* he is. He's an orphan who was taken in and raised in an obscure monster cult hellbent on triggering the apocalypse. We had a run-in with them a few years ago, and he jumped ship when he realized he was fighting for the wrong side and had been brainwashed his whole life."

"You gave him a second chance? I thought you didn't do second chances," Eve pointed out.

"No, I gave him a *chance,* and he took it. If he were to fuck it up now, there would be no *second* chance."

Eve circled back to the original point. "So, you took in a monster, but you have no idea what he is."

"We have no information on his biological family, and his genetic code is a dead end in our databases. We don't know what he is, but we know he's something not quite human."

"He doesn't know, either? Dagon said he thought he might be some kind of hybrid, but not the kind Ruth was cooking up. A born hybrid."

"Interesting. If Ramil does know, he's been hiding it."

After a brief lull, Eve revealed, "He offered his powers to me."

Fury ignited in Luc's eyes and his brows shot into his hairline. "What the fuck did you say?" Static crackled in the air.

"He suggested his powers might help me return Ruth's memories to her."

"Absolutely fucking not." Luc began to pace. "He offered himself to you while I was standing right fucking there?" He pointed dramatically toward the door.

Eve rose from her seat and caught him around the waist, hugging herself to his enormous body, forcing him to stand still. "Luc, I think you're going to have to come to terms with the fact that my power *is sex*. You can't get jealous when I actually need to use it."

She felt him stiffen at those words. In a slow, measured tone, he asked, "Do you *need* to take his powers?"

"I don't think so." Eve felt the relief wash through him, and his body relaxed. But it would be short-lived, because she followed it up with, "I need Dagon's powers."

45
There Are Mountains Even I Cannot Move

Luc began to laugh, but he was anything but amused. It was the laughter that comes from surprise, from rage, from an inability to process the emotions surging through one's soul.

This was the kind of maniacal laughter that Eve had been conditioned to fear more than any other kind of reaction. It was the laughter that came before an explosion – one that usually left bruises and scars. Adam's lessons were branded deeply on her heart, and knowing he was dead did nothing to fix the damage he'd done when he was alive. Even now, her body went immediately into defensive mode, and she quickly pulled away from Luc.

He eyed her incredulously. "Are you insane? No." He shook his head. "No. Just…no. Not fucking happening." He gestured sharply between them. "We already agreed that Dagon was a no-go."

Eve surveyed his body movements acutely, being sure to keep a safe buffer between them. Her muscles were tensed, ready to spring away from him if needed. She felt naked without the stolen powers she'd become so accustomed to having at her fingertips. Right now, she was helpless if he decided to retaliate violently. She had no power over him.

She spoke firmly, but quietly. "We agreed he wouldn't be a casual partner. This is different. I just need his powers."

"To help *Ruth?!*" he spat, flinging his arm out to gesture generally in the direction of Ruth's apartment. Eve flinched away and briefly threw her guard up, and Luc blinked in surprise at her stance. She quickly dropped her hands to her sides. Luc closed his eyes and inhaled deeply, then dropped down to the least intimidating position he could think of: sitting cross-legged on his hands in the middle of the floor between the kitchen and living room. He looked like an over-sized child in time out, and the visual snapped Eve back to her senses.

Luc wouldn't hurt her. He would never hurt her.

His voice was softer when he continued, "The risk is not worth the reward. I can't trust Dagon with you. I will not budge on this."

Eve plopped down onto the floor in front of him, facing him, her knees touching his. "I need the ability to push thoughts and impressions into the minds of others. Dagon is the only one I know who can do that...considering he can get in my dreams and make me see and experience things." And she's seen him use those powers, and she's used those powers before, though she wasn't about to tell Luc that.

"Maybe you can twist Eoduun's powers enough to accomplish that," he suggested. "If you can puppet another person, literally wear them like a damn glove, I have to imagine you can push her memories back into her head with the same power."

Eve shook her head. "Eoduun can receive, but he can't give. His specialty allows me in, and allows me to access and take memories. I can piggyback off his specialty with my own ability to take control of someone's body, but those powers don't allow me to impart or leave anything behind."

"And you believe Dagon's powers can accomplish this?"

She nodded.

Luc studied her uneasily. "Did Dagon suggest this?"

"No. He doesn't know what I'm planning. And don't forget – if I steal his abilities, then I'll be stronger than him. He'll be helpless against me, so you won't have to worry."

Luc looked away and sighed, then cast Eve a questioning gaze. "Are we even sure we *want* Ruth to have her memories back?"

Eve frowned, but she understood his concern. "I know. But I can't keep them from her forever. She has every right to them. Besides, she'll be a huge asset to the organization if she's able to tap into her full potential, and she can't do that without the foundation she already built," Eve said, touching her finger to her temple.

Luc dipped his head. "A huge asset...or a huge liability."

"What if I only gave her back the memories of her spells and how to use them, and not the memories of what made her our enemy?"

Luc was thoughtful. He pulled his hands out from under his legs and shook the tingles from them. "Is that possible? Can you do that?"

Eve bobbed her head side to side. "Maybe. Probably."

She had no idea.

Silence filled the room as Eve sat and waited for Luc to respond, meeting his hesitant expression with what she hoped was a reassuring smile.

"I don't like it, love."

"I know. It wouldn't be my first choice if I had any other option. But I don't," she admitted. Well, not entirely true. Ramil might possibly have the powers she needed, but she preferred to dance with the devil she knew.

"Even if I *were* to agree to this, which is not to say that I *would*, Bo would never allow it. You know that, right?"

He wasn't wrong. "Couldn't you just tell him he has to accept it? Don't you have the final say in all matters Knighco?"

Luc laughed. "Oh, love. You know Bo. There are mountains that even I cannot move."

"You don't think he'd be on board if it was to help Ruth?"

"Not if it puts you within Dagon's grasp." Luc smirked and leaned back on his hands, remarking, "He'd lock you in an ivory tower if he could." He cocked his head to the side. "It's funny: you bring out both the best *and* worst in him."

Eve looked down at her hands. She knew exactly what he meant. She'd seen it. "Did he tell you about killing Adam?"

"He may have mentioned it." Luc grinned. "I told him he should've brought you his head, but he didn't even want to tell you he did it. That's where he and I differ. He has no sense of drama. Presentation. The grand gesture." Luc leaned forward and brushed the dust from his hands. "But kudos to him for throwing ethics out the window and taking care of business. That is a line he rarely crosses."

Eve untangled her legs and stood up, holding her hand out to help Luc up. "I really should go talk to him. I made up with Eoduun and Z, but Bo is keeping his distance."

Once Luc was on his feet, he scooped up Eve and hooked his hands under her butt, her legs wrapping around his waist. He smiled deviously at her. "Talk to him tomorrow. You're not going anywhere until I'm through with you."

"Are you trying to distract me from finishing our conversation about Dagon's powers?"

"Is it working?" He slid one hand up her back and gripped the nape of her neck, pulling her face to his. He kissed her desperately, his lips bruising against hers. His lips still touching hers, he whispered possessively, "It seems you need to be reminded that you belong to *me*, love. I fear the consequences of you forgetting that could end up getting someone killed."

"Then don't let me forget," she whispered, smiling against his lips.

Luc pressed his forehead to hers. "God, I love you, Eve. I would burn a hole through the fucking sun for you."

Eve's heart swelled so much it hurt. She didn't doubt he could do it, and would. "I don't think I'll ever need you to do that," she chuckled. "But it's sweet of you to offer." She framed his face in her hands and leaned back so she could take in his flawless features. He was simply heart-stopping. "Goddamn, but you are a beautiful man. I wish I could put you in a box in my closet so no one else could look at you but me. I shouldn't have to share this with the world."

A dazzling, cocky grin curved his lips and lit his eyes. "Your personal closet sex slave? I could live with that."

"No, you couldn't," Eve laughed. "You'd go stir-crazy within a day, wanting to get out and burn holes in the sun."

Luc feigned offense. "Oh, so by 'box,' you meant *coffin*. Morbid, love." He then grinned devilishly. "I like it. You can kill me and keep me in your closet. I'll be your rotten little sex corpse."

He tried to lean in to kiss her again, but Eve put her hand over his face and blocked him. "Ew! Jesus, Luc. What's wrong with you?" she asked with equal parts amusement and disgust.

"Oh, come on. You love me. Kiss your rotten little sex corpse, Eve. Let me put my wormy tongue in your mouth." He stuck his tongue out between her fingers and wiggled it around.

"Don't make me gag!"

Luc pushed his thighs up against the back of the couch and rested Eve's bottom on top of the couch headrest. It was the perfect height. He tugged her hand away from his face, kissing her palm, then he pressed it to his chest. His gaze lingered on her lips, then slid up to meet her eyes. He leaned close, and as he did, he drew her hand down over his hard stomach, straight to the solid bulge in his pants. His lips brushed her ear as he confessed in a low, sultry tone, "But I kind of like making you gag."

All of the playfulness evaporated in an instant as Luc's mouth pressed searing kisses on her neck below her ear, his other hand tangling in her hair, gripping at the roots. Eve's breath caught in her throat as red-hot need ignited between her legs. She clenched her thighs around him and slid her free hand up the side of his neck while he kissed along her jawline.

Her heart squeezed in her chest as she exhaled deeply. God, how she'd missed him. The fingers of her other hand fumbled blindly with the fly on his slacks. She *needed* him inside of her. Desperately. *Now.* "You're so disgusting. You have no right to make me love you this much," she complained quietly.

His lips grazed hers, and he smiled. "I think I've earned it. And I'll work to earn it every day for the rest of your life…even when I'm a rotten corpse in your closet," he teased, then kissed her breathless before she could protest.

Luc moaned against her mouth when her hand finally worked his engorged cock free from his pants. She gripped him tightly, slowly stroking his hot length, rubbing her thumb over the thick veins popping up beneath the velvety soft skin.

She couldn't take it anymore. With her tongue still tangling with his, she ripped his shirt open – fuck those buttons – and pushed it off his shoulders. She shifted her weight on the couch and slipped her pants and underwear down over her hips, swinging one leg around so she could kick them off onto the floor. She pulled her lips away from his and kissed his earlobe. She whispered in his ear pleadingly, "Fuck me, Luc. I need you, right fucking now." She used her feet to push his pants down over his hips, and they dropped to the floor around his ankles with a soft thud. She wrapped her hand around his girth again and guided him to her entrance.

He didn't need to be told twice. He sank into her slowly, savoring every inch. "Fuck, Eve…" he purred breathily, a soft desperation in his tone. "You're so goddamn perfect."

Eve tilted her hips and pulled him deeper, her legs flexing around him. She threw her arms over his shoulders, one hand gliding up and gripping the back of his neck. She took his earlobe between her teeth and nibbled it lightly, drawing a low moan from him as his hips pulled back, then thrust back into her. She kissed along the thick, cabled muscles of his throat, his expensive, intoxicating scent filling her senses.

Still gripping the back of his neck, she leaned back. As much as she wanted to feel every inch of his flesh flush against hers, she also wanted to sweep her eyes over the masterpiece of his body. The deep V of his hips, flexing with every thrust; the hard ridges and bumps of his abs; his firm, round pecs; those strong shoulders and arms.

All those features were perfectly placed and proportioned on his enormously tall frame. He was flawless perfection.

And those hypnotizing eyes. Her body burned under his simmering gaze. He watched her like she was the most fascinating thing he'd ever seen, and he couldn't tear his eyes away. She would never get tired of way he looked at her. It sent a thrill straight through her heart.

Eve arched her back and rolled her hips against Luc, tilting her head back, reveling in the way he felt inside of her. He didn't just satisfy her body. He satisfied something deep inside her heart and soul, and he filled that need to the point of overflowing.

Her cup runneth over.

46
Ineffable

Luc leaned forward, sinking his hips against hers, pressing her into the couch headrest as the fingers of one hand dug into her hipbone. His other hand grazed over her jaw and cupped her face as his lips descended upon her exposed throat, kissing down to the dip between her collarbones. He lifted her shirt and swirled his tongue over her nipple, and she moaned softly, threading her fingers into his hair.

She wished he would bite her so she could bleed for him, so she could share in his powers right now. Did they dare, after what happened last time? How could a connection this pure and intense, this *fulfilling*, cause her curse to rage so violently? Did it sense something in him that she didn't? Did it see something she was blind to?

God help her, she loved this beautiful psychopath. Why couldn't the monster inside her get on board and accept him as well?

Luc slid his hand down to cup her other breast, tweaking the peak between his thumb and forefinger, sending a zing of pleasure through her. She moaned, "Fuck me harder, Luc."

Luc brought his mouth back to hers and kissed her once, then snatched her up from the back of the couch and carried her around to the front of it. He dropped back onto the seat with Eve on his lap. He sucked his bottom lip between his teeth as he admired her perched on his cock, and he bucked his hips. His eyes flicked up to hers. "How about you make me," he challenged.

Eve hummed and gyrated her hips, taking him deep inside of her. She pressed her chest to his, hugging her arms around his neck, and angled her mouth over his, kissing him deeply. She rode him hard, trying to focus her attention away from the rising desire to bite her tongue and bleed into his mouth. Instead, she chased the climax building in her core, her hips moving of their own accord in their pursuit of pleasure.

"Come with me," she begged, panting in Luc's ear. Her inner walls were beginning to pulse.

"Fuck yes, baby," Luc rasped. He gripped her hips and thrust up into her with force. He'd obviously been holding back until now. With a keening squall erupting from her throat, the pressure in Eve's core suddenly burst, releasing a deluge of pleasure through her whole body. Her walls pulsed and squeezed around Luc, and he threw his head back against the headrest and groaned, spilling into her with hard, paroxysmal thrusts.

When the pleasure dissipated, Eve sagged against him, resting her head on his shoulder, her forehead against his neck. Luc hugged her to him, and she felt moisture in the corners of her eyes.

"I love you," he whispered, stroking her hair. "I love you with every fucking thing I have, Eve. Goddamn."

Eve blinked away the ridiculous tears trying to form. Luc was just...overwhelming. She sighed. "I love you, too. Even if you are a fucking weirdo."

"You love me *because* I'm a fucking weirdo," he contended. He whispered conspiratorially, "Truth be told, I think maybe you're a bit of a fucking weirdo, too."

Eve chuckled. "You flatter me so."

After getting dressed and cleaned up, Eve came out to the living room to find Luc reclined on the couch, browsing Netflix. His shirt lay open across his chest, half the buttons missing from her earlier impatience. But fuck, it was a good look. She crawled over him and wedged herself half on top of him, half between him and the back of the couch. She rested her head on his chest, draping one arm over his stomach.

"Why is there so much anime in your suggestions?" Luc wondered with amusement.

"The boys." That was answer enough.

Luc flipped through the many titles, finally settling on one. "This was Bo's favorite when we were kids, as I recall," he mused as the intro music played. "I think he liked it because the main character had white hair and wolf ears."

Ruth's memories corroborated what Luc said. Ruth had sat and watched it with him as a little girl late at night, snuggled up with a blanket on the couch, leaning on his arm. Eve had seen quite a bit of this anime because the boys watched it regularly. "Half dog demon, half human, never quite fitting into either role, and a perfect, powerful half-brother he resented. I think I can see why he related to it."

"You think I'm perfect?" Luc grinned. Eve rolled her eyes and shook her head. In a less playful tone, he followed up with, "You think he resents me?"

She'd overstepped. "It's not my place to say. I wouldn't know."

"No need to stand on ceremony. He does. But he loves me, too, because I'm his little brother, and he feels morally obligated to watch over me. It's just who he is."

"Do you love him?"

Luc paused. "Of course. He's my big brother."

"And Ruthlys?"

"He still loves Ru. You know that."

"No, Luc. Do *you* love your sister?"

"'You love your sister?'" he echoed in a hushed southern accent.

"What the fuck was that?"

"*The Green Mile*. It was one of Wild Bill's lines. You can't tell me you've never seen it."

"I've seen it. But it doesn't answer my question. Do you still love your sister, even a little?"

He went silent. He was quiet for so long, Eve didn't think he was actually going to answer. Finally, he said flatly, "I don't think so. Not anymore."

Those icy words chilled Eve to the bone. All Ruth's memories of vying for Luc's attention, craving his love, revering him as some kind of untouchable god...she loved him so much. Even when she hated him, she still loved him. Even when Eve wrenched the memories from her mind, Ruth still loved Luc.

And he just...didn't?

"She's your sister," Eve challenged.

"She's a monster. Or at least, she was. Now, she's not even my sister. Not really. Now she's just somebody that used to be my sister." He glanced at her and blithely said, "Now she's just somebody that I used to know."

He was being too nonchalant about this. Did he even care?

When Eve withdrew her hand and tucked it against herself, Luc finally perceived that he was upsetting her. "Don't get me wrong, Eve. I *did* love my sister. But Ruth became something else. Something evil and unlovable, and it broke my heart. She's hurt so many people. She hurt *Bo*. He may be able to look past all of her transgressions and still love her, but I can't."

Eve wished she didn't have Ruth's memories right now, because his cold words stabbed through her as though those memories, those *feelings*, were her own. "If it had been up to you, would you have revived her at the papermill?"

He didn't hesitate. "No."

Eve tried to push away this sense of injury. If she was honest with herself, she knew that she probably wouldn't have saved Ruth if Bo hadn't implored her to. But Ruth wasn't her sister. She'd never loved Ruth.

"You don't ever want me to give her memories back, do you?" she ventured.

"I fear what she will do with them." He looked down at Eve. "I don't understand why you're so adamant about returning them to her."

"Maybe *she* could've saved Mòrag."

"No one could've saved the nuckelavee. It brought its fate upon itself." Luc scowled and looked back at the TV. "And I don't love the plan you've devised to return those memories to Ruth. You have no idea how much the thought of Dagon touching you again boils my blood. Everything about that whole scenario feels like battery acid in my stomach."

Eve chewed the inside of her cheek. She hated to even suggest it, but… "If Dagon is completely off the table, Ramil did offer the use of his powers…it's possible he may have what I need." Eve could hear Luc's heart beating furiously in his chest against her ear. "I know you don't like this," she continued. "But this is how my powers work. If you recall, you're the one who wanted me to learn how to use them. Well, now I know how. If I could do it with a simple fucking handshake, I would."

Luc sighed. "I know. And I knew then. I just thought maybe I'd have a better handle on my jealousy issues before you mastered your formidable skill." He smiled ruefully. "It seems that is not the case."

Eve stroked her thumb over Luc's rounded pectoral. "Is there going to come a day when you decide that my monstrous powers make me unlovable, too?"

Luc's eyes snapped to hers, his brows turned upward. "Is that what you think? That because I could stop loving my own sister, that I'm somehow capable of falling out of love with you?" He pried her out of her spot between himself and the back of the couch and dragged her on top of him, encasing her in his arms. He looked up at her sweetly. "You're not Ruth. The way I love you, Eve…there's no room for conditions. I know I say I don't give second chances, and I don't…but for you? You could burn the world. Eat a puppy. Put me in a coffin in your closet. I am at your mercy, and there is not a single fucking thing that will change that. My love will persist."

Eve searched his eyes for the signs of deceit that surely should be there. "You can't know that."

He gazed back at her earnestly. "I've never been more certain of anything in my life. My love for you is ineffable."

"I don't know what that means," Eve whispered sheepishly.

Luc smirked in amusement and brushed her hair from her temple with his fingertips. "It means I love you more than words can express, Eve."

"You sure about that? You have a lot of pretty words at your disposal," she teased. "Pretty words like 'ineffable.'"

It was then she noticed the voices from the television. She glanced over and watched the mismatched animated mouth movements and English-speaking voices. She snatched up the remote. "Oh, Luc, no. Inexcusable."

"What?"

"Dubbed? Dub is blasphemy. Subs only in this apartment, young man. The boys would have your head."

Luc held his palms out defensively. "Seriously? What's the difference?"

"Try watching an episode dubbed, then watch it again with subtitles, and you'll see," she said as she changed the audio settings.

"Yeah, I'm never doing that. I'll trust your judgement."

Eve relaxed against Luc again, the familiar Japanese-speaking voices matching the movements on the animated mouths, and all was as it should be.

"I wonder if our kids will inherit the eyes," Luc said suddenly in a nonchalant, conversational tone.

Eve's heart stopped. Kids?! "Jesus, Luc. It's way too early to have that conversation."

"I'm not saying let's have kids right now. I was just musing." When Eve didn't answer, he looked down at her. "You don't want kids?"

"I didn't say *that*. I guess I'm just a little surprised that you *do*."

"Why?"

Eve shrugged a shoulder. "You just don't seem like the family man type. You seem more…billionaire playboy."

"You don't want to put a ring on it and lock this thing down with a pregnancy?" he asked in a teasing tone, wiggling the fingers on his left hand.

In a remark more cutting than she meant, Eve replied, "You'd have to have the testicular fortitude to come clean to your dad about our relationship before I'd ever let that happen."

Luc, in true Luc fashion, obtusely jumped to the wrong conclusion. "So, if I tell my father I'm in love with you, you'll marry me and have my babies?"

Eve sighed heavily. "No. I'm just saying you'd have to tell him before I would even *consider* it."

Luc grinned. "So, you're saying there's a chance."

"I feel like you're getting the wrong message from this."

"I hear what I want to hear, love," he confessed unabashedly. "It's the only way to get what you want out of life."

47
Hurt So Good

Eve blinked her eyes open. She was still on the couch, lying on Luc's chest, and he was fast asleep beneath her. The anime they were watching had skipped ahead several episodes, and the clock on the wall showed it was well past midnight.

Something stirred restlessly within Eve's belly. An instinctive urge, a compulsion to get out under the open night sky. Something was summoning her outside, and it was impossible to resist. She *needed* to follow whatever this strange call was. It felt wild and hungry, but it wasn't quite the same sensation she felt when her curse raged, seeking a victim to sate it. This felt like it was coming from outside of herself, and it was *calling* to the beast inside of her.

Come to me.

Submit to me.

Give yourself to me.

Eve carefully crawled from the couch, only minimally disturbing Luc. He whimpered groggily in protest at the loss of her body against his, but when Eve took a blanket from the chair and laid it over him, he calmed after a moment, once again sleeping peacefully. Eve slipped quietly out the door.

She had no idea what she was following, but *something* was driving her on, leading her out of the apartment building. She stepped out into the cool night air, and was surprised to see how bright it was outside. She glanced up at the enormous full moon sitting low in the sky. If she wasn't mistaken, a small sliver of the outer edge had a strange, red tinge to it.

Come to me.

Her bare feet carried her straight toward the wood line, the grass dewy and cool on her toes. Her blood was rushing through her veins in nervous anticipation as she closed the distance, and the coil low in her belly began to unfurl, the promise of sweet, primal release infused into the very air she breathed.

Submit to me.

Two heterochrome, wolfish eyes burned, glowing in the darkness among the trees. As they moved toward her, she realized she recognized those mismatched eyes.

Bo stepped out into the moonlight, and Eve questioned if he was real, if any of this was real. Was she dreaming?

"What are you doing out here?" he demanded, his wild eyes fixed unsettlingly on her. "You're supposed to be with Luc."

No, this wasn't a dream. This was real.

Eve looked around. "I was...but..." It sounded so dumb to say it out loud, but what else could she say? "I felt like I needed to come outside."

He gave her a puzzled expression, then glanced anxiously up at the moon. "Go back inside," he ordered.

"What are *you* doing out here?" she asked, moving closer to him.

He held out a hand to stop her. "No, Evie. You're not supposed to be out here. You can't be near me."

She felt a tug inside of her, like he was pulling her in with his eyes, even if his mouth was telling her to leave. "Why? Is this a werewolf thing?" she asked, angling her head toward the full moon. It looked like the red tinge was spreading.

"Yes."

Eve frowned and took another step toward him. He didn't retreat. "I thought your curse only heightened your senses and affected your appearance. I thought you were immune to the rest of the effects."

"I said I don't transition, and I don't. But there are certain times, rare times, when my control and rationality…," he exhaled, his voice lowering, "…slip." He glanced at the blood-red stain blooming over the moon again.

Eve propped her hands on her hips. "Is that why you've been so intense lately?" That would explain a lot.

Bo pulled his mask down and inhaled deeply, ignoring her question. A shudder coursed visibly through his lean, muscular body. "Evie, please. Please go inside." He closed his eyes and inhaled once more, scenting her on the air. He slowly opened his eyes again, and his expression had shifted. Darkened. "Last chance."

Whatever had drawn her out here wouldn't let her turn tail now. She was trapped in the tractor beam of Bo's eyes, her fear and desire fusing into one entity, like lovers. She took another tiny step toward him. "Why? Are you going to hurt me, Bo?"

"Never maliciously. But…" Bo lowered his head, reminding Eve of a wolf's posture when it prowls after its prey. He began to stalk to her right, and she realized he was circling her. The fighting instinct in her wanted to turn to keep herself facing him, not wanting to show him her back. But the force that drove her out here urged her to stay still.

Submit.

The only thing she was absolutely certain she shouldn't do, was *run.*

Eve's heart pounded in her ears, and she cast her eyes to the ground. "But what?" she whispered as he skulked around her right side. She closed her eyes when he disappeared from her peripheral view and listened for his movements, her breath trembling in her throat.

She heard his soft footsteps as he stalked up behind her. She felt his presence looming at her back, and his breath ghosted over the back of her neck.

Her whole body was on edge, and yet, her core throbbed at his proximity. She clenched her thighs together as a tremor of eager anticipation quaked through her.

Bo's voice was close to her ear when he answered darkly, "But I can't make promises tonight, little rabbit. I'm not quite...myself."

Her eyes shot open. Fear briefly overtook her desire, and she tried to bolt.

Tried.

Bo quickly caught her with one hand around her throat, one hand around her midsection, and he pulled her back against his chest, *hard*, making the air whoosh from her lungs at the impact. His breath was heavy in her ear as he leaned down and growled, "Too late."

Oh, *fuuuuck*. His voice. His hands on her. His hard body against hers. A gush of wetness slickened her core and dampened her underwear.

His thumb brushed over the pulse point on her throat. "I can hear your heart racing, Evie. Ba-dum...ba-dum...ba-dum... Is it because you're afraid...or because you're excited?"

Both. Definitely both.

He inhaled along her neck, and goosebumps erupted over her skin. "I can smell your arousal," he remarked, the low timbre of his voice conveying deep satisfaction at that fact.

"Please don't hurt me, Bo," she whispered. But the beast inside of her begged silently, *Bite me. Take me. Make it rough. Make it hurt. Dominate me. Own me.*

His lips skimmed the side of her neck. "But I kind of want to. Just a little." His tongue swirled over the tender flesh just beneath her jaw, his teeth scraping her skin lightly. "And I think *you* kind of want me to. It drives me wild when you bleed."

He released his grip on her and stepped around to face her, keeping his hungry eyes trained on hers. "I mean to claim you right here under this blood moon, Evrys Alarie, and you will submit to me – mind, body, and soul. If that's not what you want, then this is your last chance to run." He tapped the underside of her chin with the knuckle of his hooked index finger, raising her face to his. "You can still escape this." He leaned in close to her ear and warned, "But…I can't promise I won't give chase."

She couldn't run even if she wanted to. Her legs were jelly. Her knees were weak. Her insides were molten. She was frozen in place, like a petrified rabbit, unable to tear her eyes from his.

He stepped around her again, but this time, she turned with him, until her back was to the woods. At this angle, she could see the huge, blood-red moon over Bo's right shoulder. His eyes suddenly flashed with that strange luminous iridescence she had seen when she'd looked at him with Dagon's powers, and against the night sky backdrop, it reminded her of a predator's eyeshine.

Alarm and excitement wrestled for control of her limbs as he lunged toward her. Alarm won, and she backed away from him on shaky legs. But he kept coming, his eyes focused only on her, his primal, single-minded intent clear.

He was going to fuck her like he owned her.

Eve's back slammed into a wide tree trunk, and Bo was on her in the next instant, his hands pressed against the bark on either side of her, caging her in. He leaned forward, resting his forearm above her head, his other hand moving to grip her jaw tightly. He leaned down and took possession of her mouth with a savage kiss, a low grumble sounding in the back of his throat. Bo's hand dragged from her jaw down her neck, over her chest, and he flattened his palm against her belly. His fingers slid down beneath the waistband of her baggy sweatpants and slipped into her underwear.

Eve whimpered into Bo's mouth as he shoved two thick fingers into her.

"So fucking wet for me," he praised, then kissed her again, curling his fingers inside of her. He began to stroke her front inner wall, and an intense, raw pleasure radiated like a wildfire from his fingers, making her knees buckle. Bo wedged his knee between her thighs to help support her as he stroked harder and faster. She threw her arms over his shoulders and tore her mouth away from his, gasping for breath as her whole body jerked and trembled with each stroke of his fingers.

Jesus Christ, what the fuck was he doing to her? No one had ever found that particular bundle of nerves on her before.

And she was ill-prepared for the intensity of this stimulation. "Stop, Bo, it's too much! It hurts!" she begged, the overwhelming pleasure pushing to the point of being painful. She squirmed against his hand, but it only amplified the sensation. She was afraid of the power of the climax he was drawing forth.

She was going to come so hard that it was going to hurt.

Hurt so good.

"You can take it, baby," Bo assured her. Instead of stopping, he fisted his other hand in her mane and covered her mouth with his, devouring her protests as the fingers between her legs worked her even harder.

He growled and sank his canines into her bottom lip, the metallic taste of blood spreading over both of their tongues.

Eve cried out in anguish into Bo's mouth as her core exploded in violent, beautifully agonizing spasms, and her vision briefly went starry. Her hips bucked wildly against his hand, and her abs clenched so hard, they began to cramp up. Tears filled her eyes as the sweet, torturous pleasure surged on and on as he relentlessly milked her orgasm with his stroking fingers, and it lasted so much longer than it had any right to.

Finally, the waves subsided, but when they did, a divine, lingering pleasure remained, like the tingle of peppermint on your lips after sucking on a candy cane. Eve sighed and slumped against the tree trunk as the euphoria washed over her, Bo's hand in her hair and his knee between her thighs, holding her up.

"I can't decide if that's the worst or the best thing that's ever happened to me," Eve whimpered as Bo withdrew his hand from between her legs.

He leaned down and licked the remaining blood from her lip, and another shock of pleasure ripped through Eve's core. She twisted her fingers in his shirt as her knees gave out. "Fuck, stop, Bo."

Bo nuzzled her neck, his breath hot on her skin as he declared, "Oh, I'm just getting started." He dropped down to his knees in front of her and hooked his fingers in the waistband of her sweatpants, tugging them and her underwear down in one swift motion.

"Bo…" Eve protested weakly.

He freed her ankles from her clothing, then, while still on his knees in front of her, he lifted her just enough to hike her thighs over his shoulders, burying his face between her legs.

"Bo!" She choked on her own breath and pressed her back into the tree, the bark digging into her flesh through her shirt as Bo's tongue delved into her folds and attacked her over-sensitive clit. She raked her fingers into his messy, silver-white locks and clung on for dear life. "You're…going to…kill me…" she sob-moaned between breaths, wincing at every flick and wiggle of his tongue.

God, did this feel good, or did it hurt? She didn't even know anymore. Pain and pleasure had blurred indistinguishably into one hulking monster.

Slowly, however, the scales tipped back over to pleasure, and Eve flexed her thighs around Bo's ears as he took her into his mouth and sucked hard while his tongue flicked her clit.

"Fuck, oh Jesus…Bo…fuck," Eve moaned, fisting her hands in his hair as she felt the ache quickly swelling in her core, and then she was gasping and crying out again as she climaxed once more.

Bo turned his head and bit into her inner thigh, breaking the skin, her blood pouring into his mouth.

A second burst of euphoria redoubled the intensity of the first, and Eve clenched her thighs so hard, she moved a few inches up the tree trunk. The noises that were coming out of her throat were more animalistic than they were human.

"No more, Bo," she pleaded as he shifted her thighs from his shoulders to his hips and pulled her against him. She clung to him as he stood up, but he pressed her back into the tree again.

"Yes, more, Evie," he said in a low, demanding tone as he brushed her sweaty pink hair from her face. He gazed deep into her eyes. "I want to drink every last drop of you, until there's nothing left for anyone else."

48

Pay the Piper

"I have nothing more to give, Bo," Eve insisted weakly. Her legs were quivering uncontrollably against his hips, and he smoothed his hands over them. He hummed with satisfaction.

He liked this unraveled state she was in. The state *he'd* put her in.

He ran a hand up to her throat, resting his fingers right beneath her jaw. He swiped the pad of his thumb over her bottom lip, then he stuck the tip of it between her teeth. She bit down on his thumb lightly, and his eyes met hers. A roguish grin exposed his beautiful wolf fangs. "Well, *I* have plenty more to give. All you have to do is take it like a good little girl, Evie."

The traitorous beast inside of her swooned, sending a new stirring of desire glowing warmly through her lower belly.

Bo reached between them and opened his fly, releasing his rock-hard, aching cock. Eve's legs trembled harder as he pressed the tip into her soaked sex, and he squeezed her thighs reassuringly. She wondered if he could feel her trembling inside, too.

A deep, rumbling groan vibrated through Bo's throat as he buried himself inside of her, and Eve reciprocated the sentiment with a whimpering sigh of her own. Her chest flattened against his as she rolled her hips and pressed her cheek against his neck.

Take it home, Daddy.

This. This is what she came out here for. She dug her fingernails into the back of his shoulder blades as he thrust into her, and she felt strength returning to her limbs once more. It was as though he had utterly destroyed her, and now he was raising her from that sadistically sweet perdition.

He was heaven inside her.

"God, you feel like home," he sighed into her ear. Then he growled, "You've wrecked me, Evie, and I intend to return the favor."

Oh, Bo. Too late. Mission accomplished. "Wreck me," she submitted breathily, running her hand up the back of his neck, clinging to him as he pinned her against the tree.

Bo's nails pressed into her thighs as he gripped her tightly and railed her harder. His hot tongue caressed her throat, and she felt his fangs scrape over the side of her neck. After a long, deliberate pause, he bit into her tender flesh.

Her whole body shook and pulsed around him, power and endorphins surging through her veins. A guttural groan rasped in his throat as he pistoned into her, his cock throbbing inside of her. His mouth moved further down her neck as he bit her again, sending another surge through her. And then he bit her once more on the swell of her trapezius, and again at the base of her neck.

Wave after wave, Eve rode out the crests and crashes of unbridled ecstasy, clutching at Bo like a lifeboat as his power and essence poured into her and threatened to drown her, imbuing her senses with an acute sharpness. His scent danced in her brain, and his heartbeat thundered through her ears. Electricity skittered over her skin, and her eyes blazed in fractals of yellow and gold.

Bo gazed into those strange eyes, and he smiled breathlessly, his fangs gleaming in the moonlight. Eve could see the pride in his expression.

Those were *his* eyes. An unmistakable, unique marking for all to see. Everyone knew they were his, and when she wore them, they knew *she* was his.

Eve blinked and forced them back behind her own deep brown irises.

Bo turned their entwined bodies around, so his back was to the tree trunk, and he sank down to the ground in exhaustion. Eve's bare knees dug into the dirt on either side of Bo, his spent cock still inside of her as she sat on his lap. She gently kissed the scar over his eye, then touched her forehead to his and closed her eyes, stroking her fingers through the hair on the back of his head. Her senses were beginning to return to her, and with them came uncomfortable questions.

"What are we doing, Bo?" she whispered, her voice barely audible, even to her own enhanced ears.

Bo touched his thumb and forefinger to her chin and lifted her lips to his. He kissed her hungrily, and she felt his cock twitch inside of her, beginning to swell and harden again. He met her eyes, and she saw that his wolf eye was still prominently ablaze. It hadn't gone dormant at all tonight. What kind of spell was he under? Were *they* under?

"We're following our instincts, Evie."

Without another word, he took one of her legs and swung it up and around, spinning her around as he rose to his knees and lifted her hips, pushing her forward onto her hands and knees with his cock still inside of her. He gripped her ass cheeks with both hands and began to rut into her from behind.

Lord, have mercy.

Bo leaned over her back and wrapped one hand firmly around her throat, his breath puffing over her ear as he pummeled her ruthlessly. Savagely. Primally. Her moans were harsh and staccato, matching his violent rhythm. His other hand reached under her shirt and cupped one of her perky mounds, pinching her nipple between two fingers as he held her back against his chest.

He pinched the pebbled pink peak between his fingers even harder, and at the same time, his fingers flexed around her throat as his teeth latched onto the back of her neck. She gave a strangled yelp. Impossibly, pleasure crashed over her again as he drove into her mercilessly, his orgasm riding on hers.

His palms slammed down into the dirt on either side of her as he gave one final, hard thrust, his jaws still clamped over the back of her neck. She could feel the vibrations of his groans against her skin as he emptied everything he had left into her.

After a moment, he released her from his bite, and he gave the sore spot a gentle, soothing caress of his tongue. He withdrew from her and sat back on his ankles, his hands on his thighs, his chest still heaving. Eve turned to face him, crawling on her hands and knees. He looked at her from beneath the sweaty, silver-white locks that hung down into his eyes, and she saw that his wild yellow eye had finally shifted back to charcoal gray.

He looked out toward the west, and Eve followed his gaze. The moon was no longer red, and it was just disappearing, dipping behind the horizon.

He tucked himself back into his pants and zipped them up, then reached behind him and grabbed Eve's sweatpants and underwear. He wordlessly assisted her to her feet and helped her get dressed, his eyes lingering on all the bite marks he'd left upon her skin.

She leaned back against a different tree and looked at Bo. He held her gaze with a tormented expression.

"Are you Daddy Bo again?" she asked.

He gave her a quizzical look.

"As opposed to Big Bad Bo," she clarified. "You huffed and puffed and blew my house down."

He didn't smile at her attempt to make light of what had just transpired.

After a long silence between them, he asked, "Why did you come to me tonight?"

Eve paused. "I don't know. I just…felt something. An irresistible urge. A call."

Bo worried his bottom lip with his teeth, exposing his sharp fangs. "I yearned for you, and you came to me. You know what that means?" When she shook her head, he sauntered up to her, and one hand gripped her jaw, tilting her face up toward his. "It means you chose me, and I claimed you. You've bonded to me, Evie," he revealed. His gaze dropped to her full lips, and his pupils widened, like he was contemplating kissing her again.

"Wait. *Bonded?* What the hell does that mean? How did that happen?"

Bo frowned and looked away. "It shouldn't have happened at all."

"Why not? What does it mean? Is it like Dagon and Apep being bound to me?"

"It's not the same. Only wolves forge bonds like this, and you're not a wolf. Fuck, I didn't even think I was wolf enough to be capable of initiating it."

"Bo, what does it *mean*?"

His gaze returned to her, and with a wistful look, he answered, "It means, from this day forward, there will never be anyone else for me but you."

Eve's heart didn't know whether to plummet or soar. "And for me?"

"I have no idea. You're not a wolf." Then he smirked slightly. "Like it would matter. You never follow the rules, anyway."

The weight of that revelation sat uneasily in Eve's chest. Did she just condemn Bo to a lifetime of misery? Who would ever want to be irrevocably and involuntarily shackled to *her,* and only her, for life? Luc seemed to think he did, but he would change his mind. Eventually, he would. They always did.

And he could. But Bo? This sounded permanent.

"How did it happen?" she asked quietly.

"I called, and you answered. As simple as that. You chose me…even if you didn't mean to."

"But you didn't mean for this either, did you?" Eve asked knowingly.

"I didn't know I could. I just…it just happened." Bo looked down at his hands. "I considered it was possible you had just come outside to see the lunar eclipse. I thought maybe it was a coincidence." A storm churned in his eyes as he surveyed her bite marks once more. "I'm sorry I did this to you, Evie. I wasn't myself. Luc was supposed to keep you away from me."

"He knew?"

"I warned him something could happen, so he agreed to keep you close. It's why I was in such a hurry to get back from Newbury. I could feel it coming. I'm not usually susceptible to lunar cycles, but supermoons and lunar eclipses put me a little on edge. But a supermoon *and* a full lunar eclipse? I was afraid of what urges might surface. I was afraid I was going to come after you." He gave a wry chuckle. "Instead, I made you come to me. I did not see that coming."

Bo reached up and slipped his mask up over his face, and Eve recognized his walls going up. He was withdrawing from her, ashamed of what he'd done to her.

Fuck that.

Eve hooked her finger in his mask and yanked it back down, much to his surprise. "Don't fucking hide yourself from me, Bo. You don't get to do that anymore." She wrapped her arms around his waist and rested her chin on his sternum, looking up at him. "Are you sorry to have me bonded to you?"

A tortured anguish settled in his features. "Evie, that's not it. If I were to bond to anyone, it would be you. Always and forever, *you.* But I had no right to do that."

"Why not?" she challenged.

Bo looked over at the apartment building. "Because Luc wants to marry you. He wants children with you." He glanced back down at her surprised face. "Yeah, I heard him," he admitted, tapping his ear.

"I was on my way outside – I needed some fresh air to clear my head – and I heard him talking as I passed your door. I didn't mean to eavesdrop, but I couldn't help it." He exhaled deeply. "And then all I could think about was you with *his* child in your belly, and it made me want to…behave irrationally." He cupped her face in his hands. "But don't worry. I don't feel that way anymore. It was the moon making me act like an idiot."

"Bo?"

"Hm?"

"I'm not having children anytime soon. Don't fret about it." An amused grin tugged at her lips. "But if I wasn't on birth control, I think you probably would've changed that tonight."

Bo's face flushed deeply, his wolf eye flaring up. Eve could hear his heart palpitate.

She rested her cheek against his chest. "So, what do we do now?"

He hugged his arms around her, his chin resting on the top of her head. "I don't know, Evie. I can't pretend these feelings are 'heat of the moment' anymore. I can't pretend I don't love you, and I can't pretend I don't long for you to love me."

Bo's head suddenly jerked up, and Eve caught the sound, too. She could hear Luc calling for her from inside the building.

"What do we tell Luc?" she asked.

"The truth." He sighed and squeezed Eve harder. He kissed the top of her head before releasing her from his arms. "I'll tell him. It was my doing. It's time to pay the piper." He lifted his mask over his face and began to walk toward the apartment building.

Eve looked up at her apartment window, and she saw a flash of Luc's face. Then he was suddenly outside, standing in Bo's path.

"Where is she?! What did you do?!" Luc bellowed, electricity arcing between his fingers. Bo held his hands up in a placating display and halted in place.

"She's fine, don't worry," Bo said. "But we need to talk, just you and me."

Eve stepped just out of the tree line so Luc could see that she was ok, but she didn't come any closer. Instead, she covered her ears and sat on the ground with her back against a tree trunk. She didn't want to hear this conversation.

She couldn't bear to hear it if Luc said he didn't want her anymore, or if Bo swore he'd never touch her again. It would gut her.

Eve watched the brothers' interaction, with Luc taking an aggressive stance and gesturing wildly, as he does, and Bo taking on a slightly defensive, appealing posture while still standing his ground. Adrenaline surged through her veins, making her heart race and her anxiety spike as she surveyed them. If she needed to intercede, she would, but until then, she would sit and listen to the blood rush loudly in her ears as her fingers pressed them tightly closed.

Fortunately, it didn't take long for Luc to shift from agitated gesturing to a less aggressive stance, with his arms crossed over his chest. Bo's hands went to his pockets. There was still some obvious turbulence, but the brewing storm seemed to have passed them over without unleashing too much damage.

Then they both turned their heads in her direction and looked at her expectantly. She couldn't read their faces in the darkness, but she knew they were summoning her.

As she uncovered her ears and stood, dusting the dirt off her sweatpants, she recalled the Cherokee story of the two wolves: Everyone has two wolves battling inside of them, one good, and one evil. The one you feed is the one that wins.

Eve also had two wolves battling inside of her.

One of them loved Luc.

One of them loved Bo.

And she had been feeding them both.

TO BE CONTINUED

If you enjoyed *Eve's Sins*, look for the next book in the Abomination series:

Eve's Revelations